TRUTH LIES BLEEDI

Four teenagers find t... ___
of a young girl stuffed into a dumpster in
an Edinburgh alleyway. Who is she?
Where did she come from? Who killed her
and why? And where is the baby to which
she has obviously recently given birth?
Inspector Rob Brennan, recently back from
psychiatric leave, is still shocked by the
senseless shooting of his only brother. His
superiors think that the case of the
dumpster girl will be perfect to get him
back on track. But Rob Brennan has
enemies within the force, stacks of
unfinished business and a nose for trouble.
What he discovers about the murdered girl
blows the case—and his life—wide open.

"Tony Black is one of those excellent
  perpetrators of Scottish noir... a
  compelling and convincing portrayer of
  raw emotions in a vicious milieu."
—*The Times*

Tony Black Bibliography

NOVELS:

Gus Dury series
Paying for It (2008)
Gutted (2009)
Loss (2010)
Long Time Dead (2010)
Wrecked (2019)
Long Way Down (2012; novella)
Last Orders (2013; novella)

DI Rob Brennan series
Truth Lies Bleeding (2011)
Murder Mile (2012)

Doug Michie series
The Storm Without (2012)
The Inglorious Dead (2014)

DI Bob Valentine series
Artefacts of the Dead (2014)
A Taste of Ashes (2015)
Summoning the Dead (2016)
Her Cold Eyes (2018)

Clay Moloney series
(with Matt Neal)
Bay of Martyrs (2017)

Non-Series Novels
His Father's Son (2013)
The Last Tiger (2014)

Collections
Killing Time in Vegas (2013)
The Lost Generation (2013)
The Sin Bin (2014)

NOVELLAS:

RIP Robbie Silva (2012)
The Ringer (2014)
Stone Ginger (2015)

NON-FICTION:

Hard Truths (2013; crime
fiction interviews)

Truth Lies Bleeding

TONY BLACK

STARK
HOUSE

Stark House Press • Eureka California

TRUTH LIES BLEEDING

Published by Stark House Press
1315 H Street
Eureka, CA 95501
griffinskye3@sbcglobal.net
www.starkhousepress.com

Published by Stark House Press by arrangement with the author.
Visit his website at: www.tonyblack.net.

ISBN-13: 978-1-951473-10-5

Cover and book design by Mark Shepard, shepgraphics.com

First Stark House Press Edition: October 2020

Dedication
For Jim Divine, Tony Francis,
Tom Maxwell and David Lewis

Prologue

THE GIRL'S SCREAMS WERE ENOUGH to give away their hiding place. It took a lot of noise, a racket, to have heads popping out of windows in a Muirhouse high-rise but it wasn't the noise alone that alerted the neighbourhood.

'Oh my God ...'

The young girl didn't recognise her own voice – it was loaded with an emotion she hadn't heard before. The tone was higher, seemed to tremble more. It was as if she had somehow tapped into a world she'd only encountered on television, or at the cinema. It sounded alien to her.

'What is it, Trish?'

The three teenagers surrounded their friend. They'd been smoking, drinking, having a laugh and a joke, whiling away another day that they should have spent at school. But this wasn't any other day; Trish knew it the moment she had started to scream.

'Trish, what's up?'

The girl stood rigid. When her friends touched her she jerked herself away and started to shiver. Tears fell down her cheeks soon after. They felt cold on her hot skin.

'Trish?'

She didn't answer, the words wouldn't come.

She felt the colour draining from her face. She closed her eyes tight, tried to shut it all out but the images were still there inside her head. She started to bite her lip. Her breathing altered, became shorter. She felt the corners of her mouth turning down and her whole head now seemed to be shivering out of control. More tears came. The shivers stopped suddenly, then instantly started again as she opened her eyes and held up her hands.

Trish knew the streaks of blood were spotted by the others at once. They were dark red smears moving slowly down her fingertips towards her palms. It took her some time to register the blood was actually on *her* hands – nothing seemed real now – but when she became aware of what she was looking at her mouth opened wide and her throat tightened.

No sound came from her. As the girls stared at her everything felt like it was locked inside her. Trapped.

'*Trish* ...'

Her mouth widened some more; she started to gag, wanted to be sick but nothing would come out except a noise. A shrill, desperate animal wail. The others stepped back. They watched Trish shaking as she screamed out. She stared at her hands, and felt her eyes widening at the sight of the fresh blood.

'Keep the noise down!' A man hung his head from an open window in the high-rise above the alleyway. He turned to the girls below, looked down, but didn't call out a second time.

The girls stared at each other, looked scared. One shrugged. Another ran to Trish, clamped arms around her.

As her wailing turned to sobs Trish fell into her friend, weeping and shaking. The young girl held her, trying to keep her steady on her feet but the pair were forced to slump onto the ground.

'What is it, Trish? ... What is it?'

The other two girls watched for a moment, then one of them pointed back up the alleyway. There was a large bin on wheels, a communal bin, a dumpster. A few moments earlier Trish had gone over there to drop off an empty bottle.

She watched the girls staring at each other, wondering what she'd seen. She could tell that thoughts were passing between them: they were curious.

One of the girls started to walk; the other followed.

Trish tried to call out, to bring them back, but words still wouldn't come out.

She watched them go. Tried to claw out to them, pull them back. They kept walking up the alleyway.

It was a large bin, almost as tall as they were. When they got up close they pointed to the bloody finger-streaks. Trish watched as they turned to each other as if to ask, 'What's inside?'

For a moment they stared on, frozen, then one spoke.

'Go on, open it.'

'No, you do it.'

The girls stood, unmoving. Trish tried again to call to them but all that came from her now was screams, shrill roars she couldn't control.

They looked back, then, 'We'll do it together.'

A firm nod. 'Okay.'

They reached out hands, raised the lid of the dumpster.

Their breathing looked to have stilled as their thin arms pushed the black rubber lid back. The dark interior of the vault was exposed now. For a second or two the girls peered into the blackness, but didn't seem to see anything. They drew closer, raised themselves on tiptoes.

As they edged nearer the rim, Trish remembered the sweet smell that had come from inside. She knew it would take a moment for their eyes to adjust to the darkness inside the bin, to make out the light and shade. To piece together familiar shapes, in an unfamiliar setting. To take in with their eyes what their minds wouldn't want to believe.

In the next few seconds the air filled with the screams of two more young girls; they were running from the alleyway.

Chapter 1

DI ROB BRENNAN STOOD OUTSIDE the Chief Super's door
with his fist held tightly, knuckles out, hovering beneath the brassy
nameplate. He thought about pounding the wood panel, thought
again, then gripped the handle and stomped in.

'You want me?'

Chief Superintendent Aileen Galloway, phone in hand, blasted
some poor DC about the state of his handwriting in the mileage log
for the new Cavaliers.

'If it's not a good time, I'll call back,' said Brennan.

She turned, keeping up her rant, and flagged him to sit down. It was
multi-skilling, or man-management, something like that, he thought;
something women were always better at than men. Wasn't that the
received wisdom?

Brennan walked over to the desk. It was immaculate. Little rows
of yellow Post-it notes lined up with geometric precision on the carefully stacked files. A set of pens, only two, and a photo-frame con-
taining a picture of a smiling man and two perfect young children
– looked like a mortgage advertisement from an era before the
banking crisis, before the ads had shifted towards images of cast-iron
stability, more meat and potatoes, less gloss. Or maybe they hadn't
changed at all. Maybe it was the way he viewed them now; maybe
everything had lost its gloss.

Brennan took out a Silk Cut. Not a real fag: these were for Satur-
day smokers and teenies who bought packs of ten for a sly puff between home ec and maths ... But something had to give. A lot of
things had to give, thought Brennan.

As he put the cigarette to his lips, the Chief Super hung up the
phone. 'Light that and I'll have your guts for garters!'

She probably meant it. He rolled the tip of the cig on his tongue,
held schtum. He had no intention of lighting up; it was just a gam-
bit, a needle for her. Galloway put her hands on her hips. She
seemed to have him sussed – a let-the-laddie-at-his-game look. She
smiled, sat.

For a moment Brennan stood before her. She was a thin brunette
in a tight-fitting skirt and jacket. He wondered, in other circum-

stances, could he fancy her? Doubted it – she wasn't his type. There was a harshness there, a meanness of spirit that outweighed any other physical attractiveness. She was a ball-breaker, and Brennan liked his balls the way they were.

'You called me in, ma'am.'

'Don't call me that, Brennan ... and stop playing the prick.' She put a stare on him; what should have been an attractive pair of hazel eyes managed to burrow like hungry rats. He looked away. Whatever he thought of her, she was the boss and you didn't challenge the boss ... not unless you wanted your head in your hands to play with.

The Chief Super took a file from the top of the neatly stacked pile on her desk. For a moment, she seemed engrossed; she completely ignored Brennan as she turned over the pages with her long fingernails. After some time she sat up, straightened her back and made an apse of her fingers. Brennan felt uneasy as she stared over him, spoke: 'I've been looking over your file.'

'File?' He knew exactly what she meant, but played dumb. It was the psych file compiled by Dr Fuller.

'The recommendation is for you to return to ...' she stalled, held in her words, then, 'the real world.'

Brennan felt his pulse quicken. She was riling him. 'That so?'

'How do you feel about that?' She wheeled back her chair, crossed her legs. Her heel slipped from her stiletto, the shoe dangling delicately on her big toe.

'I've told you before: sooner I'm given a proper case the better.'

Galloway stared. For a moment Brennan thought she was about to cave, then she reached out for the file, started turning pages. Every few seconds she stopped, stalled on a word or a phrase and let out a long sigh. Once or twice she wet her lips with her tongue and clicked her teeth together. She had done this to Wullie when he'd been up for early retirement and he'd said he felt the urge to give her teeth a 'proper fucking clatter'. Brennan knew how he felt.

'If this is about the murder out in Muirhouse,' said Brennan, 'I know you've got Lauder and Bryce out on the pub shooting, and there's hardly enough bods to fill the rota as it is so—'

Galloway raised an eyebrow. 'So, what, I should just bring you back into the fold because we're a wee bit short-staffed, eh?'

'No, I, eh ...'

Her tone became shrill. 'I should fucking think not. Never heard of force cooperation? I can draft in a full murder squad if I need it, Brennan.'

He knew she was bluffing now – there was no way she wanted any-one else's staff on her patch. She didn't want anyone reporting back to the competition about her. Chief constable jobs were as rare as hobby-horse shite and she knew it; like she'd mess with her prospects when the promotion board were looking at her.

'Look, I know you have some ... factors to consider.'

She laughed, near spat, 'Factors! Hah ... that what we're calling it these days?' She slammed the folder shut, got up and turned to face the window. Brennan found himself unconsciously checking out her arse. 'These *factors*, Brennan ... should they concern me?'

He rolled on the balls of his feet. 'They don't concern me.'

'The Hibs back row's your top concern, Brennan. I didn't ask what concerned *you*. Should they concern *me*, sunshine?'

The DI's palms started to sweat; he rubbed them together. There was a strong urge in him to put his hands around her neck, shake some manners into the bitch, but he resisted. 'I'm fighting fit ... Rar-ing to go, boss.' She liked that, being called boss – made her feel like one of the lads. She turned back to face him, slumped in the seat. Her body language, her posture, all screamed one thing: she had nowhere to turn.

Chief Superintendent Aileen Galloway drew another file from a drawer, scribbled in it momentarily then turned it over. She drummed her fingers on the top of the blue card- board cover. 'Ste-vie McGuire has been desking the information as it comes in—'

Brennan sparked up, 'Stevie fucking McGuire ... Is it that bad?'

Galloway frowned. 'Look, he's a DC now, Rob – give him the ben-efit of the doubt.'

'He's a DC with no experience.' Brennan's pulse fired. 'Don't tell me you're giving him this murder ... Don't tell me.'

Galloway paused, touched the corner of her mouth, then picked up the file and handed it over. Her voice came softly, slowly: 'Get down there, shake up the SOCOs ... Don't be afraid to put that big foot of yours in a few arses.'

For a second Brennan wondered if he'd heard her right. He dou-ble-blinked, took a few breaths; that seemed to put his mind back into gear. He reached forward, grabbed the folder. There was a part of him that felt like he had been released from bondage, prison maybe. But there was no part of him that wanted to rejoice. He was never pleased to hear that a life had been taken, especially such a young one. It was a wrong that was always deeply felt in him. He turned for the door, got three, maybe four steps, then:

'Brennan ...' Galloway was back on her feet now, pointing. Something about her posture, the harsh angle of her face to her neck, said she might lunge for him at any moment with those pointy fingernails. 'You fuck this up, or even hint at fucking it up, and I'll make sure you spend the rest of your days on traffic and I'll make sure every time those lights go out at the top of Easter Road, you'll be down there with a pair of white gloves, standing in the middle of that box junction.'

Brennan strode for the door, said, 'Yes, ma'am.'

Chapter 2

WAS THIS THE WAY IT was going to be? As Brennan took the case file from the Chief Super's office, and walked for the front desk, he could feel eyes burning into him. He let it pass for a few moments, then stopped flat – spun on his heels. There was a momentary interlude where everyone seemed to wonder what he would do next, then rank – the old leveller – kicked in. Phones were picked up, drawers opened, conversations commenced once more. Brennan felt a surge of pride; it was a victory all right. He was back on the force – the proper force, not sitting at some desk counting paperclips and listening to wet-behind-the-ears DCs dicking on about stuff they knew nothing about.

'You … What's your name?' said Brennan.

'Sutcliffe, sir.'

Brennan smirked. 'Got to have balls to join up with a name like that.'

'Yes, sir.'

A brown-noser; Brennan hated those. 'I want the main incident room cleared.'

'But DI Lauder—'

'Fuck Lauder! … Shift the shooting caseload to IR Three.'

'Yes, sir.' The uniform stayed put. Everyone else in the room seemed to have frozen too.

Brennan barked, 'Well, what are you waiting for?'

The assembly sprang to life. Brennan was chancing his arm, but he knew he had to make his mark right away. The whole station would be looking for weakness, waiting for the first balls-up, the first 'i' undotted, 't' uncrossed. It couldn't happen. Self-belief was an inward direction, but an outward expression. A badly timed sigh, a tremor in the voice, a challenge to his authority or any one of a hundred poker tells would have them prattling in the canteen. It was start as you mean to go on, or face the consequences. He'd learned that tackling drunks when he was in uniform: you need to shout them down, set the boundaries fast, or they arked up, got lippy. After all that had happened lately, there was too much at stake to play anything other than the firm hand. His career had been on life support for the last few months; it was time to give it the kiss of life.

In the lift he allowed his head to rest on the wall for a moment; just a moment, then his neck snapped forward and he opened the file. Straight away Stevie McGuire's bullet-point listings riled him. McGuire couldn't spell, or use grammar – if this was DC material then the public had a right to feel short-changed.

'Parents should sue the public school.' Brennan shook his head. He dreaded to think what state the scene was in if McGuire had been first on hand. Times were tough, budgets tight, but if the job was worth doing it was worth giving to decent officers. There were far too many shiny-arsed careerists about the place; too many graduates on the fast-track, and McGuire was a prime example.

The lift doors pinged; Brennan stepped out.

The desk sergeant was poring over the sports page of the *News*. Brennan greeted him in the usual manner: 'All right, Charlie.'

'Rob.' He put down his paper, thinning his eyes.

'What cars you got?'

The older man sat upright, folded his arms. 'All out.'

'You're shitting me.'

He shook his head, made a wide arc with his hand. 'Nope, all out. Crime's big business in Edinburgh … Haven't you heard?'

'So, tell me, Charlie, should I take the bloody bus to a murder scene?'

The sergeant folded his arms again; his grey moustache twitched. 'Look, don't shoot the messenger.'

Brennan slapped his folder down on the counter. 'Gimme that radio.'

'What?'

'The radio, Charlie …'

'What are you going to do with that?'

Brennan tilted his head. 'See if I can get the bloody *Archers* on it … What do you think?'

A slow, frail hand went over to the stand-mic. The desk sergeant handed it over. 'I'll bet you can't work it.'

'Don't be a smart-arse, Charl … Get me McGuire on this.'

'He's at a murder!'

Brennan snapped, 'Aye. My investigation. Now get him on.'

The radio crackled for a few seconds before the older man called out for DC McGuire. There was no reply.

'He'll be at the scene, Rob.'

Brennan tapped the counter with his finger. 'Again.'

'*Rob.*'

'Try him again, Charlie.'

The static on the line crackled momentarily, then the call went out once more. The line fizzed, then, 'DC McGuire.'

Brennan pressed the button. 'Stevie, it's Rob Brennan. I want you back at the incident room. Leave your car, I'll need that later.'

'Rob ... Did you say leave my car?'

'Nothing wrong with your hearing, then. Leave the car, and get yourself back here with uniform. Hurry it up, though.

I need a run back there.'

A lengthy gap played on the line.

McGuire came back, 'Received that, Rob.'

'That's DI Brennan ... Stevie.'

Another pause. 'Yes ... sir.'

Brennan handed over the stand-mic. 'That'll do.'

The desk sergeant shook his head. 'You're going to rattle his cage talking to him like that, Rob.'

'Bullshit.'

A sigh. 'You're the boss.'

Brennan took a deep breath, deciding not to reply. He took a seat by the front door and tapped at the blue file whilst he waited for the squad car to arrive. He didn't look up but sensed the desk sergeant going back to the sports pages of the *News*. Fucking Hibs back four, he thought to himself. Galloway had some turns. Like to see how she'd take to him commenting on her copy of *Hello!* magazine he'd seen in her Mulberry briefcase. Cheeky sow. He knew not to engage, though: the battle of the sexes had been fought and lost.

The folder in his lap called to him, but something else called louder. Brennan rose, went to the front door. He nodded as two eyes ringed with burst capillaries appeared above the paper. 'Going for a smoke.'

Nods. The paper rustled again.

Outside the sky was grey, threatening rain. Brennan liked this time of year. Not quite summer, but well out of winter. The extremes of the seasons irked him; you never knew what to wear from one day to the next. If he could pick the weather, he'd go for grey skies and a hint of a chill every time. Sunshine was overrated. The smell of cut grass and barbecues was overrated. When he'd been in uniform, he'd hated the warmer months; they brought out drunks and fly-men robbing lead off the roofs. They were nothing but trouble. Crime was crime but the petty stuff always seemed like a social problem to

Brennan. A failure of society, politicians … a waste of his time. The evil ones, the murderers, the cold-blooded killers – they were the ones he wanted off the streets, locked up. At the very least, locked up. Brennan took out his packet of Silk Cut. His heart sank. He wanted a B&H, a strong boy, a lung bleeder, but turning forty called for a few concessions. The days when he'd swap ciggies with Wullie – a Capstans smoker, no less – were well and truly over. He hoped he didn't bump into Wullie while he was hanging off the end of a Silk Cut – the shame of it. Brennan had a sly laugh to himself as he remembered the old boy; it subsided quickly.

A shaft of light broke free of a bundle of grey cloud and painted a yellow oblong on the station car park. A few patches of spilled diesel were lit in the sun's rays, little rainbow bubbles illuminated in potholes. Brennan turned his head, drew deep on the cigarette and opened the file.

DC McGuire's bullet points had been hastily keyed in.

• White female, (no age) young.
• Found in industrial-sized bin. Blood smears on bin.
• Access lane, by tower block. Car park to rear.
• Four teens (female/local) at scene.
• No statements, girls too upset. Coming in. Calls out to parents.
• No time of death, Doc called, on way.
• Scene secured, uniform on perimeters. Lab setting up.

Brennan turned over the thin sheaf of paper. There was nothing on the other side. The rest of the pages were blank too, except for some standard forms and a contacts sheet with numbers he already had in his phone. There was nothing he couldn't have received in a two-minute briefing but the modern obsession with detailing every step dictated the written word. He closed the file; it looked pathetically thin, but he knew by the end of the day it would stretch to several volumes.

The sun disappeared behind another grey cloud, the wet patches in the car park darkened once more. Brennan stubbed his cigarette on the side of the building, flicked it onto the road. The last embers in the tip sizzled on the wet tarmac. As he watched the wind take the filter tip a black Audi pulled into the space opposite him. He recognised the number plate at once. It was new; it wasn't police. The engine stilled. Driver's door opened.

Dr Lorraine Fuller wore a brown trouser suit that was fitted and hugged her thin waist. She carried a heavy case – not a doctor's case; it would be full of paperwork. Brennan made a note of her movements as she clawed her long hair from her eyes, tucked it behind her ear. She looked harassed. She took a coat and another bag, a purse, from the back seat of the Audi, then she noticed Brennan staring at her. Lorraine looked away instantly. There was no smile, greeting; but definite acknowledgement. She pointed the remote locking at the car, turned for the station. She juggled her handbag between hands before deciding on the one it had been in originally. She tucked her coat over the crook of her elbow and walked briskly, heels clacking on the hard ground.

Brennan watched her for a moment or two, then turned his gaze to the door, leaned in and grabbed the handle as she approached. There was a stalled breath's distance between them as she spoke. 'I need to see you.'

Brennan looked down. 'It's difficult.'

'Why?' Her tone was harsh.

'I'm back on the squad.'

'I know.' She let the implication hang.

'Okay. When?'

'Soon. I'll call.' She moved towards the door. Brennan eased the handle downwards, pulled. As he watched her go inside he thought about their last meeting – it was more than a week ago now, too long. He couldn't help that, though. Sometimes you needed a break from people; even those close to you.

A squad car sped into the hatched area at the front of the station. DC McGuire hurried himself, got out the passenger's door with a leg dangling over the tarmac before the car had stopped.

Brennan turned, approached the younger man. 'Stevie.'

'Sir.'

He raised the folder. 'What else you got for me?'

McGuire spoke to his feet. 'Time of death's been put at some point last night. We'll know better when they get her on the slab.'

Brennan didn't like his phraseology. His mood was already soured by seeing Galloway, and then Lorraine. 'It's somebody's daughter, lad.'

The DC checked himself. 'Sorry … There's, eh, something else.'

There always was, thought Brennan. 'Go on.'

'The body's been tampered with.'

Brennan tucked his chin onto his chest, peered from beneath raised eyelids. 'Sexually?'

'No, least, we don't think so … It's been mutilated, badly mutilated.'

Brennan could see the DC found it difficult. He watched him rub his hands together. Now he talked to his palms. 'The girl's been sawn up.'

'What do you mean?'

A deep breath, slowly exhaled. 'Her limbs were removed ... The legs, below the knee, were severed and bagged.' He looked into Brennan's face. 'We don't have the arms.'

'The girl's arms are missing?'

The DC nodded. 'They were removed ... crudely.'

'Jesus Christ.'

Brennan turned for the car. He yanked open the passenger's door, got inside and slammed it shut, lowered the window. McGuire stood still as Brennan barked at him, 'Get the incident room set up – we're in the big room.'

'What about Lauder's shooting?'

'Fuck Lauder! ... I want statements from those girls by the time I get back and have the lab primed for an all-nighter.

Okay?'

'Yeah, yeah ... Anything else?'

'Yes. Get a list together of every missing teenage girl in the country ... And you report everything that comes in to me first, not the Chief Super. Got that?'

McGuire nodded, but looked unsure; scratched his open palm.

'Stevie, everything ... No matter what she tells you. Got that?'

'Yeah ... Got it, sir.'

'Good. If you remember this is *my* investigation, Stevie, then we'll get on just fine.'

Brennan slapped the dash.

The squad car pulled out, sirens blaring.

Chapter 3

BRENNAN WONDERED WHAT was changing faster, the city of Edinburgh, or him within it. As the squad car pulled out of Fettes he grimaced at the queues of traffic clogging up the roads. Medieval cities were never meant for the motor car, but he could remember when getting about the place was a far simpler affair. One-way streets had sprung up everywhere, making every route a circuitous one. Add in the bus lanes, the persistent road works and the full-scale gutting that the recent tram installation had wrought, and driving had become a slow and effective means of torture.

'Get out the fucking way,' mouthed the uniform at the wheel.

Brennan twisted his neck – it was enough.

'Sorry, sir.'

'Would you prefer to be driving a taxi, son?'

A stall, some lip-biting. 'No, sir …'

Brennan laughed. 'Don't worry, I'm just tugging your chain. These yuppies in their Stockbridge tractors boil my piss too.'

The uniform looked relieved. 'It's the school-run mums.'

'Yummy-fucking-mummies … Making their way back home after a latte in Morningside! Bless them, probably busy day ahead. Watching *Cash in the Attic* and polishing those blond-wood floorboards.'

The constable tapped at the wheel, making an overly showy point of approval. It made Brennan wince. He knew why too: the six months' enforced psych leave had left him with an intimate knowledge of the daytime television schedules. His forays into DIY had been less successful – his father had always said he didn't know which end of a hammer to pick up. Andy wasn't much better. Neither were chips off the old block, but at least his younger brother had kept the family firm going for a while. It wasn't his fault there was nothing left to show of it. Andy couldn't be blamed for that. Could Brennan, though? He sometimes wondered; he knew his father did.

Brennan had a lot to think about right now. These times came and went. He knew they were cyclical. When Sophie was born he'd gone through a similar phase: thinking, evaluating. Life suddenly had more import, a lot that had went before was meaningless. Fifteen years later it was the other way around; nothing seemed to matter. What had changed? Was it him; was it the world? He dredged up some long-distilled lines from a philosopher about the ages of man, and viewing life and experience differently with maturity. What seemed valuable, important, was rendered worthless with the passage of time. He almost laughed at the vacuity of his younger self. But was he any better now? *Experience was the name a man gave to his mistakes*. Someone had said that too.

'Take the bus lane.' Brennan pointed at the windscreen.

The harshness of his voice surprised him. There was a lot in there, inside him, that he found surprising now.

'Yes, sir.'

The police Astra sped past the lines of traffic. A young woman on the street put her hands up to her ears. Brennan knew the older ones didn't bother – their hearing had atrophied to the stage where the sirens didn't bother them ... It was another one of those observations that the job afforded you. Very few were worth noting.

The driver was too quick into the Crewe Toll roundabout. Brennan felt some movement on the back tyres as the car spun onto Ferry Road. He felt himself automatically gripping the door handle, his right foot pumping an imaginary brake pedal. 'Try and get us there in one piece, eh.'

'Sorry, sir.'

'And stop apologising. You're far too free with your apologies ... Don't mind me, I'm a full-time prick. I point out everyone's flaws in this job.'

The main artery road was stocked with ancient figures: they were the occupants of Peter Howson paintings. Huge-knuckled working men; hard drinkers and working girls.

Smokers puffed freely, flicked dowps into the gutter. Every one of them shook their head at the sight of the speeding police car. They were *filth* round here. The fun-stoppers. The Rozzers. No one welcomed them; there was no red-carpet treatment coming their way down this end of town. It didn't bother Brennan. He'd long since lost the need to be liked – in any way – and certainly not for being a police officer. There had been a time, at the deathly dull dinner parties his wife used to hold for her circle, where spouses had tried to intellectualise their view of the police for him. 'I wouldn't like to live in a society without police,' one pot-bellied middle manager had remarked, 'for all the same reasons I wouldn't like to live in Somalia.'

Brennan remembered the remark, and the smirk the tosser had

topped the statement with; it was glib bullshit. The lot of it was glib bullshit. It was a job. A necessary evil. The scene darkened down Pennywell Road. Ginger kids, barely school age, with the arse hanging out of their trousers shot the V-sign. A few tried to spit in the car's direction. Brennan had known stones to be thrown; he was unfazed. There were middle-aged women in baffies and housecoats stood on the road, leaning over gardens and jabbering. They'd obviously clocked the police activity; the talk would be of drugs raids, whose man was being taken in, how the force victimised them. Each syllable of the schemies' chat would be punctuated by puffs on Superkings; the sight of them was as regular as the street furniture. As harrowing as the bust couch or the rusting scooters in the overgrown gardens. Brennan could have painted the scene from memory. He knew there were liberal thinkers – what Wullie called the *Guardian*-reading classes – who would gasp and deride the deprivation, but not him. This was a breeding ground for crime, a dumping ground for the dispossessed and the dafties. It was a dangerous place; no question.

Brennan shook his head, sighed, 'Another poor lassie's met her end. How many's that?'

The constable shrugged, looked like he was wondering who the DI was speaking to.

Brennan looked ahead through the windscreen, to the point on the road where the Scenes of Crime Officers had set up. The title of an old song played to him, 'Another Girl, Another Planet' ... He thanked Christ his daughter was being raised on the other side of town – no child here had a chance.

'Pull up in front of the SOCOs,' said Brennan. 'Don't want them accusing us of blocking access to their wee gang hut.'

The driver eased through the gears, slowly, and put the car in at the kerb. A small crowd had formed in the street; some uniforms paced a thin cordon. The crowd looked subdued. At once Brennan knew the word had got out.

'Look at them,' he said to the constable.

'What?'

'Their faces ... They know.'

The younger man stared out of the window. His expression seemed to mirror the sad mix of hurt and shame. Grief swayed through the assembled bodies; Brennan knew this wasn't a good sign. A community in hurt was a community in trouble, and trouble he could well do without.

The constable put on his cap, followed Brennan out to the pavement. The SOCOs paced from a small laneway, into their white van that looked like a mobile library.

Brennan watched their faces for signs, giveaways, but they portrayed nothing. They never did. Two uniforms greeted the DI. One was speaking into the radio clipped onto his Kevlar vest but he stopped when he saw the detective.

'Morning, sir.'

Brennan nodded. 'We got the doc on site?'

'He's been and gone.'

'Fucking hell. Already? Has he a holiday booked?'

The constable rubbed his cheek, tried to speak but couldn't seem to find the right words.

'Never mind,' said Brennan. 'Let's get going.'

As he paced for the lane he was T-boned by a young woman with a digital recorder in her hand. She had just ducked under the blue-and-white tape and definitely wasn't messing about. 'Are you the investigating officer?' she said.

Brennan looked at her then glanced to the uniforms. They pushed in front of her and grabbed her arms.

'Get off me!'

'Sorry about this, sir.'

Brennan watched the scene. The woman was early twenties, fresh-faced. She was also too eager for her own good.

'Do you have an ID for the victim?'

She already had too much information.

'Do you have any suspects on the girl's death?'

Brennan felt a flush of heat in his chest; he clenched his jaw. The woman prised an arm free of the uniforms, pushed out the recorder's mic. Brennan lifted a hand, covered the small, silver-coloured device. 'You seem to know more than me, love.'

She tutted, near spat, 'I'm not your *love!*'

Brennan smiled at her and walked away. Over his shoulder he said, 'Got that right.'

A SOCO approached as he walked to the lane. 'Morning, sir.'

'Is it?'

The man dropped his brows. 'Sir?'

Brennan stopped, nodding back to the scene he'd just left. 'How did the fucking press latch onto this so soon?'

Now he raised his brows. 'The press?'

'That's not a welcoming party from the *News.*'

The SOCO looked past Brennan. The young reporter was being escorted beyond the taped-off area. 'Never seen her before.'

'Get a good look. Sure you'll be seeing a lot more of her. Trust me, I'm a good judge of character.'

The SOCO had no reply. He handed Brennan a pair of blue covers for his shoes.

'Got some gloves?' said the detective.

A shrug, shake of the head.

'Typical. Come on then, let's do this.'

Brennan strode past the officer, made for the lane. As he passed, the SOCO spoke out, 'I should warn you, sir, it's not a pretty sight.'

Brennan turned. 'It never is, lad.'

Chapter 4

DEVLIN McARDLE RUBBED AN OPEN palm over his smooth head. The razor sting ignited with his touch but the satisfaction he felt with the close crop cancelled it out. 'Nice one, just the job,' he said.

The barber smiled, leaned in and brushed at McArdle's shoulders. A few strands of stubble fell to the floor. McArdle turned down the corners of his mouth, pushed away the barber's hand. 'That's enough, that's enough.' As he rose from the chair, the black robe was removed in one swift pull. He strode to the till, said, 'How much?'

A shake of the head. 'No charge, sir.' The barber made a small cross over his heart. 'Not for you, sir.'

McArdle smiled. It was only a small curl of the lip; he didn't look used to it, and stopped it almost as quickly as it appeared. As he turned for the door he saw a thin man waiting outside for him. He was tugging nervously at the cord on his jogging trousers. There was a tic queuing on his eyelid and he brushed at it with a speed that looked unnatural. Jumpy, the man was jumpy. Even more than usual, if that was possible. His whole demeanour said trouble – he was either in some kind of bother, or about to be.

At the door the man tried to catch McArdle's attention. He leaned forward and made a gesture with his shaking hand. McArdle ignored him, walking out the door and onto London Road. The street was busy. It was early afternoon; giro day at the post office had attracted a crowd. As McArdle walked he felt his thighs rub together. He had the squat build of a weightlifter, could handle himself: they called him 'the Deil'. Those that didn't know him thought it was a contraction of Devlin, a play on the Scots for *Devil*, but those who did know him knew the name was hard earned. McArdle liked people to know that about him.

The thin man followed him up the road. McArdle caught sight of him shuffling into doorways and under scaffolding as he tried to keep a respectful distance. He had told Barry Tierney never to stop him in the street; he'd warned the loser more than once. He felt his feet stamping harder with every step, wished he hadn't put on trainers – boots would have been better for bursting this stupid prick's head. His shoulders tensed as a haar shot up Maryfield on its way to the tourists trekking Arthur's Seat. He crossed over the road, onto West Norton Place, and took the side street at the old tech college. He turned to see Tierney pegging it up behind him. McArdle ducked into waste ground behind a Shell garage and waited. In a few moments he started to hear the shuffling gait, the heavy breathing. He reached out and pulled Tierney into the back of the disused building.

'What the fuck are you playing at?'

Tierney flinched, brought hands up to his head. 'I've got money … I've got money.'

McArdle slapped him; one slap, it toppled him. Tierney fell to the ground and curled up. 'I'm sorry … I know you said, but I've got money.' He dug in the pockets of his torn Adidas hoodie. 'Here, here …' It was forty, maybe fifty pounds.

McArdle snatched it. 'What's this?' He slapped the notes and his fist off Tierney's head. The force of it scraped his knuckles. Blood streamed from a gash on the thin man's forehead. 'You're into me for more than fifty quid!'

'I know … I know … I just thought—'

'You thought what?' McArdle stamped his foot on his ribcage. Tierney coughed heavily. 'I'll tell you when to think, y'piece of shit. Get it? … Eh? Get it?' McArdle was ready to end Tierney's days but the noise of a car parking up at the Shell garage changed his mind. He leaned forward, grabbed Tierney by the neck and yanked him to his feet.

'Look, I'm sorry … I'm sorry, I've got your money … I can soon get all of it!'

McArdle released his grip, poked Tierney's chest. 'What are you on about?'

Tierney gasped, stepped back. 'When, y'know, Vee and me had that deal with you – remember that time?'

McArdle's lower lip drooped. He was confused. Was Tierney saying what he thought he was? 'You mean you and Vee … ? You're not saying you want to pay me off like that again?'

Tierney stepped back. His face twitched and ticced as he brushed himself down with his bony fingers. 'Yeah, yeah. I mean, no … last time you paid more than that. More than we owe you.'

McArdle put out a hand, resting it on Tierney's shoulder. He was interested enough, but unsure if he could trust him. 'This isn't some bloody scam, 'cause if it is, I'll burst you all over this town.'

Tierney double-blinked, quick movements, unnatural.

'No. Straight up.'

'And you want to sell to me?'

'Sell, yeah. We do.'

McArdle closed his mouth, brought a hand up to his head. He ran fingertips over his crown – the tight cut of the razor felt good to the touch. He walked away from Tierney; he didn't trust him. He was trash, a junkie. His girlfriend was a junkie too, hardly the type to be doing any sort of business with, never mind one like this.

'Are you sure Vee's game for this?'

Tierney shrugged. He looked to his left, then his right; his thin shoulders poked through his top. 'Yeah, she's sound.'

McArdle felt a wariness creep up on him. He didn't like getting too involved with this sort of people. Taking their money was fine, but any more than that was asking for trouble. But he had dealt with this pair before. Maybe it would be all right. 'I'm warning you, Barry, if you're up to something and I—'

He butted in, 'I'm up to nothing ... we want paying. Nothing else. Just a few quid, eh.'

A laugh, splutters. 'You think there's a drink in it for you? You pair of greedy bastards.'

Tierney tried to smile but his heart didn't look to be in it. His teeth were yellowed and broken when he showed them. The hollows in his cheeks deepened as he widened his grin. 'Well, last time ...'

'Times change, Barry boy ... times change.' That took the smirk off his face. The state of him, thought McArdle, he'd sell his own flesh and blood for a fix with a smile on his face. Well, a sort of smile. Even for McArdle this was low; Tierney was the worst of trash. 'We'll see.'

Tierney arked up, 'But—'

'No fucking ifs or buts. We'll see.' McArdle needed to think about it. Finding the buyer was no trouble, and the money was good, but he didn't trust Tierney. Junkies were bad news. To a one, they were bad luck. Carried it round with them.

'Well, what about just now?'

McArdle shook his head, grabbed Tierney by the face. 'You scrounging, that it?'

'I gave you fifty.'

'That wouldn't clear you a week's interest on what you and Vee owe me.'

'But—'

McArdle pushed back Tierney's face. The junkie stumbled a few paces and fell onto the slabs. 'You're nothing but trash, y'know that?' McArdle dug in his pocket, pulled out a couple of wraps and threw them at the addict. Tierney scrabbled about for them, picked up the wraps fast and pushed himself up. He struggled to find any purchase, his shoes slipping on the wet slabs as his thin arms stretched out behind him. 'You won't regret this, Deil,' he said.

'Get out my sight.'

'Will you tell me soon, then?'

'I said fuck off ... Get out my sight.'

McArdle watched Tierney struggle to his feet, then saw his slope-shoulders jink round the corner. He moved to sit on a low brick wall, trying to gather his thoughts. It was simple enough taking cash for a few wraps, but what the junkie was offering was something else. It was complicated, fraught with potential pitfalls, and meant working with more people than he was used to – and he was used to being in full control, in charge. The Germans would be the ones paying up, so they'd have all the power. He didn't like that. Still, the money sang to him. It was very good money last time and maybe he could ask for more now. McArdle knew the junkie's offer was too good to be passed up. It was chancy, always was, but wasn't everything? He removed his mobile. As he delved into his contacts, and dialled, McArdle was already counting the cash in his mind.

Ringing.

The line was answered on the third chime.

'*Hallo.*'

'Günter ... that you?'

'Yes.'

'It's Devlin McArdle.'

'Uh-huh.'

'Just enquiring ... If the supply channel was to open up again, would you be interested?'

There was no sound except static on the line for a few moments, then, 'Interested? ... I believe we would be.'

'You would?'

'Yes, Mr McArdle ... I think we could almost guarantee it.'

Chapter 5

BARRY TIERNEY WAS SWEATING AND flushed when he returned home. As he slammed the front door of the flat behind him Vee appeared in the hallway. Her dirty blonde hair had been scraped back and tied in an elastic band. Her eyes bulged and watered. The edges of her mouth were cracked and scabbed. She grabbed him. 'Did you get it?'

Tierney pushed past her. 'Leave me be.' He shuffled towards the bathroom and closed the door quickly behind him. Vee followed, banged on the door. He felt disturbed to be alone in the small room; it was full of demons, but his bladder ached and there was nowhere else to go.

'Barry, you bastard ... Open this door.'

'Shut it.' As he relieved himself he heard the child start to scream in the other room. 'See to that kid, for fuck's sake.'

Vee continued to bang on the door. 'Barry, open up ... You better not be holding out on me!'

He shook out the last drops of urine, pulled up his joggers. His hands were shaking at the prospect of the wraps he'd taken from the Deil. He touched the sides of his head, tried to think, but nothing came. He ran fingers through his hair, then tucked his hands beneath his arms, but the process did nothing for him. He couldn't concentrate in this place. He didn't want to be alone in there but a racket was going on outside that he couldn't face.

'Shut it, Vee, I'm warning you, shut the noise up or I'll put you through that fucking wall.'

The banging stopped.

He heard Vee sliding down the back of the door, then her tears as she sobbed at the gap above the carpet. She had been crying hysterically the night before, but that was for another reason. She probably wanted to block it out too.

'Barry, you can't leave me here if you're holding ... You just can't.'

'Is that all you're bothered about? Eh, is it?'

Her voice lowered. 'I need a hit, Barry ... more than ever.'

'We know why that is, don't we.'

She snivelled, 'Why are you doing this?'

Tierney ran the taps in the sink, trying to drown out her shrill voice. He let the sink fill up, dropped in his hands, then splashed his face. He thought about dunking his head, blocking out the world, but he knew a better way.

'I saw him, by the way,' Tierney yelled, '… in case you're interested, I saw the Deil.'

Silence.

Slowly, the sound of Vee shuffling on the other side of the door came. 'What did you say?'

'You heard me all right.' He smiled to himself: he had the upper hand again. She was always easier to manipulate, to control, when he had something to hold over her. He couldn't recall ever having anything as weighty as this, though.

'You told him about … ?'

'Of course I didn't fucking tell him. Do you think I'm mental?'

Vee stumbled over the words: 'Th-then how … I mean, what did you say?' She sounded worried now; he could hear the fear pitched in her voice.

'I told him what we agreed.'

She had no response to that – of course she didn't, she couldn't argue with him. Tierney heard Vee start to move again. She was rocking, her back pressing on the other side of the door. With each movement the sound carried pressure towards him. He felt the walls in the small bathroom closing him in. He peered at the bath, scrubbed clean for once. Tierney couldn't remember the bath looking so clean – it was bright white, sparkling. He looked in. He didn't want to, but felt compelled to. A smell of bleach caught in his nostrils. He couldn't stay there any more, opened the door.

'Get up … See to that kid!'

Vee held on to Tierney's leg. 'Did you score? Did you? Did you score, Barry?'

He shook her off, lashed out with his foot, caught her on the solar plexus. She gasped for breath, fumbling on the carpet with her fingers splayed as if she was looking for something. 'Barry … I need some. Don't, don't …' She seemed to find strength from somewhere and raised herself to face him. She grabbed the sleeves of Tierney's hoodie. 'Please, please, Barry … I'll do anything.'

'Settle that fucking kid.'

'I will. I will. I promise … Just give me something.'

The sight of her disgusted him; he wanted her away from him. He didn't want to look at her ever again. Her face reminded him of everything that was wrong with his life and why he needed to escape from it. Tierney delved into his pocket and pulled out a wrap. 'There, get fired into that ... Get out my sight.' He watched her scurry like a rodent for scraps, padding the floor on her hands and knees. When she located the wrap her face changed instantly. She became suffused with desire. All the previous whining and begging had been for show, Tierney knew it. He hated her for it. When he was on the programme, a key worker had told him that everyone hates the one thing in others that they hate in themselves. He hadn't understood her, had asked her to explain and was told it was like living with someone who pointed out your flaws all the time: they dragged you to the mirror and showed you them. When he understood, he hated Vee more; she made him hate himself, what he'd become.

Tierney knew it didn't pay you to think. After all he'd been through, after all he'd seen, he didn't want to think. He didn't want to think about who he was or who Vee was because he knew they were both nothing. It was better not to think. Better to forget. To block it all out.

He took the remaining wrap from his pocket and went through to the front room. The curtains were drawn and the place sat in semi-darkness. He could hear the baby crying where she lay in the top drawer of the dresser, but he didn't look to that corner of the room. He climbed onto the mattress and rolled up his sleeve. A burnt spoon and a lighter fell onto the floor as he manoeuvred. He picked them up, collected the rest of his works and bit the leather belt between his teeth.

As his eyes closed, nothing mattered any more.

Chapter 6

WHEN HE WAS STILL IN uniform, barely twenty and still pimply, Brennan had made his first visit to a Muirhouse crime scene. It was nothing like he'd imagined, growing up on the west coast and watching *The Sweeney*. It wasn't supposed to be like this. The job, life. It was supposed to be better.

'I warn you, it's not a pretty sight,' Wullie Stuart had told him.

They said young Brennan fancied himself back then, said he was full of it. A typical Weegie, even though he was from Ayr. Anyone west of Corstorphine was a Weegie to this lot. 'I can handle it,' he told the detective sergeant.

'Are you sure, son? There's no shame in holding back.'

'I can handle it.'

The crime scene was in a high-rise. There had been a call from neighbours about a domestic. Loud roars, shouting and screaming. The usual. Uniform had attended and then CID had been called. Brennan had pestered the officers to get a hand-up. He wanted to learn at their elbow – it was the best way to learn anything, his father had told him that.

'Okay, then. But take a hold of this.'

Brennan looked at the sergeant's hand. He was holding out an old Tesco carrier.

'What's that for?'

'Your lunch.'

'But I've had my lunch, sir.'

'Exactly.'

When realisation dawned, Brennan shook his head. 'You're all right … Keep it.'

'Okay.' Wullie nodded. 'Okay.'

The young uniform followed the detective sergeant up the grimy stairwell. It smelled of piss and stale tobacco. The walls were daubed with graffiti, large illiterate swabs for or against Hibs and Hearts, numbers to call for blow jobs, threats of violence. None of it fazed the twenty-year-old, but something told him he was about to enter a new realm. He knew he was going to see something he'd never seen before. Would it change him? No, never. How could it? He was well equipped for anything they threw at him.

The door had been booted – the hinges hung on bent screws. Two panels had been caved in – knuckles, maybe? He'd have said a shoulder or a firm kick, but there was blood smeared there. Knuckles, then, so a junkie perhaps ... someone too out of it to know they'd broken every bone in their hand putting in the door. There was more blood inside. And a stench. A smell Brennan had never encountered before. It filled the nostrils and seemed to get right inside your head. He'd never known a smell like it; it came loaded with suggestions. It wasn't an acrid smell or an uncomfortable smell, one that made you want to put your nose into your sleeve, but it wasn't something he'd like to keep regular contact with. It unnerved him. Years later, he'd acknowledge it as the smell of poverty. The smell of lost hope, of squalor and abandonment and dissipation. Of all those things, and something else, something more sinister.

'Oh, Christ!'

Brennan knew his mouth had drooped. He felt dumb, unable to move.

'Get down!'

There was a flurry of bodies; a black flash crossed the room. There was a man at the window. He struggled with the handle, and suddenly it opened and a gust blew in. Cigarette ash flew into the room from a large smoked-glass ashtray by the ledge. Brennan felt lost.

'Who let the fucking dog in?' shouted Wullie. 'This is a fucking murder scene!'

Brennan saw the dog, a small, stout Staffordshire bull terrier type. It was on the floor tearing at something. He didn't get a full look at the dog – his eyes were fixed elsewhere. On the floor was a familiar form – it looked like a woman. There was a dress, floral-print. Yellow flowers, with white centres, splattered with dark red marks. There was a head, and hair. Pale brown hair; the colour of his mother's. But there was something missing. The face. Where the face should be was a pulpy, black mess. The eyes were there, he could see them, but not the whites. The blood vessels had ruptured and the eyes sat like black eight-balls. There was no sign of any skin, only a prominent white shard of bone set in the middle of the face where it had supported the base of the nose.

'No, leave it!' Wullie grabbed at the dog; there were growls, Wullie roared, called the beast a bastard. He pulled at its collar. It took some time for Brennan to draw his attention to the ruckus. When he did, his mind struggled to process what was happening. The dog was attached to the woman's side, tugging with its mouth; it wasn't about to let go. Sinewy, blood-red strands of flesh stretched like glue as the dog's jaws were prised apart. The corpse seemed to move, almost come to life as the contest to extricate the animal continued.

Brennan heard sounds, words: 'It's the guts!'

'*What?*'

'The dog's eating the guts.'

'Get away!'

'I'm telling you ...'

Brennan watched a cigarette being lit; one of the officers laughed at the scene before them. Then the dog broke free, ran for the door. Brennan felt it brush his trouser leg. He looked down, saw another black blur.

'You okay, son?' said Wullie.

Brennan felt his throat go dry; his head was hotter than a coke kiln. As he lifted his gaze to the sergeant a tremor passed through him from the ground. When it reached his knees they seemed to lose all their strength, folded beneath him. He couldn't remember his head hitting the floor.

It was a dark, dank lane. Not the place for a party. Not the place for a carry-out, dodging the school, getting drunk with friends. It was private, though. Brennan knew privacy had a high value amongst teenagers; in Muirhouse, a dark lane where they put the bins out was somewhere no one was going to bother them. He put himself in the girls' mindset for a moment; poor girls, he thought. A few cans, a laugh, bit of messing ... They wouldn't forget this day for the rest of their lives. He hoped it didn't scar them too much. But then, where they came from, they had every chance of more of the same to follow. Brennan knew it was the other girl he really needed to feel sympathy for – she wouldn't get any more chances.

The SOCO spoke, something trite about it being a sad way to meet her end; Brennan switched off. Words had no place here. Not at this point. There were no words to explain away what had happened. It seemed shameful to speak; beyond pointless. A life had been taken, in brutal fashion, and disposed of without any concern for the innate value of being. In situations like this, there was no humanity. There was no need for the pretence of civility, for language. Explaining away how we came to this pass was someone else's job. Evaluating man's inhumanity to man was an intellectual exercise that had no place in a dark lane where a young girl lay, lifeless, draped in her own blood.

Broken glass crunched under Brennan's feet as he neared the white tent the SOCOs had erected over the dumpster at the bottom of the lane. There was a man clad head to foot in white, a hood on his head, exiting the tent. He put eyes on Brennan then looked away.

'Minute ... Gimme those.' Brennan pointed to the box he held. It looked like tissues but held disposable gloves.

The detective grabbed a pair, said, 'Thanks.'

The atmosphere inside the tent was foetid. There was a reek of cheap lager and sugar-rich fortified wine that had mingled with the sweet smell of blood and the sweat of grown men, overdressed in too many layers of protective clothing. Brennan was used to the stench. He pulled on the gloves, snapped them onto his wrists.

He could feel people watching him as he moved. This was his show. He was the main act, the one who would make sense of this mess. Brennan slowly paced back and forth, always keeping the dumpster in the corner of his field of vision. He looked at the ground, sat on his haunches and scraped at the terrain. 'This footprint's been cast, has it?'

'Yes, sir.'

A SOCO photographer came into the tent holding a large Nikon with a mounted flash; he looked at Brennan and turned around.

'Just a minute.'

The photographer returned. 'Sir.'

'Let me see that.' Brennan took the camera from him. He flipped it over, pointed the long lens to the ground and looked at the small screen on the back. The camera had stored the crime scene perfectly. As Brennan spun the wheel he kept looking around, checking nothing had been missed. He handed the camera back.

'Get those back to DC McGuire.'

The SOCO raised the camera, spoke: 'I wanted to get a few more with the new card in ...'

'After I'm done. Wire those to the station now.' The SOCO seemed to be processing the request. 'Now, officer.' Brennan kept a stare on him; the man backed out of the tent.

'You.' Brennan pointed to another suited-up officer, on his haunches holding a small brush. 'This printed?'

'Yes, sir.'

Brennan stored the response, then ignored the officer. Prints were rarely of any use in this kind of situation, but a necessity. Brennan knew the number of murder cases he'd made use of prints was a low scorer. They were nearly always partials – a bit of a thumb, a palm.

The good prints – the full hands, the clearly identifiable fingertips – were only useful if their holders were on record. Fine, if you were working housebreakings, where the local skag-heads and scrotes were always slipping up; but murder, that was different. Killers knew the stakes were higher. Even in a state of panic, they knew to clean up, cover their tracks.

There was a swish on the tent flap. DS Collins appeared. He had one hand in a protective glove and was wrestling the other one on.

'Fucking things, hate them … Like johnnies.'

Brennan turned. He didn't appreciate the stilled ambience he'd created being disrupted. 'They irritate pricks, you mean.'

Collins grinned. 'Yeah, something like that, sir.'

The DS walked towards the dumpster, jerked open the lid, flicked his head. 'You seen our stiff?'

Brennan felt a flicker in his chest. He turned towards the bin. When he drew even with Collins, he shook his head. 'Your mother must have been a lovely woman.'

The DS frowned, clearly confused. Brennan took the weight of the lid from him, pushed him aside.

As he looked inside, Brennan exhaled slowly. The girl was small, tiny. Her flesh was pale; white. Dark welts had been made at the corners of her mouth; black contusions detailed where her teeth had been clattered. Her mouth presented a dark rictus; dried blood sat at its edges and pooled in the hollow of her neck. Brennan was disturbed by how still she looked. She was almost peaceful, at rest.

'I hear Ian Lauder's gunning for you, boss,' said Collins.

Brennan stared at the girl. 'That so?'

'Fair pissed you turfed his shooting out the big room.'

Brennan huffed, 'Tough shit.' He put a stare on Collins.

The DS was chewing gum; it annoyed Brennan. He waited until his jaw stopped moving and then he pulled his gaze back to the girl.

There was a deep incision on her forehead, running round to her temple. Her pale blonde hair had been matted by dark blood which had stuck her to the black refuse sack she lay on.

Brennan reached in, moved some of the rubbish around her. He saw her milky-white body, arms truncated at the shoulders. 'Do we have her arms?' he said.

'Nope.'

'How do we know they're not in here, then?'

'We don't.'

Brennan lifted the edge of a black plastic refuse sack. The raw butt where her arm once sat seemed to have been ripped and torn by a jagged edge.

'What you think – saw?'

Collins leaned in. 'Fucking cheapo one ... Not electric – too rough.'

'Why go to the bother?'

'Doesn't want her ID'd, obviously.'

'If she's from the scheme we'll ID her without prints.'

'Might take longer though. That's what they're thinking, I'd say.'

Brennan delicately lowered the black plastic. 'That's a lot of thinking for a pack of skag-boys.'

Collins didn't seem to be giving the DI his full attention. He started chewing on the gum again. 'Look, maybe it's a trophy take.'

'Fuck off, Collins, you can't draw that from one corpse.'

The DS exhaled loudly, reaching into his pocket for a packet of Embassy. He took one out the pack and wrestled the rubber gloves off. 'Well, what do you reckon, sir?'

Brennan shrugged. 'Panic, probably. If she's local, and she's been offed by another local, and our murderer had a bit of nous, they'd want to make it look different to every other square-go gone wrong.'

Collins moved out to the flap over the entrance. He had a cheap plastic lighter in his hand, shook it as he spoke to Brennan. 'Maybe. Maybe ... But you're forgetting one thing.'

'What?'

'That girl wasn't killed around here ... There's not enough blood for this to be the crime scene and the time of death doesn't tally.' Collins lit his cigarette and stepped out of the tent.

It riled Brennan, but the DS was right. 'So the girl was hacked up to make her easier to move.'

'Put a body in a bag, it's gonna stand out.'

'But put it in two or three ... could be anything.'

Chapter 7

BRENNAN STOOD LOOKING AT THE silent, cold body of the dead girl. She couldn't have been much older than Sophie. He felt a strange urge to check where his daughter was; it made his heart quicken for a moment and then it passed. It was instinct, a mad spiralling of thought that denied the solipsist in him. He brushed it aside: Sophie was safe and sound. Brennan knew that it wasn't her lot to end up in a dumpster at the end of a dark lane in a grim public housing scheme. He knew it was the fate of the poor, the indigent. They lived the types of disorganised, chaotic lives that led to heavy drinking, promiscuity, crime, violence and a higher likelihood of murder. The facts couldn't be denied. It didn't mean she deserved any of it.

'Right, get that girl out of there,' he hollered. 'I want that bin tipped and every inch of it gone over … Anything that even looks like it might have been a murder weapon – including a ginger bottle – I want it tested.'

The SOCOs stood up, watched Brennan cutting the air with his palms. 'And if there's so much as a jaggy steel comb I want it looked at … She's had her fucking arms sawn off – where are they?'

Brennan slapped the bin. 'Come on. Move it.'

The group headed for the dumpster, white-suited arms tucked into rubber gloves gesticulating over how best to remove the debris. Brennan watched for a moment, then left them to their work. Outside the tent he followed Collins down the lane.

'Bri, hold up,' he said.

The DS removed the filter tip from his lips, spun on his heels. 'What's up?'

Brennan resisted the urge to state the obvious, said, 'I think you're right.'

'Sir?'

'My gut says she's local.'

Collins looked around him, flagged an arm to the high-rises. 'Welcome to the Killing Fields.'

'Until we have an ID we need to go with what we have.'

'We've got fuck all.'

Brennan put his hands in his pockets, leaned towards Collins. 'We think she's local ... Most murder victims know their killer very well. If we have to shake up every bastard within a country mile of her, we will.'

Collins scratched his head, puffing out his cheeks. 'Look, shouldn't we wait and see what the SOCOs turn up?'

'We don't have time on our side, Bri ... Get your boys knocking on doors now.'

As Brennan walked away he heard Collins mutter something, but he couldn't make it out. When he turned round the DS was flicking ash onto the ground and kicking at a pothole. Brennan removed his left hand from his pocket, looked at his watch. 'Find out when those bins were last emptied,' he pressed his points home with a finger in the air, 'quiz all the taxi drivers, any that were out here between the time of death and the discovery, bring them in ... If anyone on the scheme still gets milk delivered, I want to know what their milkman had for breakfast ... Get searching every verge, hedge, gutter, gully and fucking rabbit hole from here to the black stump. And when you've done that, you can turn over the tramps.'

Collins swayed where he stood, staring at the pothole. 'Anything else, sir?'

Brennan smiled. 'Not just now ... But don't make any plans for the weekend, eh.'

When he reached the end of the lane the reporter was still there. Uniform were keeping a close eye on her now. She spotted Brennan and started to shout at him. He missed what she said because his attention was distracted by a press photographer leaning over the roof of a squad car to get a shot of him. Brennan upped his pace towards the blue-and-white tape, ducked under and started to make his way towards McGuire's car. As he unlocked the door he felt relieved to be leaving the scene, but couldn't resist a final glance towards the lane. The thought of the young girl lying in the dumpster jabbed at his heart but he knew any emotional response had to be locked away. Emotions had their place, but they got in the way of rational thinking. There was a killer out there, and it would take a slow, methodical approach to catch the bastard.

Brennan put the key in the ignition and engaged the clutch. As he turned at the end of the street he spotted a small child, two, three maybe, peering through the palings of a poorly maintained fence. The child had a colourful ball in her hands. When she saw Brennan staring back at her she dropped the ball and smiled, a wide heart-melting smile.

For an instant, Brennan forgot where he was, why he was there. The future seemed full of possibilities for the small girl; life was an adventure that had just begun for her. As he pressed the accelerator pedal and sped past the child, he looked into the mirror. She was staring, waving now.

Brennan lost his smile about the same time as his vehicle drew even with the lane's opening.

'Where's the fucking justice?' he muttered.

On the road back to the station, Brennan lit a Silk Cut. The taste was minimal, but he needed something to stop him grinding his teeth. It felt good to be back on the job, to be off desk duty, but he knew this case was going to test him. It was a feeling, a sense of uncertainty. Wullie had said he knew the tough cases within the first five minutes. It was an exaggeration, but Brennan knew what he meant. This job, this life, was all about following your instincts. Your head was prone to distractions, and your heart wasn't to be trusted.

Brennan's gut told him there was more to the young girl's demise than was first apparent. There were too many factors at odds with each other. He felt as if he'd entered a familiar room, but some of the furniture had been rearranged – and he'd been blindfolded. He hadn't had a case for over six months, since Andy's death, but something told him that had nothing to do with how he felt about this case.

Brennan hadn't wanted the leave; the Chief Super had insisted on it. She'd wanted to put him out because he wasn't a yes-man. Galloway was a typical careerist: she surrounded herself with the types that were no challenge to her. People like the boy, Stevie McGuire. He was a no-hoper, perfect material for promotion in Galloway's ranks. More like McGuire beneath her and her ascent was assured, carried high on their shoulders. Providing she could keep the likes of Brennan in check, that is. She still needed to rely on someone providing the clear-up rates if she was to get the Chief Constable's job.

Galloway was going to be watching him closely, he knew that. It was all about the long game with her. All about the mental battle, wearing people down, bending them to her will. It was a power struggle, and she wanted to man the controls. That's what the leave had been about. Brennan knew that the Chief Super wanted to break him – time off wasn't good for someone like him. Time to yourself wasn't good, it wore you down, made you morose. Too much time made you introspective, made you question your motives, your past, your future.

Brennan lived for the job. The job kept you busy, stopped the mind's relentless need to go over old ground. It was impossible to replay alternative scenarios when you were holding down a DI's job. Galloway knew he'd collapse under the weight of all that free time, thought Brennan. She knew what she was playing at from the start; it was all part of a plan.

He tried to figure out what her next play would be, but stopped himself. That's what she wanted, surely. To have him checking himself, to have him editing his every move, second-guessing what her response was going to be. There was only one way to play it – to do what he always had done. No changes. No genuflecting to her. He knew everything rested on this case, but it was small feed in comparison with finding justice for the girl in the dumpster. No one had been looking out for her. Brennan could be the last man on earth to care about her passing. The thought leapt in him.

As Brennan pulled into the station he checked the car park for Dr Lorraine Fuller's black Audi but couldn't see it. When he switched off the ignition, he took out his mobile phone. There were no messages. He wet his lips, toyed with the idea of calling Lorraine, but couldn't quite summon the strength. He knew he needed to speak to her. He knew she'd been in to see Galloway and he wanted the inside track on their meeting – what had been said. What her plans were.

What she was playing at now. But he knew any delving into those waters would mean diversions into choppier currents. Lorraine wanted to talk, and so did Brennan, but the conversations they wanted to have wouldn't come to the same conclusions, he was sure of that.

At the stairs, the desk sergeant called out, 'Rob ... got a minute?'

Brennan stepped down, turned towards the front of the building again. 'What is it, Charlie?'

The older man stroked his moustache, leaned over the counter. 'I was up the stairs earlier ...'

Brennan nodded, saw he was waiting for confirmation. 'And?'

'There was a ruckus ... Lauder and—'

Brennan tilted eyes to the ceiling, took off. 'Bollocks to Lauder.'

Charlie ran to the end of the counter, lifted the lid and waylaid Brennan at the foot of the stairs. 'He was raging and calling you for all you're worth.'

Brennan stopped, put a hand on the sergeant's shoulder. 'Thanks ... but I'm not worried.'

'I know ... I know, but ...' Charlie touched his mouth, wiped a wrinkled hand down his cheek. Brennan was close enough to count the liver spots.

'What is it, mate?'

Charlie lowered his voice, looking up the stairs. 'Lauder was in with herself raising merry hell.'

'About me?'

'Everyone heard it ... Couldn't miss it.'

Brennan turned for the stairs again. 'Is that so?' He was used to being the fount of gossip and knew how to release the tension from these little crises. He kept his expression stone, eyes front, as he went up.

On the top floor, he approached the vending machine, dropped in a fifty-pence piece and selected a black coffee. The cup was still being poured when Chief Superintendent Aileen Galloway appeared in the door of her office.

'Rob, in here.'

He looked up from the cup, pointed to the coffee pouring in.

Galloway pinched her lips, slapped the door. 'Now. Right now.'

Chapter 8

DI ROB BRENNAN WATCHED HIS Chief Super staring at him
across the room. He could feel the burn of her gaze – she'd slit her
eyes for effect and Brennan wasn't convinced by it. If she was mad,
really angry, she'd have no need to embellish it. After a hard slap on
the door she started drumming her painted fingernails, seemingly
impatiently, but Brennan wasn't buying that either. He had grown
accustomed to her bouts of high drama. It was a show; she loved an
audience. What was it Wullie had called her? An actress. One of the
lads from the Met that he'd been on a course with – a prat, full of
management-speak – had known Galloway in her early days, before
she'd got on the turkey runner. He'd said: 'She likes the visibility, but
lacks the credibility.' Brennan had stored the statement away, but
thought it an overly ornate way of describing what Wullie had managed with one word.

Brennan refused to let his emotions play on his face. He knew his
shoulders had tensed automatically but there was nothing he could
do about that and he knew it wouldn't be seen through his outdoor
coat. Galloway had her audience: a WPC and some civilian admin-
istrators halted their actions to better view the goings-on. The one
nearest, a matron-type with a twinset and dripping Morningside
smarm from every pore, slid her glasses down her nose to better peer
at him. It took a strong concentration of the will not to snap fingers
in her face and put her back in her place, but Brennan resisted.
There was nothing to be gained from letting anyone else know
what you were thinking – you did that, you lost your edge. Keep
them guessing, keep them wondering. If you gave anyone any information, they only used it to judge you on. In the workplace this
was especially true: the forced union of opposites indeed bred contempt and no one was immune to the typecasting that went on at
water coolers and in the canteen.

He was a so-and-so … Such-and-such are all the same … He'd
heard it all.

The trouble with people, Brennan thought, is that they don't really
like each other. All contact is false, and forced. They wear masks, different ones for different occasions. When the masks come off, or you

get a peek behind them, the truth comes out. We are all out for what we can get, we are users and after a certain level, or is it age, all we are capable of is measuring our self-worth against each other. It was pathetic, sickening even. He knew there were exceptions, he knew he wasn't a misanthrope because he could still be amazed, moved, shocked even, when he was proven wrong. However fleeting and rare the occurrence.

Brennan took his change from the coffee machine. He heard the nozzle fizz, cease pouring, and he watched the bubbles set on the brim of the plastic cup but didn't pick it up. As he straightened his back, he put his change from the coin slot in his trouser pocket. He kept his hand there as he walked towards Galloway's office.

The Chief Super watched Brennan approach for a moment then backed inside. The DI had expected her to glance into the wider office to see how much attention she had garnered – this was her usual way. She would carpet someone from her door, then yell to the room, 'Get back to work.' It was the curtain-fall on her theatrics that the workforce had come to expect, but she seemed to be playing it cautiously with Brennan. He started to worry about what had passed between Lorraine and the Chief Super earlier in the day. He was sure Lorraine still had his best interests at heart, but he'd tested her mettle lately and she had a temper. She was still holding all the cards. As his force-appointed therapist she could decide when or if he rejoined the ranks permanently; at least, she had the power to influence the decision.

Brennan stepped into the Chief Super's office; it felt like getting into a bear pit. He removed his hand from his trouser pocket and reached for the door handle. The blinds on the back of the door, and all round the glassed office, had been drawn.

'Sit down,' said Galloway. She was curt, brusque even. She stood over her desk with her arms folded. Brennan had heard somewhere that this was a defensive posture. He didn't think that was her style, though – Galloway was a classic 'attack is the best form of defence' type and they both knew it.

Brennan pulled out the swivel chair, sat. 'Is there something wrong?'

'We'll come to that ... What's the SP?'

The DI relayed the details of the case: a summary of the crime scene; the position of the corpse; the SOCOs' findings; his assessment; his instructions so far.

'I think she's probably local,' he said.

'You do?'

'It's Muirhouse and looks sloppy. I don't think there's any reason to believe that someone planned this, dumped her there—'

Galloway cut in, 'Why?'

'Exactly ... You'd go somewhere less obvious. I think the girl was killed near by and then dumped close to the scene. The removal of the limbs could have been to make the drop less obvious – smaller bags are easier to carry about.'

Galloway leaned over the desk; her heady perfume attacked Brennan's nostrils. 'Then why the move to obscure the prints and dental?'

Brennan leaned back, took a deep breath and slowly exhaled. 'I don't get that at all ... Maybe it's to throw us off the scent. Or a last-minute cover-up. It says hurried, rushed to me. That kind of obscuring of ID would only make sense if the girl was known to us ... Of course, maybe she is – we don't have the arms yet.'

Galloway tutted. 'Yes we do.'

'What?'

'A paper boy's dog found them in an Aldi carrier bag ... Was just a couple of streets away.'

Brennan felt a firework go off in his head. 'When did this come in?' He had expressly told DC McGuire to report all findings to him straight away.

'Don't have a cow, Rob. It came in about half an hour ago.' She leaned back again, put her hands on her hips and pushed out her breasts. 'Or are you more upset that DC McGuire disobeyed you and told me first?'

Brennan riled, 'I'm the investigating officer.'

She slapped her hands on the desk. 'And since when does that give you the right to call all the shots? ... You've some balls, Brennan.'

He stood up, laughing. 'Flattery's not going to get you anywhere with me, ma'am.'

'Sit!' She pointed at the empty seat. 'I am far from finished with you.'

Brennan snapped, 'Well, you better make it quick because I want to find out what else I've missed out on in the last half-hour.'

Galloway removed her chair from under the desk. It was luxuriously padded and covered in black leather. Slowly, she eased herself down. Brennan heard her cross her legs below the desk. Her voice came low and flat: 'Rob, don't think about undermining me, I won't stand for it. You're old enough and ugly enough to know how this works – I will not think twice about a public crucifixion if you piss me off.'

Brennan looked away. It was on his mind to tut, but he let it pass, drew in his composure, said, 'I understand. I'll be a good boy.'

Galloway's tone changed again, brightened: 'I hear you've dropped another rung on the station's popularity rankings as well.'

'Come again?'

She smiled. There was pink lipstick on her front teeth.

'Lauder was in here pissing on your chips.'

Brennan shook his head. 'He's just a whining bitch.'

Galloway seemed to object to the remark. 'I thought he had a point ... Were you trying to get his back up turfing him out like that?'

'No. Look ... Lauder's had the shooting case on the go for long enough and produced squat all. The next move for that case will be a filing cabinet and you know it.'

The Chief Super looked at the watch on her wrist then spoke up. 'This doesn't have anything to do with your brother's shooting, does it?'

Brennan felt his jaw clench, then release. 'I don't know what you mean.'

'Don't play coy, Rob. You know Lauder was on the Strathclyde team then.'

Brennan didn't like to delve into the past; he had enough trouble with the present. He certainly didn't like discussing his brother with Aileen Galloway – who the hell was she to bring him up? She wasn't family, and it wasn't any of her business. Brennan started to gnaw at the inside of his cheek. He resented the fact that she'd taken the conversation in this direction, but he felt he couldn't avoid commenting. 'And what a team they were – hardly the fucking A-Team.'

'I've seen the files: it was a thorough investigation.'

Brennan had seen the files too. He'd pulled strings and indebted himself at the favour bank for years to come, but he couldn't let on about that. Instead he called her bluff. 'Really?'

Galloway crossed her legs again. 'Yes, I asked for the file when you were on sick leave. I thought it responsible in my position to be apprised of all the variables.'

Christ Almighty – Brennan knew she was looking for something to burn him with. It was a typical management witch-hunt – she'd done the same with Wullie. Galloway wanted young blood in the station, easily pliable types, fodder. Bright new pins that were going to shine for her.

Dipping into Andy's murder file was a new low, though.

Brennan felt the bile heating in his gut. He rose from the seat, swallowed hard, said, 'Well, it's clear you know all there is to know now, so if you don't mind, I'll get back to work.'

He strode for the door.

Galloway stood up. 'Rob, some free advice: you're running out of friends fast around here. Mind how you go when you get out that door.'

'Don't let it hit my arse on the way out, you mean?'

She flicked her hand in the air. 'Whatever.'

Chapter 9

BRENNAN CLOSED THE CHIEF SUPER'S door harder than he should have. The blinds rattled on the windows. A couple of heads bobbed up, but this wasn't a part of the show anyone wanted to see. The main attraction was over. Any further viewing was likely to come back with an icy blast from Brennan – his stride suggested it.

As the DI walked he was heavy on his feet. He held his hands at his sides as though he expected to swing at someone, or fend off a blow, perhaps. His mind was awash with competing emotions, anger predominant, but he was intelligent enough to know there was no redeeming feature of anger. He had never seen his own father give in to anger; Gregor Brennan wasn't a quiet man, but he was a calm one. When Brennan was about fifteen he recalled a fight with his brother; as the Scots say, Brennan had *lost the rag*. 'Son, if you lose your head, you lose the argument,' his father had told him. He wasn't a man given to much wisdom or eloquence, but the few times he'd expressed his inner workings had stayed with Brennan.

At the edge of the corridor, towards the main incident room, he spotted a pile of cardboard boxes, brimming with manila files. A few had spilled out. There was a loud exchange taking place in IR One and Brennan couldn't face it. He touched his stomach. The other emotion, hurt – hurt at the thought of Andy's death being bargained with – seemed to rest beneath his palm. He stroked his stomach, up and down, thought there might be a chance of sickness but dismissed it as unfeasible. Brennan couldn't remember the last time he had actually been sick. Still, he needed to gather himself before facing the squad, and McGuire especially.

Brennan walked towards the Gents toilet; he felt lighter on his feet now. Perhaps he felt lighter in the head too. The toilet block was empty. He ran the nearest cold tap, cupped water in his right hand and splashed it on his face. The chill of it was a shock at first. He recoiled, closed his eyes and drew back the edges of his mouth. The second attempt, closely followed by a third, was more successful. Brennan brought both his hands together, filled them with cold water, and seeped his tired face. As he did so, in the darkness, he saw an image that took several seconds to materialise: it was the girl. Brennan stared at the murder victim's pale flesh again and quickly dropped his hands towards the sink. His heart rate quickened as he shook off the drips, wiped at his brow.

'Shit. Shit.'

It was not good, seeing things. There was enough talk about him circulating in the station. Brennan put his hand back on his stomach. It hadn't settled, but the churning was drowned out now by the beating of his heart. He moved his palm towards the fast-moving muscle in his chest. Someone had once said he had a good heart; who was it? He knew it was Joyce, but which one? The one he met and fell in love with, or the one he married and fell into domesticity with?

'Get a grip, man,' Brennan scolded himself. He was giving in to the same demons that had given Galloway the upper hand. He stared at himself in the mirror. He looked different. The face hadn't changed much – he'd kept his hair, the jawline was still firm – but it was the expression he didn't recognise. This man looked miserable, worn down by life. What was his problem? He had his health, a settled home, daughter, wife, and the career he'd craved all his life was still there, despite everything that had happened. He even had Lorraine, the ultimate midlife crisis accoutrement; though she was far from a guilt-free vice.

As Brennan stared into the mirror, assessing his lot, he realised none of it added up to who he wanted to be. There was a void he couldn't fill. He turned from the mirror, looked towards the row of cubicles and selected the one nearest the door. As he entered, Brennan put down the toilet seat, sat. He leaned forward and slid the bolt into the catch. As he eased back he sighed. For a moment he let his head rest on the cold wall tiles, then he removed his wallet and the newspaper cutting he still carried inside.

He read the date; it never changed: Thursday, 11 June. The paper hadn't had time to yellow yet. He unfurled the cutting at its crease. It seemed pathetically small for such an important piece of news. Important to Rob Brennan. The edges of the paper were starting to deteriorate, little nicks and tears making it look flimsy; it would soon be too fragile to touch.

He read the headline first: POLICE PROBE LOCAL MAN'S SHOOTING. That always made him shake his head; they were still probing the case. There was a subheading on the article which read: FORCE BAFFLED BY DAYLIGHT KILLING AT FARM-HOUSE. He had almost memorised the rest:

The shocking midday shooting of a much-loved and respected

Glasgow builder was being investigated by Strathclyde Police today.

Andrew Brennan, 37, was shot three times at point-blank range in what police have confirmed bears all the hallmarks of a 'gangland hit'.

Mr Brennan, a father of two, was undertaking refurbishment work at the farmhouse on the outskirts of the city when the incident occurred at around 2 p.m.

yesterday. His wife and children were said to be in shock after the news and being comforted by friends and family. Floral tributes appeared outside the family's Bearsden home soon after the news broke and well-wishers continued to gather on the doorstep until late in the evening.

Those who knew Mr Brennan described him as a popular and much-loved local figure.

Councillor Tom Fulton, who worked alongside Mr Brennan in the construction industry, said it was 'heartbreaking news'.

Cllr Fulton commented: 'I knew Andy since he was a boy. He came up with his dad, Gregor, and took to the business with great enthusiasm. He was a lovely, decent, solid bloke and this news is just heartbreaking.

My thoughts and feelings are with his family and Jane and the boys right now.'

Police confirmed they were not investigating any links Mr Brennan may have had to underworld activities.

They said no positive identifications had yet been made but several witnesses had reported seeing a 'limping man' in the area and they appealed for anyone with any information to come forward.

Detective Inspector Ian Lauder confirmed: 'We are exploring all avenues but proceeding on the assumption that this tragic incident was a case of mistaken identity.

'There is no indication of any wrongdoing on Mr Brennan's part whatsoever and likewise we have been unable to establish any connections to organised crime.'

He added: 'Several people did attest to there being a man with a pronounced limp in the area and we are keen to locate him in order to eliminate him from our inquiries.'

No funeral arrangements had been released at the time of going to press.

Brennan smoothed down the edges of the newspaper cutting, stared at it without taking in the printed words. It was becoming an artefact, a holy relic of the brother he once knew. Brennan berated himself for being so weak, for allowing himself to torment his emotions, self-flagellate. Why did he carry the story around with him? He knew every word of the short piece by rote. Reading it again and again didn't make him feel any better, but he knew what it did do: it kept his anger aflame. He needed these little reminders to himself that no one had solved his brother's murder, and the longer it went on, the less likely it was that his killer would be found.

The door to the Gents banged open; loud chattering bounced off the walls. For a moment Brennan was thrown. He was still deep in his reverie, but then the tones took on a familiar sound. He knew the voices, and they were two people he'd have paid to eavesdrop on. Slowly, he slid the newspaper cutting back into his wallet, and his wallet into his jacket. He raised his shoes from the floor and tucked them on the rim of the toilet pan; it was an uncomfortable seating arrangement but necessary. The door latch was loose and slid from its catch easily; it would show green for vacant on the other side if anyone looked.

The voices cackled. The most prominent was Lauder's.

'I'm sure Galloway fancies me, you know that?'

'Oh, really.' It was McGuire, playing the straw-man role.

'Every time I'm in her office she's leaning over me, flashing the flesh an' that.'

McGuire laughed, played up: 'So, you think it's her *orifice* she wants you in?'

Loud guffaws. Brennan sneered inwardly.

'You could say that, Stevie, you could say that ... You see, the thing with me is, I get a lot of women coming on to me like that.'

'I see ...'

'They want me for a shag, think I'll be good for a bit of the old wham-bam-thank-you-man ...'

'No strings attached, eh?'

'Exactly, I just give off that kind of vibe, y'know, and I'm discreet – ask your missus, she'll tell you.' Lauder burst into laughter. He sounded like a teenager to Brennan.

When the laughter subsided, the topic of conversation touched on something that was more interesting to the DI in the toilet cubicle.

'What about Brennan, then? Must have put the shits up him to see Aylish from the *News* there,' said Lauder.

'I hear he wasn't chuffed ... Apparently she near lamped him with a voice recorder. Jesus, what a picture that would have been. Galloway would have his arse for a hat!'

McGuire's voice halted.

'What is it?' said Lauder.

'Nothing.'

'No, come on … What's up?'

McGuire exhaled loudly, his words coming out like a puncture. 'I'm getting kicked about on this case already.'

'How do you mean?'

'I just …' He held schtum. 'Look, it doesn't matter.'

'No, say …'

McGuire sounded livelier: 'They say Brennan's a top operator, don't they?'

Lauder bit: 'Do they?'

'I mean, that's the word about the station, that he's a good cop and has landed some good collars in his day.'

Lauder arked up, 'You fucking fancy him now?' The DI raised his voice: 'I'll tell you this, I don't rate him and I've been in this game long enough to know who the top operators are, son.'

McGuire didn't respond. The atmosphere in the toilet block seemed to have cooled. Brennan felt his legs start to ache. He knew he wasn't going to be able to hold them up for much longer.

The sound of a tap turning, the splash of water, took over from the silence. A hand dryer blew out a violent blast.

'I'll catch you later, Ian,' said McGuire.

Lauder didn't answer.

Brennan waited for the creak of the door. He let the hinges sigh and the wood kiss the jamb before he stood up. Lauder had started to whistle; as Brennan opened the cubicle door he saw the DI pitching up on his toes as he relieved himself into the urinal. He had his head facing the tiled wall, but cocked it sharply to the side as his colleague appeared.

'This'll be where the pricks hang out then,' said Brennan.

Chapter 10

DEVLIN McARDLE WAS SITTING IN the Wellington Café on London Road when the cabbies came in, asked for the television to go on. They saw McArdle and nodded, took some more nods from the bloke behind the counter and moved to sit at the rear of the premises where the dusty windows faced the street. The PVC seats squealed as the men lowered themselves down. The cabbies looked over the greasy, laminated menu and clawed at the new prices that had been stickered over the old; there was already a rim of sauce and crumb-dust ringing the white tabs. McArdle looked the other way, towards the television. He waited for the midweek football results to come on. He was only interested in the fortunes of Heart of Midlothian but in the absence of a fixture for his team, scanned the rest of the division. They were all losers to him – anyone not on the Deil's side was a loser.

'Can you believe the run United are having?' said the bigger of the two cabbies.

'Dundee United?' said McArdle. 'Fucking Scum-dee ... Who cares what kind of a run they're having? Do they even have a stadium up there? Does the manager take the strips home for his missus to wash? There's only one team: Hearts ... The fucking glorious Jam Tarts!' McArdle felt his face warming as he spoke. He knew his voice had risen because there was an old couple sitting at the front of the café who looked at him. They had to crane their necks over a rack of vinegar bottles to see him. Their effort bothered McArdle; he didn't like being put on show. 'What do you fucking want, Granny?'

The elderly couple turned away immediately, dropping gazes back to their fish teas. The cabbies laughed it up. The bigger one spoke: 'Nice one, Deil ... Showed them!'

'Fucking pair of p-r-i-c-k-s-s-s ...' He stretched out the word for effect, savoured the sound of it on his tongue. For a moment he seemed satisfied within himself, but the expression soon changed. 'Right, what you pair got for me?'

The cabbies dropped hands in their inside pockets, removed rolls of banknotes. They were mixed denominations, tightly bound and held by elastic bands.

'These are a bit fucking light,' said McArdle.

The thinner of the two, a stubbly chin and chalk-blue eyes, said, 'No one's got the money, big man.'

'What do you fucking mean, no one?' McArdle's gaze firmed. He showed his bottom row of teeth – they were yellowed, stubby.

'It's the recession an' that,' said the other man.

McArdle slammed his fist on the table. The elderly couple flinched; the woman dropped a knife. 'Since when did schemies feel the pinch? They're on the dole, on the rob.'

The pair looked at each other. McArdle knew he had them scared. He grabbed one by the shirt front. 'Don't you be coming to me for gear, taking the fucking gear, and then not selling it. I'm not a fucking charity, right?'

'Yeah, I know … I know.'

'Well, what are you going to do about it?'

'We'll go back out.' The cabbies turned to each other, nodded. 'We'll go back out. No bother.'

The old man and woman crossed to the counter to pay up. They hadn't finished their meals. McArdle blared, 'You're fucking right you will. Get down to the Links and crack onto the brasses. There's no recession for punters looking for blow jobs last time I heard. And if they're not on it, get them on it … Right?'

The pair nodded. 'Yeah, sure. Sure.'

McArdle stood up and the two men followed. As they did chairs scraped on the laminate flooring and put a scare on the old woman. She hurried towards the door. 'Boo!' yelled McArdle. The couple increased the speed of their steps and McArdle laughed as they fumbled with the door handle. 'Night-night, you old p-r-i-c-k-s-s-s.'

As the door closed McArdle returned to the cabbies; his demeanour went to assault mode. In a flash he fired out a fist. It caught the large man clean on the nose. His head shot back on contact and he stumbled into the orange plastic chair he'd just left. The back of his thighs caught the tabletop and stopped him from falling to the floor. He was dazed, his eyes rolling wildly in his head.

'Take that as a taster,' said McArdle. He held up a roll of cash. 'You come back to me with a bundle like that again and it'll not be your nose I'm bursting next, it'll be your fucking head with one of those big cleavers out the kitchen.'

The man behind the counter laughed as he turned a dishtowel over his shoulder. The cabbies turned for the door, the bleeding one helped by the other.

McArdle raised a thumb to them. 'What do you make of that pair of pussies?'

Shakes of head. 'Can't get the staff, eh?'

'Hard times, I tell you … Hard times.'

McArdle sat back down and the waiter brought him over a mug of coffee. As he counted out the takings, separated it into denominations, then clear plastic money bags, McArdle glanced idly at the television. The football scores had finished and the Scottish news headlines were being read out by a pretty young girl in a red party dress.

It was the same old stories: job losses, strikes. Some eighty-year-old in the finals of a talent competition. None of it interested McArdle. He only liked the news when there were serious crimes reported. Then he would shout at the screen, blast the criminal's idiocy. He knew better than most how to make crime pay. No one was ever going to put the Deil behind bars again. He'd spent the eighties in Bar-L, had a stint in the Nutcracker Suite. He'd learned all he needed to know in there about staying out and he'd put it into practice every day since.

The Scottish news turned into the local news and immediately McArdle's interest was gripped. The top story was an eye-catcher.

The girl in the party dress said, *'The body of a young woman was found on an Edinburgh housing estate today.'*

So what? thought McArdle.

She went on, *'Police have yet to identify the victim but witnesses confirmed the badly mutilated body was found in a communal bin in Muirhouse. Residents described being alerted to the grisly find by four young girls who stumbled across the body.'*

The newsreader made the familiar tilt of the head that indicated the screen was about to change. Some new footage started up, fronted by a less-attractive male reporter at the housing scheme.

His piece to camera was backgrounded with some shots of police cars coming and going at the crime scene.

McArdle laughed out, 'Fucking plod! Useless bastards.'

The reporter said, *'Lothian and Borders Police are remaining tight-lipped about what is believed to be a brutal murder scene in the Muirhouse area. Of course, this locality has had more than its fair share of murders over the years but the teenage girls who stumbled upon the body revealed some particularly horrific details for me when I spoke to them earlier … I do warn viewers some of the comments they made to me are of a graphic nature and not for those of a deli-*

cate disposition.'

The camera angle changed again.

'Hey, turn this up, mate,' said McArdle, 'sounds good, this.'

The four girls were huddled together in the front room of a small council flat. A picture of a crying Spanish orphan hung on the wall behind them. One of the girls had a cigarette in her hand, which trembled every time she brought it to her lips. The other three competed for the camera.

'It was pure nasty ... Loads of blood an' that,' said the loudest, a small freckled girl who seemed to be wearing too much make-up.

McArdle sang out, 'Wee fucking tramp!'

Another girl spoke: *'I saw her first, well, second likes, after Trish, but it was me that saw the arms were missing. They'd been pure sawn off so they had.'*

McArdle chuckled to himself. 'Christ, it's a braw laugh seeing folk from the town on the telly.'

The screen changed again, the reporter handing over to the studio.

McArdle stood up, took the first sip of his coffee and put it back down. 'Right, I'm off.'

The man behind the counter nodded.

'Put that on the tab, eh.'

Another nod came.

On the street McArdle's strides were full of purpose. The cash in his jacket wasn't enough, takings had been sliding down of late, but there was another option now that might come good. It was a bit more risky, and he still had his doubts, but he hadn't been turned over in a long time. This was Edinburgh as well, where they chopped the limbs off young girls and dumped them in bins at the end of dark lanes. The filth had enough to be getting on with just keeping the streets free of folk killing each other. What were the chances of them taking an interest in his activities? So long as he played by the rules he'd set himself, then what could go wrong? Muirhouse was a long way from Germany and once he'd collected the cash, bunged Barry Tierney enough to keep him quiet, then the evidence would be out of the way. Well out of the way; the filth could say and do all they liked, but the evidence would be out the country.

McArdle's car was parked outside the post office. He turned the key in the lock and eased into the driver's seat. The clock on the dash said it was after six now. That meant Tierney had had the best part of five hours to shoot that shit into his veins. It might just be worth giving him a rattle, making sure there was a deal to be done. You just couldn't take a junkie's word for it; these things had to be checked out. He started the ignition, engaged first gear and pulled out. The traffic was light on the roads, hardly anybody walking about either. Funny that, thought McArdle. He wondered if it had anything to do with the young girl's murder he'd just seen on the news.

Chapter 11

BARRY TIERNEY BRUSHED DRIED VOMIT from his face. He couldn't recall being sick, but there was no disputing the fact. At some point in his stupor, somewhere between taking the works from the Deil, going home to Vee, and shooting up, he'd thrown up. It was a milky sick, like a baby's. He was familiar with the sight of baby sick lately, though this was a new occurrence and not entirely something he was happy about.

The child was crying again.

Barry pushed himself up. His sick-wet hand slipped on the greasy mattress and he fell towards the floorboards. The motion sent his brain swimming in his skull. He felt another heave in his gut; more puke rose in his throat and appeared in his mouth. He delivered the mouthful onto the mattress. He didn't care whether it stained or smelled, he'd long since lost all desire to care about such matters.

The child continued to cry, loud breath-filled shrieks. She'd be hungry again. Why the hell did they need so much feeding and changing? Did it never end?

Tierney suddenly felt cold. He started to shiver. He wiped his mouth with the back of his sleeve and tried to rub warmth into his arms and shoulders with the palms of his hands. It didn't seem to be working. The cold he felt was too deep. There was no heating in the flat – they had no money left for power cards after paying McArdle for their hit.

Several attempts later Tierney got up. He swayed on his feet, like a much older man, and clutched the wall for support. His vision was weak, tired. He could never understand this – how could his eyes be tired when he'd just woken up? He scratched at his eyelids with blackened fingernails. His eyeballs burned. He wanted to scoop them out, drop them in cold water, iced maybe. He wanted another hit – the aches and pains disappeared as soon as he had a hit. He looked around the room for Vee. He couldn't see her. All he could see was the kid, lying in a drawer, crying again.

'Shut the fuck up.'

He staggered to the other wall, felt his way to the door.

'Vee ... Vee, where are you?'

There was no reply. She was supposed to be looking after that kid, that was the idea – and it was her idea. Tierney knew he'd played his part in bringing the child into their chaotic lives, but he didn't want it to be like this. He didn't want to have to think about the hows and the whys. He only knew it shouldn't have been like this – it was wrong, all wrong.

'Vee ... Get up to that kid!'

He dragged himself from the sitting room. There was no sign of her. Had she gone out? Where? If she had gone out she was whoring or scoring. Tierney tried to find strength to hit the wall but his dull thuds were barely audible. He saw the bathroom door ahead, sat ajar.

'Vee ... you in there?' He edged closer, his aching limbs dragging.

At the door to the bathroom Tierney's heart rate picked up, only a little at first, but as he touched the woodwork his blood raced. 'Vee ...'

He wondered if she was in there – why would she go in there? After last night Tierney could hardly bear to take a piss in there. 'Vee.'

There was no reply. As he edged inside the door, the hinges creaked. The mat caught behind the door as he pushed it open, tugging and dragging. Tierney felt moisture gather on his brow – he was sweating. His hands felt clammy as he turned towards the bathtub. The shower curtain was drawn shut. Mould and mildew grew at the top but at the base, where the bleach had been splashed about, it was white, bright. Tierney paused before the unusual cleanliness. His mouth dried over. He could see Vee's pale feet resting beside the taps. Oh Christ, what had she done?

He whispered, 'Vee?'

His voice cracked but seemed above his normal range in the small room. Oh Jesus, what had she done? Was it too much for her? If it was too much for her, it was too much for him. Where would he go? What would he do?

He heard the child's cries again. 'Oh, Jesus, Vee ... what have you done?'

Tierney gripped the curtain and pulled it back. Vee looked pale and still. Her head rested on the rim of the bathtub; Tierney could see the blue veins in her temples. He wanted to shake her, to poke at her and wail, tell her to get up and stop being so fucking selfish ... It was all her fault, after all. Everything was her fault.

'Vee ...' Tierney's voice rose, became a growl. 'Vee.'

There was a twitch in her brow, a curl of her lip, and then her head turned. Tierney leaned over her. 'Fuck's sake, Vee!' He grabbed her face in his hand, squeezed hard.

'You're out of it!'

Vee groaned. She seemed to try and open her eyes but her head lolled from side to side with the effort. Tierney pulled her hair, banged her head several times off the rim of the bathtub. Vee groaned, but failed to come round.

'You selfish bitch!' roared Tierney. 'You lazy, selfish piece of shit.' He drew a fist, aimed it at her face but stopped himself. 'You'll keep.' He turned from her, went to the shower unit and flicked on the switch. Thin streams of water jetted onto Vee where she lay, fully clothed in the bathtub. She mumbled at first, then her mumbles became moans as she tried to wave away the water.

Tierney left her to come round. Somebody had to look after the kid; she wasn't capable, that was clear. He pushed at the door. It stuck again on the mat. He struggled harder and freed it. As he forced his weight into the door the action made the hinges squeal, then a layer of dust was dislodged from above the frame as the door slammed into the jamb and rebounded back towards Tierney.

'Fuck's sake!'

Vee had started to react to the pelting of the water on her. She screamed out, seemed to have found a surprising amount of strength. 'Turn it off ... Turn it off.'

'That'll be right.'

'Barry. Barry, get that off.'

He started to laugh as Vee tried to fumble for the shower, hands outstretched like a blind woman; the scene was comical to him. 'Serves you right, leaving me to mind that kid.' He left her slipping, stumbling, ungainly in the bathtub, trying to escape the pounding of the thin jets of water.

Tierney plodded back towards the hallway. He found himself coughing loudly after his exertions. A wisp of mucus trailed from his mouth as he raised a hand to steady himself on the wall. There was no strength left in him. He found his head ached once again. There was a dizzy spell queuing behind his eyes and he needed to sit down. As he stumbled towards the living room he put his hands out in front of him in preparation for a flop onto the filthy mattress he had left only a few moments ago. Once he was inside, the baby's cries attacked Tierney like jabs. He couldn't lock them out. The child was Vee's responsibility, not his, he thought. But somebody had to see to it. He couldn't let any harm come to the baby – there was far too much at stake for that.

Tierney walked over to the dresser. The baby lay there in the top drawer, wrapped in an old coat. Her cheeks were puffed and the colour looked too red to be natural, like a plastic toy. The little hair on her scalp was stuck down. He leaned over, picked up the child – she felt damp. 'Fuck's sake.' She was wet again. He raised her on his shoulder, gently patted her back. She was a young child and cried all the time. 'Come on now, settle yourself down.' He'd heard somewhere that the thing to do was put a drop of whisky on the baby's dummy, put them fast asleep apparently. He'd heard that from a woman he once knew, so it had to be true. Women knew about babies, they were the ones to look after them, not men. 'Vee. Get your arse through here!'

He heard movement in the hallway. The shower had stopped. That made him smirk again. He bared a row of cracked teeth at the child; already the baby seemed to have settled somewhat in his arms.

'Vee ... get through and feed this kid.'

The handle of the door to the living room turned slowly. As Vee came through she was still dripping wet but now she was wrapped in an old, fraying blanket that was dotted with stains and cigarette burns. She carried herself like a figure from a tragedy. Her thin, pale arms, exposed above the blanket, were bruised and scarred and her eyes were bloodshot and tired-looking. Tierney looked her up and down; he saw her feet sticking out beneath the blanket. He had always hated her feet – they were too big and her toes were crooked after years of forcing them into smaller shoes with high heels she wore to walk the Links. The sight of those feet was like incitement to Tierney. He wanted to knock her down for bringing them before him. He knew it wasn't just the sight of the feet that poked the anger in him, it was the sight of her, what she had done to him and what she had made him do.

'Get this fucking kid off me.' He handed Vee the child and she put a hand under its legs, raised it onto her shoulder.

'She's hungry,' said Vee.

'Well, fucking feed her.'

Vee craned her neck to the side, as if she was trying to hear something far away, said, 'The bottle's in the kitchen.' It was only when she spoke that Tierney realised she was indicating that he was to prepare the milk. He watched Vee with the child for a moment and felt something stir inside him. It was a feeling he wasn't sure he had known existed before. It was close to duty, but he knew he wasn't doing it for Vee, or the child.

Tierney dragged his legs back into motion, made for the kitchenette and started to fill a pot with water. There was a small gas burner with a blue canister. He lit it and placed the pot over it to boil. As the water heated he walked back to Vee and the child. 'The Deil better sort us out.'

'Do you think he won't?'

He shook his head. 'He's not sure.' He raised an arm, a thin finger extended towards the child in Vee's arms. 'About that.'

'He was before.' She seemed nonplussed, already looking towards the possibilities.

Tierney nodded. 'He's not sure now … He said he was, but then …'

Vee moved the child to her other shoulder, jutted her jaw.

'But then what?'

Tierney heard the water boiling up, turned. Vee grabbed his arm as he moved. 'But fucking what, Barry?'

'Got to get the milk.' He pulled his arm away.

As he went to the kitchen, Vee followed him. She watched him take off the saucepan, drop in the bottle of milk.

'Barry, we can't mess this up. We need to get sorted out or he's going to lose patience. You know what that means.'

Tierney faced her. 'I know.'

He didn't want to think about being in debt to Devlin McArdle. He'd seen what happened to people who had run up sums they couldn't pay back to the Deil; the idea he might join them scared him. He had thought he had the answer but now he wasn't so sure. It had all gotten out of control, so much so that he couldn't think of a way out. He couldn't see any possibilities.

As the pair stared at each other there was a loud knock on the door. It sounded twice, then became a thud. Next was the sound of the post-slot being rattled and a familiar voice yelling in for them, 'Open the fuck up!'

Vee stopped patting the baby's back. She was the first to speak: 'It's him … the Deil.'

Chapter 12

BRENNAN WATCHED LAUDER. His lips were pinched but he had ceased to whistle. As he stood, an arc of piss sprayed the urinal. The expression on his face was hard to analyse – somewhere between startled and slightly chuffed. He turned away, looked down, shook, then zipped up. He regained composure quickly, began whistling again. It was an irritating tune, some chart rubbish, thought Brennan, something that might once have been worthy but had been milked dry by a television talent show.

Lauder brushed past Brennan, left him in no doubt about what his impression of the DI was – as if he was in any doubt after catching his comments from beyond the cubicle door.

Lauder said, 'If you think I care two shits for you hearing any of that, you're wrong.'

Brennan turned slowly. He removed his hands from his pockets and folded them behind his back as he faced Lauder in the wall mirror, said, 'Do you think I do?' He managed a sneer on the last syllable. He was sure it had the effect he was after.

Lauder pushed the soap spray, put his hands under the taps and got a lather going. He'd abandoned the whistling completely now.

'This is a new low even for you, is it not?' said Lauder.

Brennan held schtum.

'I mean, you know I don't rate you as a cop, but I never had you down as a cock-watcher.'

Brennan laughed it up, kept his powder dry.

Lauder continued, 'I know you had that little flip-out there, nice bit of leave, but seriously, are you sure you're right in the head yet?' Lauder walked round Brennan. He shook the excess water from his fingers as he went. At the towel rail he pulled the blue cloth tight and smirked.

The scene had played just how Brennan had predicted it so far. There had been a time, in his younger days, when he might have given the lank streak of piss a slap, cracked a few ribs maybe. But not now. He'd passed that stage. Learned to control himself. The rough stuff, the physical blows, were rewarding but short-lived. He wanted to leave Lauder wondering, keep him guessing, and it was best to file his comeuppance away until a later date. There was always the satisfaction to be drawn from the knowledge that Lauder didn't have the intelligence for it, and he could be mentally tortured for a long stretch of time.

Brennan tapped his hands where he held them behind his back. He returned the sly smile to Lauder, spoke: 'Game on.'

'What?' said Lauder. He turned from the towel rail. 'What are you saying to me?' He took two steps closer, expanded his chest and dropped his head in a combative stance.

Brennan widened his smile, keeping his posture firm. He felt secure enough in his capabilities if the confrontation became physical, but he was in control and kept up the mental assault. 'Funny what you pick up if you keep your ears open, isn't it, Lauder? I mean, I thought that reporter had been tipped off, but you can never be sure, can you?'

Lauder twisted his expression, brought up a finger, pointed it. 'Look, if you've got a mole, that's fuck all to do with me!'

Now Brennan stepped up. He brought his hands round and slowly rubbed them together. 'If I've got a mole, Lauder, I'll find him ... And when I do, he'll be lucky to stay on the force as a dog catcher.'

There was a moment of silence between the two men. The filling of the cisterns could be heard, the drip of ageing pipes. 'Ah, fuck this,' said Lauder. He sidestepped Brennan and stomped away. As he grabbed the handle the door clattered off the wall; the swish of it pushed a breeze towards Brennan. He watched Lauder leave and turned to the mirror.

For a moment his eyes failed to register the man staring back at him in reflection. When they did he moved closer, placed his hands either side of the wash bowl and sighed. As he emptied his lungs Brennan knew that things had just got more difficult for him. He knew his first priority was to find a killer. There was a dead girl. A young girl, not much older than his own daughter, had been desecrated. There would be a family, people who needed answers. Hurt, confused, desperate people in a state of helplessness. He knew how they felt – there was no misery in the world like it. And, as ever, there would be a murderer hiding somewhere, wondering if the police were coming; honing survival instincts. It was Brennan's job to catch that murderer, to find justice for the girl and her family. He took his job seriously. It galled him to know there were people on the force like Lauder who just didn't get it.

Not like he did. They didn't come close.

In the corridor Brennan straightened himself, headed for the incident room. As he opened the door there was a cackle of voices, some movement, activity – everything stilled for a second or two as he walked to the front of the room and stood before the whiteboard. Some pictures had come back from the photographer and had been stuck up. Brennan looked them over. There were more on the desk in front of the board; he picked those up. The girl looked even paler than he remembered. Her light-coloured hair, stuck fast to her brow, seemed to have darkened in contrast. The images were stark. He placed them back on the desk. The team started to assemble themselves around him, awaiting a formal address. He gathered his thoughts, looked up, eyes front.

'Right, you don't need me to tell you this is a particularly brutal assault on a young life ... Even by Muirhouse standards.'

There was no reply; they listened.

'We have an approximate time of death and all the likely causes of death stand out. We have theories, but no leads ...' Brennan turned to McGuire. He had avoided eye contact with the DC since entering the room and now he put him on notice that he was expected to perform: 'Stevie, what did you get from the prints?'

McGuire held a blue folder at chest level, then lowered it as he spoke. 'Erm, as you know, the arms were removed from the victim and recovered approximately ...' He turned to the folder, toyed with the idea of opening it but thought better of it. He continued, 'Well, close to the scene the arms were recovered. We've no prints on file.'

Brennan spoke: 'Okay. So, that's an unidentified victim ... Listings, Stevie ... What did you get on the missing persons?'

'Right, well, I have a list.' McGuire went to his desk, produced a bundle of pages. 'There are upwards of maybe three hundred girls missing in the country right now.'

'How many matching our victim's description?'

McGuire turned to a WPC, presented a palm. She answered, 'I've been through most of the list, and got about a dozen possible ... but—'

Brennan cut her off. 'Get that list to Stevie right away.'

'Yes, sir.'

Something in the corner of the room seemed to have attracted a small clique's attention. 'What is it?' said Brennan.

'The TV news, sir,' said a PC. 'They're running an item on the case.'

The team gathered round the small screen. 'Turn it up,' said Brennan. There was a hush in the room as the item played. Brennan caught sight of the footage of himself turning up in the squad car.

There were a few giggles around the room.

'That's enough,' he said. 'Hardly fucking Hollywood.'

The incident room watched the broadcast. Occasionally the scratching of a pencil tip was heard, a comment made, but mostly the mood was attentive until the girls who found the corpse appeared.

'Oh Christ Almighty,' said Brennan. 'How the fuck did they get to them?'

Heads dipped, bowed.

'Thought as much ... Bloody hell, Stevie, tell me we've got statements.'

McGuire squirmed. 'Erm ... yes, from the scene.'

'I know we had statements at the scene – I thought you were bringing the girls in!'

'Erm, I thought you were dealing with that, Lucy ...' McGuire turned to another WPC.

Brennan immediately spotted the blame-shift. 'Don't fucking leave it to Lucy ... Get them in!'

McGuire, subdued, said, 'Yes, sir.'

When the news item was over Brennan picked up the remote control, pointed it at the television. The screen fizzed, went blank. His mood was serious. His tone sent electricity round the room. 'Right, the media's out the traps on this already, so we're going to have to move it,' he said. 'Stevie, get a statement out through the press office.'

'Yes, sir.'

'Nothing fancy, just the basics ... Appealing for witnesses, that sort of guff.'

McGuire offered an opinion: 'It could actually play to our advantage.'

'Is that right?'

'I mean, we might get some leads from the telly slot.'

As Brennan watched McGuire write down his instructions, he knew he would have to have a word with him.

More than a word, perhaps.

'Or it might send our murderer running for the hills,' said Brennan. Media interest was only useful up to a point. Mostly it meant added pressure, thought Brennan, and that he could well do without on this case. He hoped McGuire, naïve though he was, might be right, but he knew the top brass got fidgety when the news crews took an interest.

McGuire nodded, spoke up: 'Yes, sir.'

Carpeting the DS was a risky strategy after the run-ins with Galloway and Lauder. Brennan didn't want McGuire to go marching back to Galloway and give her more ammunition, but then he might do that anyway.

He watched the top of McGuire's head. There was a strange parting there – hair sort of half spiked and half fringed. Brennan knew he didn't understand this generation, couldn't work them out – they seemed to be wired up differently. If that was the case, he'd have to rewire DC Stevie McGuire soon. The job at hand was too important not to.

Chapter 13

DI ROB BRENNAN KNEW MOST people were miserable. The first
time he had encountered Thoreau's dictum 'The mass of men lead
lives of quiet desperation' was like an epiphany. Life is drudge; it af-
fords the majority of people just enough comfort to stave off the nagging rage at the injustice of their existence. A bellyful of cheap
booze; escape through vicarious sporting victory. It is a pathetic life
for them, he thought. He passed judgement not in a critical, arrogant
way – he meant it in the true meaning of the word, worthy of pity.
It was what got him through the day. Dealing with the ignorant and
ill-mannered was workable if you didn't lower yourself to their base
emotional states. He had always frowned on those who reacted to
rude waiters or receptionists or bank tellers – what was the point?
With people so low on the life-rewards scale, you can't reason. Every
action and reaction is aimed at redressing their low rating, clawing
back some modicum of self-worth, levelling the world they despise.
You can try to remonstrate, take them on on your terms, but it always ends the same way: with the rolling up of sleeves. It is easy to
be brought down to their level – impossible to raise them to yours.

Brennan knew he had a difficulty with DC Stevie McGuire. The
lad, and he was a lad, had never impressed him. He didn't take the
job seriously, and this was a job you could not take any other way.
He had McGuire's number, as they say, and it didn't amount to a frac-
tion of what it should. The boy was typical old-school Edinburgh: the
type whose first question – once they've passed a favourable judgement on your accent – is what school did you go to? They never ask
out of idle curiosity, or to make conversation like other people; in Edinburgh, they ask to see if you are part of their club. Brennan was
a part of no club; he did not join in.

McGuire's actions bothered him. It wasn't his background – that was
something he'd learned to deal with, couldn't alter so didn't try – but
the sense of entitlement he carried soured him. Brennan held on to
his rank with a similar sense of entitlement but it was different in one
main regard: he had earned it. McGuire felt due rewards he hadn't
grafted for – or, so far as Brennan could see, was ever likely to, or capable of. If the lad had shown promise, or enthusiasm even, he would

have gladly pushed him up the ranks, but his attitude as it stood created the opposite effect in him: Brennan wanted to expose his flaws. Was this wrong? Was it a failing on his part that he couldn't warm to McGuire? Did he have some deep-seated class prejudice that kept him from identifying any good qualities in him? Surely not.

Brennan knew when he was being hard on himself. It was almost a speciality. What he was being was analytically critical. He had to be. The life he led demanded it. There was your opinion, then there was the polar opposite, then there was every shade and nuance in between, and Brennan knew well to check them all out, because you never knew which one was going to get the job done.

'Stevie, when you've a minute.' Brennan nodded to the glassed-off office at the back of Incident Room One.

The DC looked up from the desk he was leaning over. The WPC he'd been speaking to turned as well. McGuire nodded. He straightened himself and walked towards the back of the room, tucking a yellow pencil behind his ear as he went.

Brennan moved behind the desk, removed his suit jacket and put it on the back of the chair. There was already a pile of files waiting for him to go over. He loosened off his tie and then undid the top button on the collar of his shirt. As he turned over the first file he saw more pictures of the murder victim. On the glossy photographic paper she looked unreal, like an image in a magazine, some celebrity still or a screen-grab from a movie. It unsettled Brennan to think like that. Did he have to remind himself that only a few hours ago she was flesh and blood? It annoyed him that modern life had desensitised so many people, himself included.

'You want to see me, sir?' said McGuire. He seemed breezy, almost smiling as he brushed in.

'Shut the door,' Brennan indicated the seat in front of the desk, 'and sit down.'

The temperature of the room seemed to have lowered several degrees all at once. McGuire looked as if he'd just awoken from a premonitory dream. Self-preservation seemed to kick in. 'Look, before you say anything, I just want you to know that I never went to Galloway about the arms.'

Brennan sat back in his chair. The backrest creaked as he let it take the weight of his frame. He placed his elbows on the armrests, crossed his fingers over his belly. 'Is that so?' The tone of his voice said much more than the words.

McGuire scratched his ear. 'I, well ... She had pulled me up when

I came back from Muirhouse and told me to report everything to *her* first ... not you.'

'And you told her you had other plans, I'm sure.' Brennan allowed a crease to appear in his cheek; tilted his head. He knew McGuire was too weak to stand up to the Chief Super.

'Erm, well, not exactly.'

'No?' Brennan uncrossed his fingers, leaning forward.

He tried to make his demeanour look interested. 'Well, what did you tell her, Stevie?'

The DC's eyes flickered. He touched his brow with the hand he had used to touch his ear a moment earlier. 'I said ... I would do, y'know, what she asked.'

Brennan leaned back again, allowing himself a full smile now, a headlamp grin. 'Oh, I see, Stevie boy, I see ... You thought you'd play both sides!' He wagged a finger at him.

'No, it wasn't that.'

'Looks like it to me.'

McGuire put his hands on his thighs, stretched out his fingers and looked towards the window. He seemed to have changed shape, grown smaller. It was as though a light had gone out in him.

Brennan lowered a hand into the pocket of his jacket that hung on the back of his chair. He withdrew a packet of Silk Cut and a lighter. For a moment he tapped on the box, let the intention rise, then withdrew a cigarette. He lit it, blew out smoke. He offered the pack to McGuire.

'It's a no-smoking office, sir.'

Brennan took another pelt on the cigarette, blew out some more smoke. 'Arrest me.'

McGuire stayed silent. Rubbed his palms some more.

Brennan spoke: 'No, you've not got the balls to take me on, have you?' He took another draw. 'Why don't you go and tell Galloway? Get her to arrest me.'

The DC clenched his jaw. He seemed to know what Brennan was playing at, and didn't like it. By contrast, Brennan was very happy with where he had him. He laughed out, 'For fuck's sake, don't chuck your toys out the pram.' He rose, stubbed out the cigarette in the paperclip tray. He moved round to McGuire's side of the desk, rested his backside on the edge.

'I had a wee chat with your buddy earlier,' said Brennan.

'Who?'

'Lauder ... He seemed to think I had a mole.'

McGuire firmed his jaw again. 'Did he now?'

'Oh, yeah ... Thinks that's the only way the girl from the *News* would have got to Muirhouse before the investigating officer. Got any thoughts on that?'

McGuire looked back towards the window. It seemed to be too uncomfortable for him to sit on the seat – he gripped the armrests tightly but he didn't get up. 'That's a very serious accusation.'

'Who said it was an accusation? ... I didn't say he'd accused anyone. At this stage, it's merely a theory, speculation. Not even in the realms of allegation ... Unless, that is, you have something you want to tell me.'

McGuire stood up, faced the DI. Brennan looked him up and down, noticing the knuckles on his hands were white where he had been gripping the chair. 'I did not fucking tip off the press.'

Brennan watched his eyes. He was close enough to see the irregular brown flecks in the blue irises. He stared for a moment then moved away, returning to his seat. He was satisfied.

'Okay. That'll be all.'

McGuire blinked. His mouth widened as he ran the back of his hand across his lips. He seemed to be looking for the right words but didn't find them; that or the courage to say them was lost. 'Yes, sir.'

Brennan picked up the files again. He looked at them as he spoke: 'Choose your friends in here very carefully, Stevie. The ones you think have your best interests at heart rarely do.'

McGuire opened the door. He was still twitchy; said, 'Yes, sir.'

Chapter 14

IT HAD BEEN A LONG DAY. If this was what it was like being back on the squad, DI Rob Brennan wondered if he wasn't better off shuffling paperclips. No, bollocks to it – this was what he had been born to do. There was no moment he could remember from childhood where he was suddenly aware of wanting to join the force; it had always been there. When they were boys, Andy had wanted to be an artist. Brennan could still see him now, pens and pencils spread over the kitchen table. They were fabulous pictures – colourful, sprawling. He'd had no shortage of imagination. Why he'd abandoned it to help Dad with the family firm was something Brennan could never figure out. Was it selfish to follow his own dreams? He didn't know; it didn't feel selfish. But Andy had been selfless, that was his failing. He'd put Mum and Dad before his own ambitions. Brennan could never have done that, not for anyone.

His mobile started to vibrate. The caller ID said Lorraine.

'Shit,' he mumbled. Brennan didn't want to talk to Dr Fuller. He wanted a report from her. It annoyed him that people outside the force couldn't be commanded within the normal regulations. Life would have been so much easier if they could be.

He pressed the answer button, 'Hello there.'

'Don't sound so surprised, I told you I was going to call.' She was scaling the limits of Brennan's patience.

'I'm still at the station.'

'I saw you on television.' It was as if she hadn't heard the previous statement.

A sigh. 'You'll know why I'm here then.'

She tapped something down on a hard surface; it sounded like a wine glass. 'I've had a hard day too.'

There were hard days and there were hard days – he was prepared to wager hers were nothing like his. 'Really?'

He heard movement. She sipped, then, 'Well, there was the call to attend Her Majesty … the Queen Bitch.'

She was referring to Aileen Galloway. Brennan needed to know what had been said. Life around the office was already difficult enough – getting the inside track when it was available was a necessary advantage. 'I'll try to get round—'

A tut. 'On your way *home*.' She let the sarcasm settle into her last word; her voice seemed to tremble.

Brennan knew it was pointless to take her on when she was like this. A row had been brewing for weeks, since he had failed to leave his wife and daughter on her first request some months ago. Subsequent requests had always resulted in bitter acrimony. Lorraine was prepared to sacrifice her career for him, to leave her job right away and avoid the ethical dilemma, not to mention the boys from Complaints. 'How much have you had to drink?' As soon as he'd asked the question he knew it was a mistake; he was getting tired, careless.

'It's not so much the quantity that's the trouble, Rob, it's the drinking on your own that's the real danger.'

She always made her points in roundabout ways. She was a classic smart-arse, thought Brennan. She had been hard to work out at first, and that was interesting. And she was an unquestionably attractive woman – the mixture of mystique and beauty had been a lure worth testing at first, but Brennan now had his doubts. He knew many married men who had – what was the euphemism? – strayed; on the force it was almost an epidemic. But there was a difference between what Wullie used to call 'being busy' with someone, and making emotional attachments. That was an altogether different form of betrayal – that was adultery to Brennan. The other stuff, the physical side, that felt more like something you could easily detach yourself from. You could almost pretend it was nothing, beyond your control. He knew it wasn't, he knew he'd made a conscious decision to pursue Lorraine, even though she was the force psychiatrist. He knew the consequences, but he never thought he would have to face them. People got together at the station all the time, it was just the way it was. Officially it was frowned upon but blind eyes were turned. You couldn't expect people not to form attachments in such circumstances. Bonds form in the face of tragedy, isn't that what they said during the war when people were getting it together in underground stations?

'I'll be there, as soon as I can. That's all I can say.'

'When?'

'I can't say when, you know that.'

'Why? Why can't you?'

'Because I don't fucking work for Standard Life.' At once he knew this was a low blow. Lorraine's ex had worked in insurance, some hot-shot who had left her to set up home with an actuary in Basingstoke.

She hung up.

Brennan looked at the phone. The call had been timed at one minute thirty seconds: the rows were getting briefer, if not fewer. He sighed loudly, placing the phone in the inside pocket of his jacket. He lifted the jacket off the back of the chair by the little loop on the neckline and slotted in his arms. He scooped up the files on his desk and held them under his elbow as he headed for the office door, turning out the light in the small glassed-off room. He was just exiting when one of the team approached.

'Sir, one of the street sweepers ...' He was breathless.

'Yes, what?'

'We have a possible murder weapon ... A saw – we have a saw. The lab boys have it.'

This was something. Things were suddenly moving in the right direction. 'Where was it picked up?'

'Muirhouse, sir.'

'Christ Almighty ... everything's been thrown to the winds. We got the arms in the same manner too.'

The young officer looked perplexed. Brennan patted him on the shoulder. 'It's half-arsed ... It's either a half-arsed attempt at concealment by a fucking moron or it's a half-arsed attempt at making someone look like a moron.' He shook his head, walked away from the officer. 'Get me on the mobile if we get an ID off that saw.'

'Yes, sir.'

'Or anything else. Right away.'

'Yes, right away ... Don't you want to see it? It's at the lab.'

Brennan shook his head. 'No, I'm going to the morgue. The preliminary report's in.'

As the DI walked through the incident room he looked about. There was a lot of leaning on elbows, chewing on pens. Tomorrow would be different. He could already hear Galloway screaming for updates on the hour, the press office passing on requests for interviews. He stopped at the desk of the WPC that McGuire had given the missing persons job to. 'How's the list coming along?'

'We've got it narrowed down ... There's been some calls, after the telly, sir.'

'And?'

'Two very good possible ... erm ...' She shuffled some papers on her desk, picked up a black notebook with an elastic fastener. 'This one's

been missing for six months.
She's from Leith.'
Brennan leaned in. 'Go on.'
'Elaine Auld ... She's sixteen and been seen about Muirhouse before. She's not been seen for six months, though, like I said.'
The Muirhouse connection was promising. Brennan had it in his gut that the girl was local. Leith was close enough to Muirhouse for her to have known associates there, but it bothered him that she had been missing for six months.

That was a long time – common sense told him people didn't disappear for that length of time in their own town without some kind of sighting.

'What's the other one?'
The WPC put down the notebook. 'Hang on, I was just printing that up now.' She rose from her chair and walked over to the small printer that sat on the desk next to hers. As she walked back she read the page: 'This is from Northern Constabulary, sir ...'
'What?'
'She's from Pitlochry ...'
Brennan curled down the edges of his mouth. 'Why do you think she's a possible?'
She turned over the page. There was a badly pixelated picture of a young girl. It seemed to have been taken from the internet, a social-networking site perhaps. The image had been printed in black and white and it was difficult to make out any more than the fact that she was female, and blonde. 'She's the right weight and height ... age too.'
The detective took the page, scanned the print. 'There's no city connection ... She might never have been here.'
'But if she's a runaway, sir.'
She had a point, but it didn't do to concede points to juniors in the ranks. 'I'm not buying it.' He handed her back the page. 'Keep looking. I want an update on my desk before you go home. All possibles, with the favourites on top. Okay?'
'Yes, sir.' She looked crestfallen.
'Good work, though. Keep it up.' Brennan spoke loud enough for the room to hear as he left. He caught sight of McGuire in the corner of his eye. The DC was frowning.

Chapter 15

DI ROB BRENNAN TOOK THE car McGuire had been driving that morning but he had since claimed. He had already put the seat back to accommodate his heavier frame, had adjusted the steering wheel slightly, but it still didn't feel like a vehicle he should be driving. The VW Passat started on the first turn of the key. The noise beneath the bonnet betrayed the fact that it was a diesel engine. Edinburgh had too many diesel engines, thought Brennan – taxis, buses, they were all rank, stinking up the city worse than any brewery. The place didn't need any help on the grime front; it had been doing well enough for centuries. He engaged the clutch and pulled out.

A smattering of rain hit the windscreen as Brennan turned onto Comely Bank. He put on the wipers. By Raeburn Place the rain was coming down in torrents. He slowed his speed through the Circus. He liked the New Town. The symmetry, the organised geometry of the buildings, suggested order. He knew that disorder was the more common currency where people were concerned, but he liked to believe the New Town was different. This was where R. L. Stevenson grew up. Brennan liked to imagine the young writer storing up material for his stories among the grey granite walls and cobbled streets. He knew for sure there were plenty of Jekyll and Hyde characters in Edinburgh. On the west coast, where he grew up, people were plain and simple. Agrarian, almost. Bastards were bastards and you saw them coming a mile off. In Edinburgh, he never tired of saying, people would piss down your back and tell you it was raining.

The morgue was on the other side of the city. The Old Town had more heart and soul on display, medieval spires and dark closes – the stuff of tourist dreams and the people who lived there's nightmares. When Brennan had arrived in Edinburgh he had thought the hotchpotch of pends and wynds was like nothing he'd ever seen before. He fell for the romance of the city's history, instantly. It made him proud to be a Scot, for once. The country hadn't always been the arse-end of the world, the seat of an ersatz parliament that watched the nation's wealth siphoned off by its larger neighbour. The only country in the world to discover oil and get poorer. Brennan's capital city had once spilled over with men of towering intellect. The place still dined out on their achievements, lauded them on every street in stone and bronze.

It was the infamous Deacon Brodie that best summed up the city for Brennan, though. The respectable businessman persona Brodie adopted by day contrasted starkly with the burglary trade he plied by night. The deacon seemed to embody the schizophrenic air that the city choked on still. It was a mix of stoic kirks and grand cathedrals, of bold achievements and great plans; but it was also the place where innocent-looking teenage girls wound up, beaten and bloodied, in grimy piss-smelling back alleys. They just didn't put that stuff in the tour guides.

Brennan eased the VW over the juddering mix of potholes and worn-out cobbles of Calton Road onto the roundabout. On Horse Wynd he was expecting to be stopped by the lights. As he drove on, squeezed between the Palace of Holyroodhouse and the half-billion-pound new Parliament building, he didn't know which way to spit. Both buildings, on opposite sides of the road, were not there for the likes of him. Brennan was a working man. There were times when he might not be able to look himself in the mirror, but he could always reassure himself that he benefited the public good. How many of those wankers could say that? he wondered. He did the job he did, not just for him – though he was born to it – but for everyone else walking the streets and paying his way. Royals and politicians were parasites. 'Come the revolution, those bastards will be first against the wall!' Wullie had said that many a time. The thought made Brennan smile. He could hear his mentor's voice, the inflection rising, the grin spreading. He missed the old man.

It was well after clocking-off time. The parking bays on Holyrood Road were empty. Brennan parked outside the morgue and removed the key from the ignition. The car's engine rattled a few times before it stilled. Stevie had been gunning the motor, overrevving. It was a new car too – had the lad no respect for anything? Brennan frowned and removed his seat belt, got out the driver's door. The rain had eased but was still fierce enough for him to run towards the little unassuming building. Unless you knew it was there, you could miss it. The city morgue looked like a public toilet or a small community library. There was nothing to distinguish it except a small plaque, which you couldn't read from the street – the building was set back about twenty yards and was in a small, gated garden.

At the path's bourne, by the gate, Brennan pressed the buzzer. The staff inside had stayed on and were expecting him. He was buzzed in right away. At the door an Asian woman smiled and opened up. She wore a green set of overalls like a surgeon.

'Hello, Rob.'

'Misa, how's things?'

She looked at her watch. 'I'm on a tightrope … Pete's mum's had to pick up the kids.'

Brennan got the message. 'I'll be as quick as I can.'

The pathologist led Brennan through to the waiting corpse. When he saw the still, cold body laid out on the mortuary slab, he felt his throat freeze. Her hair had been combed back from her head. It made her look older, but she was still such a very young girl. Her head lay against a wooden rest, like a chopping board, and her brow glistened where a damp cloth had wiped away the muck and blood. No matter how many times Brennan saw the dead like this, there were still occasions when he could be jolted. The old jakeys, the middle-aged, there was a hint that they had lived, seen something of life. It was as if their corpses confirmed this. To look at this young girl lying there stilled Brennan's blood: she looked as though she had been robbed. Her life had been stolen away from her. She didn't look at peace; she wanted answers too.

Misa spoke loudly, in technical terms about what she had done with the girl's remains. The DNA database had turned up no matches. The legs, below the knees, had been laid out and the arms similarly placed; it looked like an unwholesome jigsaw. Brennan stopped the pathologist: 'You're blinding me with science, Misa. Keep it simple, eh.'

She smiled. She had very white teeth. Brennan wondered why such a nice, seemingly normal, young woman would want to spend her waking hours poking about in the entrails of dead people. The thought passed. 'It's been a blow to the head, a blunt instrument.'

'Like a hammer?'

Misa creased her nose. 'No. More like something pointed. I'd expect a larger skull cavity with a hammer. We had large fragments but a hammer blow can look like that …' She made a circle with her thumb and forefinger.

Brennan nodded, moved around the girl's body. 'What about this?' He pointed to the knees, where the legs had been removed.

'Hacked off … I got the JPEG from Stevie with the saw. I'd say it's as close as you can be to a match. The bones have been ripped at with metal teeth. It's a no-brainer.'

The detective moved to the top of the slab, stared down at the girl's face. 'What are these?'

'Contusions ... There's a lot of heavy bruising, consistent with a fall. The knees are blackened, but here, look at this ...' Misa took up the girl's arm. There were small penny-sized black dots on the forearm's underside. 'That's fingertips, bet any money.' She lowered the arm and repeated the action with the other arm. 'Here too, and the front – that's a palm grip.'

Brennan felt his Adam's apple rise as he swallowed a breath. 'She was in a fight.'

'With a woman, I'd say ... or another girl.' Misa directed Brennan to take a closer look at the bruising. 'Those punctures, the small crescents, that's from sharp nails.'

'So we're looking for a female?'

'Or a trannie,' Misa laughed.

Brennan returned a smile, but couldn't find it in him to laugh with her. 'Okay, love, get off to your kids.'

'You sure?'

'Yeah, get away home.'

Misa pulled a green heavy-cotton cover over the corpse. 'Okey-dokey, pleasure doing business with you.' She started to wheel up a trolley as Brennan left the room.

On the steps outside, Brennan put his hands in his pockets.

The packet of Silk Cuts rested against his knuckles. He removed them, sparked up the lighter. After two or three consoling puffs, he took out his mobile phone, called the office.

DC Stevie McGuire answered. 'CID.'

'Stevie ... Brennan.'

'Hello, sir.'

'Have you got those young girls in for questioning yet?'

There was a pause, a squeak of a chair. 'They're coming in first thing tomorrow, boss.'

Brennan wasn't impressed; rolled eyes. His voice came like a growl: 'Stevie, get a couple of uniform right away and fucking drag them into an interview room if you have to. Tonight, do you hear me?'

'Yeah, sure. What's the rush?'

Brennan didn't like his authority being questioned. 'Do you need it gift-wrapped with "urgent" stamped on the front? Fucking do it and don't question me.'

'Yes, sir.' McGuire sounded contrite.

'Good. Now, Misa will be sending over the preliminary pathology report. Looks like our victim had been in a fight ... I want those girls given the full forensic. If we can link a flake of fucking nail polish to them we'll do them.'

McGuire stayed quiet for a moment, then, 'Sir, there was something else ...'

'What is it?'

'Linda was compiling the missing persons list earlier.'

'Yeah, and?'

'The girl from Pitlochry ...'

Brennan rolled his eyes, sighed, 'Yeah, what about her?'

'Well, her parents called up – they saw the item on the TV news and want to come down.'

'Our girl's local, Stevie.'

'Well, what should I tell them? They're coming down in the morning.'

Brennan shook his head. He had too much to do without playing nursemaid to the parents of a missing teenager. 'Well, add that to your list. Take them down, lay their fears to rest ... Right now, I'd be taking bets on our girl being local.'

Chapter 16

THE MINISTER SAT FACING THE train's window. His wife, opposite, seemed to be gazing at a different landscape. Frieda had always been a taciturn woman, even before they had married and she'd buried herself in the household's chores. She was never one to express what was going on behind those pale-blue eyes of hers. She had been a calm young woman, a bit of a wallflower, they used to say, but he liked that about her. The way she had seemed uninterested in having a large circle of friends, or socialising even, had appealed to him. They had their own little coterie, church folk and family, and until recently they'd had Carly.

'What are you thinking, my dear?' said the minister.

Frieda raised herself slightly in the seat. She looked uncomfortable. It wasn't a long journey – it was being away from the manse and familiar surroundings she had never liked. Surely a missing daughter rendered all of that meaningless, though; other things were on her mind. Should be, anyway.

'Do they have a buffet on this train?' she said. The words came out cleanly and crisply, as though she had been practising them over to herself for some time.

The question wasn't expected. The minister flustered, 'I-I don't believe so.' He looked over to his wife. She had opened her bag and removed a small handkerchief. 'There might be a trolley, you know, with sandwiches and the like.'

Frieda patted at the corner of her nose with the handkerchief, then folded up the small white cotton square, returned it to her leather handbag. The clasp made a loud snap as it shut. 'They'll be expensive.'

Everything she said seemed unnatural to him. He hoped to God she wasn't going to break; he couldn't stand to see that. 'It doesn't matter.'

She returned her gaze to the window. The minister followed the line of her vision. There was rain falling on the green, open fields. In the middle distance, some sheep were huddling under a copse of trees; they looked wet and miserable. The thought wounded him. For days he had been filled with visions of Carly out in the wider world.

The image of the animals – huddled against the harsh elements – seemed to signify his worst fears.

They had made mistakes with Carly, he was sure of it.

They were only human, with feet of clay – how could they not? But he did not know what they could have done any differently. Carly had always been a headstrong girl, he thought, but she was stable. She worked hard at school and got good examination results. She was a prefect – they didn't make just anyone a prefect – so the teachers had to see something in her.

The minister smoothed down the sides of his moustache. He repeated the action three, four times and then he felt conscious of his wife watching him. 'What is it?'

'You're making a habit of that.'

He withdrew his hand, smiled. 'I'm sorry … I wasn't aware of it.'

She didn't smile back. 'Don't be doing that when we get to the police station … They'll think there's something funny about you.'

For the second time, he was shocked. 'What do you mean by that?'

Frieda pinched her mouth. She seemed to be wearing more lipstick than usual, or was it a different colour, perhaps? 'You know what they say about the police – always suspicious.'

The minister shook his head. 'We have a missing daughter, and they have found a child who …' He stopped himself. He could feel his breath shortening. 'I'm sorry.' He leaned out, touched his wife's hand. 'I don't mean to snap at you.'

She brought her other hand over his, patted it softly. 'No need to apologise.'

They sat in silence for the remainder of the journey. When the train arrived at Waverley Station in Edinburgh, the reality of the situation suddenly gripped the minister. He took the small overnight bag that his wife had packed for them down from the overhead rack and placed the strap over his shoulder. Frieda put on her raincoat and fastened the buttons. He watched her tighten the belt and admired her cinched waist. His wife was a fine woman. She didn't deserve this. As he took a slow breath he made a silent prayer that God would spare her any misery, that Carly would not be the girl, the poor unfortunate murdered child they had come to see. He knew at once, as he made his wish before God, that if she was not his child, if it was not Carly who had suffered that cruel end, then it must be another mother's daughter. He was, in effect, wishing misery on someone else and this was surely no way for a minister of the church to think. But he thought it and prayed to God Carly was safe.

On the station concourse the number of bodies, rushing about, running for trains, made him feel uncomfortable. Pitlochry was a quiet town, peaceful. This was the big city. He did not want to be here. The reason for his visit made this obvious, but it was as if the entire population and every building conspired to make him feel unwelcome. Edinburgh had always left the minister cold, all large population centres had, but he knew he would never again be able to feel anything but unease here.

As they passed through the ticket barriers Frieda seemed to slow at his side. She placed an arm on his own. 'What is it?' he said, 'Is everything okay?'

For a moment she seemed to look blankly at him, and then her arm slipped from his and she swooned forwards. The bag on his shoulder swung round, slipped to the ground as he lunged to catch his wife. She had fainted; without warning she had lost consciousness. The minister tried to hold her up, stop her from hitting her head on the cold tiles. She was surprisingly light in his arms, but as the heavy bag threatened to topple them over he realised he couldn't hold her up.

'Can somebody help me, please?'

A man in a business suit brushed past. Two young women, chatting, turned away.

'I'm sorry ... Please could you ... ?'

More walked on. He was losing his grasp. He could feel the grip he had on Frieda's coat slipping. His knees started to wobble. 'Please, somebody?'

From the other end of the station a young man sprinted towards them. He grabbed the minister's wife and eased her onto the ground. He supported her head with his hand, then spoke: 'Are you John Donald?'

The minister kneeled down beside the young man who was loosening off his wife's coat. 'Yes, I am.'

The young man extended a hand. 'I'm Detective Constable Stephen McGuire ...' He touched Frieda's brow with the back of his hand. She seemed to be stirring. 'I think she's going to be fine – just a wee turn.'

'She's never fainted before.'

The DC raised himself on his haunches, said, 'I'd say she's en titled in the circumstances.'

'Indeed, yes.'

McGuire pointed to the car parking area. 'I have a car waiting ... But if you'd prefer to go to the hotel, get freshened up first ...'

The minister looked at his wife. She held out a hand, tried to sit up. 'Frieda … We'll get you to the hotel, rest up for a bit.'

She pushed the DC away, flagged her husband aside. 'No. No. We'll get this over with. Right now.'

The minister took his wife's hand as they settled into the back of the policeman's car. Her fingers felt cold; her hand was trembling. He wished there was something he could say, do, but nothing presented itself. There had been hundreds, thousands of family tragedies to deal with over the years. He'd found the right words for all of them; they came naturally, with ease. None had ever been in this situation, though. This was new territory for him. He tried to tell himself that he was not alone, that God was with him – the thought did calm him, but there was still the nagging feeling he carried in the pit of his stomach that he couldn't shake. It was the *what if?* What if the girl was Carly? The minister found himself squeezing his wife's hand tighter. She reciprocated, turned.

'Were you praying?' she said.

He smiled – not a wide smile, a thin crease. 'No, not really.'

'Will we pray together?'

He nodded, closed his eyes. They touched heads and prayed in silence. As he began to relay the familiar words to himself, and God, the minister felt his mind wandering. He couldn't remember this ever having happened before. Even as a very young child he had always been able to concentrate. What was happening to him?

His wife was first to break off, remove her head. 'There, that's done.'

He opened his eyes. 'Thank you.'

'Do you feel better?'

'Yes …' It was a lie. 'Much better.'

The journey through the city was slow – traffic clogged up the old streets and stopped the car every fifty to sixty yards. The minister didn't remember it ever being this bad. There had been bottlenecks on his previous journeys but there seemed to be double the number of cars now. It was apocalyptic, he thought.

'So many cars,' he said.

The young policeman agreed, 'It's been like this since they decided to bring back the trams.'

He'd seen something about that on the television; trams seemed a step back to him. 'Why are they bringing them back?' he said.

'Search me.'

The reply struck him as strange. After all, if a policeman in the city didn't know why the entire place was being dug up, who did? 'Maybe you should investigate it.'

The young man laughed. 'And I wonder what we'd find! ... The trouble with this city is the people at the top do what they like. The rest of us are treated like mushrooms: kept in the dark and covered in muck!'

The minister and his wife smiled. He was grateful for the release. 'Yes, that sounds familiar.' He looked out of the window. The lights had changed and a mass of people were bustling from one side of the road to the other. All so busy, he thought. All rushing, going somewhere. He envied them their uninterrupted routine. He pulled his gaze back, returned to the DC: 'Not sure about this trams plan, y'know.'

They couldn't have been so great if they got rid of them the last time round.'

The officer nodded to the rear-view mirror. 'Good point.' He seemed to catch sight of something that forced the look on his face to change – the minister followed the line of his vision and knew it was his wife. She had grown pale and wan. 'First trip to the city for a while?' She turned to her husband, didn't seem to have the vocabulary to answer.

'No, no ... I get down regularly. We have Assembly meetings here.' He held firmly to his wife's hand. 'Frieda's here less regularly, isn't that right, my dear?'

She turned away. Her lip started to tremble. She ferreted for something in her sleeve, removed a handkerchief. She was too slow – the tears had begun before she could get the small white hand-kerchief to dab at them.

'Come on now,' said the minister. 'We'll be fine. Everything will be fine; put faith in God.' He reached an arm around her, gripped. It didn't seem to be enough. Her head lolled back and her mouth widened. He watched the gape open silently and expected to hear sobs, wails, but nothing came. The hurt was trapped inside her. He turned back to the DC – he was looking away, his expression said he felt to blame.

'I'm sorry, officer,' said the minister, 'it's all a bit fresh ... the wound.'

The young man nodded. 'I understand.'

The minister patted his wife's back, smiled at her. 'Come on, now ... Let's not get carried away. Sure, we don't even know who the poor girl is – it mightn't be Carly.' He turned to the policeman. 'Isn't that so?'

The officer was engaging the gears, the traffic clearing. 'That's right. We have no positive identification yet.'

Chapter 17

THE MINISTER KNEW THE GIRL was some poor mother and father's child but he hoped, more than ever now, it wasn't theirs. Frieda couldn't cope; she wasn't a strong woman. The minister had seen weak people collapse under far lesser tragedies and he knew his wife wasn't able to carry such a burden with her. They would all suffer, had suffered already, but if that child was Carly, he knew, then there would be more than one death in the family this day. His wife's demise would be slower, over years maybe, but no less painful.

'John … do you ever think about things?'

'What do you mean?' He wiped a tear from her cheek with his fingertip.

'The way we treated Carly when we …'

He knew what she referred to, but they had never spoken about this. They had never questioned the way they had dealt with it. The minister had followed what was in his heart, a good Christian heart; he had never questioned his faith.

'Frieda, please don't punish yourself.'

She straightened before him, turned to face the window. She seemed to be about to speak, but held herself in check.

The minister began, 'Frieda, we did all we could for her … We have nothing to reproach ourselves for. Don't do this, Frieda, please.'

She kept her neck straight and firm and her eyes level with the crowds passing the car window. 'But I do.'

The remainder of the journey passed in silence. As they reached the Old Town the occupants of the car were jolted on the cobbled streets. The minister knew they were nearing Holyrood Road, where the morgue was situated. On the Royal Mile he glanced at Knox's home, and a pub called the World's End. He knew the name but it took him some time to register why. When it returned to him, he recalled the pub featuring in a lengthy murder investigation that had been in the news for some years. The thought chilled him.

'Not long now,' said the policeman.

He was trying to be helpful, but the words only added to the minister's tension. He gripped his wife's hand again, patted her wrist. The car turned the corner at the box junction on St Mary's Street;

the road ahead was clear. It seemed like they had hardly travelled any distance at all when the vehicle pulled alongside the kerb. The policeman turned off the engine and swivelled on his seat to face them. 'I'll go inside, see if they're ready. You can take a few moments, maybe stretch your legs.'

'You're very kind,' said the minister.

The young man nodded to them, opened his door and headed for the pavement. He looked back when he reached the gate, then pressed the buzzer. He seemed to be very comfortable in his surroundings and the minister wondered about what he had to block out when he went home at night. No one should have to take home things like death and murder. Of course, in the midst of life, there was death. But there was also evil, and that was what occupied his thoughts as he got out of the car and walked round to open the door for his wife.

This city smelled of evil. Could a city smell of evil? He knew it couldn't but the familiar smell had come to be associated with the concept in his mind now. Would he ever be able to rid himself of that notion? Would this place forever be the home of all that was unwholesome, unholy?

The minister opened the car door. 'Come on, my dear, let's get you out of there.' Frieda swung her legs over the car's sill. Her shoes had been polished – they shone. She held on to her husband's hand as she eased herself towards the pavement. As she tried to stand she made a slight stagger. 'Everything all right?'

She nodded.

'Just take it easy. I know it's been one shock after another these last months ...'

Her hand went up to her mouth, seemed to hold in words she didn't want to say. She kept it there for some moments, then dropped it to her side and clutched at her handbag.

'It's not Carly, is it, John?'

'No, of course not.' He smiled at her.

'Do you mean it?'

It was like talking to a child. She was more fragile than he had ever seen her. 'Yes. Yes. It's all formality.' He started to walk. She stayed still, her feet fixed to the pavement. 'Come on, it'll be fine.'

She wasn't convinced. 'Are you sure? ... It's not her, is it?'

He eased her into a first step. 'Come on, my love.'

DC Stephen McGuire had appeared at the gate once more. He pointed up to the entrance. 'Let me know when you're ready. There's no rush.'

The minister nodded. 'We're on our way.' At first he had to drag his wife a little. It was like when Carly was a child and she didn't want to go to the dentist. The thought wounded him.

On the stairs to the morgue the couple held on to each other; they must have looked like some four-legged beast, he thought. Moving slowly, taking the steps one at a time. At the doorway stood a young woman, an Asian with a pretty smile. She seemed very welcoming and he was glad to see her comforting presence. The young policeman had been very good, but there was something perfunctory about his demeanour in comparison with the woman.

'Hello, Minister,' she said. 'I'm Misa, the pathologist.'

The word seemed to have a physical presence as they stood on the steps, in the cold. *Pathologist* – he had never met a pathologist before. There was a reason why he had to meet one now and it hung over the step with him like a pall. The minister removed his right hand from his wife's arm and extended it towards the woman. 'Hello, Misa.' He couldn't say he was pleased to meet her; that would be wrong. It wasn't that it would be a lie, though it would. It was because the statement was out of sorts with the situation. Meeting someone who had the potential to deliver news like Misa had was no cause for joy. He thought of the woman standing before him, and what must have been on her mind when she was presented with the remains of the girl. Had she felt any grief for her? Did she place herself in the minds of the girl's family? Or had she been doing the job so long that it had become no more than a perverse sort of butchery?

Misa edged backwards towards the door. She went inside the squat building and ushered the way in for the minister and his wife. The police officer followed behind them. 'Just right the way to the end of the hall there. Follow the carpet down to where the tiles start.'

They walked slowly. Gripping each other. The place was dark and gloomy. A smell like bleach lingered in the air. It seemed to have been masked with something, a patchouli oil, perhaps. Whatever it was, it hadn't been strong enough. The odour reminded him of decay and of his days as a schoolboy in the science labs. He followed the line of the wall, where it met the carpet. It was an industrial colour of grey – like they painted battleships. Why didn't they brighten the place up, he thought? Would it be too much trouble to have some brighter colours about the place? Flowers, perhaps? That's what they did at funeral services. It reminded everyone that even in death there was still much to be thankful for on God's earth.

'And round to the right here, Reverend.' The girl had a sweet voice, like a nurse; he could hear the compassion in her tones.

As they turned the corner he saw the large double doors. They had heavy plastic skirts along the bottom and two circular windows. As the neared the doors the minister felt his mind suffused with a weary fog. The closer they came he saw the scuff-marks and scratches on the doors where he assumed they had been pushed open by heavy trolleys. It suddenly occurred to him that they were similar to the doors of an operating theatre, though this was no place where life was extended, or saved.

The DC spoke: 'Now, if I could just have your attention for a moment, please.'

Misa slid past him. 'I'll go through now.' She edged into the door like before, creasing her lips as she went.

The minister felt his wife gripping tighter to him.

'The pathologist has prepared the ...' the police officer stalled, 'young girl for your visit, but ...' He paused again. 'I should warn you, her appearance might be a shock to you, whether you can identify her or not.' He hurried the last words.

The minister nodded. 'We understand.' He did not turn to his wife again as they were led through the doors. He could hear her sobbing already, tried hard to steady her gait, but by now his own steps were faltering.

The room was large and well lit. Misa stood in the centre by what at first glance looked like a bed, but on closer inspection appeared to be more like a kitchen counter with shiny steel coverings on the sides. There was a heavy wooden board at the end and a tap that could be raised like a shower head. On top was a small, green bundle. At once the minister knew what must be under the covering but it seemed too small. His mind stilled – it couldn't be her.

As they reached the centre of the room, and the side of the mortuary slab, they all stopped and stared at each other. It was as if no one wanted to be the first to speak.

DC McGuire broke the silence. 'If you'd like to let me know when you're ready, Misa will remove the sheet.'

The minister and his wife held firm to each other; nothing in this world seemed real any more. A flurry of emotions he didn't recognise swept over him. His mind returned to bright days in the summer months when his daughter played in the garden, in a paddling pool or with a badminton set. She was such a lovely child. She had always been so content, so playful as a young girl. And as a young woman, even when she was tested by circumstance, she had been brave. If there was one thing the minister wished from God it was to return to those sunny days of the past when they were all so happy, when there was nothing but peace in their home, but they were gone. He braced himself for God's will and nodded towards the young woman. Her hand moved slowly towards the green cloth. As she removed the covering there was a flash of blonde hair – thin wispy hair scraped back in an unfamiliar style. The minister stared but did not recognise the face before him. The skin was pale, blue almost, and the eyes were blackened. A dark line of stitching ran the length of her brow. The eyes were closed – if they had been open, it might have made a difference.

He turned to his wife. She seemed as still as the girl. She seemed to have stopped breathing. The minister grabbed her shoulders. 'Frieda. Frieda …'

There was no reply.

The officer moved into his view. 'Reverend Donald.' He placed an arm on his wife's back; the minister brushed it away.

'Leave her alone!' The harshness of his tone surprised him. 'Frieda. Frieda.' His wife didn't reply.

As the officer stepped back, Frieda lost her balance and slumped away from him. She fell into the officer and he grabbed her; in one smooth movement he took up her weight and lowered her to the floor. The minister watched as his wife lay lifeless. The pathologist ran to her side, supported her head. 'She's fainted. She'll be okay. She'll be just fine …'

As the minister looked at his wife on the cold floor of the mortuary, he knew she would never be fine again.

Chapter 18

DI ROB BRENNAN HAD GONE straight home from the morgue the night before. Despite a loose agreement to meet Lorraine, he'd driven directly to his Corstorphine address and spent the night with two tins of Stella Artois and a peaty malt as his wife and daughter kept their distance. He would have liked to be able to switch off his mobile phone but the job didn't allow that, so he had kept it on vibrate and let the two calls from Lorraine go to voicemail. He knew this was storing up trouble for himself but he was content to let that sit in the back of his mind whilst the rest of it filled up with thoughts about a young girl lying on a mortuary slab, and her killer walking free.

Brennan was woken by Joyce shouting at Sophie about being late for school and looked at the clock. It was nearly 9 a.m. He rubbed his eyes and looked again, tried to make sure he hadn't made a mistake. No, it was nearly 9 a.m. His mobile phone sat next to the bed, still on vibrate. He had missed another call but this time it was from the office.

'Shit.'

He would have to call back, but decided on a quick shower before he did so. As he walked to the en suite he could still hear Joyce and Sophie rowing in the kitchen below. His daughter should have been at school by now, there was no way she would be anything but late. He could already hear Joyce telling him in that hard, demanding tone to 'speak to your daughter'. He had done too much of that already. She needed something, but it wasn't speaking to.

In the bathroom Brennan started the shower. He looked at himself in the mirror and contemplated running a razor over his stubbled chin but the thought was enough to discourage him. He stuck out his tongue – a grey-white layer of velvet sat on the surface. As he stared he could smell the malt whisky seeping through his pores. Did it matter? It did if Galloway thought to call him on it. She never had, but after recent run-ins with the Chief Super nothing would surprise him. He replayed yesterday's words with her, and then the encounter with Lauder in the toilets. It felt like there was a storm coming. He didn't know which direction it was going to arrive from but it was imminent. He let the thought trail off; he did this on purpose. Brennan knew that his main focus was the job. When he was working a case like this – no matter what else was going on in his life – if he left his thoughts to run their own course they always came back to the case. Even in the bad times, the worst times, when he was low and lost, he had always been sure of that one irrefutable fact. The job was his life and everything else was a distraction.

Brennan showered and dressed. He chose a navy blazer to match the grey chino-style slacks he still wore. He knew they were no longer fashionable, but he didn't care. He was carrying a little more weight than he had in the past and the wider leg and pleats were comfortable. There had been a time when he had been a keen follower of the latest styles, but the older he got, the less it had meant to him. Fashion was an irrelevance, for trivial minds. Brennan occupied his thoughts with serious issues – the width of a trouser leg was something for other people to worry about.

In the kitchen Sophie ignored her father, as she always did these days. She was eating a piece of toast and watching the moronic presenters on breakfast television dissecting the weekend's *X Factor* talent contest. Brennan hugged her. She pulled away, rolling her eyes.

'You might try speaking to your daughter,' Joyce greeted him in her usual way.

'Good morning, Sophie darling.' He knew he was using the girl as some form of emotional ammunition.

'That's not what I meant,' snapped Joyce. Her face had set hard already. The dew was still on the grass and Joyce was moaning, thought Brennan.

'What would you like me to say to her?'

'Well, how about why are you not going to school?'

Brennan mimicked her: 'Why are you not going to school?' He paused, added, 'Sophie darling.'

The girl kept her eyes focused on the television screen, said, 'I don't feel well.'

Brennan turned towards his wife, repeating, 'She doesn't feel well.' It was their first exchange of the day and already he knew that the next one would be no improvement.

Joyce turned away, went to the kitchen sink and turned the tap on to fill an empty pot. When the water was tipping over the brim, she turned the tap the other way. She dropped cutlery and other household items on top of the pot. Each one clanged loudly, each one echoed her mood.

Brennan started to fasten his tie, to pocket his keys and coins from the counter. Joyce turned. 'If she's going to stay off school, *allegedly* sick, then she can at least tidy her room ... Have you seen the state of her room?'

Brennan wasn't given an opportunity to answer: Sophie stood up, glowered at her mother and stated, 'Why should I tidy my room when the whole world's a mess?'

Joyce put her hands on her hips, turned to her husband. 'Are you going to let her talk to me like that?'

Brennan shrugged. 'She has a point.' He walked out the door.

In the car he contemplated calling in to the office but figured he would be there soon enough anyway. If there were any important developments he would find out when he got in.

The roads were heavy with traffic again. Cyclists weaved in and out of the bus lanes and made gestures at drivers when they thought they were being denied ample road space. The commute to the station always seemed like a worthless task to Brennan. All time spent travelling was like intellectual and emotional stasis for the detective. He had never been able to adhere to the adage that it was better to travel than to arrive. Travel was dead time; arrival was all about the commencement of action, and Brennan was all about the action. By Ravelston Dykes he had started to drum his fingers on the wheel. He had tried to go over things in his mind that he had to do, but he knew the landscape shifted so quickly that any assessment he made of the current situation could have changed by the time he reached the office. He still felt the girl was local; his instinct was to question the teenager, Trish Brown, and see what she really knew. He hoped McGuire had got onto that like he had told him.

At Fettes station, Brennan put the car into second gear and rolled the VW Passat into the nearest parking space.

As he got out of the driver's door he reminded himself that he was going into the bear pit. He needed to have his wits about him and he needed to be aware of the potential dangers. There was more than one person in the station who would be cheering his downfall. The thought of thwarting their attempts was enough to make him grin at the challenge.

At the front door Charlie looked up over the *News*.

'Hey, Rob, come here.'

Brennan walked over to the counter as Charlie lowered the paper. 'Morning, Charl.'

'Aye, fuck that. You seen this rag?'

The DI glanced at the paper's front page: they had splashed on the murder. The headline read: ANOTHER BRUTAL MURDER. The picture was of the alleyway, artfully strapped off with blue-and-white crime scene tape. In the subheading the newspaper claimed: PO-LICE BAFFLED BY GIRL'S KILLING.

Brennan sighed, threw down the paper.

'She's seen this, I take it?'

Charlie furrowed his brow. 'What do you think?' He pointed at the paper. 'She's after the Chief Constable's job, y'know ... She's not going to like this kind of thing blotting her CV.'

Brennan turned back to the paper, clocking the reporter's byline: Aylish Dunn. He stored it away then took to the stairs, thought: Will the day get any better?

At the top of the steps he unbuttoned his jacket and loosened his tie. The temperature in the building was always too high but he imagined it had gone up a couple of notches this morning. As he walked through CID there was little of the usual chatter. He could see ahead into the door of Incident Room One. There were a few people standing around chatting but he couldn't see DC Stephen McGuire. Brennan managed a few steps closer to the incident room when he heard the door of the Chief Super's office open. As he turned he caught sight of Galloway. 'Rob, a moment.'

He thought she looked stressed, hair pulled back tight – it wasn't a look he had seen on her before and it worried him. As he got closer to her office he could see McGuire in there, sitting down. The DC looked even worse than Galloway did.

As Brennan entered the office, the Chief Super closed the door behind him. The blinds had already been shut. He looked down to where McGuire was sitting but the DC kept his gaze front. There was a copy of the *News* on the desk in front of him.

'Right, Rob, glad you're here.'

He wondered if this was sarcasm.

'Oh, yes.' He pulled out the chair next to McGuire, sat. 'Morning, Stevie.'

'Sir.'

The Chief Super walked round to the other side of the desk, smoothing her hair as she went. 'There's been some developments ...' She sat down and opened a blue folder on her desk.

'There has?'

She looked up; her eyes widened. 'We tried to contact you. Was your phone off?'

'No, I, erm ...' Brennan knew he was squirming, 'I missed a call.'

'Never heard of calling back?'

'I was on the way to the office.'

She seemed unconvinced, but let it slide. 'Look, Stevie has the details. Why don't you fill Rob in?'

McGuire coughed nervously. He looked unprepared for the honour. 'Eh, sure.' He sat fidgeting in his chair, uncrossed his legs. 'We have a positive ID.'

Brennan leaned forward. 'The teenager – Trish whatever – she came good?'

Galloway interrupted, 'No, Rob … That theory of yours was pretty wide of the mark.'

He felt stung. Looked first to Galloway, then back to McGuire. 'I don't understand.'

'No, I don't think you do,' said Galloway. 'Go on, Stevie.'

By the time the DC had finished detailing the fact that the parents of sixteen-year-old Carly Donald had been able to identify their daughter without any doubts, Brennan's mind had shifted from disbelief to stupefaction. He had dropped all the facts into the personal computer that was his brain and the answer had came back the same every time: local girl. If he was wrong, and it seemed he was, then he had lost his touch – that, or this murder investigation was shaping up unlike any other he'd been involved in.

'Have you got that, Rob? … She's not a local girl,' said Galloway. Brennan twisted on the chair. 'Yes, I heard the boy.' The news had came as a shock to him, but the method of receiving it had come as an added embarrassment. He had told McGuire to relay all developments to him first. There was the missed call, and he could use that to cover his arse, but the lad had fucked him over for a second time and he didn't like it. Putting Galloway in the picture about every new development on the case before him was going to make it impossible to operate, and the thought burned Brennan. He needed to get away, get out of the Chief Super's office and try and make sense of all of this.

Brennan stood up. 'Right, I want the full SP, Stevie.'

McGuire looked at the Chief Super first – was he waiting for her say-so? thought Brennan. 'So, let's get moving … Now, Stevie.'

Galloway nodded and the DC rose, turned for the door. Brennan followed. He got as far as the other side of the glass, handle in hand, before the Chief Super called him back. 'A word before you go, Rob.'

He halted. 'I've got my hands full here.'

She pointed to the seat he'd risen from. 'A word, Rob.'

Chapter 19

BRENNAN FELT THE MUSCLES IN his shoulders tightening as
he went back into the Chief Super's office. He didn't give her the satisfaction of seeing him lowered before her – he brushed aside the offer of the chair and stood, hands on waist. 'What is it?'

Galloway rose to face him. She wasn't going to give him a height
advantage when she was wearing four-inch heels, he thought.

She picked up the *News*, dropped it again. 'They're having a fucking field day.'

Brennan shrugged. 'Tell the press office.'

She pointed a maroon fingernail at him. 'I'm telling you.'

He looked her in the eye. 'What are you telling me, ma'am?'

That riled her, the ma'am bit, always did. Brennan knew he was
in no position to be cocky. To be cocky, you needed something to back
it up, or big-time supporters, and he had neither.

Galloway upped the volume a notch. 'I'm telling you that if there's
another set of headlines like that, I'll be wearing your balls as ear-
rings. Do you get me?'

He smiled. 'I think they might stretch your ears.'

She didn't flicker, held her face stone. 'I'm warning you, Rob …
You're on probation, don't forget that. As easily as I handed you this
case I can take it away.'

It was a bluff, he was sure of it; who else was there to take over?
The squad was stretched too tight. Not even her golden boy Lauder
could take on another case. He was sound. Brennan stared at her for
a moment: she was no more police than Stevie McGuire, she was a
shiny-arsed careerist. A manager; an actress like Wullie said. But she
had rank, and the force was all about rank. He held himself in check,
said, 'Nobody wants this bastard more than me.'

She made a moue of her mouth. 'I know that, but there's a difference between wanting something and getting it.' She'd made her
point, asserted herself. As she sat down again she picked up the
newspaper, folded it in two and dropped it in the waste-paper basket beside the desk. 'No more headlines, Rob.'

Brennan nodded, turned for the door.

DC Stevie McGuire was waiting for him outside the Chief Super's office. 'Rob, can we talk?'

Brennan walked past him, heading for the incident room. 'Oh, we'll talk Stevie. Soon enough.'

Brennan walked fast, his stride powerful enough to lift the carpet at his heels. As he reached the room, the door was already open. One or two officers approached; he could tell they sensed the shift. Brennan flagged them down, said, 'One minute.' He made for the end of the room, stood looking at the board where the pictures of sixteen-year-old Carly Donald had been pasted up. There was a lot of white space.

As Brennan placed his jacket on the back of a chair a small crowd began to gather. He noticed DC Stevie McGuire lurking at the back and motioned him to the front.

'Right, listen up.' Brennan's voice reverberated around the room. 'We have a positive ID for our victim. I don't need to tell you that we have our nuts over the fire, and the press are pouring on the petrol, so we need to get moving.' He turned to McGuire, who had reached the front of the crowd. 'Right, Stevie … Fill them in on our victim.'

There was silence in the room as the DC cleared his throat, and read from the file. 'Carly Donald was sixteen, a schoolgirl from Pitlochry.' Some audible surprise was registered.

'Listen up,' said Brennan. 'Go on, Stevie.'

'She's the daughter of the Reverend John Donald, and his wife, Frieda, a housewife. They've formally identified the body.'

Brennan took over. 'Right. That's it so far. Not much to go on but we'll be interviewing the parents in due course.

Meantime, I want this girl's world turned upside down and anything that falls out put on my desk. I want you out there knocking doors, now. Friends, teachers, hockey team-mates, youth club members, the man she bought her Smarties from – I want them all spoken to. Got that?'

The group answered together, 'Yes, sir.'

Brennan held the crowd rapt as he moved on to disseminate specific instructions. 'Brian, I want you to grab all the CCTV. I want footage from the train stations, the bus station, taxi ranks, BP garages, truck stops … Anywhere you might think she'd show if she was coming here from the north.'

'Yes, sir.'

'Lou, get onto the homeless shelters in the city. She had to be staying somewhere. Check out all the halfway houses, the cheap hostels in Hillside and elsewhere. This was a young girl away from home …

Think where she'd go, think where she'd end up.'

'Sir.'

Brennan looked round the room again. His eyes lighted on another face. 'Davie, find out how she supported herself.

Was she brass? If she was working the streets, who was pimping her? Call the faces in – *all* of them.'

'Yes, boss.'

The room remained quiet, still, as Brennan leaned forward, rested his elbows on the back of his chair. 'I don't need to remind you that this is a young girl from a respectable family. She's been cut up in the most brutal fashion imaginable. The media are already interested. When they get the full details they are going to go ape-shit. I want you all to work fast, but stay alert. Don't let anything slide, don't think twice about throwing stuff up to Stevie or me – we'll look at all of it. Now, one more thing: I'm cancelling all leave with immediate effect.' He paused, expecting to hear groans. None came. 'Good, I'm glad you understand. We need to move like lightning. Our killer has already tried to cover their tracks and I want this bastard behind bars. Right, get to work.'

The group scattered. Brennan yanked his jacket from the chair, headed for the office. As he went, he called out, 'Stevie, in here now.'

DC McGuire followed him in.

'Shut the door.' The young officer pressed a hand on the glass panel; there was a gentle click as the door closed.

McGuire was speaking before he turned round: 'I didn't go to her. I went to you, but your phone rung out … What was I supposed to do?'

'How about fucking try again?'

McGuire's mouth opened, closed quickly, then words seemed to come through clenched lips: 'I did. I did. Look, she was here, in the office and asking questions all night. I could hardly …'

Brennan got the picture. He conceded that McGuire hadn't gone out of his way to shaft him. At least, he gave him the benefit of the doubt on this occasion. Too much had happened in the last twenty-four hours to think about settling scores right now. The case had to be first priority.

'Did you haul in Trish Brown last night?' said Brennan.

'Yes, I did. Look, boss, I saw the initial pathology report too and I thought about the indicators but I just don't think—'

Brennan interrupted, 'Good, I don't fucking want you to think. Did you get her swabbed and dabbed?'

McGuire nodded. 'Yes. Should have results around late morning.'

'Where's she now – Trish?'

'Downstairs. We're holding her and the other girls. Sir, I have to say, they knew fuck all.'

Brennan shook his head from left to right. 'Not a hint?'

'They were silly wee girls, just talk, y'know. Lou and me, we went through them till the wee hours. Got nothing. I think we're barking up the wrong tree.'

He was probably right, thought Brennan. If the victim wasn't local, the chances of her knowing the girls that found her remains looked slim now. He said, 'Wait for the lab boys. If you get the all-clear, let them go. But if there's any dubiety, I want to know.'

'Yes, sir.'

'And you warn them to keep their traps shut in front of the fucking press!'

McGuire nodded. 'Of course, sir.'

Brennan told the DC to type up the interviews and have them on his desk by close of play, then, 'Tell me about Carly's parents, Stevie.'

He moved forward, pulled out a chair. 'Queer fish if you ask me.'

'How come?'

'Well, they're your typical sheep-shaggers for a start – northerners, y'know. Full of religion.'

'He's a minister – I'd be surprised if they weren't.'

McGuire sat on the edge of the chair. 'Nah, it's more than that. There was a couple of times I thought he hushed her up, like she was going to say something he didn't want to get out. They were very guarded, cautious.'

Brennan leaned forward. He scratched his brow. 'You think they're not letting on about something?'

'I don't know … It was just a feeling I got.'

Brennan had learned to trust those feelings. 'Then we should get them on the rack.'

McGuire seemed doubtful: 'They were a nice couple.'

'I don't give a flying fuck, boy. Their daughter's been killed – you know most victims know their murderers, don't you?'

McGuire looked at his hands, turned over his palms. 'Yes, boss.'

Chapter 20

DC McGUIRE STOOD UP. He was turning for the door when it was suddenly flung open. Dr Lorraine Fuller stood in the jamb.

'I'll get you in the car park, Stevie,' said Brennan.

'Yes, sir. Do you want me to call ahead?'

The DI nodded. 'Yes. Do that.'

As McGuire left the office Lorraine walked towards Brennan's desk. He offered her a seat. For a moment Brennan wondered if she was going to cause a scene, then he remembered who he was dealing with – Lorraine was far too collected for that kind of thing. Then there were the consequences; neither of them wanted black marks on their employment records at this stage.

'Would you like something? A coffee, maybe?'

'I'm not here for tiffin, Rob.' She lowered herself onto the office chair, crossed her legs. Brennan noticed her calf – she had very defined muscles.

'If it's about last night ...'

'You know bloody well what it's about.'

Brennan sighed. The heavy rise and fall of his chest didn't go unnoticed by the psychologist. Lorraine rolled her eyes in response. When she brought them back to Brennan he had eased himself onto the corner of the desk. A siren howled from beyond the window. 'I had every intention of coming round but I stopped off at the morgue on the way home and ...'

She looked at him as he spoke; her lips widened momentarily then dropped slightly. 'I didn't realise.'

'The victim was a young girl, barely sixteen.'

Lorraine stood up. 'Look, I shouldn't have come. I know this must be very stressful for you after ...'

Brennan smiled. 'It's my job. It's not stressful in the slightest for me, you know that ... I hope that's what you told Galloway as well.'

Lorraine leaned over, picked up her briefcase. As she did so, Brennan noticed more buttons than usual were open on her blouse. 'Aileen only listens to what she wants to hear.'

'We need to talk about that ... and a few other things.'

Lorraine turned from him, walked for the door, said, 'You know where to find me. I'm home alone most nights and the number hasn't changed.'

Brennan placed a hand on her arm. The act made him feel self-conscious and he ceased it quickly. 'Let me get a handle on this case ... Once I've done that ...'

She nodded. As she held her head firm a small muscle twitched in her neck. 'Look, Rob ... I have something to say.'

'Well, say it.'

She lowered her grey eyes; her lids closed for a moment and then she lifted her head towards the ceiling in one swift movement. Brennan knew she was searching for strength.

He was about to prompt her again but she seemed to find some steel, raised up her briefcase on one leg and popped the fastener. She appeared to know what she was looking for and found it quickly. As she removed her hand, Brennan spotted the small piece of card. She put it to her chest for a moment, shielded it, then turned it over and handed it to him.

Brennan took the card – it was a picture. Black and white, a bit fuzzy round the edges, but he'd seen something like it before. 'What's this?'

Lorraine stayed quiet, stared at him.

'Is this a scan?'

She nodded. 'I didn't expect you to be overjoyed but I thought you might take it better than this.'

'You're pregnant.'

A tut. 'Ever the detective.'

Brennan didn't know what to say. He offered the picture back to Lorraine; she shook her head. 'Keep it, I've got others.'

'Lorraine, I-I ...'

She turned around. 'Take your time ... You'll find the words.'

As she left the office, Brennan tucked the picture in his pocket. He put on his jacket and collected the blue folder from his desk. His mind seemed to be ablaze, unable to settle on one set of thoughts. He took a moment to look out the window towards the city streets; it was cloudy, but there was no rain. He pitched himself on the rim of the ledge to see further into the distance but the view had no appeal. Brennan turned away and sighed. He knew Lorraine had every right to feel angry with him: she had stood by him, helped him straighten things out with the review board and with Galloway. She had even offered to resign her job so they could formalise their relationship, and he'd rewarded her how? By treating her like a tart.

And now she was carrying his child. He had felt something for her, genuinely. He may not have known just what it was but there was a definite connection. Had it passed? Was it just another phase he was going through that made him think he had no more time for Lorraine? He didn't know. All he did know was the situation had suddenly got more complicated than ever.

Brennan rubbed the stubble on his chin. So, there was more than one difficult situation that needed his attention, but they would all have to wait. Until he had that young girl's killer before the courts, everything would have to wait. He headed out.

In the car park Brennan lit a Silk Cut and waited for McGuire to work out that he was waiting to be collected from the front of the building. He got three or four good pelts out of the cigarette before the silver Cavalier drew up beside him. He let McGuire sit with the engine running for a moment or two as he took short draws on the filter tip.

He still couldn't get a decent smoke out of the Silk Cut but he persisted. Life was all about perseverance, wasn't it?

In the car Brennan opened the file and looked through some of the notes that had been made by Galloway that morning. She had scribbled some inane remarks about the pathologist's preliminary report and double-underlined instructions to make the kind of checks even the most wet behind the ears on the squad would do without thinking. The woman infuriated him. She was completely unaware of her own unsuitability for a life in the force and seemed to be in full receipt of the kind of arrogance that made her stupidity even more galling to all those who noticed it. She was, however, racing up the ranks. She obviously had her protectors and backers and it wouldn't be wise to get on the wrong side of her. Certainly not in a probationary period.

Brennan was first to break the silence in the car. 'Where are they staying?'

'The Travelodge, sir.'

'Which one?'

'The new one ... Out at Cameron Toll.' Brennan felt relieved – there was also a Travelodge on the same street as the morgue; staying there would have been more than a little odd.

'You say they're a bit ... strange?'

McGuire spun the wheel through his hands. 'A bit, yeah, you could say that.'

'Well, you did. So explain it.'

The DC took a lower gear, rode the clutch a little. 'Well, if it was me, and I'd lost a daughter like that, I'd be ropeable, but he just dragged his wife away and, well, seemed to want to shut her up, really.'

Brennan sized up the DC's response. 'But that's you, Stevie. Different strokes for different folks.'

McGuire smiled, started to work his way back up the gears as the road cleared. 'Yeah, I know. I guess you had to be there. It was all very odd, that's all I'm saying. I had this gut feeling that the bloke had something to hide.'

Brennan went for broke. 'Do you think he killed his daughter?'

'Christ Almighty.'

He pressed, 'Well, do you?'

McGuire was braking for a traffic light. He paused before he brought the car to a halt. 'Are you asking me do I think he did it?'

Brennan shrugged.

'I can't make a wild guess like that, sir. I mean, I just can't. But if you were asking do you think he was a possible, at this stage, going on what I'd seen of him I'd say he's definitely suspicious enough.'

The lights changed. McGuire overrevved; the engine nearly cut out. He cursed as he found first again and heard the gears bite.

For a moment or two, Brennan replayed what he'd just heard from the DC. It did seem a bit odd, for sure, but weren't all religious types a bit odd? And then they were from the north – stranger still. There was nothing solid to go on. Brennan had seen parents so shocked at the loss of a child that they entered a virtual state of catatonia upon hearing the news. There was no standard way of dealing with that kind of blow. He knew he would have to reserve judgement until he'd thoroughly quizzed the parents.

Brennan spoke: 'Did either of them seem surprised to discover their daughter in Edinburgh?'

'No. Not really … In fact, I can't say there was a flicker. Why?'

Brennan frowned. 'Isn't it obvious?'

This was a test – McGuire appeared to know it. He squinted, seemed to be searching the recesses of his mind for the answer. None came. 'Not to me, sir.'

'Well, where did you say they were staying?'

'Travelodge.'

'Not with friends, then?'

'No.'

'Well, could be because they don't know anyone here … In that case, what the hell's their daughter doing this far away from home, in a strange city, where the family has no connections?'

McGuire's eyes flickered. 'I see. I didn't think of that.'

'Get the boys back at the office to check out any school- mates, boyfriends or the like that have left her hometown recently. Anyone that the girl might have had a connection to, or reason to want to tie in with down here.'

'Yes, boss.'

McGuire drove to the car park for the shopping centre at Cameron Toll and pulled up outside the front entrance. As they got out he pointed to the hotel across the road. It was the first time Brennan had seen the place; the last time he had been up this way it was a half-derelict building. It seemed like the city was changing everywhere he went. If you strayed into an area where you hadn't been for some months, or weeks even, the chances were that you wouldn't recognise the topography.

At the hotel Brennan left the formalities to McGuire. He listened as he spoke to the receptionist, requested she call the minister's room. There was no answer.

'Perhaps they've gone out,' said the receptionist. She had a heavy Eastern European accent.

'Have they dropped off a key?' said Brennan.

The girl looked under the counter. 'One moment, please.'

Brennan gave one of his looks to McGuire. It was a look that said: If you've lost the pair of them already then I'm putting your arse in a sling. The DC drummed his fingers repeatedly on the front desk.

'Erm, no ... they haven't dropped off the keys. They might be at breakfast. I'll check, if you'd like to wait.'

'We'll wait in the lounge.'

'Yes, that's fine,' said the receptionist. 'Would you like some tea?'

McGuire nodded, smiled.

'No, thank you,' said Brennan. 'We'll be fine as we are.'

The DI strode off.

Chapter 21

BRENNAN LOOKED AROUND THE NEW hotel, sneered at the fittings. These places all looked the same to him. He was glad he wasn't a travelling salesman, or someone who had to spend any length of time in places like this. They were soulless. What was the point in travelling around the country, the world, when you stayed in joints like this? You'd be as well staying at home, saving the money.

It had been some time since Brennan and his family had been on holiday. Sophie was too old for that kind of thing. In the last few months she had turned into a small adult. It just occurred, almost overnight. She woke up and suddenly she was no longer his little girl. It scared Brennan how alike they were: at Sophie's age he had been just as wrapped up in himself. He'd wanted to make a difference, hadn't wanted to be like everyone else. The idea of the nine-to-five existence had terrified him. He couldn't see himself poring over the minutiae of business in some corporate black hole. He'd wanted to be out in the world, where life was. There had been lots of run-ins with his father then. He'd wanted his son to go into the family building firm but the idea horrified Brennan. His father had never got used to his son's career choice; it had always smacked of rebellion, nose-thumbing to him. His father couldn't understand that it went a lot deeper than that. Andy had known, his brother had understood, but then Andy had been an exceptional person; the thought burned Brennan again. It surprised him how fresh the wound remained at these times. It was something you never got over.

DC Stevie McGuire rose as the minister and his wife came into the foyer. They had been in the dining room but looked as if they might have just walked from a funeral service. Brennan eyed them cautiously; he could see what McGuire meant at once – they were queer fish. Their faces seemed expressionless, as though they spent their lives rationalising their every move. Even their clothes – deeply conservative brogues and tweeds – looked to be from another era. They unnerved Brennan. He stood up, approached them.

McGuire spoke first: 'Hello, Minister, Mrs Donald.' He nodded and extended a weak hand. Formalities over, he turned. 'And this is Detective Inspector Brennan.'

'Hello,' he said.

The minister replied, 'Hello, Inspector.'

'I hope I'm not intruding, but I'd like to offer my respects.'

A nod; the slightest of turns showed on the minister's mouth. 'Thank you.'

Brennan continued, 'If it's convenient, I'd also like to ask you one or two questions.'

The minister looked at his wife. She seemed horrified at the suggestion, her eyes moistening and several shades of colour draining from her cheeks. He replied, but seemed to be speaking to his wife: 'Well, I suppose it's quite necessary … In the situation.'

Brennan stayed quiet, watched them both for reactions, then, 'It might be best to go to your room, if you don't object.'

Mrs Donald walked away, headed for the lift. The minister spoke: 'Yes. That would be fine.' He watched his wife at the other side of the foyer, said, 'You will have to excuse my wife, officers, I'm afraid she is in a state of some shock.'

'I understand,' said Brennan. He waved a hand towards the lift. The doors pinged and Mrs Donald walked in.

The room was surprisingly large. Part of the original building was Victorian and they had struck lucky with bay windows and high ceilings. The bed had already been made and stood at the far end of the room, tucked beside a writing desk decked out in hotel stationery and leaflets for all the usual Edinburgh tourist attractions – zoo, castle, palace.

Brennan watched the minister point to the chairs in the window. 'Please, take a seat, gentlemen.'

As Brennan and McGuire sat themselves down in the window's lee, the minister and his wife stationed themselves on the edge of the bed. The minister took his wife's hand. They looked like a very old oil painting as they sat before the officers. Brennan glanced out the window as the pair shared a brief moment of reassurance; there was a dull sun breaking through the clouds.

'I know this will be very difficult for you,' said Brennan, 'but I hope you understand we need to move as quickly as possible to build a picture of what happened to Carly.'

The couple seemed to grip each other tighter. 'Yes, we understand,' said the minister.

Brennan realised he had not heard a single word from the minister's wife yet. 'If I can begin by asking you a little bit about your daughter.'

The pair nodded.

'Can you tell me when you became aware Carly had left home?'

'It was a Sunday, the twenty-fourth,' said the minister. 'I remember because I was at the second morning service when Frieda alerted me.'

Brennan looked to the quiet woman. 'You discovered she had gone?'

A nod; she deferred to her husband.

'There was a note, of sorts. Her room was empty.'

'Do you have the note?' said McGuire.

'I'm afraid not – it was very brief. No more than a goodbye really.'

'And there was no subsequent contact with her, after the twenty-fourth?'

'No, none.'

Brennan let the pair settle again, continued: 'Did she give any indication as to why she was leaving, or where she was going?'

'No.'

The information Brennan wanted was not forthcoming.

'Why do you think she chose Edinburgh?' he said.

'I have no idea. She knows … knew … not a soul here.'

Mrs Donald seemed to be getting tired of the questions – she put down her husband's hand and stood up beside the writing desk, resting a finger on top and staring out over their heads to the sky.

'It would be best if I could get both your opinions,' said Brennan.

'Why would that be?' said Mrs Donald. It was the first time Brennan had heard her speak and he was surprised by the calm in her voice. It was as if she'd decided the way forward was to block it all out. 'Nothing's going to bring her back now, is it? This is all pointless.'

Brennan stood up, indicated the edge of the bed where she had been sitting. 'Please, Mrs Donald …' He never got to finish his sentence – the minister turned and nodded and his wife returned to her seated position.

'Was there any upset in the home, or school, at the time of Carly's departure?' said Brennan.

Head shakes in unison: 'No, none.'

Brennan was tiring of the staccato answers. As he eyed the couple he tipped some grit in his voice: 'Nothing at all?'

The minister answered brusquely, 'Nothing.'

'It seems very unusual that Carly would be so happy at home and then just leave, don't you think?'

There was no answer from either of them. They held firm before the officers.

Brennan let the silence stretch out, watched their faces, then, 'You don't think that's unusual, Minister?'

'I thought that was a rhetorical question.' He seemed to have grown irritable, his tone testy now.

'I'd like an answer if you have one.'

'Then no. I don't think it was unusual.' He blurted his words – his breath had shortened; he finished on a sigh.

'Why would that be?' Brennan watched Mrs Donald turn from her husband and raise a hand to her mouth.

'She was a very headstrong child at times ... She could be wilful when she wanted.'

'In what ways?'

The minister rose from the bed. 'Inspector, is this really necessary? I don't see how this is helping us. My wife is very distressed.'

Brennan looked at Mrs Donald. She lowered her hand, placed it within her husband's – he brushed it aside and sat down again. Brennan took this as his cue to continue: 'Did your daughter ... Had she made any enemies, had a row at school or something of that nature?'

'I don't think so.'

'So it's possible?'

'I suppose so, yes ... I didn't follow her around every minute of the day.'

The minister's abruptness lit a fuse in Brennan. He had reached the limit of his patience and thought it was time to reveal the fact. He turned to McGuire, shook his head, then rose and made for the door. As he looked back he spoke: 'I'm going to need a full list of everyone that Carly had contact with in the weeks and months leading up to her death – friends, family, teachers, boyfriends. Everyone. I'd like you to compile that before you leave the city.'

The minister and his wife followed Brennan's actions as he buttoned his jacket.

The detective continued, 'I'll also need full access to Carly's personal effects, her room, diaries, computer, everything.' He paused. 'I am conducting a murder investigation here ... I don't want to have to go through this with the parents of another child any time soon.'

As the DI exited, McGuire followed at his heels.

The officers got as far as the foyer before Brennan spoke. 'I see what you mean.'

'Boss?'

'Queer all right. It's what's at the back of it that worries me.'

'You think they're hiding something?'

Brennan glared at him. 'I'd bet money on it.'

As he turned for the car park, Brennan's phone rang. He answered straight away: 'Yes.'

It was Galloway. 'There's been some developments.'

'Go on.'

'Where are you?'

'At the hotel ... I've just interviewed the parents.'

'Good. You'll want to bring them in now.'

Brennan swapped the phone to his other ear. 'Come again?'

'We just got the full pathology report in. The girl had given birth.'

'What?' Brennan's thoughts seized. He felt his breath shortening.

'Carly Donald had a child, and we're talking about a very young child at that ... Our victim had not long ago had a baby.'

Chapter 22

MELANIE McARDLE SANK INTO THE heavily padded white sofa. There was a slight buzzing in her head, but not enough. She reached for the Beaujolais bottle and tipped some more into her glass – the bottle's rim chinked on its lip and she giggled. 'C'mon, Mel … Keep the party clean!' Her giggles descended into full-on laughter as she made another attempt to fill her glass. Some liquid escaped and fell on her chest, ran down into the lacy bodice she wore beneath her dressing gown. Melanie laughed harder now, sat up.

'Jesus Christ, doll …'

As she wiped away the wine, wrung out the edge of her cream-silk sleeve with her fingertips, Melanie's laughter subsided. It was another item of clothing ruined; some wine had splattered onto the sofa too. 'Oh fucking hell.' She put down the glass, rubbed at the stains with her hands. It made no difference – only pressed the redness deeper into the fabric. Devlin would go mad. He would be home soon and see the state of the place, the state of her, and go mad. Melanie slumped onto her knees, lowered her head. He hadn't hit her for weeks, since the hospital. When she came back with her face stitched he'd said that was it, no more. He'd said sorry – even looked apologetic – and she'd believed him, but that seemed like a long time ago now.

Melanie shook herself, pulled a foot under her. Her head spun a little – she liked it, had another giggle to herself. She dragged her other foot forward, steadied her arms on the front of the sofa and pushed herself up. It wasn't so hard to stand after all. She rested a hand on her hip and pointed the other to the ceiling in a victory salute. 'C'-mon, girl, you can do it!'

As Melanie twisted, her foot caught the glass of Beaujolais resting on the floor and the contents flew into the air. They seemed to hang there for a moment as she watched the liquid escape, then the light caught the wetness and the scene became real again. When the wine landed there was an almost imperceptible splashing noise, and a three-foot red streak was etched in the pale carpet.

'No. No. No.' Melanie brought her hands to her head, scrunched her eyes. The image was still there when she opened them, however. She cried out, 'No. God …' She flopped to her knees again, began rubbing with the sleeve of her dressing gown, but the stain only spread further into the fabric. As Melanie rubbed, she felt her wrists ache, her arms grow tired. She could feel the pressure on her knees as the carpet burned into the skin. Devlin was coming home soon. He would in all certainty go mental.

'Oh Jesus, please no.'

As she rubbed harder she felt her head spinning faster. She kept up the movement for a full minute, then slumped, exhausted. The carpet looked worse, far worse than when she had begun. She had managed to ruin the sofa and now the carpet. Her bodice was stained and the sleeves of her dressing gown were blackened. Melanie reached out for the bottle and raised it to her mouth. She slugged deep. The wine spilled from the tip of the bottle and overran her lips, dribbling down her front. She chugged harder, downed the contents as quickly as she could. If the Deil was coming to beat her senseless, she would get there before him. She finished off the wine and felt her head swim in response. She liked that feeling, the dislocated swirl that said nothing could come between you and true happiness. She knew it was an illusion, that it never lasted, but she didn't care.

Melanie threw aside the bottle. 'Fuck you, Devlin McArdle!' She staggered to her feet, swayed a little, then headed to the kitchen. As she went, she steadied herself on the walls. She knocked a lampshade on her way through the door; it made her grimace. The kitchen tiles felt cold on her bare feet but the sensation wasn't altogether unpleasant. As she reached the refrigerator she had a craving for more alcohol. Her eyes were starting to slow-blink and her mouth had curled into a louche smile. She tugged the dressing gown round her as she opened the door, stared in. A bottle of Absolut vodka seemed to wink at her from the shelf. She reached for the neck. It was cold as she raised it, slammed the door shut in one swift movement.

Melanie removed the cap and threw it on the ground. She downed a mouthful and wiped her lips with the back of her hand. 'That's the trick!' She let out a long exhalation of breath as she steadied herself on the countertop. She took another deep swig and then she walked, shakily, towards the breakfast bar and sat down with the bottle of vodka in front of her.

For a moment she stared at the clear liquid swirling in the bottom and then she sighed, raided the mug rack and poured until the brim was overflowing. She raised the mug, drank greedily until it was drained. 'Fuck, Mel ...' she laughed at herself for a moment and then, inexplicably, her laughter turned to tears and she lowered her head in front of the bottle.

Melanie didn't know how long she'd been asleep, leaning on the breakfast bar, but when she heard the sound of car tyres on the gravel of the driveway, she knew it had been some time. The sky outside had darkened and the only light in the kitchen was coming from the cooker's digital clock and some shafts through the windows where the garden security lamps had come on.

Her mouth felt dry, her tongue harsh. She rubbed at her head – her temples burned. She had been slumped forward and the nape of her neck ached like it had been in a vice. She raised herself, tried to straighten her back, but her head swam, threatening to drop her on the floor. The physical discomfort was intense, but nothing compared to the realisation that she had returned to the real world – the drinking bout had done nothing but delay the fact that she had to face up to her actions, and Devlin.

Melanie shuffled towards the sink, ran the tap. The water came out too fast, too hard. At first she threw up her arms, shielded herself as it splashed off the plates and cups and wetted her face and chest. When she gathered herself, she turned the tap the other way a little, diminished the flow. She cupped her hands underneath and splashed the cold water on her face. It made her eyes smart. As she fanned her hands under the tap, the beads of moisture seemed to rouse her. She recouped her senses and retreated.

Melanie was running her hands through her hair, tucking stray strands behind her ears, as the front door opened. She heard the heavy thud of the door closing, then Devlin's keys being thrown on the little table nearby. She had expected to hear shouts, bellows after that, but as his footfalls made the living room she heard an altogether different noise to the one she expected.

It sounded like a baby crying.

She tugged the cord of her dressing gown round her waist and tapped the sides of her cheeks in an effort to waken her senses yet further. *Shushing*, she heard Devlin *shushing*. His voice seemed lower than she had ever heard it; unnatural.

Slowly, she edged herself towards the kitchen door.

The floor felt cold beneath her feet as she walked but once through the door the carpet was soft. She was so intrigued by the noises coming from the living room that she managed to push the accident with the wine out of her mind. As she turned the corner into the seating area, she straightened the lamp she had knocked earlier, and switched it on.

Light flooded into the room. Melanie felt her mouth widening but no words seemed to be forming on her lips.

'Hello, dear,' said Devlin.

Melanie pointed to him. 'What the hell is that?'

He turned towards the light and held out a small bundle.

'It's, well, kind of ...' He was searching for the words but none came. 'It's a baby, Devlin.'

'Yeah, that's right.'

Melanie walked towards her husband. He shook the small child up and down to try and calm it. 'Come on now, that's enough.'

It was clear to Melanie he had not a clue how to look after a baby. Something rose in her; she took the child in her arms.

Chapter 23

THE BABY CALMED IN MELANIE'S arms, gurgled. She looked at the small round cheeks and the pink nose and thought how cute they were. The child was like a toy, a squirming noisy toy. She lifted the baby onto her shoulder and started to walk around the living room, shushing and cooing. McArdle watched for a moment or two then threw himself down on the sofa. He seemed unaware of, or unconcerned about, the red wine stains.

Melanie watched her husband as he took out his mobile phone and checked his calls. He scratched the back of his neck and sighed, returned the phone. 'You all right with that nipper for a bit, doll?' he said.

Melanie turned round, looked him in the eye. 'What do you mean?'

McArdle sat forward, rested his elbows on his thighs.

He looked, if not troubled, at least not his usual self.

Melanie had expected shouting, screaming about the wine stains but he wasn't bothered in the slightest. He seemed to be preoccupied; there was something troubling him. 'It's like this … I'm minding it, for a pal.'

Melanie felt her brows crease, her jaw sag. He made the poor child sound like a car or something that was stolen from a building site – a generator or power tools. It was a child. 'What the hell do you mean, minding it for a pal?' she launched into him.

McArdle rubbed his neck again, brought his hand up the back of his head, smoothed his palm over the stubble on his crown. His eyes darted from left to right; he was about to lie to her, she could tell. 'See, there's this couple and they have a bit of a problem and can't mind the kid for a bit, so—'

Melanie arked up, 'So you said you would!' It didn't sound like Devlin McArdle to her. It sounded like a decent thing to do and she knew he wasn't capable of a decent action. If he had taken this child he had done it for some other reason. 'Oh, come on, do you expect me to believe that?'

McArdle flared his nostrils, opened and closed his mouth, then, 'Mel, you can believe what you want.'

Was he testing her? She knew he was playing at some kind of game

but she couldn't work out the rules. He liked his psycho logical spar-
ring as much as the physical, but this was all new to Melanie. She
understood that someone had to look after the baby – and that someone was going to have to be her – so McArdle needed to keep her onside. If he lost patience with her, he'd have to look after the child himself, and that obviously wasn't part of his plan; neither was letting
someone else look after the child. If he had intended to leave the child
elsewhere he would have already. There was a reason why he had
brought a baby back to their home and Melanie wanted to know
what it was.

'I want the truth,' she said. Her voice betrayed the seriousness of
the situation, sounded harsh. The tone had surprised Melanie. Was
she standing up to McArdle? She knew she would never do that herself, but she seemed to draw strength from the situation.

'Okay, okay … Come here.' McArdle motioned her towards the sofa.
'Come and sit down, Mel.'

'I mean it, I want the truth … This is a baby, not some knock-off
gear you've brought home.'

McArdle breathed in. His chest rose as he spoke: 'I was out at Muirhouse today …'

'I fucking knew it. You're not doing anyone a favour!'

Melanie stood again. She felt light-headed.

'Sit down, love.'

'No. No way.' Her adrenaline spiked at the mention of the scheme.
Nothing good came of McArdle's doings there. She knew he dealt
drugs, but he had a small army of people to do that for him. If he'd
been visiting the badlands it meant trouble: someone hadn't paid up,
or an old score had been settled. She prayed he hadn't taken some
poor mother's child to put a scare on a bad debtor.

As she walked away from her husband, Melanie McArdle suddenly
wondered to herself, where was she going? She could flee to the
kitchen, the upstairs bathroom maybe, but that was as far as she'd
get. The thought stilled her. She turned, faced him. McArdle was fid-
dling with his watch strap. His teeth clenched as he readied himself
to deal with Melanie's rebellion. She felt her nerves shriek. The realisation of her situation was like a hard ball being bounced on her
head. She scrunched her eyes and looked away. When she returned
her gaze, McArdle had reclined in the sofa, crossed his legs; she could
see the Adidas symbol at the top of his socks.

He patted the cushion beside him. 'Come on, Mel …'

She sucked at her cheeks, pressed her tongue against the back of her teeth. She tried to keep her mouth closed, but the words wouldn't stay in: 'What's going on?' She wanted to know, she wanted to hear the truth, but at the same time she felt helpless to do anything about the situation. She couldn't stand against him – he would kill her before he tolerated that.

McArdle tweaked the tip of his nose with his finger and thumb, spoke: 'Well, if you're ready to listen, I'll tell you.'

She nodded; hugged the baby close.

'As I said, I was in Muirhouse … Now, it's not what you think. I had some legitimate business there and, well …' he paused, cleared his throat, coughed into his fist, 'well, how can I put this, love …'

Something was wrong, she knew that the second he started to call her love. He was lying. McArdle never stalled for words. He was lying to her because he needed her to help him out of a fix. She'd seen the look before, when police were involved. It put a shard of ice in her spine. She gripped the child again.

McArdle continued, 'There's this couple there and, well, they have their addictions … Nothing serious, mind, they take a bit of grass and a bit of skag and they're payers, good payers, I've no worries with them on that score if that's what you're thinking.' He rubbed his knuckles, fiddled with a heavy gold sovereign ring. 'Melanie, it's like this … The social services are coming down hard on them, threatening to take the kid away. Really shook them up, so it has …'

Melanie couldn't look at him any longer. She turned her head away, spoke: 'So you said you'd take the kid … Why?' It didn't make sense to her.

'Because, love, they need a break and they don't want to lose the kid … Look, they've no family to speak of, so the social would just put the nipper into care. I couldn't let that happen, could I?'

She huffed; who was he kidding? Since when did Devlin McArdle give a shit about the people he supplied drugs to?

He cared if they didn't pay him. He cared if they short-changed him, lied about having money when they didn't, or bought from someone else, but that was all. He wasn't a social worker, and he thought about one person and one person alone: himself.

'Mel, please … Hon, it's not going to be for long. A week at the most. You can look after the kid for that long, can't you?'

Melanie stared at her husband. The blood surged in her veins. He had reached a new low and she hated him for it, but she knew she was powerless to do anything about it.

He spoke again, his voice a pathetic low paean: 'Mel, I know you can do it ... I know you can, one week, that's all I'm asking.'

She felt a spasm in her neck tug her gaze from him. She took in the full horror of the wine stains. Before she knew what she was doing, Melanie had answered him: 'Okay.

One week.'

Chapter 24

DI ROB BRENNAN PAUSED ON the way to the interview room, gathered his thoughts. He leaned against the wall and watched the flurry of activity around the station. The momentum of the case had seemed to stall not long after finding the body, then accelerated once they had identified her as Carly Donald. Things had lunged forward rapidly once more, but the mood of the investigation had altered.

Nothing was being taken for granted.

He had worked hundreds, thousands of cases in his time on the force but Brennan had never encountered anything like this before. There was, for sure, a reason why Carly's parents had kept the details of their granddaughter Beth's birth to themselves, but he couldn't fathom what it might be. A child was a gift from God, in any circumstances – his mother had said that when Sophie was born, and she was not a religious woman, but the sheer significance of the event had prompted a spiritual outburst. How could a so-called man of the cloth carry on like that? It felled Brennan to think of it. Was life so cheap?

He knew, when the case was over, complete, tidied up and all the loose ends put together into one nice neat bow, things would make perfect sense. They always did, then. The reasons for seemingly inexplicable behaviour always became clear; motives presented themselves. Sometimes it was money, sometimes lust. He had seen just about every variation in between, but for Reverend John Donald and his wife to lose not only a child but a grandchild too, and to keep quiet about it before the investigating officers, was perplexing. Brennan thought about the picture Lorraine had handed him earlier. He placed his hand into his pocket and removed the small photograph and stared at the tiny shape, barely recognisable as human. A small smile spread from the corner of his mouth. He touched the picture with his fingertip, then hurriedly returned it to his pocket.

A siren sounded in the car park and Brennan was poked back to the waking world. He watched as a young WPC worked the photocopier. She retrieved her copy then walked off, getting only a few paces before returning to the machine to raise the lid and retrieve the original. She smiled at Brennan on her way back to her seat.

They knew; they all knew. This case was turning out to be a thankless task: the kind of crime that had a clear victim, but that was all that was clear. Brennan had decided early on that the girl in the dumpster was local to Muirhouse – it looked that way, everything pointed to that – but now he had to reassess his assumptions. He had to go back to the start, look again. Was he missing something? He knew he must be, but what? All he needed was one break, one pointer, something to set the ball in motion and the rest would gather in its wake. If he was a religious man himself, he thought, prayers might not be a bad idea.

As he paced through Incident Room One he saw Lauder coming from DC Stevie McGuire's desk. Brennan approached him, stood in his path: 'What are you doing in here?'

Lauder grinned. 'Who promoted you to hall monitor?'

Brennan stood his ground. 'This is my investigation, Lauder, and I'd like it solved.' The bustle of the room ceased – they had an audience. Brennan sensed himself becoming a gladiator, all eyes upon him for a reaction as Lauder replied.

'I'd ask how you were getting on, but I think I'll just catch it on the news later.'

It was a low blow, designed to rattle Brennan. He returned a volley of his own: 'We're doing fine here, so you can take yourself elsewhere, Lauder, I don't want you fucking up our mojo.'

Lauder riled, 'What's that supposed to mean?'

Now Brennan smiled. 'How's the shooting case going?'

Lauder shook his head. 'That's a complex investigation; it would take me too long to explain to you, Rob.'

Brennan walked past him. 'Broad-daylight shooting, in a public place ... Sounds it!'

Lauder looked ready to spit as he turned for the exit.

Brennan knew he was storing up trouble for himself if he didn't ease off on him, but he didn't care. The man had messed up the investigation of his brother's murder and the thought rankled, more than a bit.

Outside the interview room Brennan stalled, looked in the peephole. The minister sat silently inside, head bowed. Brennan lowered his eye, rested his forehead on the door for a second or two, then jerked his neck back and walked into the room opposite. DC Stevie McGuire was sitting inside. He had a sandwich box open on the desk and a styrofoam cup filled with grey coffee halfway to his mouth. When he saw Brennan he lowered the cup, said, 'Sir, how's it going?'

'It's me that should be asking you that.'

McGuire took a quick sip of the coffee. 'Well, I warmed him up for you but didn't get much.'

'What's he saying?' Brennan sat on the edge of the desk.

'Not a lot.' McGuire exhaled slowly. 'He said he was going to tell us about the baby ... in due course.'

Brennan smirked. 'Oh, really ... When, exactly?'

'That he didn't say.'

'What else?'

'Nothing much. I didn't go in too hard, just wanted to give him a foretaste, make him think, y'know.'

Brennan knew exactly what he meant – he was leaving it to him, didn't want to mess up. 'And the wife?'

'I'm just going in there now. Thought I'd question her whilst you took the husband. We can compare notes.'

Brennan made a conscious effort to keep his expression blank, register nothing. He rose from the edge of the desk, turned for the door he'd walked through a moment earlier. He was about to close it behind him when he retreated a step, said, 'I saw Lauder through there.'

McGuire's eyes widened. 'You did?'

'Yes. I did.' Brennan let the statement hang in the air for a little while, then, 'If there's any media enquiries come in, say nothing.'

McGuire's lips parted. He seemed to be unsure of his answer, then: 'Yes, sir ... Of course.'

Brennan closed the door behind him. As he turned for the interview room, he took a moment to think about his strategy: he was going in hard, studs first. There was nothing to be gained from holding back. They had treated the minister with too much civility already. A man that hides the fact that he has a missing granddaughter, in the wake of his daughter's brutal killing, deserves no leeway.

Brennan reached for the handle, turned it briskly and strode in. He did not acknowledge the minister, merely removed his jacket and flung it over the back of the chair. There was an empty plastic cup on the table. It toppled in the draught the jacket's landing threw up; a little sliver of brown tea spilled on the table. The minister stared at it, seemed unsure of what to do next. He righted the cup and returned his hand to beneath the table.

Brennan spoke: 'Who was the father?'

'*What*? I-I've no idea.'

'You never asked?'

'She wouldn't say.' The minister looked away.

'And you accepted that?'

A nod. 'It seemed irresponsible to press her, she was very unsettled then.'

'She must have had a boyfriend, someone you suspected?'

'No, no one.'

Brennan raised an eyebrow. 'Well, it was hardly an immaculate conception, Minister.'

He riled, 'I have no idea who the father of the child was, Inspector.'

Brennan paused, took a deep breath. He had already been through all the possibilities and their permutations in his mind. 'We can have that checked.'

The minister nodded. 'I'm sure you can.'

The line of questioning had stalled. It gave Brennan an opportunity to change tack: 'I see you're in line for the big league.'

'Excuse me?' His voice sounded tired.

'You didn't expect that to escape us, surely ...' Brennan turned his cheek, squinted. 'I'm talking about the job – Moderator of the Church of Scotland.'

The minister nodded, brought his hands out in front of him and laid them on the table. 'You present that like it is an important piece of the puzzle, Inspector.'

Brennan smiled. 'Maybe it is.'

'And why would that be?' His tone grew cockier.

The detective settled himself in the seat, made a show of turning up the cuffs on his shirtsleeves. 'Do I need to paint you a picture, Minister?'

A head tilt. 'I'm afraid you might have to, because I don't see any connection between my career prospects and this unfortunate turn of events.'

' "Unfortunate turn of events" ... You make it sound like your washing machine's on the blink.' Brennan sat forward, rested elbows on the table. 'Your daughter has been murdered and your grand-daughter – Beth – remember her? *She's* missing.'

The minister looked away, his pallor faded.

Brennan let the implications of his words settle. He rose from the chair and paced the room, spoke: 'Now, here's how I see it: you're up for the top job in the Kirk, and young Carly is *unfortunate* enough to get herself pregnant. Now, how does a respectable Church of Scotland minister deal with that? Does he throw a party in the manse?

Take an ad out in the paper? ... I wonder.' Brennan stared at the minister – he was looking away. 'No, here's what I say he does: he thinks about how this will look for *him*. Oh, now, the parishioners won't like it, he thinks. No, no. They'll talk, they'll complain, they'll put words in ears, maybe even write letters. No, no. That would never do. Am I painting a clear enough picture, Minister?'

'Yes, very clear.' His speech was blunt, brisk.

The DI leaned over him, shouted, 'I doubt it. I doubt it very much.' He didn't like the minister's demeanour – he was acting as if he had some cards in reserve, and Brennan knew full well he had no such thing. He fired on, 'You see, when I found out you were in line for the Moderator's job, it made me think. What did it make me think? you're wondering ... Well, it made me think that if an opportunity like that presented itself, an opportunity of a lifetime, you might say, some people would do almost anything to stop it slipping through their fingers.'

'No, this is wrong ... You are wrong about that,' said the minister.

Brennan returned to the table, leaned over. 'I doubt it.

You see, I watched you talking about your daughter and I think I learned one or two things about you, Minister. You are a very secretive man, you like to keep your private life, as the saying goes, private. Am I right or am I wrong?'

The minister nodded, said, 'Is there a law against that, Inspector Brennan?'

A smile, wry one. 'No. Not against that. But there is a law against murder.'

The minister's eyes flared. He rose. 'This has gone far enough. I demand to have a lawyer, now.'

Brennan eased back, lowered himself into the chair. 'You can have a lawyer any time you like, but jumping the gun a bit, aren't we? No one's charged you with anything.'

The minister sat down again, ran fingers through his thick grey hair. 'This infernal questioning is leading nowhere.'

'I'll be the judge of that ... and more besides.'

'Meaning?'

'*Meaning* I'd like you to start answering some questions, with some straight answers. Like why didn't you tell us about Beth?'

The minister laced his fingers, looked at his palms, turned them over. The actions seemed perfunctory. 'That would seem like an error now.'

'I'd say so. But you're not answering my question.'

The minister raised his eyes. 'My wife and I, well, we were in so much shock ...'

Brennan wasn't buying any of it. 'Why did Carly run away?'

A sigh, followed by a deep breath. 'We discussed with her about putting the child, erm, Beth, up for adoption.'

'And Carly wanted to keep her.'

'No. Well, not at first ... Before the birth, Carly was in favour of adoption.'

'But then she had the child, she held Beth in her arms and changed her mind, is that it?'

The minister nodded his head.

'So, you pressed her to have the child adopted?'

'No. Not at all ... It's very complex, Inspector.'

'Then explain it.'

His gaze turned away from Brennan; his eyes drooped in time with his shoulders. He spoke: 'We ... removed Carly from school when the pregnancy was uncovered. We tried to keep her from prying eyes.'

Brennan knew exactly what he was saying, and wasn't saying. 'You were ashamed.'

The minister's lower lip curled into his mouth, sat over his teeth for a moment, then subsided. 'There was some element of that, yes.'

'You were ashamed, and you were afraid you'd miss your chance to be Moderator.'

The minister didn't answer the question, said, 'It was very ... complex.'

Brennan rose from his chair again, began his pacing ritual. 'And then Beth was born.' The child's name seemed to unsettle the minister every time he heard it.

'Yes. Carly had the child at home. My wife was a midwife when we met and ... It was a simple procedure for her.'

'And the adoption?'

'We had made all the arrangements.'

'Go on.'

Talking like this was a trial for the minister – each word was drawn from a deep, dark well. 'Somewhere along the way, Carly had a change of heart. She didn't want to give up the child and ... there were words.'

Brennan turned, pointed to him. 'You laid down the law.'

He raised his voice: 'You told her she was giving up her child whether she wanted to or not!'

The minister raised his hands to his head, lowered his brow towards the table. His words were inaudible. Brennan watched as he rested his eye sockets on the heels of his hands.

'Well, this is all very interesting, Minister … All very interesting indeed, wouldn't you agree?'

Chapter 25

DC STEVIE McGUIRE WAS WAITING for Brennan as he left the interview room. He had a blue folder pressed to his chest, said, 'I have a media statement back from PR ... Do you want to cast your eyes over it?'

Brennan took the piece of paper, read:

Lothian and Borders Police investigations into the death of a young woman on the Muirhouse Housing Estate in Edinburgh are ongoing. Police are treating the matter as suspicious. The victim's identity will not be released until all family members have been informed. Police are keen to hear from anyone in the locus between the hours of ...

Brennan returned the paper, pinned it to McGuire's folder. 'Release the name.'

'What?'

'You heard.'

He walked off; McGuire trailed him.

'Sir, are you sure that's—' He broke off as Brennan spun round.

'Look, Stevie, how many calls from the hacks have we had on this?'

The DC shrugged. 'A lot ...'

'More than that, son. We've given them nothing and they're getting antsy. If we hold off on the ID then they're going to know we're playing them hard ... We'll be upping the pace, but we need to keep them onside, make them work for us.'

McGuire nodded, said, 'You're the boss.'

Brennan placed a hand on his shoulder, squeezed. 'Don't you forget it.' He smiled at McGuire. There was another reason behind his thinking, and he wanted to relay it: 'Look at it this way, Stevie – we might be jumping the gun a bit, but we'll piss off our mole something rotten.'

The pair shared a brief laugh as they walked towards the incident room; Brennan wondered if he was coming round to the DC. Phones were ringing, uniforms running to and fro. There was a message coming through the fax – a WPC waited for it. Brennan nodded to the crowd who looked up as he entered. He pointed to one of them. 'Lou, what's the go with the door-to-doors?'

A short man in a Markies shirt and tie, open at the collar, bedraggled, spoke: 'I'm about fifty per cent through them.'

'And?' Brennan moved his fists in a circular motion.

'And ... nothing, sir.'

'*Nothing?*'

'No one at the halfway houses saw anyone matching our victim. There's a few left to try but we're drawing blanks.'

Brennan shook his head, jutted his jaw. 'Did you start these before or after we had the full pathology report?'

Lou leaned back against the wall, touched his brow. 'Erm, bit of both ... Some before, some after.'

'Right. The ones you covered before, go back and ask if they saw anyone with a kid.'

'Yes, sir.' He pushed his shoulder blades off the wall, returned to his desk.

Brennan started to move fists again, halted, pointed.

'Brian ... what pictures you got?'

A shake of the head.

'Nothing?'

'Not so far. I've not got them all in yet, we're halfway through the train stations footage and haven't started on the buses ... The community centre's wasn't running.'

Brennan arked up, 'Oh, for fuck's sake.' He smacked a fist in his open palm. 'How many bods have you got screening?'

'Four on the early shift, two the back.'

'Double it. I'll worry about the overtime later.'

Brian nodded, ran fingers through his hair and picked up the phone's receiver.

Brennan paced round the room. He looked at the whiteboard.

There were more photographs of Carly now; her name had been added in red marker pen. Brennan's gaze hung for a moment, then he turned swiftly.

'Okay, Davie ... you're up.'

When the DC rose, he was a full half-foot taller than the rest of the room. His arms seemed too long for his body and his elbows poked out at an unnatural angle as he spoke: 'I hate to say it, boss, but I've got even less to report than the others.'

'Jesus Christ.' Brennan shook his head.

'I've pulled in the pimps working the Links but they're giving nothing away.'

'Are they holding back?'

A shrug. 'Hard to say ... They're never forthcoming at the best of times.'

'Haven't you got any brass that talk?'

Davie scratched his earlobe with a long bony finger. 'I tried that too
– nothing.'

Brennan threw up his hands, kicked out at a waste bin.

'Right, get them in … take a meat wagon and round them up.' He
turned, pointed again. 'Davie, you can head up the interviews and
I want them started today. Go on through the night if necessary …
Tell Charlie to clear some cells.'

'Sir, do you know how many sex workers there are out there?'

Brennan hated the phrase, it was too PC. He preferred the tried
and tested handle – seemed to fit. 'Get them all in, all the brass and
ass walking Leith, and interview them. One on one. A young girl has
died – someone knows something. And in case anyone has lost sight
of the fact, there's a child, a baby girl called Beth that's missing …
When I get my balls put over the coals on national television I want
to be able to tell the country that every single man and woman in
this room is doing everything they possibly can to find that child and
her mother's killer.'

The room fell silent. Heads were bowed.

Brennan continued, 'This might turn out to be the biggest case any
of you will ever work on. We have a seriously deranged killer on the
loose and don't think for a second the press and public are going to
let us forget it.' He walked to the window. 'Look out there – that's
where our killer is. There are people who know him, or her, and
they'll lead us right to where the bastard is hiding. I want every single one of you to up your game – the stakes have never been higher.
I want this bastard, and I want that child out of harm's way.'

The room was still quiet.

Brennan slammed his fist down on a desk. A cup and some pens
jumped. 'Do you hear me?'

Together: 'Yes, sir.'

'Good, now get to work. I want results … *Nothing* else will cut it.'

Brennan put one foot in front of the other, paced through to his
glass-fronted office. He slammed the door, more for effect than anything. As he sat at his desk he watched the bodies pass his window;
he knew they were a long way from finding out anything. The case
had him mystified. He knew there was some piece of the puzzle that
hadn't yet come into view, but he didn't know where to begin looking for it. What had happened to that girl back in Pitlochry that
made her pack up her belongings and head for the big city? It had

to be more than a tiff with her parents. Yes, the minister was a queer fish, as Stevie described him, but he wasn't a monster. Surely there was family support there for the girl, and if it wasn't there in sufficient quantities then she'd had some options available to her. At what stage did the best choice become to uproot herself from friends and family, with a baby, and head out into the unknown?

The more Brennan played over the events in his mind, the more it baffled him. Who was Carly Donald? He needed to find that out. He needed to get under the skin of the young girl from Pitlochry who had ended up in cold storage in the capital city. Brennan could see the whiteboards through the glass front of his office. The name of Carly's school was listed at the top of a number of contacts that had been deemed worth chasing. Teachers, friends, a hockey coach and the family doctor.

'Bullshit,' mouthed Brennan.

He would have to check this out himself. He had to start pushing a few buttons; the information was out there, it always was, it was just a matter of finding it. The girl had a child, Jesus, a child that no one knew where to look for. Who had the child? Was the child still alive? The questions mounted but the answers remained elusive. A thought of Lorraine cross-hatched with the case: he was soon to be a father again – how would he feel if his child was missing?

Someone had fathered Carly's child and Brennan wanted to know who. It was his experience that in small towns, information like that was never far from the lips of gossips; even if they were wrong, there were always theories. He didn't know where finding the father would lead him, or the investigation, but that was the way things went. You upturned every stone, in the hope of finding what you were looking for there. It was when you left stones unturned that you ran into difficulties.

Brennan felt his conscience pull. He picked up the receiver of the phone, dialled home. His wife answered after a few rings.

'Hello.' Her voice immediately chided him for his infidelity. She didn't need to say the exact words – his guilt drew its own meaning.

'It's me, Rob.'

'Oh, decided to return my call, did you?'

He turned to his blotter to see if there were any messages.

'What call? … First I've heard of it.'

'I called about an hour ago.' Joyce's tone was indignant.

He'd tired of that tone, and more besides. Even the things he had once admired and enjoyed in Joyce had become tiresome. The way she did her hair, the books she read, her pet phrases; her familiarity bored him. Lorraine was a very different woman; she didn't need to be, all she needed to be was someone other than Joyce, but Brennan hadn't realised that at the time.

'What is it, then?' he said.

A sigh. 'What do you think, Rob? It's your bloody daughter.'

Sophie had been testing her parents lately, but Brennan had more to worry about. Joyce could handle a stroppy teenager, surely. 'Look, you know what she's like … What they're all like at that age.'

The volume seemed to have risen on the other end of the line. 'Well, yes, I do know as a matter of a fact, because it's me that's dealing with it every day of the week, Rob, whilst you get to go off playing cops and robbers.'

That was unfair. 'Is that right?'

A pause. 'Well, it's how I feel. I'm tired of all of this, tired of being the only one who raises our daughter and I'm tired of getting no support … I want to know what the point is, Rob? What's the point any more?'

He didn't have an answer for her. He stared into the open-plan office and searched for something to say, but nothing came. Maybe there was no point.

'Well?' said Joyce. 'Are you just going to leave that one hanging?'

He watched one of the DCs walk over to the whiteboard and scribble something in red ink. He found some words: 'I'm going away for a few days.'

A tut. 'Well, that's just great. Just bloody—'

He cut her off. 'Joyce, shut up. I'm investigating the death of a young girl and her baby is missing. I'm going to interview her friends and people who knew her. She came from Pitlochry.' He blasted his words. 'Is that all right with you? Do you think you can manage a day or so with Sophie and her tantrums whilst I try and find out who cut up a young girl and left her body in a rubbish bin and what the fuck they've done with her child?'

There was no reply for some moments, then, 'If you're interested, Sophie, your own daughter, who was supposed to be sick and took the day off school, has left the house. She's taken a bottle of vermouth and some of my housekeeping money … In case it's of any concern to you, I thought I should let you know. I'll be scouring the streets for her when I put down the phone.'

Brennan had no time to reply before she hung up.

Chapter 26

BRENNAN JOTTED DOWN THE NAMES listed as Carly's 'known associates'. He halted before placing a full stop, touched his tongue with the tip of the pencil, then planted it in the notebook.

'Right, listen up,' he addressed the team.

The room fell quiet.

'DC McGuire and myself are going to be out of the office for a day or so ...'

McGuire perked up as his name was mentioned; Brennan hadn't told him he was going to Pitlochry.

'We're leaving for the north and we'll be tracking down some of Carly Donald's known associates, seeing what we can find. I do not want to hear anything second hand. I repeat: anything comes in, you dial this!' Brennan held up his mobile phone. 'You tell me right away if there are any developments in my absence. Got it?'

Together: 'Yes, sir.'

'Lou and Dave ... I want you to handle the media.'

'Sir.'

Brennan frowned, shook his head. 'Now, what do I mean by that? This: you take it straight to the press office ... After you've told me, of course.'

Both grinning: 'Yes, sir.'

'I don't need to remind you the media are going to start jumping up and down as soon as they discover we have a missing child on our hands. We want to delay that eventuality for as long as we can. Hopefully, the first the press know about it will be when we announce the child is safe and well, but we have to be prepared for the worst. Understood?'

'Yes, sir.'

Brennan tucked his notebook in his jacket pocket, threw the jacket over his shoulder and paced for the door. 'Come on, Stevie, we can collect your Clearasil on the way ...'

The team jeered the DC. 'Go get 'em, Stevie ... Shag a sheep for me, mate!'

Brennan allowed himself a smirk. The way things were progressing on the case, there would be precious little room for laughter. He knew if he didn't find Carly's child soon the chances were slim that he ever would. He couldn't allow that to happen. He wouldn't have another young life on his conscience. He felt a surge of pity and tapped at his breast pocket where he kept the scan picture Lorraine had given him.

In the station foyer Brennan was stopped by the desk sergeant. 'How's it going, Rob?'

Brennan inverted a smile. 'You know, Charl.'

Charlie leaned over the desk, acting conspiratorial.

'What's Princess Prada saying?'

He knew better than to feed office gossip. 'Just the usual.'

'Oh, yeah?'

Brennan motioned McGuire to get the doors, threw him the car key. 'Bring round the Passat, eh?'

'Yes, sir.'

As the DC left, Brennan leaned over the counter, lowered his tone. He could see Charlie's eyes lighting up. 'You know Lauder thinks she's got a thing for him.'

'That right?'

Brennan showed teeth. 'I shouldn't say, but I heard him talking about her coming on to him.'

'Get away.' Charlie's mouth drooped.

Brennan straightened himself. 'Probably just idle chatter – wouldn't pay it any heed.'

The desk sergeant nodded. 'You're right. That's how rumours get started, mate.'

Brennan winked at him as he headed for the door. Charlie's old face was unreadable; like a piece of clay on a potter's wheel, it waited for a new form to emerge.

Outside the wind cut. Brennan buttoned his jacket, stamped his feet on the pavement. He could smell the brewery on the breeze; he hated the smell. It was the city's scent, the defining characteristic that seemed to sum the place up for him. Where he grew up the air was clearer; Ayr was famous for it. The wind that washed over the Irish Sea brought clarity, the smell of seaweed and promise. Edinburgh had none of that. It was the smell of squalor and confusion and desperation that summed up the city for Brennan. They said it was warmer on the east coast but he didn't believe it. Growing up in Ayr it seemed to have been all sunny days, golden summers and smiling and joking with Andy. Those days were gone.

McGuire lowered the window on the Passat as he pulled up.

'Ready to go, boss. Want to drive?'

Brennan walked to the passenger side, stayed quiet. When he was in he put on his seat belt and nodded. 'Come on, then, let's get going.'

It took them an age to get out of the city, onto the main road. When they started to pick up speed, Brennan opened his window a few inches. 'Don't mind if I smoke, do you?'

he said.

'Well ...'

'Because if you do, there's always the bus.'

McGuire nodded. 'No, it's fine.'

Brennan took out his cigarette packet, looked at the purple square on the front and frowned. 'Got to get some proper fags.'

'Sorry?'

'Silk Cut ... Think they're for folk with sore throats.'

'Trying to give up?'

'Cutting back.'

'They'll kill you, y'know.'

Brennan pushed in the cigarette lighter, said, 'There's a lot of things that'll do that.'

McGuire nodded. He put on the blinkers to overtake a heavy goods vehicle. There was an unfamiliar expression on his face. 'Sir, can I ask you something?'

The lighter pinged; Brennan removed it. 'If you like.'

'Why did you join the force?'

Brennan lit his cigarette, held it between his fingers and exhaled his first drag slowly. 'What kind of a question is that?'

McGuire took his eyes off the road, glanced at the DI then back to the car in front. 'Most of the people I ask these days talk about the pension, or some bullshit about never seeing a policeman lose an argument ... But I'd say you were different.'

Brennan took another drag, squinted at McGuire through the cigarette smoke. 'Oh, I'm that.'

McGuire put the Passat into fifth gear, planted his foot. 'You don't rate many at the station, do you, sir?'

Brennan knew where this conversation was going. 'Like Lauder, you mean?'

'Well ...'

'Don't concern yourself, son. Me and Lauder have a score to settle, that's all.'

McGuire coughed on the back of his hand. 'Is that your br—'

'Stevie, change the subject, eh.'

'Sir.'

They drove in silence for a few miles. Brennan noticed how the fields and trees altered his mood. It was a release to be getting out of the city. He wound up the window, stubbed out his cigarette. There was a twinge of regret building in him for the way he had treated McGuire. The DC was trying hard to make an impression. He was just a boy after all; Brennan could remember being his age, once.

'I always wanted to be a police officer, even when I was very young. My brother wanted to be an artist then, but we were both told early on that we'd be going into the family business. My old man was a small-time builder – we were both to get trades. I was having none of it. I joined up as soon as they'd have me and that was that.'

McGuire smiled. 'You rebel.'

'Yeah, something like that.'

'What about your brother – did he become an artist?'

Brennan looked out over the fields again. The sun splashed a yellow glow on the grass. 'No … Andy went into the family firm.'

McGuire seemed to have sensed it was difficult territory for Brennan – talking about his brother; he changed the subject now. 'So, Pitlochry … Never been. Has it got its fleshpots?'

Brennan laughed. 'Don't be daft, it's like any other small Scottish town.'

'A shit-hole, then?'

At McGuire's age, Brennan had thought every small town in Scotland was a shit-hole; it was funny how your opinions changed with maturity. 'I suppose it depends what you're looking for. We're not going to paint the town red, Stevie, we're investigating a murder.'

'Yes, sir.'

Brennan was happy that the tone had returned to a familiar formality. He withdrew his notebook, scanned the names he'd jotted down back at the station. 'What sort of impression did the local woodentops make on you, Stevie?'

McGuire breathed out slowly, slapped his hand off the steering wheel. 'Well, they were a bit shocked to get my call at the start, to be honest …'

'More used to dealing with calls about some young farmer up to his nuts in a ewe!'

McGuire laughed, slapped the wheel again. 'Nice one!'

Brennan clawed him back in: 'Anyway, once they got over the shock of having a murder squad on the way up …'

'Erm, quite cordial, I suppose.'

Cordial – where did he get these words? Brennan never used words like cordial, certainly never at McGuire's age. The benefits of a private education no doubt, he thought.

'Well, we'll be putting their hospitality to the test, so we'll find out. I hope they've got a phone line.'

'I brought a whistle, just in case.'

Brennan put his notebook back in his pocket. 'I want to start with Carly's best friend. Lynne Thompson.'

'Right, I'll get her brought into the station.'

'No, don't do that. We'll go to the home ... Want her to be comfortable enough to speak, not frighten her off.'

'Yes, sir.'

'Have you spoken to the Thompson girl's parents?'

McGuire creased his brows. 'No, Lou did ... They were very helpful, apparently.'

'That's country folk for you.'

'Yeah, apparently the poor girl's devastated. Off school, not eating.'

'Did she give anything away?'

McGuire shook his head. 'Sorry, boss ... She's bemused, by all accounts. They were best friends and the pair of them didn't really mix with the rest of the youngsters in the town, so she's a bit lost without her.'

Brennan lowered his voice. 'She must have known about the pregnancy, then ... Maybe she'll know the father.'

McGuire nodded. 'Yes, maybe. What you thinking? Local boy?'

'One thing's for sure: if she was seeing someone, a friend like Lynne would have heard about it. Teenage girls don't keep that kind of thing from each other.'

McGuire dropped a gear, put the blinkers on again, pulled out to overtake a slow-moving caravan. 'Why do they let those fuckers on the road?'

Brennan agreed; but steered the conversation back on course. 'What about the head?'

'Staggered. Seriously strung out. Carly hadn't been at school for the last few months. She'd been kept off with – get this – depression. The school had no idea she'd given birth.'

'*Depression?*'

'Certified ... I spoke to the doctor: he said she was depressed after the birth and it was quite normal.'

'What about before? If he was signing her off school with depression before the baby was born then he must have had his reasons.'

McGuire eased the car back into lane. 'He's a family doctor, sir. Said there were a lot of issues surrounding the birth. He didn't want to stress the mother out in her pregnancy with worry about small-town gossip and thought it was better for all if she was kept off school. Seemed genuine, and fair enough to me.'

Brennan drummed his fingers on the windowsill. He dipped his head, pushed in the cigarette lighter once more.

'Okay, the girl first, then ... Let's hope Lynne's got something that we can use to find out who killed her best friend.'

They spent the rest of the journey in silence, punctuated only by the pinging of the cigarette lighter and McGuire's overrevving of the engine.

When they reached Pitlochry it was just as Brennan remembered it. He'd been there on a family holiday – when they still took family holidays – to the Highlands a few years back. He'd taken the road off the A9 to check the place out and remembered Sophie complaining because she wanted to get to the hotel to watch *Friends*. The town was small but not without its appeal, he thought. It had once been a popular tourist spot with the Victorians, who took to the scenic setting and the proliferation of spires and sturdy Scots baronial architecture. The town centre said solidity, a Presbyterian longing for respectability. Knowing what he did, it seemed like hypocrisy to Brennan.

'Nightmare to get parked here,' said McGuire.

Brennan soaked up the feel of the place – it screamed to him of a vanished country. The days of men in tweed and brogues were gone, he thought – that was all just dress-up for the hunting, shooting and fishing mob – but there was something about Pitlochry that said the look was still de rigueur. 'Check out the Barbour jackets.'

McGuire sighed. 'Christ, thought I'd seen the last of them at uni.'

Brennan shook his head. 'The last time I came up here I thought it was quite, what's the word ... quaint?'

'I'd bet if you stopped and talked to one of the Barbour mob they'd be Home Counties ... Or Notting Hill. This part of the country's just a playground for the seriously well-heeled.'

Brennan agreed. 'Makes me a bit queasy now.'

'What's changed you?'

He shifted eyes. 'Maybe I suddenly developed awareness.'

McGuire dragged the gears. 'Traffic's seizing up.'

Brennan nodded to the road. 'Over there – it's our home from home.'

McGuire turned towards the small building with the police sign, blue with white lettering. 'By the Christ … It's like something out of *Dixon of Dock Green*.'

'Is a bit,' said Brennan. 'Let's get this over with.'

McGuire steered the car towards the station, parked outside with two wheels on the kerb. As he got out of the driver's door he eased his hands onto the base of his spine and leaned back. Brennan exited on the other side of the Passat, rubbing his neck. He was relieved to get the journey out of the way but apprehensive as to what to expect on this visit. He was an outsider in unfamiliar territory. Much as he despised the city, he had grown accustomed to its ways and felt comfortable there. Pitlochry was an unknown quantity and he expected it would take time for both of them to get used to each other.

Brennan headed for the front door of the station. He watched McGuire stretching on the pavement and nodded gravely. 'Come on, we're going in.'

'That sounds ominous.'

Brennan squared his shoulders. 'Let me do the talking.'

'That sounds worse.'

A frown, thinned eyes. 'I hope you've got my back.'

McGuire laughed, patted the detective's back. 'No worries.'

The station smelled of mould and bleach, the cheap industrial bleach that comes in powder form. Brennan flared his nostrils as they approached the desk. There was a black plastic pen sitting in a pen holder the same colour, that looked as if it would be more at home in a branch of the TSB circa 1975. Some crime- prevention leaflets were piled next to a small Perspex rack. There was a bell, like a front-door bell, screwed into the counter. Brennan pressed the button; a buzzer sounded.

There was no movement. He toyed with the idea of pressing the button again, then a stout man in uniform, three stripes on his arms, approached. He seemed to be ignoring Brennan as he leaned over the counter and showed him the top of his bald head. Brennan turned to McGuire, raised an eyebrow then removed his warrant card and dropped it in front of the uniform.

For a moment the bald head remained in place, then slowly it was raised and a hand with ginger hair sprouting from the knuckles picked up the card. 'Inspector Brennan … You must be the boys from Edinburgh, eh?' If there was any hint of a welcome, Brennan missed it.

He played it calm; he was on foreign soil. 'That's right.'

The uniform took two steps to the left, released a catch under the counter and raised a section that sat on two hinges.

'This way.'

Brennan nodded McGuire through first. On the way past the uniform he retrieved his warrant card and said, 'How long have you been on the desk?'

He leaned forward. 'Too long.'

'You got that right.'

Brennan turned. As he walked through the small vestibule his shoes sounded loudly on the pine boards. He thought the place could do with a lick of paint, but concluded that was probably low on the list of things they needed.

McGuire found a door on the other side of the room that led through to a corridor. The uniform called out from behind them. 'Out there, left then first on the right. Can't miss it. Fergus is your man.'

Neither of the officers thought to thank him. They headed through the door and walked up the corridor. At the end, on the right, a panel door held a small grey plate that read DS NAPIER. Brennan knocked on the door.

'Come.'

Once inside, the officers were greeted by a head of curly brown hair that sat over the top of a copy of the *Press and Journal* newspaper. Napier had his feet on the desk and a pair of argyle socks showed below three to four inches of pasty white leg.

Brennan approached. 'This is DC McGuire and I'm DI Brennan from Lothian CID ...' He had thought this would be enough to prompt some kind of a reaction, but Napier remained still.

Brennan looked at McGuire – he shrugged.

'Right then, if you can just show us where our office is—'

'Office?' Napier chuckled. 'You're bloody well standing in it.'

Brennan put his hands in his pockets. 'Well, that makes one of us ... When you're finished checking the day's form, Detective, I'd like to see what you've been doing up here with the information my colleagues have supplied you with surrounding the murder of Carly Donald.'

Napier uncrossed his feet, lowered his legs. As he moved he folded the newspaper and positioned it on the corner of his desk next to two empty coffee mugs.

Brennan eyed him impatiently. 'Did you hear what I said?'

Napier replied. 'Oh yes, I hear you ... sir.'

Brennan could feel his heart rate increasing. He had come a long way and was prepared to be as amenable to the local customs as he could be, but he wasn't going to be pissed about, certainly not in front of one of his staff. 'Good. Nothing wrong with your hearing then; shame I can't say the same about your fucking manners.' Brennan removed his hands from his pockets and leaned over the desk. 'You might as well get your arse out of that chair, fella. If this is where we're working from, I'll be having the desk.'

Napier rose. As he walked around the officers, Brennan straightened himself. 'Hold on.'

'Yes, sir?'

'You'll need these.' He picked up the empty coffee mugs.

'I'll take mine black but I believe DC McGuire is partial to a drop of milk.'

Napier took the mugs and walked to the door, glancing back at Brennan and McGuire before going through and closing it gently behind him.

'Bloody hell,' said McGuire. 'I hope this isn't going to be like *The Wicker Man!*'

Brennan ran a finger over the desk, collected a burr of dust, held it up. 'Welcome to the country.'

McGuire rolled eyes. 'I think we can kiss goodbye to any cooperation from the local boys, then.'

Brennan barked, 'Don't be fooled. They all like to test the boundaries. I'd say they know where they are now.' He picked up a blue folder: CARLY DONALD was written on a white label on the front. He opened it – there was one page inside.

'What is it?' said McGuire.

Brennan turned it over, held it between finger and thumb.

McGuire peered at it, dropped his head.

The page was blank.

Chapter 27

DI ROB BRENNAN KNEW IT was true that the older you get the more cantankerous you become, but he drew the line at agreeing with the adage that age also gives you more clarity of thought. Some people, no matter what age they are, just aren't capable of reasoning beyond tying their own shoelaces. He listened to Napier praising the minister and the town and dismissing any suggestion that anyone with a connection to the family could have been involved in Carly's murder. He watched Napier's moustache become flecked with spit as his temper, and face, darkened the deeper he got into his rant. Then, enough was enough.

'At what stage are you going to move from conjecture to fact, Napier?'

The rotund man halted in his speech. 'What do you mean?'

Brennan kept his tone monotonous: 'I asked you for a summary of the case.'

'And that's what I'm giving you.'

'No, you're not. You're giving me a bunch of assumptions and prejudices that you've come to, Christ knows how, and I couldn't care less, but none of it is based on empirical research.'

Napier closed his mouth; he looked like a scolded child.

Brennan rose from the chair. The boards beneath the chair legs creaked. 'Since you're doing nothing else you can take us to the manse.'

'Well, I am actually running an investigation of my own—'

Brennan cut him off: 'The case of the open gate and the sheep on the road can bloody well wait. Get your coat and your car keys.'

'Sir.' Napier went to the corner of the room, removed a wax jacket from the stand. He checked in the pocket and produced a set of keys, said, 'This way, gentlemen.'

McGuire smiled, cast eyes in Brennan's direction as they left the office.

Napier led them to a navy Mondeo with mud splashes at the wheel arches. Inside, the car was covered in empty McCoy's crisp pokes and Mars bar wrappers. As Brennan moved his feet an oily carton from a chip shop stuck to his shoe, adding to his distaste for the vehicle's interior. That was the tipping point. 'Jesus, Napier, when did you last clean this car out?'

'Eh, this morning.'

'Well, I'd hate to have seen it before then.'

McGuire handed over an empty bottle of Bell's whisky from the back seat. 'Hope you weren't driving when you tanned this.'

Napier snatched the neck, said, 'That's going to the bottle bank!'

They drove in silence; Brennan lit a cigarette.

Napier wound down his window, spoke: 'This is a real shock to the whole community, you know.'

'I'll bet.'

'We've never had anything like this before, nothing even close … It's sent a shiver through us all.'

Brennan remained silent, took a pull on his Silk Cut, looked at the tip.

The manse house wasn't far away – a substantial red sandstone building to the rear of the kirk. Brennan eyed the comfortable residence and tried to calculate in his head how many millions it would fetch in Edinburgh. Several, was his answer. The gardens surrounding the property were extensive and clearly well maintained.

'Who does the lawns?' said Brennan.

Napier shrugged. 'Don't know, to be honest.'

As they walked towards the front door, McGuire called to the inspector, 'There's someone in.'

Brennan stopped on the path, followed McGuire's finger-point.

There was a light on and curtains twitched in an upstairs window. There was a man standing there. 'Who's that?'

Napier squinted. 'Looks like Pete.'

'Who?'

'Odd-job man … Maybe he does the lawns. You want me to ask him?' Napier waved to the man at the window.

A weak reciprocal gesture came.

Brennan strode for the door, pressed the ringer. In a few moments he heard footsteps, then the sound of the lock turning.

'Hello.' The man was in his thirties, short, shaved head and a muscular build beneath a Glasgow Rangers shirt. He looked first at Brennan, then peered over Brennan's shoulder to Napier. 'What's all this, then?'

Napier eased through the door. 'Just procedure, Pete. These officers are up from the city.'

The man's gaze intensified, his hands dropped from the door's edge and he retreated inside. 'I see.'

Brennan spoke: 'Forgive me, I don't have any record of a ... What is it you do here?'

'I do the maintenance, whatever's needed really.' The man's face seized.

Brennan nodded to McGuire – the DC removed his notebook. 'What's your full name, sir?'

'Peter ... Peter Sproul.'

Brennan made sure McGuire had a note of it. 'And how long have you been employed at the manse?'

Sproul put his hands on his hips, seemed to be counting back the time. 'I'd say it's coming on for a year, now.'

'A year, really?'

'Yes. A year.'

Brennan watched as Sproul fidgeted, then folded his arms across his chest. 'I suppose you'll be here about Carly ... Dreadful business.'

'You must have known her very well.'

'Yes, well, I don't know about very well, but I certainly knew her. I live out the back.' He turned, pointed to the rear of the house. 'A granny flat so to speak.' He smiled; no one returned the gesture. 'Just a dreadful business, terrible really.' He unfolded his arms, turned towards the kitchen. 'Can I get you some tea?'

Napier's face lit up.

'No. We won't trouble you,' said Brennan. 'If you can just point out Carly's room.'

Sproul walked across the parquet flooring. He wore training shoes and they squeaked on the polished surface.

Brennan watched him pitch himself on his toes and felt his curiosity piqued. 'You're not from round here, are you?'

Sproul grabbed the badge of his football shirt. 'It's not St Johnstone!' He smiled again, but it vanished quickly. 'No, I'm from Glasgow, well, Paisley really. There's a difference but you get tired of explaining it after a while.'

Brennan turned to McGuire, checked he was still writing the details down. 'Mr Sproul, this is DC McGuire ... He's going to ask you a few questions.'

'Oh, really.'

'Yes, *really*.'

McGuire stepped forward, indicated the door to the kitchen. Sproul led the way as Brennan went upstairs.

'What will I do?' said Napier.

'I saw a shop across the street – go get yourself a Mars bar.'

The stairs creaked as Brennan ascended. He felt a strange sensation, like he was going backwards in time. It reminded him of a famous point on the Carrick Hills near his hometown called the Electric Brae. Tourists went there and switched off the engines of their cars, let the handbrake off. As the cars rolled down the people inside felt like they were rolling up the hill. It was all an illusion of course; the world was full of them, thought Brennan.

The manse was an old property. It could have done with redecorating, maybe even modernising, but that would destroy the feel of it. At the top of the stairs the carpet had worn thin. Brennan looked down at the torn surface, straggled wool fibres sticking up, and thought it was a trip hazard. He didn't think anyone would care now – the occupants of the house had worse things to worry about.

He moved on. There was a picture on the wall he recognised: a small blonde girl leaning against a wall while a rough collie, ears pinned down, waited at her back. The image seemed intensely familiar and at the same time utterly alien to him. It was like seeing a flash of memory from childhood – a time, or a place, that wasn't there any more – that existed only in the annals of his mind.

He looked away. His eye caught a door with a large paper sunflower stuck on it. The flower had a face drawn in the middle and the petals bore letters; they spelled out:

CARLY S ROOM

Brennan felt his throat freeze as he thought of Carly. Until now she had been a corpse to him. At best, a pale young girl on a mortuary slab. She didn't exist in the real world. She existed in blue folders and on whiteboards. She existed in pathology reports and photographs and newspaper stories, but Carly Donald, the young girl who once had a family, friends, a life, didn't exist to Brennan in any real sense, until now. As he stared at the door to her room, he knew he was about to bring her to life for him. It always happened this way: he'd shut out the reality of murder as long as he could; the case, the investigation, came first. After a while, sometimes sooner rather than later, the victim showed up.

The detective took a deep breath, touched the handle on the door and walked into another world.

Chapter 28

DEVLIN McARDLE SAT WITH HIS head in his hands. 'Can you not shut that kid up!'

Melanie paced the living room with the screaming child on her shoulder. 'I'm trying.'

'Not hard enough!'

McArdle got up, grabbed his black leather coat from the hall stand.

'Where are you going?'

'Out.'

'Out where?'

'Just out … Away from that.' He pointed to the red-faced baby in Melanie's arms.

'Then bring back some Pampers …'

McArdle flared his nostrils, let out a grunt. He pulled open the front door and headed for his car. He could still hear the child screaming as he got inside the vehicle and flung back his head. He couldn't live with this for much longer. It wasn't the noise – he could handle that. It was Melanie: she was changing. She'd stopped drinking and he didn't like that – the drink made her bearable to be around. When she was sober she was full of questions. He couldn't handle questions, he didn't want to be quizzed about the child especially. The baby had to go, soon.

McArdle picked up his mobile, searched his contacts, found the one he wanted and pressed Dial.

Ringing.

Then, '*Hallo.*'

'Günter … It's Devlin McArdle.'

'You have your money?'

'Yes … The first payment got here fine.'

'Then why do you call?' The German sounded irritated, his voice crisp, serious.

'I need to know when—'

Günter interrupted, 'I told you, I would collect the child as soon as I can. There is a lot to organise at this end. I can't just jump on a plane.'

'I know, but—'

'There is no buts, Mr McArdle. Our agreement is that you hold the child until we collect.'

'But when?'

A tut, throat-clearing. 'Soon. I said soon. Now be patient, Mr McArdle. I'll be in touch.'

The line died.

McArdle threw the phone on the back seat and hit the dashboard with the heel of his hand. His elbow caught the horn and Melanie came to the window. McArdle frowned at her, started the engine and pulled out of the driveway. He took the car straight to Muirhouse. The light was failing but he could still see enough of the neighbourhood to pass comment.

'Fucking shit-hole.' McArdle had been raised in Sighthill, another Edinburgh dumping ground for losers on the lowest rung, but he'd left. He remembered growing up in the scheme, people would tell him that when the flats were built they were highly sought after. The new high-rises replaced cold-water tenements with outside toilets. The boxes were nothing to look at but they had hot running water, toilets and bathrooms and – beyond luxury – fitted kitchens. People were easily bought, thought McArdle. He knew he was right in the case of Barry Tierney and Vee Durrant.

He had bought their first child and now he was taking another one from them for the same price. He tried not to think about the transaction. He didn't fool himself that he was being benevolent; it was business, but he wanted it out of the way.

A mangy dog barked at him as McArdle got out the car. He stamped his foot on the ground and the beast went running. As he walked towards the open door that hung on one hinge, McArdle tapped the inside of his pocket. He was tooled up, knew better than to come down here without a chib, but he was also carrying the payment for Tierney and Vee.

A junkie on the stairwell asked him for a fag.

'Fuck off.' Scum. Just trash, he thought.

As he ascended the steps McArdle scrunched his nose – the stair smelled of piss and vomit. He hated being back in schemes like this. It was almost an insult to him, but at the same time it made him feel good to know he'd got out. He was better than the wasters that stayed there. He was the Deil; he was someone.

At Tierney's door he thudded on the panel with the outside of his hand.

'Open up, y'prick.'

He heard movement, coughing. He could already imagine the weak frame of the skinny man stumbling towards the door. There was a rattle of chains, a key in the lock, then a latch being slid. As a chink of light appeared in the gap between door and jamb he forced his way in.

'Took your fucking time.'

Tierney smiled, a toothless grin. 'Sorry, man. Sorry ... Was, er, taking a dump, eh.'

McArdle poked him in the chest. Tierney recoiled. 'Do you think I want to know what you get up to in here?' He grabbed Tierney's jaw, squeezed his lips together. 'Keep that shut!'

Vee came through from the living room, draped in a long grey cardigan. She held herself in her arms and leaned on the wall for a moment. Straight away, McArdle knew she was wasted. 'Look at the fucking state of you ... Not going to get any punters paying for that skanky arse, are you?'

Vee slid down the wall. As her legs folded her buttocks rested on her heels. The belt of her cardigan curled behind her like a tether.

McArdle walked away from them shaking his head. In the living room he put his hand to his nostrils. 'Jesus, it stinks in here ... Can you not open a window?'

Tierney came scurrying behind him, grabbed the handle and pushed – a gust of air blew in from the sea. 'Is that better, Deil?'

A nod was fired in his direction, but there was no real approval attached to it. 'You live like animals, do you know that?'

Tierney shrugged. He looked over his shoulder to see Vee coming in on all fours.

'Look, look at this ... She even walks like a fucking animal.' McArdle laughed hard, dropped his head and smacked his palm off his forehead.

'If you say so, Deil ...' said Tierney.

The laughter subsided. McArdle strolled around the room. He passed Tierney and grabbed the dazed Vee by the hair, twisted hard. It took her a few moments for the pain centres to register, but when they did she screamed out and flapped hands around her head.

'See this, see what I'm doing here ...' said McArdle. He twisted harder. 'This is just a bit of fun.' He dragged Vee to the open window. He could see Tierney growing anxious – the thin man drawing his hands to his mouth.

'Deil, what are you doing?' said Tierney.

McArdle silenced Vee with a backhander; the force of the blow raised her on her knees for a brief moment and then her head struck a harsh angle with the floor and she collapsed, splayed out like a rag doll. McArdle suddenly grabbed her round the waist and tipped her over the edge of the window.

'No! No!' yelled Tierney. 'Deil, please … No!'

McArdle held Vee by the ankles as he dangled her out of the highrise. She was lifeless for a brief spell but when she regained consciousness she started to scream.

McArdle laughed, shook her legs, watched her head bang off the roughcasting on the side of the building; little stone chippings escaped. He could hear the dog he'd seen earlier barking as the chippings fell to the ground. 'Is this not a bit of fun, Vee … eh?' He felt Tierney approach, place a hand on his shoulder. McArdle released one of Vee's ankles and swung a fist at Tierney. 'Get back!'

He turned again, looked at Vee dangling over the window, and lost interest in tormenting her. He pulled her ankles in one quick sweep and dropped her back inside the flat. Tierney ran to her side and started to pat her back. She brushed his hand away.

McArdle watched the junkies, wiped his brow. He'd had some fun with them and he knew there was no other reason to come here, unless he was making money. He reached inside his jacket, removed the envelope with the cash and threw it in front of them. 'Here … don't spend it all in one shop.'

Vee was still shaking as Tierney lunged forward and ripped into the envelope. He tipped the contents into his hands, spread the notes apart, counted. 'What's this, Deil?'

McArdle loomed over them, spoke: 'Your money, isn't it.'

'But … we agreed more.'

McArdle adjusted his jacket, brushed down his sleeves.

'That was before.'

'Before what?'

McArdle leaned over, pointed. 'How much do you think it costs to keep a kid? Eh? I'm forking out a small fortune on fucking nappies and rusks and Cow and Gate this and that!'

Tierney put the money back in the envelope. 'We agreed more.'

'Are you complaining?' He approached the pair again.

Vee spoke: 'We agreed.'

'Well, if you've got a better offer, I can always take the money back.' McArdle reached out for the envelope. Vee snatched it and rose. She stared at McArdle; he could see the veins pulsing in her neck. 'Nah, didn't think you had,' he said.

McArdle turned for the door. As he went, Tierney and Vee held the envelope between them and watched him.

Tierney spoke: 'That's us quits.'

McArdle raised a hand above his head.

'We're quits!' shouted Vee.

McArdle turned, stared at them. 'If you say so.' He took two steps forward, locked his fingers briefly, then stretched his arms, palms out towards them. 'What a way to settle your debts ... You people disgust me.'

He unlocked his fingers and spat at them.

Tierney and Vee didn't move.

Chapter 29

BARRY TIERNEY LEANED INTO THE bar, raised himself on the little brass rail that skirted its base. The barmen were ignoring him.

'Prick's not wanting to serve us, Vee.'

Vee twiddled the black straw in her vodka and Coke. She looked uncomfortable in the George Street style-bar, twitching and jerking at her new blouse.

This part of town was for people with money to spend, lots of money. It was for the bank workers and the young professionals, thought Tierney. They didn't want him there; they hated him and he hated them back.

'Hey, you going to serve me?' he shouted.

One barman was polishing a glass, looked over to Tierney and sighed. The action sparked something in the junkie. He wanted to take the glass from the barman's hand and thrust it in his face. The bastard, the cheeky bastard looking down his nose at me, he thought.

'Look at this, Vee … He's talking to his boss.'

Vee put down her glass, slapped the bar. 'Hey, you serving here?'

The bar staff looked around them, approached Vee and Tierney. 'If you don't keep the noise down, I'm afraid we'll have to ask you to leave.'

'Eh, what you on about?' said Tierney. 'I'm just trying to get a few drinks in here.'

The barman who had been polishing the glass rolled eyes, said, 'I think, perhaps, you've had enough, sir.'

'Oh do you, *perhaps*?' Tierney spat out the last word.

Some flecks of spittle landed on the barman's black waistcoat.

'Right, that's it. Out!' The other one pushed forward. He slid past the cappuccino machine and opened up the bar counter. He stood hands on hips as he called over the door stewards.

'Fuck this,' said Tierney. He launched himself at the man behind the bar. He could feel himself being pulled back as he lunged and immediately realised the door steward had caught a hold of him.

'Right, don't make this hard on yourself.' He sounded Australian, or South African; he was foreign.

'Get your hands off me, you're not even Scottish … Get back to your own fucking country.'

Vee threw over the last of her vodka and Coke and joined the melee. She smashed the glass over the steward's head and screamed, 'Leave him, you bastard!'

Shrieks went up around the bar. Chairs scraped on the floor as people moved away.

'Get them out! Get them out!' shouted the manager.

People ran to left and right, headed for the edges of the room to be free of the scene. A group of reinforcements – more stewards – arrived from the front door and Tierney and Vee were bundled onto the pavement. Tierney struggled with the men in black jackets, lashed out and kicked. As Vee was dragged she lost one of her new shoes and removed the other to hit at her attackers.

'Fuck off ... Bastards!'

When they got them far enough from the bar, the stewards dropped the pair on the ground and backed off, brushing down their jackets as they went.

Tierney ranted, 'You're fucking dead, you are!'

'Calm down, just calm down,' said the biggest steward. 'We've called the police and they're on their way.'

Tierney got up, jutted his head at him. 'You're dead! Do you know who I am? Barry Tierney, ask about town. I'll be back to do you in.'

Vee swung her bag as the men retreated indoors, shaking their heads. 'You've lost it, love,' said one of them.

'Let the cops deal with them,' said another.

Tierney watched them go inside. The blood rushed in his veins. He felt his adrenaline spike and looked around for something to throw at the window. There was nothing, no brick or an ashtray even. He scoped about – further up the street there was a chrome stanchion, outside the next bar. He ran over and unhooked the red cord. The stanchion was heavy; he struggled with it down the street but somehow managed to get it onto his shoulder.

'Vee, get ready to run. I'll show those bastards.'

Tierney edged closer to the window and started to spin with the stanchion in his arms. When he felt he had enough momentum he released his grip. The noise from the smashing window was like the one o'clock gun. Tierney and Vee ran off, laughing and jeering.

The pair made for Hanover Street and kept going until they were completely out of breath.

'Did you see their faces?' said Tierney.

Vee struggled to stay upright, gasped. 'Yeah ... Total fucking idiots.

You showed them, Barry.'

'I showed them.' Tierney felt proud of himself; no one was going to talk to him like that. It was a great feeling to have a few quid in your pocket. He didn't want to think about how he'd come by it, but that didn't matter now. He was free of his debts to the Deil, he'd scored enough to see him through the weeks ahead and he had a new set of clothes and more money in his pocket to spend.

He stepped into the road and flagged a black cab. 'Come on.'

'Where to?'

'The night is young, so it is.'

Vee giggled as she was dragged into the cab. Tierney gave the driver the name of another bar – he couldn't sober up. Not now. As he sat in the back of the cab his mind returned to the events of the last few days and he felt his bolster subside.

'What is it?' said Vee.

'Nothing.'

She knew well what it was, he thought. As he looked at her, eyes slow-blinking, out of it as ever, he knew she was going to be a constant reminder to him. He looked away, out to the road, the hum of street lights and the blur of shopfronts and takeaways on Broughton Street. He felt sick – not physically, deeper than that. He felt sick in his soul.

'Barry, what the fuck's up now?' said Vee.

'Shut it,' he snapped.

The driver's eyes appeared in the rear-view mirror.

Tierney flagged him down. 'It's okay, mate. No bother here.'

Vee tugged at his arm. 'You've gone all moody again.'

'I told you to shut it.'

The driver was getting anxious, kept looking back.

Vee spat at him, 'You're not telling me to—'

He snapped, grabbed her head in his hands and screamed in her face, 'I told you, shut it. I don't want to hear your fucking voice again.'

The cab screeched to a halt. 'That's it!' shouted the driver.

Tierney watched the cabbie open his door and walk round to his side of the street. He pulled the handle and opened up. 'You can walk from here.'

Tierney squeezed Vee's head in his hands, then banged it off the seat. 'That was your fucking fault. It's always your fault!'

As he got out he eyeballed the cabbie, who reached behind him and helped Vee to her feet. 'Hey, she can walk herself ...' Tierney watched the cab driver help Vee and felt a knot tighten in his stomach. He let out a fist that connected with the back of the man's head and he fell to the ground. Where he lay Tierney started to kick him; when he tired of kicking he started to stamp on his head. Soon he was too exhausted to continue, panting and wheezing, his chest aching.

When Vee got out of the car she staggered over the cabbie.

He spluttered blood as he tried to speak, raised a hand.

Vee looked at Barry and then she brought her foot down on the cab driver's face. There was an audible crunch, the breaking of bone, and she laughed out.

Barry watched her for a moment. She was lining up another blow, balancing herself by holding the taxi's roof to give her more purchase. She looked enraged. Barry wondered why.

'Vee, pack it in.'

She didn't listen as she tried to drive her heel into the cabbie's face.

'Vee ... leave it,' Barry roared, but the words had no effect.

A crowd had started to gather, a few muttering and gesturing to others to intervene.

Barry knew it was time to move on. He grabbed Vee's arm. 'Come on, let's go.'

'Go where?'

'Away ... away from here.'

Chapter 30

THE FIRST THING THAT STRUCK DI Rob Brennan about the inside of Carly Donald's room was how unremarkable it was. He didn't
know what he had expected to find in there but the familiarity of the
place seemed to dig at his heart. On the small single bed there was
a pink bedspread that was covered in little mauve flowers; it looked
like something Sophie would have once picked out, before she had
entered the phase where she wanted everything to be black. Over
the window was a draw-blind with butterflies on the edges and a
long pull tassel. Everything seemed so normal, so simple, almost like
a film set or from a TV show for teenage girls.

Brennan eased himself in. The place smelled of lavender and
vanilla. He wondered if it was a trait of every girl to have a room
smelling just like the first floor of Jenners. He eased up to her desk.
There was a red organiser for pens and pencils; she had tied red elastic bands – like the ones the postman drops – into a little ball. Brennan picked up the ball, rolled it in his palm and started to squeeze
it. The item was a connection to Carly and he felt some strange
power holding it.

'Okay, Carly ... What am I looking for?'

Brennan opened a drawer. There was some writing paper in there,
pink again, and more pens, felt-tips. He removed the cap from one
– it had dried out; the entire collection was probably left over from
when she was younger. Sixteen was too old for colouring in.

There was nothing else that caught Brennan's attention on the
desk. He closed the drawer and moved to the wardrobe. A tall, free-
standing pine box that looked like flat-pack but was probably more
substantial. He opened up and immediately smelled a stronger
waft of perfume. It was a different smell, not rose – apples, maybe.
He liked it. The first thing that caught Brennan's attention in the
wardrobe was a school blazer. He took it out. The jacket was well
kept; it had been brushed regularly and looked in good shape. The
braid on the sleeves was yellow and bright. It struck him that
dressing children in uniforms was a strange thing to be doing at this
stage of human development. It was almost tribal. In Edinburgh, the
rich kids stood out a mile in their uniforms, but then, that was the

idea, wasn't it? When you were paying £25,000 a year for your kid's education, you wanted it to be as conspicuous as the Bentley Continental you drove to work.

Brennan looked further into the wardrobe. A lot of jeans. Simple tops, spots and prints. There were some boots beneath the clothes, grey suede. Brennan thought they were called pixie boots but he was no good with fashion. There were some trainers too, sports socks rolled into a ball and a hockey stick propped against the back. He closed the door.

The DI returned to the bed, sat. He hadn't found anything worthwhile, but he had found something of Carly. The room had presence, she had put her stamp on it and Brennan drew on that, took it in. She may not have been there in person but Carly had made an indelible impression on him. He felt an attachment now; he understood more about her. She seemed a middle-of-the-road type; some might say plain. Her dress sense was unimaginative, but then she was only sixteen. Had she had time yet to fully form her personality, develop a style of her own?

On a whim, Brennan looked under the bed. There were some magazines, *Heat*, *OK!*, *Closer*, and some books on childbirth. He rubbed the cover of one – the pages were dog-eared. There were items in the book ringed in red marker pen. Baby chairs and prams, clothing. Was this the action of a girl who was going to see her child adopted? Carly had wanted to keep the baby, he sensed it, knew it. Brennan replaced the magazines and books, got off the bed and smoothed down the bedspread.

He stood for a moment, stared at the posters on the walls. One of them was a *Pop Idol* winner, or was it *X Factor*? He didn't know, but he recognised her face – Leona something? There was another larger poster of a boy band. Brennan didn't know who they were – he thought they looked like tossers, though. All the posing and gesturing made him wonder what was going on in their heads. He bounced the elastic-band ball off the poster, said, 'Come on, Carly, give me a sign here.'

Nothing came.

He stood for a moment longer, turned, went to place the ball on the desk but something stopped him. He felt some kind of comfort holding it, a connection he didn't want to lose. Brennan held the ball in his hand for a moment longer, stared at it as if there was a message inside. He'd felt this before, a strange channelling from artefacts of the dead, but he always dismissed it as the mind playing tricks. He smiled, shook his head, then put the little ball back on the desk and headed downstairs.

In the kitchen McGuire and Napier were talking over cups of tea. There was no sign of Peter Sproul. When Brennan came in their chat ceased at once.

'Hello, boss.'

Brennan nodded.

'Anything?'

A shake of the head. 'How far is this Thompson girl's house?'

Napier put down his cup. 'Just a minute or two away.' He twisted his neck, raised a thumb over his shoulder. 'Round that way.'

Brennan fastened his jacket. 'Finish your tea. I'll wait in the car.'

McGuire rose and took his cup to the sink. Napier followed him.

In the car Brennan drummed fingers on the dash, held his thoughts in check. There was a call he had to make. He didn't want to speak to his wife but Sophie was on his mind now. He needed to know she was okay, that she had come home and her antics had all been another attention-seeking prank. He knew his daughter was too sensible to get mixed up in anything that would bring real worry to her parents – she'd been well briefed on the subject – but Brennan couldn't help his concern surfacing.

He dialled home.

Ringing.

An answer, 'Hello.'

'Joyce … it's me.'

'Yes.' Her tone was frosty. Had she kept the mood going all this time? he wondered.

'Did you get hold of Sophie?'

A sigh. 'Where's this sudden concern came from?'

Brennan snapped, 'Stop messing about, Joyce!' He had just sat in a murdered schoolgirl's bedroom and was in no mood to joust with his wife. 'Is she home or not?'

Joyce's voice lowered: 'Yes. She's home. You can go back to your job now with a clear conscience.'

Brennan hung up. As he did so McGuire and Napier returned, got in the car.

'Okay, sir … Ready to roll,' said McGuire.

'This Sproul character, what's his story?' said Brennan.

McGuire took out his notebook. 'He's a kind of factotum.'

Brennan shook his head at the DC's pretentiousness. 'An odd-job man.'

'Yes, sir. Got a background in the trades, moved about a bit. Plenty of praise for the minister – says he gave him a job when he was at a low ebb ... Sounded grateful.'

'What kind of a low ebb?'

McGuire put his pencil in the corner of his mouth. 'Erm, he didn't really say ... Unemployment, I think.'

Brennan turned round in his seat, put fierce eyes on McGuire. 'Run him through the system.' He turned round again, addressed Napier: 'And you can keep tabs on him.'

Napier nodded. 'Okay, sure. He's sound though, Pete – plays in the dominoes league down the Lion.'

Brennan snapped, 'I don't give a shit if he helps old ladies across the road or rescues kittens. I don't like the bloody look of him.'

'Yes, sir.'

Napier started the engine, pulled out. In a few minutes they had arrived outside a semi-detached house. It looked to have been built in the seventies – utilitarian architecture for families on budgets. The officers assessed it and then got out the car, walked up the drive. A dog barked inside as Brennan rang the bell. It sounded like a small dog, pitching itself above its size. Napier eased himself to the rear of the group, stepped back.

As the door opened a small white flash dashed past them, a Jack Russell ran into the garden, barking. The animal seemed to have a routine, turning left then right, before circling the group entirely.

'Penny, get in!' A small woman in a blue fleece and wellington boots greeted them: 'Hello, you must be ... the police.'

Brennan introduced himself, produced his warrant card.

'I hope this is a good time to call.'

The woman had very red cheeks. As the dog rushed in at their feet she tilted her head and placed a hand on her hip; she gesticulated with the other hand as she spoke. 'I just don't know what the world's coming to ... I really don't, when something like this happens.'

Brennan looked down the hallway behind her. He saw a thin girl with dark hair held back by a white Alice band.

She watched the officers then moved out of their line of vision.

Mrs Thompson continued, 'Carly and Lynne were like that' – she crossed her fingers over. 'Our Lynne's lost without her. I can't hardly get her to eat or anything. It's terrible, just terrible.' She brought her arms together, crossed them over her chest and touched one of her shoulders. 'That poor girl, such a good family too ... They must be devastated.'

Brennan spoke: 'Do you think Lynne would be up to talking to us?'

She turned, eyes widening. 'Oh, yes. Of course … Come through. Can I get you some tea or coffee?'

'No, we're fine,' said Brennan. He could tell the enormity of the situation hadn't registered with the woman – had we all become so desensitised? Were people inured to murder now? He wanted to tell her that it wasn't like *Prime* bloody *Suspect* showed it on the television.

In the kitchen Lynne sat at a small folding table. There was a fruit bowl in front of her and she stared over it at a blank wall.

'Lynne, this is the police officer I was telling you about.'

Mrs Thompson turned to Brennan. 'Sorry, what did you say your name was again?'

'Brennan … Rob Brennan. Hello, Lynne.'

The girl remained still in her seat, absorbed in herself.

She looked fragile enough to shatter into tiny pieces if the slightest breeze blew her way.

Mrs Thompson rubbed the girl's back. 'Come on, love.'

Lynne turned to her; still not a word.

Brennan pulled out a chair, sat. He placed his hands on the table in front of them, spoke softly: 'I hear you were good friends with Carly.'

A nod. No eye contact.

It was something, a start, thought Brennan.

'In the same class at school?'

'Yes.' Her voice sounded forced, too quiet, even for such a delicate frame.

'Best friends?'

Lynne nodded again. 'I don't have any friends now. There was only me and Carly.'

Brennan got the picture: the pair of them weren't top of the popularity stakes. He could see neither of them had that air of confidence that was required of class favourites. They were not part of the crowd of beautiful people, not performers soaking up adulation; they were followers, not leaders. 'I know this must be hard for you, Lynne … Can you tell me, is there anyone that you can think of who might want to harm Carly?'

She looked at her mother, then back to the detective. She shook her head.

'Are you sure, Lynne? … It's very important.'

She shook her head again, began to pick at her fingernails.

Brennan sat further forward. He glanced at the fruit bowl – the oranges were developing a grey fur. 'Lynne ... did Carly have a boyfriend?'

She shrugged. 'I don't know.'

'Are you sure about that?'

Another shrug; she turned her head away. A cat leapt onto the window ledge.

'You knew Carly was pregnant, didn't you?'

Lynne blushed. Her mother rubbed at her back again.

'I guess.'

'So, she didn't get pregnant by herself ... did she, Lynne?'

The girl started to bite her top lip. 'I don't know anything.'

Brennan knew she was holding out. He'd seen far better liars than her in his day; the girl didn't even look as if she was trying. 'Are you sure, Lynne? You wouldn't be protecting anyone, would you?'

Mrs Thompson put an arm round her daughter, leaned in. Lynne spun in her seat and buried her face in her mother's chest, sobbing. Mrs Thompson waved a hand at Brennan, said, 'I'm sorry, she's a bit emotional.'

Brennan leaned back in his chair. The wood creaked. 'I understand.'

'Maybe you could come back another time.'

The girl sobbed harder. It was all too early for her, she was too delicate to press any further. 'Of course.' He rose, motioned the other officers to follow.

In the car Napier spoke first: 'Well, that was a waste of time.'

Brennan fastened his seat belt. 'Not at all. We know for sure and certain she's covering up for somebody.'

'*Who?*' said Napier.

'If I knew that, I wouldn't be contemplating spending the night in Pitlochry.' Brennan lowered his window, removed his cigarettes. 'You can take us to a half-decent B&B ... if you can find one.'

Chapter 31

BRENNAN SPENT A RESTLESS NIGHT. The bed sheets were too tight, like a hospital or one of the hotels he had stayed in as a boy, with his parents, and brother Andy. He couldn't remember having slept in such tight-fitting sheets as an adult; at home he had a duvet and was used to more freedom of movement. Although the temperature dropped in the night-time, Brennan had been forced to get up and tug everything free. The action had given him more room to move about in the bed, but didn't feel quite right either. Perhaps it was the fact that he was away from home, in unfamiliar surroundings, he thought. When they were young, Andy and himself had never been able to sleep on any of their trips away from home; it had been too exciting, like the time before Christmas or the day preceding a birthday.

Andy would have liked Pitlochry, thought Brennan. It was like their hometown – at least, how he remembered it before the economic collapse. They had now shuttered up all the shops in the high street, and all that was left was pound stores and bargain-basement outlets. The place used to have more prestige, when they were young.

Brennan could see Andy now – it was a summer holiday memory and made him smile. Andy was playing Swingball in the back garden in a Scotland football strip. His legs were stick-thin but he wore the red socks pulled tight below the knee, the white diamonds at the top turned over with precision. He was always very precise, thought Brennan.

The vision of his brother seemed to fade. The thought saddened Brennan; he wanted to return to the warm glow he felt when he remembered his brother but there was a part of him that said it was wrong to stay in happy moments for too long. Life wasn't about the happy moments – there was too much sadness in the world. He knew that for every fond memory he had of Andy there was an unhappy one lurking close by; and now one appeared.

It was summertime again.

Brennan had come home from school, his papers signed by his housemaster – he was leaving.

Andy knew at once. 'What's going on?'

'Nothing.'

'You're lying.' Brennan could never lie to his brother; he always knew when he wasn't telling the truth.

He told him what he had done. 'Do you think Dad will crack up?'

Andy tutted. 'Bloody hell, what do you think?'

'I want to go into the police. I've got no interest in the business.'

Andy looked away. 'Do you think I do?'

Brennan pulled him back. 'Did you hear what I said?

I'm joining the police.'

'I heard you ... Everyone listens to you, Rob. It's me nobody pays any attention to.'

Brennan registered the point. 'Andy, the police is a job, it pays ... Who's going to pay you to paint pictures?' He smirked, felt cocky, too sure of himself.

Andy didn't answer. He dropped his gaze. Brennan watched him walk off. The collar on his blazer had been turned up and as he went the wind caught it, ruffled the back of his hair. He watched his brother walk to the end of the driveway, then turn right into the street. He could only see the top of his head above the hedgerows for a few moments but the look on his face was something he had never forgotten. The memory stung as Brennan recalled it now; even twenty years ago, Andy was thinking of others before himself.

Brennan knew that he had thought of no one except himself when he had decided he wasn't going into the family business. He was going to be a police officer and nothing was coming between him and his ambition. As he thought of Andy he wished he could have reversed the decision; even for a little while, to have given Andy some time to follow his own dreams like Brennan had followed his.

Brennan rose from the bed, sat on the edge and ruffled his hair, then surveyed the stubble on his chin. Before he met Lorraine, and started the therapy, when he got into moods like this there was no way out. He could spend hours, days in despair, blackness. Now he had developed what she called coping mechanisms. He had trained himself to think of distractions. Why was he here? What was the purpose of Rob Brennan's life? The answers to those questions depended on the time of day, he thought. He knew, as he mulled over the answer now, that his purpose was to find the killer of a young girl. It wouldn't bring back Andy, but it might make him feel like part of the human race again, and that was something to cling to.

Brennan showered and shaved. He dressed in a crisp white shirt from Burton and a sober navy tie. When he looked at himself in the mirror he saw the sleeves of the shirt were a little creased and crumpled. He had ironed the shirt himself. The days of Joyce taking care of such domestic duties had passed a long time ago – ironing shirts for a spouse was an act of love and there was precious little of that left in their relationship. If it wasn't for Sophie, he knew he would have left her already. That's what Lorraine wanted; she had pressed for it many times. Brennan didn't like being pressed but there were other factors to consider now. He removed the picture of the baby scan she had given him, held it up. He permitted himself a smile – he was going to be a father again. The smile left as quickly as it had appeared; as happy as the thought of a new child made him, he knew it was going to bring complications.

Brennan removed his mobile, searched for Lorraine's number.

He put the phone to his ear. It was ringing.

'Hello, Rob.'

'Lorraine, I don't … I still don't know what to say.'

'Maybe there's nothing to say.' He hated the way she framed her responses like open-ended questions. It was shrink-speak.

'There must be plenty. We have to talk about this … About what we're going to do.'

Lorraine sighed. He could hear her moving on the bed, the sheets rustling, the springs sagging. 'We've done all the talking, Rob. It's time for action.'

He knew what that meant, but he didn't know if he was ready for the next step. 'It's not so easy.'

'You always said you couldn't leave because of Sophie. Well, now you're going to have another child to think about, Rob … Are you going to put Sophie before our child?'

'Lorraine, don't talk like that.'

She stayed quiet for a moment, then, 'It's a choice you have to make, Rob.'

'It's not as simple as—'

She interrupted, 'Yes it is! It's very simple.'

'Lorraine …'

Her voice dropped: 'I have to go, I have appointments in an hour.'

There was nothing more to say. The call had played out just as he'd expected it would; like all their talks recently, it left him feeling more lost than when they started. He wished he hadn't bothered, but knew the effort was necessary, and there'd be more required.

Brennan hung up.

He stared at the phone for a short time, then put it in his pocket and rose. He tried to clear his thoughts, let his mind still, but he knew he wouldn't be able to put off a decision for much longer. In the job decisions came easy – without thinking, even; it was in the wider world where he found most trouble deciding on the right path.

Brennan walked to the dresser, collected his wallet and some coins, put on his jacket and went down to breakfast.

McGuire was already at the table, finishing off a cup of coffee.

'Morning, sir.'

Brennan nodded.

'Any word from Napier?'

He lowered the cup. 'You're kidding – it's barely gone eight in the a.m. And there was a match on last night – Inter Milan.'

Brennan sniffed. A waitress came over. He ordered tea and eggs, some toast with butter. She smiled sweetly and left for the kitchen.

'You sleep okay, sir?' said McGuire.

'Now *you're* kidding. I was wrapped up like King Tut … Guess the duvet revolution hasn't reached Pitlochry.'

As he watched McGuire grinning, Brennan's phone began to ring in his shirt pocket. The caller ID showed it was from the office. He flagged McGuire quiet, answered: 'Brennan.'

'Have you seen the *News*?' It was Galloway. She sounded irate, her voice shrieking down the line like a harpy.

'I'm in Pitlochry.'

'Well, think yourself fucking lucky … You're page one in Edinburgh.'

Brennan didn't like the sound of this. McGuire tilted his head, opened his mouth quizzically.

'What's this?'

Galloway shuffled the paper. 'They have the scoop on the case. Missing child, the works.'

Brennan rested his brow in his hand. 'Shit.'

'Yes, you may well fucking curse, Rob.' Galloway rustled the paper some more, slammed it down on a hard surface.

He could hear her stomping around her office, high heels clacking, as she blasted, 'Now, I know it was your bright idea to give the press the victim's name, but tell me you didn't release the fact that her baby's missing.'

Brennan sat back, steadied himself. 'You've got to be joking.'

'Well, somebody did.' The paper was rustled again.

' "Police sources say" … Who the fuck are these *sources*, Rob?'

McGuire's face started to grow firm. His eyes had begun to widen but now thinned into slits. He looked perplexed, but in no doubt that the news Brennan was receiving was not good. The look of the DC unsettled Brennan. He flagged him away, mouthed a 'fuck off'.

'Look, Chief, none of this came from me or anyone authorised by me.'

'So you have a mole – who is it?'

He steadied his tone: 'I don't know.'

'Oh, I dare say you've pissed off so many people that it'll be hard to narrow down, but you better start.' Galloway paused to draw breath for another onslaught. 'I want you back here as soon as, Rob. Do you hear me?'

'I've got a few leads I'd like to pursue if that's—'

'Back now, Rob!' Her voice rose to its highest pitch. 'Get this force off the front pages of the papers, do you hear me?'

Brennan knew the chances of that were slim. When the press got hold of a story like this they tended to run with it, build it up and up. The only way to stop that snowball in motion was to solve the case, and he didn't see any chance of that happening by the time of the *News*'s next edition, not without a dramatic breakthrough.

He lied, 'Consider it done. I'm on my way back now.'

Brennan hung up. He could sense Galloway lining up another barrage of criticisms but he didn't give her the chance.

As he put down the phone the waitress arrived with his eggs. He looked at them but had lost all appetite.

Chapter 32

BRENNAN OPENED AND CLOSED HIS FIST. He did this a few times before he noticed the elderly woman at the table next to him watching his actions. He smiled and moved his hands out of view. He sat for a few moments, simmering. His inclination was to batter at the wall with fists, shout. He'd have been happier to batter at someone's head, shout in their face. The someone was Lauder. He was pretty sure his only other suspect for tipping off the press, McGuire, had been on the level all day yesterday. He'd been busy too; not too busy to contact the press, of course, but absorbed enough in the case to convince Brennan that his intentions were sound. As the call from Galloway was coming in Brennan had noted McGuire's expression, and the look of real and genuine stupefaction convinced him the DC wasn't the culprit. Of course, Brennan knew the dangers of jumping to conclusions without hard facts to back them up.

He got up from the table, folded his napkin and placed it over the eggs – they were untouched.

In the hallway Brennan spotted McGuire looking out the open front door. A taxi was dropping off some golfers.

'Well?' said McGuire.

Brennan tested, 'Well what?'

'Well, something's up ... That was the Chief Super, pissed, I presume.'

Brennan watched McGuire's pupils for signs of dilation.

'The press found out about the missing baby.'

McGuire clenched his teeth, then opened his mouth wide as he pointed his chin in the air. He emptied his lungs then straightened himself. Brennan studied his every movement. 'Fucking hell.'

'Watch your language, eh.' Brennan motioned to an elderly couple welcoming the golfers by the front door.

The DC traced the line of an eyebrow with his finger, began tapping a foot on the floor. 'Well, that's all we need.'

'Nothing we can do about it.'

'Yeah, but all the same, makes life difficult for us.'

Brennan shrugged, said, 'I wasn't aware it was ever easy.'

'Easier, maybe ... How did they find out?'

A frown. 'Search me.'

McGuire stopped tapping his foot, looked at his watch.

'So, we can expect another witch-hunt when we get back, I suppose.'

Brennan glowered; two creases like warpaint appeared at the sides of his mouth. 'I doubt there'll be time for that.

We're going to be seriously up against it. The scrutiny will be intense. If we don't get rolling, get some leads soon, we can forget about getting a result.' The thought of Carly's murderer getting away from him burned Brennan. He didn't want to see the case written up in a trashy true-crime book with Carly's life and death reduced to no more than titillation. He'd seen too many cases go unsolved. He didn't want Carly to be another Andy.

'Right. Get your kit packed up – we're back down the road,' said Brennan.

'We're going back to Edinburgh?'

'Chief Super's orders.'

McGuire visibly slumped: his shoulders drooped, a deep sigh deflated his chest. 'I can't believe this.'

'Believe it.' Brennan turned for the stairs. 'Hurry it up.

I want to see if the sheep-shaggers have clawed in any info on our man Sproul yet.'

McGuire followed him, rested a hand on the balustrade.

'You didn't like the look of him, did you?'

'He's a Paisley buddy.'

'Is that supposed to mean something?'

Brennan laughed. 'I haven't met one yet that wasn't crooked as two left feet.'

On the way to Pitlochry station Brennan rolled down the car window, lit a cigarette. He couldn't get any flavour from the mild Silk Cut and wondered if he'd wrecked his taste buds with the full-tar alternatives. He seemed to have wrecked a lot lately, he thought; nothing would surprise him. He considered his marriage and he considered Lorraine and the baby again – he knew there were no immediate answers coming to him – the case had to come first; it always did. The rest could wait.

Inside the station Napier was making himself a cup of tea. An unopened pack of HobNobs sat beside the kettle.

Brennan spoke first: 'Morning, Napier.'

A nod, nervous cough. 'Ah, hello, good morning, sir.'

'You'll be relieved to hear we're getting out of your hair soon.'

'Oh … really.'

Brennan smiled. 'Don't go all teary-eyed on us, eh.'

The kettle boiled and Napier poured out his tea, offered the others a cup; they declined. 'Suit yourselves.'

The office was in the same state of disarray as the day before: a dusty old computer terminal, tea-stained tabletop, and piles of case files on the floor. There seemed to be too much dark wood about the place, and too little light; it looked like the land that time forgot. Brennan took a chair, pointed to the fax machine. 'Anything come in?'

'Oh, the Peter Sproul stuff … It's over there.'

Brennan motioned McGuire to pick it up, returned his gaze to Napier, said, 'What did it say?'

A shrug, palms levelled in the air. 'Don't know, I'm just in … No use till I've got a cuppa down.'

Brennan rolled his eyes. 'Read it out, McGuire.'

'Sir … I don't think you're going to like this.' He walked towards the desk. Brennan eased forward, propped himself on his elbows. He watched McGuire turn over the top sheet, then hand him a mugshot: it was Sproul.

'He's got form.'

'Lots of it,' said McGuire.

Brennan stood up, took the list of charges.

'Christ All-fucking-Mighty. He's a time-served nonce!'

'*What?*' Napier was sipping on his tea, spluttered. 'Pete Sproul?'

McGuire creased the corner of his mouth. 'And you didn't even know. Play much dominoes with him, did you?'

Napier put down his cup, picked up the list of convictions that Brennan had just laid down. 'I can't believe it.' He turned to McGuire. 'Some of these are spent. He's been inside for a fair few years.'

'Yes … He's been in Peterhead.'

'Bad as that. Bloody hell. When did he get out?'

McGuire skimmed the fax pages. 'Hang on … Oh, right, here it is. It looks like he got out about a year and a half ago.'

'I do not like the look of that. What the hell was Donald thinking, putting a paedo up in the family home?'

Napier's meaty neck quivered. 'Maybe he didn't know.'

'Oh bugger off, man, not everyone's as lax about these things as you.'

Napier threw up his hands. 'Look, I never saw him on the offenders' list … He wasn't on it.'

Brennan sneered. 'Maybe you were too busy making tea and stuffing your face with HobNobs. Or maybe it was just in joined-up writing and it fucking confused you.'

McGuire jumped in, shaking his head. 'Or you were playing dominoes.'

'I-I'm not clocking the movements of everyone in the town.' Napier's cheeks coloured – he flushed red from the jaw up. 'If he came in under the radar how was I to know?

How was I to know?'

Brennan made for the door. 'Oh, stop your bleating, Napier – and just leave the police work to us, eh.'

McGuire was still shaking his head at the officer as they left the building. They broke into a jog on the way to the car. Brennan took the keys from McGuire and opened up.

He had the flashing blue lights on as he spun the tyres on the tarmac and headed for the manse.

McGuire held on to the door handle as Brennan sped down the street. There were far fewer cars on the road than in Edinburgh, and the ones that did hear the sirens got out of the way quickly. It was as though they had never seen a police car before, thought Brennan. As he drove, old ladies with shopping bags and umbrellas stopped in their tracks and stared. Brennan didn't want to contemplate another balls-up. He didn't want to see the Chief Super's face if Sproul had shot through, but the way things were shaping up he began to wonder if the investigation was jinxed in some way.

The whole town seemed to have been transfixed by the speeding VW Passat as Brennan pulled in to the manse. He put two wheels up on the kerb, yanked on the handbrake, left the engine running and got out. McGuire followed and ran to the rear of the property without instruction.

At the front door Brennan wasted no time on the doorbell. He plucked a stone from the rockery and smashed one of the windowpanes; it shattered into tiny fragments. As he reached in, grabbed the latch, he was aware at once of the emptiness of the building. When he walked in the place was quiet. He could hear the pounding of his heart on his shirt front.

As Brennan moved around the property there was not a sound. The place was still. He ran first to the living room, then the kitchen. McGuire was at the back door – Brennan opened up and pointed him to the stairs. Brennan checked the dining room and the minister's study. All were empty. He pulled open the cupboard under the stairs and flicked on the light, but it was empty too. As a last resort he returned to the kitchen and opened the larder, then the press. There was nothing but tins of soup, beans, and packets of flour, bags of sugar.

Brennan walked to the window and looked out into the back garden. For a moment he felt lost, unable to gather his thoughts, and then the momentum that had been gathering for the last few days struck him. He folded over the sink and gasped for breath. His heart was pounding harder now, adrenaline rushing in his veins. He stood, crouched over the sink, staring at his hazy reflection in the polished stainless steel basin, and suddenly became aware of someone else in the room with him.

McGuire appeared at his back.

'Sir, I found him.'

Brennan pushed himself up from the sink. He turned, rested his hands on the rim of the table; he had to ask McGuire to repeat himself. '*What?*'

'Sproul's upstairs, in Carly's room.'

'Upstairs ...' He started to move to the hall, pushed past the DC. 'Why have you left him alone?'

McGuire raised his voice: 'Because he's dead, sir.'

Chapter 33

BRENNAN LUNGED FOR THE STAIRS. He could feel the veins pulsing in his arms as he ran, each step increasing the pressure on his cardiovascular system. He reached the landing light-headed, breathless. There was no indication that the scene had changed in any way from his first sight of it the day before; the only difference was the door to Carly's bedroom was open this time. Brennan paused on the worn carpet for a second. He wiped the sweat from his eyes and started his slow paces towards the door. As he walked Brennan's mind lit on what McGuire had said – he couldn't seem to take it in, to register the new facts. It didn't make sense to him, but then, the further he went into this investigation the less he understood. Nothing seemed to be stacking up. No sooner had he set his mind to one course of action than he needed to alter it. He started to feel his breath shortening once more and stalled before the open door.

The hinges creaked slightly as Brennan eased the handle further away from him. Light escaped from the room, landed on the hall carpet. When he placed his foot in the girl's bedroom his heavy leather sole sounded noisy on the bare floorboards. He breathed deep as he brought his second foot forward. There was already a different atmosphere in the room, unwholesome. Did he imagine that? The smell of flowers seemed to have gone. There was a new scent in there; Brennan didn't like it as much – it symbolised change, a turn of events, and not a good one.

He looked towards the wall and saw only the posters and the small chest of drawers with little golden handles; they were suitable for a girl's room, but a much younger girl. Brennan's thoughts were already with Carly – not the girl in the dumpster, or on the slab – the girl who was living her life in this room, until recently. He looked to his right, and over his shoulder he caught sight of a pair of heavy working man's boots. They were similar to hillwalking boots, the outdoors type people wear for trekking. The boots were muddy and worn, and attached to a pair of legs covered in faded and torn blue jeans. The knees of the jeans were flecked with grass cuttings, filthy, looked to have been patched. As Brennan's eyes went up the legs he noticed the blotches of dark blood splattered on the knees. A few inches higher the small marks turned into long smears that ran down the outsides of the thighs. Beneath the motionless body the bedlinen was a sodden mass of dark wet blood.

Brennan turned his gaze to take in the whole frame. He could see the entire scene now. It was Peter Sproul; there was no mistaking the face was the man he had spoken to yesterday. The features were emotionless, the eyes staring blankly now, but the gaunt and hollowed cheeks, the unshaven chin and the cracked, twisted lips were unmistakable.

As Brennan stared his mind seemed to jump from thought to thought. It was as if a light switch was being flicked on and off behind his eyes – one second he saw it all, the next, darkness.

Sproul's wrists had been cut, probably with the serrated knife that now lay on the floor at an acute angle to the bed legs, smeared with blood. It looked like a kitchen blade, but Brennan found it hard to tell as a pool of blood had formed under the bed and the knife was in shade. He leaned towards the body. There was no sign of a struggle having taken place, no bruising or cuts and scratches. It looked like a clean scene, a suicide.

McGuire appeared behind him, his footfalls ending some metres from the bed, and the blood. 'I called it in, sir.'

Brennan didn't acknowledge him. He held his thoughts for a moment then looked about the room. Everything was as he remembered it yesterday. Nothing seemed to have changed, or been moved. The only difference was the dead body of a serial sex offender lying in Carly's bed. Brennan stared on, tried to make sense of it all. Why? They hadn't pressed him; they'd given him no real indication he was a suspect. It didn't make sense. But then, nothing that went on in a pervert's mind made sense to Brennan.

'What do you think?' he said.

McGuire answered quickly, 'I think the bastard took the easy way out.'

'Why?' He turned, put eyes on the DC.

'He knew we were onto him.'

Brennan snapped, 'No he didn't.'

'Come on, he would have guessed for sure, sir. He's not exactly new to dealing with police – he knew we'd go away, check him out and haul him in.'

Brennan looked at the corpse, felt nothing, said, 'So he was in and out of prison for years, he knew what to expect – does that explain it?'

McGuire didn't flinch. He knew Brennan was working through possibilities; maybe testing him too. 'Maybe his last stint put the shits up him; didn't want to repeat it.'

Brennan walked round to the other side of the bed, crouched down. He looked at the floorboards, ran a finger along the ground and inspected the tip. There was nothing there but dust. 'Maybe he heard about the *News*'s report.'

'You wouldn't get that rag up here.'

Brennan looked up. 'Never heard of the internet?'

'Right enough … But why's that going to make a difference? He'll have seen the previous stories before now, surely.'

Brennan stood up, put his hands in his pockets and looked left to right along the line of the corpse. 'None of them mentioned the fact that Carly's child was missing.'

Sharp radial lines creased the corners of McGuire's face. 'You think he knew something about the kid going missing?'

Brennan shrugged. 'Maybe.'

'He was a paedophile.'

'That's true.'

McGuire's mobile phone started to ring. He answered: 'Yes.'

Brennan watched the DC talking into the handset.

'All right, Brian. Yes, he's here.'

Brennan shook his head.

'Er, he's just left the room right now, you can tell me. What you got for us?' McGuire smiled into the phone. 'Very nice indeed … Right, thanks for letting us know, he'll be pleased.' He hung up. 'That was Brian.'

Brennan spoke: 'What's he got?'

'Good news, sir. They've unearthed some CCTV footage from the bus station and Carly's in it.'

'Brilliant!' Brennan made for the door; he wanted to put distance between himself and Peter Sproul. 'Tell me more.'

'She's been positively ID'd and she's talking to a man, some random punter in the station … And get this: she leaves with him.'

'Did she have the baby?'

McGuire grabbed his earlobe. 'Ah, I, er, didn't ask.'

'Fucking hell. Get on the phone to Brian again and get the details.' Brennan's voice was forceful. 'I want the media kept in the loop and I want you to tell them we need this footage aired on all the news channels tonight.'

McGuire leaned back, scratched his jawline. 'Big ask, sir.'

'I'm all about the big fucking ask, lad. Do it.'

'Yes, sir.' McGuire spun, halted as Brennan began to speak again.

'Might just piss off those wankers at the paper – put them off our mole.'

McGuire looked ahead, spoke: 'Sir, you never told me what your theory was.'

Brennan stared at him, full on. 'Who said I had one?'

'But you think Sproul might have known about the baby?'

'I'd say he knew very well about the baby. If he was the father I'd say Donald would feel compelled to let him know ... Be the Christian thing to do, wouldn't you say?'

McGuire followed his boss as he took long strides towards the stairs. 'This is wrecking my head, sir.'

Brennan stalled halfway down the first step, turned. 'Expect it to get a lot worse when we get back to Edinburgh. I can't see Galloway being overly pleased that we let a possible suspect slip through our fingers, even with the footage card to play.'

McGuire bit his lip. 'But he killed himself, sir.'

The DC was running ahead of the facts; Brennan reined him in. 'Did you see a note, Stevie?'

'Well, it looks that way ...'

'It does indeed, Stevie, but let's not jump to conclusions.'

Chapter 34

DEVLIN McARDLE GLANCED AT THE clock. It was approaching six. He'd spent the day waiting for a call from his German contact, but it never came. He knew these people were secretive, had to be because the filth were all over their activities, but he didn't like waiting for the rest of his money, or the child to be collected.

Melanie walked through from the kitchen. She was carrying a baby's bottle, smiling as she said, 'Why the long face?'

McArdle pressed his back hard to the sofa. He had his leg over the arm of the chair and he lowered it when his wife spoke. 'What you on about?'

Melanie tipped her head, jauntily. 'You look like you've lost a pound and found a penny.'

It was a stupid phrase, the kind of thing Melanie always came out with when she wasn't drinking. When she was drinking it was bearable – she was bitter and ranting. He knew where he was with her; she could be manipulated, controlled. This new state of mind unsettled him. 'Away and see to that kid,' said McArdle. 'I want to watch the news.'

As Melanie sauntered off McArdle picked up the television remote control and directed it at the screen. Anne Robinson was hectoring the contestants on *The Weakest Link*. Just the sight of her was enough to make McArdle curse. He flicked the television to off.

In the silence of the room he felt grateful the baby he'd taken from Tierney and Vee wasn't making its usual racket, but he was far from happy. McArdle wasn't going to be settled until the Germans took the child and did whatever it was they wanted to do. McArdle knew what they were, what they were capable of. He wasn't a fool. He'd met their type in prison; the others called them beasts. No one on the inside would dare to associate with a beast – they were beneath contempt, not real people. There was a hardcore of cons who made it their business to wipe out beasts. Shanks, sharpened spoons, anything that could be used as a weapon was useful currency among those who wanted to wound, or worse. McArdle had read stories in the papers about the beasts; he knew how they operated and what they were after. Snatching children off the street and subjecting them to all kinds of torment and indignity before suffocating them, if they were lucky, beating them to death if they weren't.

He started to fidget on the sofa as he thought of the things he had heard and read about beasts. They were called beasts because they were just that – animals. Fucking beasts. McArdle pressed his lip against his bottom teeth and paced the living room. When he reached the far wall he let out a blow with his fist. The action set a standing lamp quivering and when he withdrew his knuckles he saw there were three little declivities in the plaster.

'Fuck it!' he roared.

He heard Melanie stir upstairs. She moved to the landing and hung her head over the banister. 'Dev, what's going on?'

He looked up, shouted, 'Nothing. Nothing. Get back to that kid … Get saying your goodbyes – it'll not be here much longer.'

Melanie seemed to stall for a moment or two before moving off. She made no reply.

McArdle moved back to the sofa and threw himself down. He had a pack of Carlsberg sitting on the seat beside him and pulled a tin towards himself, cracked the seal. 'Fucking German beasts,' he muttered. 'Get me my money and get the fuck out my face.'

They could do what they wanted with the child; that wasn't his concern, he thought. No one had ever looked out for him. Why should he care if no one was looking out for that kid? They could have their fun with it and drop it in a pit; he didn't care. It's not my lookout, he thought. The kid's nothing to me. He knew he had watched his wife bond with the baby over the last few days and he didn't like that. He never let his emotions get in the way of business, and that's all this was, business. He'd sold a child to the Germans before and they had paid promptly. They had collected promptly too, however, and he wondered why they were taking so long this time. Was it the price? He'd increased the price, of course he had, but not by that much. It made him nervous.

McArdle knew how they treated beasts inside, had seen it first hand. He didn't want to be associated with them. Even though he was certain in his mind he was nothing to do with them – it was business, that's all – there would be people who would see it differently. The police, for sure.

He didn't like the waiting. It unsettled him, made his mind seek out possible reasons for the delay. Every minute of the day that the child stayed in his keep was a minute too long. He needed to get rid of it, fast.

McArdle supped on his tin of Carlsberg, put it back on the arm of the sofa and removed his mobile phone. He checked his calls to see if he had missed one from Günter, but there were no messages at all. He went into his contacts, looked out Günter's number and contemplated ringing him again, and then his mind froze. If the filth were watching him, they could be tracing his calls. He knew he couldn't take the risk. The thought lit a taper in him; his anger erupted again and he rose, kicked out at the sofa. The tin of Carlsberg went over and poured onto the cushion.

'Fuck it! Fuck it!'

He wiped at the lager with the back of his hand, sprayed the majority of it onto the carpet and worked it in with his foot. He didn't care about the mess. Melanie could clean it up later … if she was ever finished with that fucking baby.

He touched his brow, dabbing away the line of sweat that had formed below his close-cropped hairline. He ran his lower lip over the tops of his teeth and tried to think but there was nothing close to a solution in his mind. The frustration started to create a burning feeling in his chest; the beat of his pulse increased its rate. He was getting worried, irrational now – he knew the signs. He needed to calm himself, keep a level head, that's what he'd always been told. It was the ones who lost it that got locked up.

McArdle lowered himself back on the sofa and picked up the remote control, pointed it at the television screen. *The Weakest Link* had finished and the news was on now. He watched the day's headlines and the endless jousting of political rivals that went on every night of the week, and felt somehow secure enough in his own home once more to let his mind settle. The world was a mad place, he thought; you did what you had to do to get by, find a way through the madness.

By the time the Scottish news headlines came on McArdle had relaxed enough to open another tin of Carlsberg. The pounding in his chest had subsided and his thoughts seemed to have settled into a more peaceful commentary on the day's affairs. Everything changed when the newsreader shifted to the next item. It was as if her voice had been altered to impart the seriousness of the story she was relaying. As she spoke a picture appeared behind her head. Whatever it was she was saying seemed to be cancelled out by the image for McArdle. As he leaned forward and placed his elbows on his knees he couldn't quite take in what he was seeing. The photograph, obviously blown up from a CCTV image, was of a face he clearly knew.

McArdle felt his breathing alter right away. He leaned back and tried to compose himself but his surging blood wouldn't let him. He felt as though he was drowning, like his head had been shoved under water and his mind was being flooded with strange memories, sensations, premonitions.

He knew the sight of Barry Tierney's image on the television was the beginning of a nightmare.

McArdle grabbed up the remote control, pumped the volume as he dropped to his knees in front of the television screen.

The newsreader's words came like arrows: *'Police investigating the murder of Pitlochry schoolgirl Carly Donald have today released images of a man they would like to identify. The footage, taken from inside Edinburgh Bus Station, shows Carly, who was sixteen at the time of her death, and her baby daughter, Beth, who has been missing since her mother's murder, and an unknown man.'*

McArdle put his hands to his mouth. He couldn't believe what he was seeing. It was Tierney. The bastard. 'What the fucking hell has he done?' he blasted. McArdle sensed the seriousness of the situation at once. It was on the evening news, for Christ's sake.

The woman on the screen introduced another man, a police officer. His name was printed along the bottom of the picture: DETECTIVE INSPECTOR ROBERT BRENNAN.

The officer spoke: *'Lothian and Borders Police are very keen to trace the man in the picture. These images were taken only the day before Carly Donald's remains were found in the city's Muirhouse housing scheme, and we believe he may be able to help us with our inquiries.'*

The reporter spoke: *'What should people do if they recognise this man?'*

'They should get in touch with police, or Crimestoppers, in complete confidence ... I should state again, there is a very young baby missing and we need to locate the whereabouts of young Beth as soon as possible, so any information, however small, will be of use to us.'

McArdle felt himself grimacing before the screen. He could feel the heat pulsing in his neck as his veins bulged. His eyes were wide in disbelief. He knew exactly what 'help police with their inquiries' meant – Tierney was dead meat. The filth were probably tearing the city down looking for him already. If they got to him, McArdle knew he was finished. Tierney would do anything to try and save his scrawny neck.

McArdle looked at the cop speaking on the screen. He could see the determination in his eyes. He knew this was a man he couldn't cross; he'd met his sort before. He was old school, not like the by-the-book mob who ran shitless from a fancy brief. McArdle was scared; he rocked to and fro on his knees. 'Fucking hell! Fucking hell!' he roared. 'Tierney, you bastard, I'll fucking kill you. I will fucking put a bullet in you.'

McArdle knew his only chance was to get to Tierney before the police. If he didn't, he was looking at a jail cell in Peterhead, where they put all the beasts.

He rose, turned to collect his phone. As he did so, he noticed Melanie standing behind the sofa.

'How long have you been there?' he said.

She didn't answer.

Chapter 35

DECLAN KILLEAN DIDN'T TRAVEL ACROSS the water without good reason. He'd flown on the first available flight, after a call from Devlin McArdle. He hadn't known the Scotsman, but McArdle had supplied a list of names he could check him out with. They all confirmed he was, if not trustworthy, careful, and, more importantly for Killean, a payer.

The stewardess smiled as he left the plane. They weren't as good-looking as they once were, he thought. 'Thank you very much,' he said. Manners were important – it was the ones without manners that stood out, got remembered. He didn't want that.

Killean carried no luggage in the hold, so made his way out as everyone else stood at the carousel. He passed through customs in the green channel and found himself in the main concourse of Edinburgh Airport; the place had changed, he thought. Was it progress? Possibly, though if he was back in this country, there couldn't have been that much progress.

He eschewed the Avis and Hertz car rental desks and made for the bus stop that took tourists to the city centre. It was a short ride, twenty minutes. There was still daylight when he got on the vehicle, but by the time he alighted at St Andrew Square the sky had darkened and a gaudy, bright moon was up. He followed the late-evening crowds onto York Place and made for the pub McArdle had mentioned on Broughton Street. As he walked, Killean remembered why it had been so long since he'd been in Scotland. He didn't like the place. Edinburgh especially was a strange city – too English; he didn't trust a Celtic town that had given away so much of its identity. Then there was the smell. Dublin could blame the Liffey, but what was Edinburgh's excuse? He wanted to get his visit over with quickly, and get out.

In the bar, Killean ordered an orange juice and stood with his bad leg resting on the foot rail. A squat man with a shaved head and a nervy manner approached, spoke: 'You must be my visitor.'

Killean collected his change from the barman, nodded.

'Let's take a seat in the corner.'

As they walked Killean tried to get the measure of the Scotsman.

He was hard, but what did he have to back it up with? And what was with the swagger? Those bloody Scots always had to wear their status on their sleeve, he thought. In Ireland, people knew you were hard by reputation. You never needed to advertise; if you did, you weren't that hard. Killean had earned his status in the Cause and had no call to parade himself. If anyone doubted it, it would be easy enough to prove them wrong.

McArdle took a seat. He was drinking lager – some spilled over the brim as he placed the pint on a beer mat.

'You come highly, eh, recommended.'

Killean wasn't there to talk about himself. 'You have something for me.'

McArdle nodded; a roll of flesh quivered beneath his neck as he reached into his back pocket and removed a copy of the *Racing Post*. He placed it on the table. Killean raised his glass to his lips, quaffed a large draught of orange juice then returned the drink to the table.

McArdle opened the cover of the *Racing Post* – inside was a padded envelope. 'Don't you want to count it?'

Killean shook his head. 'Why would I need to do that?'

'You wouldn't.'

There was a gust of wind as the door to the pub was opened and jammed on its hinges; a middle-aged woman with over-dyed blonde hair rose and wrestled the door shut. Killean watched her as she moved – her arse must have been a yard across.

'Have you put the details I need in there like I said?'

McArdle nodded. His hands seemed to be jittering as he spoke: 'They're in a flat I've got down in Dean ... Told them to wait until dark, then make their way along the water to Canonmills for the car.'

A nod, confirmation. Killean picked up the *Post* and put it under his arm as he finished his drink.

McArdle started to rub his fingers on the table. 'The cunts have got it coming,' he said.

Killean put down his glass, pointed to McArdle's mouth.

'Keep that fucking shut. I don't want to hear.'

McArdle settled further back into his seat, shook his head. Killean rose from his chair and walked for the door. As he left the pub he didn't look round to farewell McArdle.

In the street he transferred the *Racing Post* to his bag. He walked a few more steps and hailed a taxi – he had another appointment on the other side of town. As the driver turned into Leith Walk Killean transferred money from the padded envelope into another smaller envelope. He made sure to do this within the confines of the bag resting on his lap, out of sight of the taxi driver. When the cab reached the Shore, Killean passed the driver the fare and left a tip of one pound; he always left a tip of one pound. Any more was ostentation; any less could be deemed parsimonious.

Killean swung his good leg from the black cab's bay and followed with his other, allowing the first to take the weight of his frame. He crossed to the other side of the road and made his way to the edge of the car park where a silver Toyota was waiting. As he closed in on the car he saw a man with a beard in the driver's seat. He avoided eye contact and made his way to the passenger door; as he turned the handle the bearded man started the engine. The car pulled out.

There was no talk between the pair until they reached the first set of traffic lights on Commercial Street. 'That stuff's in the boot.'

Killean nodded.

'It's all there, like you asked for.'

Killean kept his eyes front as the driver engaged the clutch, proceeded to first gear. He didn't want to engage in conversation, that had been one of his requests, but the driver seemed to be relaxing now, getting curious.

'That ammo took some getting hold of. Make much of a difference, does it?'

Killean felt a nerve twitch in his temple. 'Can you please keep your ignorant fucking mouth shut.'

The bearded man turned towards him. His lips were parted, on the verge of words, but he held them in. Killean sensed the man's fear – there was no mistaking the emotion.

On Ferry Road the car stopped at more traffic lights but the driver kept his head facing forward and jerked quickly through the gears as the lights changed. By the time they reached Dean Village a full ten minutes of silence had passed. When the car came to rest, Killean opened his door and made for the boot. He removed an oversized black bag and closed the boot up, walked away. He did not speak again to the driver as he headed for the Water of Leith.

Killean balanced the bag on his left shoulder, the other side being unable to bear that amount of weight. When he reached the water's edge he looked down towards the first bend, a copse of trees. He glanced back and forth, tried to estimate the distance between the point he occupied at present and the spot where the trees provided cover. He thought it must be two hundred yards at most – that was a good distance, an easy distance.

Killean set out for the copse, the bag cutting into his shoulder. His left leg dragged on the pavement and his thigh burned. The moon had gathered some cloud covering now and the sky darkened, but the water still reflected enough light to make the job easy, thought Killean. As he stationed himself behind a sycamore he lowered himself towards where the bag rested on the ground, unzipped. Inside he removed the rifle covering and attached the scope-mount. He seized the barrel and looked down the stock, tested the sights to see they were clean and then he lowered the rifle.

He opened the box of ammunition and checked it was as he'd specified, then he loaded the gun.

Killean rested the rifle against the sycamore, removed his overcoat and turned it inside out. He took the coat to the slightly elevated edge of the copse and lowered it onto the ground, outside facing up, then returned to collect the rifle.

As he settled onto the ground, on top of his overcoat, Killean raised the rifle's scope-mount to his right eye and put the water's edge in his sight. He had a clear view of the path and enough light to identify anyone who came into view. He rested in that position for a few seconds, making minor adjustments to his shoulder and elbow position, and then he held himself steady, firm.

Killean waited for approximately fourteen minutes, then fired his first shot. The second followed within seconds.

Chapter 36

THREE BODIES IN TWO DAYS – that was all DI Rob Brennan
needed. He closed the car door and took the road towards the twist-
ing path that led down to the Water of Leith. Uniform had been out
with the blue-and-white tape, sealed off the entrance. It hadn't
kept out the reporter from the *News*; Brennan caught sight of a
young WPC leading her by the arm towards the brow of the hill. She
hadn't seen Brennan; he was grateful for that. He hadn't caught the
morning's paper yet, but he knew it wasn't going to include hearts
and flowers for Lothian and Borders Police. He had ordered McGuire
to keep the latest find from Galloway until she arrived at the office.
She had her promotion board interview this week and that made her
unpredictable. Brennan knew the Chief Super might choose to take
the case off him, hand it to someone else. She could also make good
on her promise to transfer him to traffic, but Brennan was hoping
she might do neither and opt not to attract any attention to herself
before the interview. If she landed the job, chances were her mood
might improve – she'd be demob happy – and leave him alone. If she
didn't get her promotion – that didn't bear thinking about.

Brennan pushed his way through the cordon of uniforms, approached the SOCOs in their white tent. He noticed the tent was
larger than the standard size he'd been used to – he stared for a moment, not quite sure what to make of the makeshift structure.

'Sir.' It was McGuire. As he emerged from the tent he pinned a yellow rubber-tipped pencil behind his ear, pulled off a disposable
glove and put it in his pocket.

'What have you got for me?'

McGuire removed his other glove, repeated the process of putting
it in his pocket, then opened a black notebook. 'It's our boy from the
bus station footage ...'

'You sure?'

Nods, a gesture towards the tent. 'There's a wallet and cards in the
tray, got his name stamped all over them: Barry Tierney.'

Brennan sighed. 'Bastard's not going to be much good to us now,
is he?'

McGuire shook his head. 'Lou ran his name through the system

last night after the calls came in off the television news slot. He's got
a colourful record.'

'Fucking Technicolor, I bet, and his bit of stuff.' Brennan took the
notebook from the DC, ran a finger down the spine. 'This the other
one?'

McGuire peered into the page. 'Durrant ... Yeah, she copped a bullet too.'

'Fucking hell. You kept this from the Chief Super, I hope.'

McGuire curled his nose up, nodded, then turned to the side and
spoke: 'She'll be in sooner or later, boss. I can't keep blanking her for
ever.'

'As long as we've got something to fend her off with, we'll be in with
a shout.'

McGuire retrieved his notebook, stared into Brennan's eyes. 'It's not
looking good, is it?'

'That's nothing for you to worry about.'

McGuire dropped his voice to a whisper: 'I don't want to see you
taken off the case now; you've come too fucking far for that.'

Brennan wondered if the remark was genuine or arse-kissing; decided on the former. He tapped McGuire's shoulder. 'Don't worry
about me, son. I know the ropes so well my palms are red.' He took
off, headed for the tent, called out on his way, 'Get Lou and Brian going door to door with the victims' neighbours.'

'Already on it, sir.'

Brennan stalled, turned and shouted, 'Don't tell me you're learn-
ing now.'

McGuire raised his middle finger in a salute. Brennan laughed.
'Known associates ... Pull them, then. I want to talk to everyone who
knew Tierney and Durrant. Even their fucking window cleaner.'

In the tent the SOCOs dressed in white overalls busied themselves
trying to erect a trestle. Brennan eyed their movements for a moment or two, then turned to the pale corpses on the ground. It had
been a cold night and the flesh had quickly lost colour – as he
kneeled closer he saw the lips of the man, Barry Tierney, had turned
blue. There was a dark black hole in the top of his left temple where
a bullet had entered and ended his life instantly. The sight of the bullet hole set Brennan's nerves jangling, and his memory lit. When he
had gone to identify his brother's corpse there had been a bullet hole
in the left temple. It was higher up, closer to the hairline, but it had
looked similar and the sight of another one jolted Brennan. He recalled looming over Andy's face; the life force had departed – there

was no sign of his brother. He had touched his cold flesh and had tried to hold back his tears for Andy. He had tried to warn him about taking that job at the big house. He'd told him about Grady, about his Ulster connections, about the ongoing investigations …

Brennan took a deep breath. What was the point of going over old ground?

He got up and looked to the other body. They were about four yards apart; the reason for the bigger tent seemed obvious now. Brennan called out, 'When are you moving these?'

A shrug. 'When we're ready.'

Brennan walked towards the white-suited SOCOs. 'What you got there?'

One of them held up a little clear plastic bag; inside was a piece of metal. As Brennan took the bag, moved it towards the light that was streaming in through the front of the tent, he turned the item over. It was a bullet casing.

'You know what that is?' said a tall SOCO.

'Oh, yes … Do you?'

The SOCO smarmed: 'Are you serious?'

Brennan pointed to the bullet. 'And this?'

'Some kind of residue.'

'These bullets are *gold-washed* … I've seen this before.'

The SOCO took the bag back, peered deeply. 'I think you could be right.'

Brennan smarmed back: 'I fucking know I'm right. These bullets are serious – this was a pro hit.' He left the SOCO staring at him as he walked out of the tent and found McGuire. The DC was on his mobile; he hung up when Brennan approached.

'Well?' he said.

Brennan halted in his stride, motioned up the hill to his car. 'Back to the office.'

McGuire followed on his heels. 'I'm waiting …'

'It's a professional hit, no question. High-calibre rifle.

Gold-washed ammunition. Close range.'

'What's that about the ammo?'

'Makes it all the more lethal; rare as hobby-horse shite. Only serious craftsmen insist on it. Someone had this pair of dafties knocked off, and paid a high price for it. I want to know why.'

McGuire jogged ahead of his boss, raised the blue-and-white tape. 'Any ideas who?'

Brennan looked at him. 'I'd say someone who's fucking shitting themselves.'

As he spoke, the reporter from the *News* approached. She came running from the edge of the road with a digital recorder in her hand. 'Detective, are these killings related to any other ongoing investigation?'

Brennan halted, stared at her. 'Who's pulling your strings, love?'

'Excuse me?'

'Don't come the innocent.'

She lowered her hand; the digital recorder dropped out of range. 'I'm just doing my job.'

Brennan put his hands in his pockets, tilted his head to one side. He loomed over the reporter. 'So am I. My job's about catching murderers and scum, keeping the streets safe. What's yours for?'

She looked perplexed, narrowed her eyes. '*What?*'

Brennan eyed her up and down. He'd had just about enough of seeing her at his crime scenes. 'If you don't know the answer to that question, maybe you're in the wrong job.'

As he walked away and got into the car, Brennan caught sight of the reporter again. She hadn't moved from where he had left her. When he started the engine she jutted a hip and slapped a palm off it. He knew he'd given her something to think about: it was never a good idea for reporters to get on the wrong side of the police.

'She's not pleased with you,' said McGuire as they pulled out.

'Good. She'll get hers.'

'You still think she's being fed a line from inside the station?'

Brennan took second gear, pulled from the side street.

'I'd bet a pound to a pail of shite she's going flat out, probably on her back, to work her contact.'

McGuire laughed. As he did so, his mobile phone started to ring. He took it out his pocket. 'Shit. It's Galloway. Do you want me to answer it?'

Chapter 37

BRENNAN LOOKED AT McGUIRE, who held out his mobile. 'Dump her,' he said.

'You sure?' The DC looked pensive now.

Brennan nodded. 'As shooting.'

They continued back to the station. Brennan turned things over in his mind. First there was the situation with Peter Sproul. The plan had been to pull him, rattle some details about his living situation with the Donalds in Pitlochry. But finding him in a pool of his own blood had put paid to that. He couldn't see the minister revealing anything about him – he had been too wary of letting details of his life slip. Brennan wondered if the Donalds knew more about Sproul than was good for them. If they believed the sex offender to be the father of their grandchild then perhaps that was why they had been so cagey. It was a delicate situation, thought Brennan, but the time for treading gently was over. Time had run out.

Brennan gripped the wheel tighter the closer they got to Fettes. He had thought he wanted back to the city when he was in Pitlochry but now he'd got home he realised how wrong he was – the sensation was like picking up a cold beer on a warm day, and finding the bottle empty. He rolled up the window. The air outside was heavy with fumes; he could almost taste the diesel. As he stared out the buildings looked dirtier than he remembered. Everywhere he looked the stone was grey or blackened. The streets were awash with litter, the bins overflowed and spilled into the gutters – cans, fag dowps, crisp bags, all blowing like bunting in the fetid wind. He worked though the gears as he hit a quiet stretch of Orchard Brae. 'We have to call in the minister, find out what the hell was going on there.'

McGuire stretched round in his seat to face Brennan. 'For a father to take in a repeat sex offender, with a young daughter at home, defies logic.'

'Just what I was thinking.' Brennan knew the minister was blinded by some sense of religious duty – that had been obvious from the start – but why had he kept Sproul's presence a secret from the police?

McGuire said, 'Unless he wanted to rehabilitate Sproul. Y'know, if he was taken in by a sob story, perhaps some claim about him being a changed man.'

Brennan smirked. 'Or having found the Lord in Peterhead.' The DI had answers of his own, but he knew he would be making a mistake applying his logic to the minister's situation. Carly was dead, though. A man's daughter had been killed and he'd shielded a potential suspect from the investigating officers. Why? Worse, Beth was still missing. The minister's granddaughter, his innocent flesh and blood, was who knows where and still he hadn't revealed Sproul.

Brennan knew the case was in chaos. Nothing was fitting together. He knew there was a bigger picture, something that linked up the missing pieces of the assassinations at the Water of Leith, but he couldn't pull it into focus. They were drawing near to the station. He lowered his speed as he went into the car park, pulled up. He turned off the engine and moved to face McGuire.

'Why?'

'Why what, sir?'

Brennan's voice rose: 'Why have two minor-league scrotes professionally hit?'

'Someone wanted them knocked off quickly.'

'Obviously. But who? And why?'

McGuire looked straight ahead. 'Well, for a start, someone with the money to pay for it.'

It didn't make sense; their necks weren't worth the price or the trouble. 'If someone higher up the food chain was going to put up money to have that pair wiped out then they must be scared shitless.'

McGuire returned his gaze to Brennan, tapped the top of the gearstick. 'You know, they've most likely seen the *News* piece and thought we were getting close ... Shat themselves.'

'Are we getting close?' said Brennan.

McGuire turned up his palms. 'Maybe we're closer than we realise.'

Brennan hoped he was right. He turned to face the windshield, looked at the station. He felt his stomach tighten, sighed, 'Galloway's waiting in there to kick our arses all over the place.'

'You're right there, sir.'

'Get your phone, call Lou ... See what he's got on the door-to-door.'

McGuire reached into his coat pocket, removed the phone and dialled. Brennan watched his movements and facial gestures. The DC spoke to Lou for a few minutes then hung up.

'So?' said Brennan.

'You'll like this. Flat above says they heard a baby screaming all hours for the last few days.'

Brennan's head snapped to the side. 'Really?'

'More yet – folk next door said they saw a young girl with the woman ... No positive ID as Carly but a definite maybe. They haven't seen the girl again; she just disappeared.'

Brennan slapped the dash. 'That bastard's had his, Stevie ... We might just be getting closer.' He opened the car door, leaned out. 'Come on then, let's go face the dragon!'

As he opened the station doors, strode in, the desk sergeant got up and called Brennan over: 'Rob, hear about Lauder?'

'Not now, Charlie.' He waved him away, made for the stairs.

The sergeant sat back down as Brennan and McGuire took the staircase.

Chief Superintendent Aileen Galloway was waiting for Brennan and McGuire as they reached their floor. She was dressed in a black trouser suit and a cream-coloured silk blouse that had elaborate collars pulled out across the shoulders. As ever, she wore heels that added an extra three inches to her height. Brennan composed himself for a confrontation, tried to make a straight eye contact but Galloway turned her head and pointed a palm to her office. Brennan and McGuire led the way with the Chief Super following, her heels clacking on the hard flooring like a tribal drumbeat.

As they entered, the door was closed quietly behind them and Galloway directed them to seats. The atmosphere in the office was heady; added intensity came from an expensive perfume that the Chief Super had applied liberally. She was always groomed, thought Brennan, but today she looked like something from an eighties soap opera. *Dynasty* or *Dallas* – one where the shoulder pads came from the AFL.

'Quite a body count you've amassed over the last two days, is it not?' said Galloway.

Brennan crossed his legs, undid the button fastening his jacket. He turned to McGuire. 'Stevie, perhaps you could fill the Chief Super in on Peter Sproul.'

'I know about Sproul, I've seen the file,' she bit back. 'What I don't know is how he ended up dead in Carly Donald's bedroom.'

McGuire cut in: 'It was a suicide: the lab have confirmed the wounds were self-inflicted and we have a note of sorts which he added to a social networking site.'

Galloway's face held firm; her lipstick seemed to have been baked on. 'So, let's have a stab at tomorrow's headline in the *News* ... "Repeat Paedo Tops Himself in Murder Victim's Bedroom and Leaves Message on Facebook." '

Brennan turned to McGuire. Neither was smiling. 'It's our belief Sproul had good reason to want a fast route out of the picture.'

'Oh, you think?' Galloway put a finger to her chin and pulled a ditsy expression. 'Why? Maybe he didn't want to go back to Peterhead ... I've read that report too, the one about the sharpened chicken bone he got in the lung.'

'I think, in time, we'll establish Sproul's involvement.

It's my assumption he might be the father of Carly's child.'

Galloway slapped the desk. 'I'm not fucking interested in assumptions, Rob. Yours or anyone else's. I'm interested in facts and what we can prove to the Fiscal, and more than that I'm interested in having a murderer under lock and key and a missing child back with her family. I'm interested in proper police work and not having my force traduced all over the papers.'

Brennan rose, closing up his jacket. 'Then I'll get back to work.'

Galloway got up too, faced him. 'You'll do what I tell you, Rob.' She turned to McGuire. 'Go and gather the team in Incident Room One, Stevie.'

McGuire eased himself from the chair. He looked at Brennan, said, 'Yes, ma'am.'

The Chief Super watched McGuire as he went. Her eyes were wide, piercing. 'Tell them I'll be in there in a minute. I want as many of the team as you can find.'

McGuire closed the door.

Galloway leaned over the desk and put a bead on Brennan. He spoke first: 'What are you doing?'

'My job, Rob ... Some of us still care about that.'

He leaned over the desk too, staring her down. 'You're not the only one in this room who's given more than they'd like to consider to the job.'

Galloway sat down. She seemed to be gathering her thoughts, choosing her words carefully. 'I haven't seen much evidence of a result coming any time soon.'

Brennan pushed himself away from the desk, put a hand in his pocket. 'The footage flushed out Tierney and Durrant. When the SOCOs have been through their flat we might have our murderers. I'd call that a fairly definite result.'

Galloway thinned her eyes. 'It's not a result yet ... And we still have a missing child.'

Brennan looked away, exhaled slowly. He felt an urge to grab her by those floppy collars and shake some sense into her but he held firm. There was too much at stake. He had come this far with the case and wasn't about to let a burst of temper ruin everything. After all, that's what she wanted, and he hated giving in to her.

'Tierney's neighbours have confirmed a baby crying in their flat and there's a possible sighting of Carly at the address. I have Lou and Bri hauling in all of Tierney's known associates. I anticipate a result imminently.'

The Chief Super closed her mouth, pouted. She seemed to be running her tongue over the front of her teeth. She was definitely thinking. 'Do you know what today is?'

Brennan answered quickly, 'It's your final interview for the Chief Constable's job.'

She smiled. 'Oh, it's that all right. I wasn't referring to that, though.'

Brennan shrugged his shoulders. 'What were you referring to?'

She got up again, walked towards the water cooler, took down a small paper cone and filled it. 'Today's the day we wrapped up the pub shooting ... Or should I say Lauder did. Haven't you heard?'

The news must have just come in. Brennan chided himself for not stopping to talk to Charlie on the way up. 'Oh, really?'

Galloway drained the paper cone, dropped it into the bin.

'Yes, really. So, you see, I do have one clear-up to be happy about.'

'Congratulations,' said Brennan. 'Is that a first for Lauder?'

Galloway flicked her hair back. 'Tut-tut, Rob, you really shouldn't be jealous just because one of my inspectors has got a result. In the nick of time too: this force needs some positive press, wouldn't you say?'

Brennan felt his mouth dry over. He had no words. She was playing him, goading him. She had tried everything else and seemed to be delighted that her latest approach was getting the desired result – Brennan was riled.

The Chief Super straightened her jacket front, brushed her sleeves at the elbows, said, 'Now DI Lauder will be presenting the case to the Fiscal, but that's a lot of his workload reduced. I'm wondering if perhaps he would be put to better use on the Carly Donald case.'

Brennan let his hands fold behind his back, scrunched them into fists. 'I'd sooner not disrupt the team dynamic.'

Galloway laughed, tipped her head back again. Her hair floated behind her. 'Jesus, Rob, where did you find the management-speak?'

He bit down hard on his back teeth, then released his jaw. 'Let me put it another way, then: my team is tight and won't take kindly to a glory hunter coming in at this stage and stealing all the credit for their hard work.'

Galloway tilted her head towards her shoulder. Her eyes were wider than ever as she spoke: 'Well, well, harsh words indeed, Rob. Perhaps we should ask the team just what they think … Let's go see the troops.'

Chapter 38

INCIDENT ROOM ONE WAS QUIET as Brennan walked in, two paces behind Galloway. As she entered, he noticed her stride became a strut. The woman loved the attention her rank afforded her; it was probably why she was in the job, he surmised. It certainly wasn't to catch criminals, protect the public, or keep the streets clean.

'Right, listen up,' said Galloway.

The people in the room had already gathered round the end desks, in front of the whiteboard, where the images of the victims had been stuck up. A couple of WPCs looked at each other, whispered, but most of the team were held in awe of Galloway. She moved in front of the board, took a glance, allowed her jacket to flap open and then attached her hands to the desk as she spoke: 'Is this it?'

McGuire nodded. 'We have two teams going door to door and there's a few more here and there.'

Galloway looked out on the group, raised her chin at a right angle with the floor and then she opened her mouth wide. 'I am not in the habit of shaking up investigations for the hell of it, but it is clear to me you are pretty far from a result in any shape or form …' A murmur went round the room. '*Quiet* … Thank you. So I am here to tell you all that as of oh-nine-hundred hours on Monday I am putting DI Ian Lauder in charge of all investigations arising from the murder of Carly Donald.'

A flurry of voices went up; heads shook, papers were slapped on the table.

'That's enough,' said Galloway. It didn't calm the room.

'That's enough … I'd like to thank DI Brennan for his hard work—'

'Here! Here!' No one could place the first male voice, but a chorus of approval rang out.

'Right, Rob, over to you.' Galloway exited the room. Her strut seemed to have left her; each clack of heel on floor resounded with less force than before.

Brennan stood by the edge of the photocopier, leaning on his elbow. He could feel his neck expanding in his shirt collar, a pulse beating hard on the knot of his tie. His first instinct was to push up off the copier, steady himself, but he didn't seem able to engage his brain in time to meet the eyes around the room that waited on his words to follow.

Brennan tucked a finger behind his tie, loosened the knot, and then undid the top button of his shirt. The relief was instant, but seemed at once to be replaced by a craving for nicotine. 'Right, you heard the Chief Super … You have very few days left before we hand over to Lauder. If you want to avoid that fate, you better get bloody moving.'

Brennan found his legs heavy as he went towards the office at the end of the incident room. Galloway had undermined him in a public fashion. He had seen scores of senior officers throw their weight about, it was nothing new to him – it was the way she had done it that rankled. The inference was that she wanted the case solved. But turning it over to a new DI wasn't the way to go about that. What Galloway really wanted was to show him – and everyone else – who was boss.

Brennan was two paces inside the door and lighting up a cigarette when McGuire came in.

'This is a joke …'

Brennan took a deep draw on his cigarette. He looked at McGuire then pushed past him and called out to a PC, 'Ben, gimme a fag!'

The constable took up a packet of Marlboro and handed them to Brennan. 'Yes, sir.'

'Thanks.' He removed a cigarette and put it in his mouth, lighting it with the tip of the Silk Cut. He made to return the packet but the PC held up his hand.

'Keep them, sir …'

Brennan returned to the office, closed the door.

DC Stevie McGuire was sitting down now, rubbing the back of his neck. 'What are you going to do?'

'What can I do? She's got our balls in her handbag.'

McGuire leaned forward in his chair. 'You can raise a complaint.'

Brennan grimaced. 'Don't be bloody daft. She has her promotion board today; she'd really be gunning for us after that.'

McGuire moved his hand from the back of his neck, met it with his other and placed them over his face.

'It's not that bad,' said Brennan.

'Isn't it?'

'We still have a few days.'

'And then?'

Brennan took another pelt on the Marlboro – he approved of the strength of it. 'I'm not thinking that far ahead.'

'You can bet Ian Lauder is …'

'You've changed your tune. I thought you pair were mates.'

McGuire tutted. 'I just think we've all worked far too hard on this case for Lauder to come in with Bryce and all the rest of his boys and start calling the shots.'

Brennan removed his jacket, put it on the back of the office chair. He took a quick pull on the Marlboro, then put it on the edge of the desk, ash out, as he rolled up his sleeves. He sat. 'Leave Lauder to me, Stevie. I've got a funny feeling he'll not be as popular with the Chief Super in a little while.'

'Eh? How come?'

Brennan crossed his arms over, leaned on the back of the chair. 'Do you trust me?' He retrieved his cigarette.

McGuire perked up. 'Yes, 'course I do!'

'Then when I give you the nod later on, be ready to help me out with a little bit of extracurricular activity.'

'Like what?'

'I thought you trusted me.'

McGuire bit: 'I do. Count me in.'

'Good, then wait for the nod.'

Brennan held the cigarette in between his thumb and forefinger, took repeated little drags, then stubbed it on the back of the stapler and dropped the dowp in the bin. 'What stage are the team at with Tierney and Durrant's known associates?'

McGuire scratched his head. 'Not getting far …'

'How come?'

'They're, eh, in lockdown. No bastard's talking.'

Brennan squinted, pointed a finger at McGuire. 'Right, the next lot they bring in, I want you to do the interviews, rough them up a bit … This lot are scum; Tierney and Durrant were the worst of the lot. They had dealers and they had pimps and they knew a string of ex-cons who don't want to go back inside – hit them hard, rattle their cages. Put the heavy threat of the force taking a serious interest in their day-to-day activities if they don't give us what we want and make sure they know we're not pissing about.'

McGuire smiled. 'Yes, sir.'

'But go canny, eh … Don't have her down the way quoting us the tale of the slippery steps.'

'Sir.'

Brennan tweaked the end of his nose. 'And where's our minister?'

'He's still at the Travelodge. Knows not to stray too far.'

'Right … Bring him in this morning, soon as.'

'Sir.' McGuire rose, turned his back to Brennan and walked out the door, closing it behind him.

In the empty office, Brennan felt a twinge of shame creep up on him. He was close to losing the case to Lauder and he knew that wouldn't look good among his colleagues. Wullie had said there was no way back for you in the force once people started to see you as someone who can't come up with the goods any more. He had told him about an old hand who had started to lose respect when his wife developed mental illness. Simpson was a respected DI, had worked the big cases like Bible John, had brought in some big faces in his day, but when his wife started walking about the town in her nightie and slippers he was never the same man.

'You know what Simy's problem was, Rob?' he'd said.

'What was that?'

'He lost respect for himself.'

'What do you mean?'

'He got to the stage where he was so worried about what folk were saying about him, that he questioned his own abilities. The mind's a funny thing, Robbie lad, it's all about tricking it into believing that you're the bee's knees. If you can convince yourself, who else is going to doubt you?'

Brennan knew Wullie was right. He needed to keep his fears to himself. If he started to show weakness the entire force would be on him like a pack of wolves that had scented blood. There was just no place for self-doubt on the job – it was lethal. He had to be smarter than that, he had to search out others' weaknesses, Lauder's, and hold them up to public ridicule.

He raised the phone, dialled an internal number.

Ringing.

It was answered: 'DS Bryce.'

'Hello, Brycey.'

'Rob, how's it?'

'Not bad. I hear congratulations are in order.'

Bryce's voice quavered: 'Yeah, we cracked the bastard late last night, full confession.'

'Always good to hear another one's off the street. Well done, lad.' Bryce wasn't a bad bloke, thought Brennan, just a little dim – like a forty-watt bulb to Lauder's sixty-watt.

'Look, Rob, you'll have heard about the handover. Got to tell you, it wasn't my idea, mate.'

'Brycey, don't worry about it. It's just that cow playing divide and rule.'

Bryce's tone rose: 'Setting man against man, that's it.'

'Look, I thought we should have a chat anyway, about the handover, so if you want to grab your boss and head up …'

'Can go one better than that: why don't you join us for a beer tonight? Having a few after work to celebrate.'

Brennan smiled into the phone. 'Might just do that. The Bull as usual?'

'Yeah, say about six, seven …'

'See you there, Brycey.'

He hung up.

As he put down the phone the door to the office was flung open. DC Stevie McGuire stuck his head in. 'Minister's on his way, sir. Be here in a half-hour.'

Chapter 39

BRENNAN ORDERED McGUIRE TO GO and prepare the interview room; he had a phone call to make. He knew it would have been
better to meet face to face with Lynne Thompson, ask her the question he wanted to know about her friend Carly that she had been so
reluctant to answer, and it would be clumsy with her mother there
on the line, but he had no choice. Time had almost defeated him on
the case, and he knew if he didn't get a result before Lauder took over
he was as good as finished.

Brennan dialled the number.

The phone started to ring.

He knew there was no advantage to be gained from showing the
Reverend John Donald that he had unearthed a secret, something
he and his wife had tried so hard to keep from everyone, the police
included, but it would give him something to prod the minister with.
And he needed that. Brennan needed to have the minister onside for
his next move. Without him, he felt pretty sure that the case was going nowhere; certainly not before Lauder pushed him out.

'Hello.'

'Hello, Mrs Thompson, it's Detective Inspector Rob Brennan.'

A pause. 'Oh, hello there.'

'And how are you keeping?' Brennan loathed the formality of
these situations, the small chat; life would be so much more straightforward if everyone just said what they meant.

'I'm well, thanks … And you?'

'I'm fine, Mrs Thompson. You'll no doubt have seen the news.'

A clearing of throat. Her voice lowered a little: 'Yes, I saw the, er,
news about Mr Sproul.'

Brennan listened to her intonation carefully – she seemed to have
put a stranglehold on her vowels. 'I think I mentioned on my last
visit, about speaking to Lynne again.'

'I'm not sure about that.'

Brennan tugged at the phone line, started to twist it into little
kinks. 'Oh, really.'

'She's very upset about everything, as you can imagine, Inspector.'

Brennan cleared his throat. 'Yes, I can understand that, Mrs

Thompson, but I'd like to stress how important your daughter is to our investigation … A young girl has been killed and her child is missing. We still have no idea of the whereabouts of …' He suddenly became aware of a silence on the other end of the line that made him wonder if he was speaking to himself. 'Hello?'

There was no reply, then, 'Lynne, here, take the phone.'

'Hello, Lynne … Do you remember me?'

'Yes, of course.' The girl's voice came loaded with nerves but short on actual words.

'And how have you been keeping?' Formality again; it irked him.

'Okay, I guess.'

Brennan dropped the telephone cord, sat upright in his chair. 'Lynne, I don't want you to think too hard about what I'm about to ask you, all right?'

'Okay.'

'I think, by now, you know there's nothing you can say that's going to harm you, or get you into trouble …'

'I suppose.'

'If you are going to think about anything, you need only concern yourself with your best friend, Carly, and her baby, Beth. You knew all about Beth, didn't you, long before anyone else did?'

There was a gap on the line. It stretched out too long and Brennan jumped in again: 'You knew about Beth before Reverend Donald and his wife, didn't you?'

The girl's voice lowered yet further: 'Yes.'

Brennan raised his eyes, thanked above. 'Now, remember what I said: no one can hurt you now, Lynne … Peter Sproul was the father, wasn't he?'

A gap. Brennan imagined the young girl looking at her mother and then a defiant nod coming. 'Yes.'

Brennan scrunched his eyes, and smiled into the receiver. 'What happened, Lynne? … What happened with Carly and Peter Sproul?'

The young girl started to cry. Brennan felt an enormous guilt for upsetting her. He heard her mother making encouraging noises, then, 'He … he … raped her.'

Brennan froze. The facts of the matter had crossed his mind many times before but hearing them uttered this way somehow gave them more power. 'Did she tell you about that, Lynne?'

More tears, sobbing. 'Yes. More than once. He used to come into her room … She told her …' The girl paused.

Brennan prompted: 'Carly told her parents – is that what you were going to say?'

'Yes.'

The thought of what Carly Donald had gone through in the months before her death welled up in Brennan. He felt his chest ache for her hurts. He wanted to be able to take the culprit and wring the life out of him, like Carly had surely had the life wrung out of her. The girl had faced a trial of misery. Brennan knew who to blame for some of it, and thought he knew who to blame for the rest.

'Okay, Lynne, that's enough now. Go back to your mum. You've done well. Thank you.'

The young girl started to cry again as the phone line died. Brennan placed down his receiver, rose from the chair and picked up his jacket. Something drew him to take the picture that Lorraine had given him from the pocket. He stared at the familiar shape for a second or two; he was responsible for bringing another child into this world and the thought gored him. Could any of the children be protected from the beasts that were out there? Brennan shoved the scan back in his pocket. As he put his hand in the sleeve of his jacket he spotted the Reverend John Donald being led towards the interview room by DC Stevie McGuire.

'Right, Minister, let's see what you have to say for yourself now,' he muttered.

As Brennan left the office for Incident Room One he was stopped by a WPC. 'Sir, I have the lab on the phone for you.'

'What do they want?'

'I think you should take it.'

Brennan picked up the phone. 'Hello.'

'Rob?'

'Yes, what is it?'

'I just thought you'd like to know that hunch you had about the ammunition …'

'What about it?'

The boffin's voice rose an octave: 'You were absolutely right: the bullets were gold-washed.'

Brennan liked to be proven right; it hadn't happened enough lately. 'Pro hit all right. Told you. Thanks, Mike.'

He hung up, turned the phone over to the WPC, said, 'Did you get anywhere running that ammunition through the system?'

She lowered the receiver, reached over a pile of blue files for a loose sheaf of paper, then another. 'There's a few, sir.'

'How many?'

She curled down the corners of her mouth, showed a row of milk-white teeth. 'I haven't counted but I'd say over the country, I mean Scotland, fairly few ... but in the UK and Ireland we're into the dozens, especially in Ulster.'

'Those Troubles have blocked our job.'

A smile. 'Do you want me to cross-ref with over the water, sir?'

'It's a hit with military precision on our patch. They have enough on their own to still clear up without going out of their way to help us, but give it a go.' Brennan nodded to her. 'Good work, Constable.'

'Thanks, sir.'

On the way out, Brennan picked up his pace. He didn't want the minister to get too comfortable. He wanted him on edge. As he swung open the door, the minister was standing in the corner of the room with his hands behind his back.

Brennan was the first to speak: 'Would you like to take a seat?'

'I'd sooner stand, unless you have something to tell me.'

Brennan indicated the chair. 'I have plenty to tell you and I'd like you to be comfortable but, please, suit yourself.'

The minister removed a grey-to-white handkerchief from his pocket, wiped his nose, then moved forward. As he sat down Brennan noticed the redness at the edges of his nose. 'Can you tell me what this is about, please, and how long you will be keeping us under house arrest?'

Brennan turned over the cover of the blue folder sitting on the desk, said, 'This is about the murder of your daughter and about your missing granddaughter, you know that ... You also know you are not under house arrest, but merely helping us with our inquiries. I should have thought, Minister, in the circumstances, you would be more than happy to do that – am I wrong?'

The minister crossed his legs, showed grey argyle socks. He checked his watch as Brennan shuffled papers.

'Will you need me long?' he said.

Brennan tilted his head, huffed. 'Are you in a hurry, Minister? Got somewhere to be?'

He looked away, frowned. Dark semicircles had appeared under his eyes in the last couple of days.

Brennan started again: 'It's not the Moderator's job, is it? ... My boss has an interview today. I know how nervous they make some people.'

'Can we just get on with this, please?'

Brennan slapped hands on the desk, smiled. 'Glad to. Shall I start with the investigation update?' The minister nodded and Brennan ran through the events that had transpired since they'd last met. He watched the older man for signs of interest but none showed; he seemed to Brennan all too keen to get out of there. 'For me, Minister, the most interesting piece of information I turned up was from Carly's best friend.'

'Oh?'

'Yes, Lynne Thompson.'

'I know the girl; she's from a good family.'

'Very good,' said Brennan. 'They are all devastated at the loss of Carly. You knew Carly confided in Lynne?'

'They were young girls.' The minister crossed his legs the other way. 'I'm sure they talked a lot.'

Brennan leaned back in his seat, turned eyes upwards. 'She told me something very interesting about your *man about the house*.'

'Are you referring to the late Peter Sproul?'

Brennan nodded. 'Who else?'

'Well, I'd sooner not talk about the deceased if you do not mind. Suicide is such an unfortunate business.'

Brennan was stunned at his defence of Sproul. 'The man was a convicted child molester. He'd spent years behind bars for raping children and you let him into your home.'

The minister's tongue flashed before his grey lips. He retracted it quickly, searched for words. 'I do not judge people on their past mistakes, but on what they hope to make of the future.'

Brennan stood up, walked round to the minister's side of the desk, sat on the edge. 'He was a serial child sex offender and you let him into your home. He raped and impregnated your daughter and you did not reveal that to anyone, even when she came to you …'

The minister stayed calm. 'What proof do you have of that?'

Brennan was incredulous. He leaned over the minister.

'Your daughter told you he raped her, she was pregnant – what more proof did you need?'

The minister turned away. His voice was flat, bereft of emotion: 'Is this what you heard from Lynne Thompson, a teenage girl who heard something around the town and repeated it?'

'No one in the town knew Carly had a child – you did a good job of covering that up.'

'This is all hearsay.'

'Sproul's record wasn't hearsay. He killed himself in your daughter's room.'

The minister shook his head. 'This is helping no one.

Why have you not found my granddaughter yet?'

Brennan stepped away from the edge of the desk, spoke: 'I wondered when you were going to ask about Beth.'

The mention of the baby's name seemed to poke a spear into the minister. He laced his fingers and placed them on his thighs.

Brennan said, 'We had a good response from the television news item.'

'Another two people killed – is that what you call a good response, Inspector?'

He didn't bite, closed down the minister: 'We need to give this case a public face. We need to put out a plea and I want you to do it, today.'

The minister rose from the seat. 'That will not be possible.'

Brennan got up, faced him. 'Why? Think it'll play havoc with your prospects of getting the Moderator's job?'

'That's ridiculous!'

'I thought you'd say so.' Brennan picked up the telephone, buzzed the switchboard. 'I'll take you to meet our media people. They'll coach you through what you'll say at the press conference.'

Chapter 40

MELANIE McARDLE HAD GIVEN UP on her husband coming home any time soon. She had waited for him the night before to bring home the list of things she'd given him for the baby, only to be disappointed to see him carrying in tins of Carlsberg Special Brew for himself and nothing else. She had grown tired waiting and upset herself listening to the hungry child's screams. Melanie knew she was disobeying her husband to go out with the child, but she also knew she had no choice.

In the garage she fitted the baby carrier that they had bought a few years back. It was at the time Melanie had fallen pregnant. She remembered those days as she strapped it into the back of the four-by-four; she had been so happy. McArdle had never come round to the idea of her having the child – he'd accused her of trying to trap him and then he'd denied it was his. When the bump started to show he didn't want to look at her and that's when the real trouble had started.

Melanie bit her lip as she stepped away from the back seat of the car. She looked over the baby seat and checked it was in place but she couldn't help the tears starting to come now. Every time she thought of the child she had lost she started to cry. Alcohol usually stopped her mind from reaching such lows but she couldn't drink when she now had a baby to look after.

She wiped away the tears, went inside. The child was lying on its back where she had left it in the sleeper. She reached over, tickled its tummy. 'You poor lamb. Hungry?'

The baby smiled a broad toothless grin.

Melanie picked her up, put her on her shoulder as she went out to the car. As she fastened the baby into the carrier she rubbed her own stomach and remembered how it felt to be pregnant. She remembered too how it had felt when she had lost the child; she was sure McArdle had been upset about it, but he would never let on.

Melanie reversed the four-by-four out of the garage and onto the driveway. The shopping centre wasn't far away but she didn't know how the baby was going to be in the car for the first time and she kept up an idle chatter to distract her. 'Not to worry, just going out to the shops to get you a few nice things.'

The car stalled on her first attempt to reverse out of the driveway, the scree scrunching beneath the wheels, but after she turned the ignition again the vehicle moved smoothly down. 'There, no trouble at all, little one.'

As Melanie drove, her thoughts turned back to McArdle. He hadn't been himself lately. The other night he had been ready to rip the television off the wall and then he had stormed out and hadn't returned until after midnight. He'd gone straight to the kitchen and drunk beer from the fridge and had collapsed on the couch an hour or so later. It wasn't like him. She was the drinker. McArdle only drunk like that when he had something on his mind.

'Don't worry, darling, there soon.' Melanie slowed the four-by-four at the traffic lights and turned towards the baby – she had started to tug at one of her socks. 'No, leave that on.' The child grinned that toothless smile again. 'Okay, fine, suit yourself.'

At Sainsbury's Melanie drove straight to the parents' parking spaces out front. It made her feel like she was somebody – she could do that because she was responsible for another life; society approved. As she lifted the baby out of the back-seat carrier she quickly attached the harness and watched as the little one reached for her beads. 'No, don't be touching those.'

In the supermarket Melanie felt sure she was unlikely to see anyone she knew, but the thought of coming out with a baby and no proper explanation alarmed her. What would she say if anyone asked about it? She'd have to lie. She had never been very good at lying; McArdle had always caught her out. When she thought about it, she had never been very good at anything, but she somehow felt right for the job of being a mother.

'Now then, let's get some shopping done,' she said.

The child played with her beads and looked content. Melanie smiled back at her. She felt happy with the baby, something she hadn't really thought about for a long time. The feeling stayed with her all the time she wandered round the store, nodding and sharing knowing looks with other mothers. The thought of being happy lingered all the way home in the four-by-four right until she pulled into the drive, behind McArdle's car. He was at the window when she got out the vehicle. He stared at her for a moment and then threw down the curtain as she released the baby carrier.

Melanie knew her husband was furious when he appeared at the door, even before he spoke. 'What the fuck are you doing?' He flapped his hands in the air, grabbed her arm; she pulled it away.

'Get off me.'

McArdle looked around. 'Get inside. We'll see about this in the house.'

Melanie lifted up the child and closed the car door. The shopping bags rested on the ground and she picked those up with her free hand. As she walked towards the front door, McArdle seemed anxious, rushing her forwards with his hands. 'Come on, move ... Get in.'

'What's the big rush?'

'Just get in that fucking house!'

Melanie could feel a knot tightening in her stomach – when McArdle got this angry he was likely to strike out. She wasn't scared for herself, though; she'd felt his punches too many times for that. She was afraid for the baby. If anything happened to the child she would be destroyed now. 'Don't talk that way, Devlin, you'll upset the baby,' she said.

He let her pass and pushed the back of her head down. 'Shut up.'

Melanie spun round. She found strength she didn't know she had. 'You lay one finger on us and I'll call the police.'

He looked stunned, his eyes bulging from below their heavy lids. 'What did you say?'

Melanie held firm. 'I mean it – you harm one hair on this child's head, Devlin, and I'll see you fucking hang.' She felt as if her words were travelling on fire. She had never dared stand up to her husband before but she meant everything she said and she could see by the look on McArdle's face that he believed her. He was shaken. He stepped aside and walked towards the house with his hands in the front pockets of his jeans. When he reached the doorstep he looked back, said nothing, then entered.

Melanie followed behind her husband and went into the kitchen, laid down the shopping bags. She returned to the living room and put the baby in the cot. McArdle was sitting silently on the sofa, gripping the armrest with his hand. She watched him for a minute and then she went back to the kitchen and started to unpack the shopping. She called out to McArdle as she went, 'Where have you been all day?'

There was no answer.

She walked to the open door. 'Devlin, where have you been?'

He looked distracted, miles away.

'Just here and there ... You know.'

Melanie held up the carton of baby milk. 'You were supposed to get the stuff for the baby … What's she supposed to eat?'

He looked at her; his mouth drooped. 'I was too busy.'

The answer didn't suit her. 'Devlin, that's not good enough. If you want to bring a baby back to this house for me to look after—'

He jerked from the seat, cut her off. 'Melanie, for fuck's sake, what are you playing at?'

'*What?*'

'You're just supposed to be looking after the fucking thing for a few days – you're not adopting it. I told you not to go out. What were you thinking?'

She walked forward, faced him. 'That we needed stuff?'

'What if someone had seen you?'

'Well, so what if someone had? … Look, what's going on here, Devlin?'

He touched the sides of his head; his shoulders shrank. 'You wouldn't understand …'

Melanie put down the baby milk, grabbed her husband's arms. He flinched, pulled away from her and returned to the sofa.

'Devlin, I'm not bloody stupid. There's something going on here and I want to know what.'

He grimaced, looked like a small boy putting his hands over his ears because he refused to be confronted with unpalatable truths. 'Shut up!'

The baby started to cry.

'No, no … I won't. I want to know what's going on.'

McArdle rose. His chest inflated as he grabbed Melanie by the arm, waving a fist at her. 'Since when did you get the guts to talk to me like this?'

She started to squeal: 'You're hurting me, let go!' The baby's crying intensified. Melanie could see the child's face reddening. 'Let me go.'

'I fucking well told you not to go out the house, Mel.' He pulled her towards him and she struck out with her hands, clawing at his face. The three scratches flashed white on his skin for an instant and then the blood coloured them. McArdle dropped Mel's arm, threw a hand to the scratches. 'You fucking bitch …'

There was a sudden snapping noise, a pain in her stomach and then Melanie crouched over. The room seemed to have emptied of air, but then the realisation that she was struggling for breath came to her. As she looked up from the floor she saw McArdle holding a tight fist and she knew she'd been hit. As he drew it back and bowed over, her hearing became distorted. There was a flash of white light that seemed to block everything out and then it disappeared as everything went black.

Chapter 41

WHEN MELANIE McARDLE CAME ROUND her first thought was to check the baby was okay. As she tried to open her eyes, however, they felt stuck together. She tried again – nothing. She rubbed at the lids – they felt caked in something that crumbled to tiny particles as she touched it. When Melanie finally got her eyes open she looked at her hands and saw they were covered in dried blood. She felt the side of her head and found the gash that was responsible. It seemed to have stopped bleeding now, but there was a throbbing pain that increased when she touched it, making her feel sick.

Melanie put her hands out in front of her, raised her head. She felt woozy now; there was a metallic taste in her mouth and her tongue was dry. When she managed to get her head far enough off the carpet to take in the room she saw the baby sitting up in the cot; her face was flushed and her eyes looked red and sore. The child was wet and hungry, but Melanie was glad she was okay – she knew she couldn't count on that situation lasting much longer.

As she dragged herself onto her knees, Melanie felt her stomach turn over, then a strange sensation like a wave pressing on her knocked her down again. Her head landed on the carpet and her eyes glazed for a second, but she was still conscious enough to hear McArdle laughing at her. She understood now he had kicked her in the back; as he stood looming over her she wondered what he would do next.

'That's you learned your lesson, is it?' he said.

Melanie tried to speak, but her mouth felt numb, her lips were too swollen.

McArdle stepped over her, went to sit on the sofa. He didn't look at her as she tried to rise again. It took some effort. Her head was heavy on her shoulders, much heavier than usual, and she thought she might fall again but she got to her knees and dragged herself onto the arm of the sofa, pushed herself up. On her feet she stood for a moment and watched McArdle point the remote control at the television. He found the news, put down the controller and started to rub at his reddened knuckles.

'What are you looking at?' he said. 'If you're up now you can go and get me a beer from the fridge.'

Melanie stared at him, her face burning and throbbing where he had hit her – she wanted to scream at him. But she didn't have the strength. She felt more hate towards him than she ever had as she turned for the kitchen, dragging her battered body as though she was beginning a slow death march.

At the sink, Melanie ran the cold-water tap and tried to catch enough in her open palm to wet her lips. Her hands were already bloodied from rubbing her eyes and as she ran them under the tap the water she collected took on a pinkish hue. She stared at the cold liquid and splashed some on her face. It stung. The second attempt stung a little less but she could now feel the swelling under the skin. The thought of her battered features made her start to cry but she steadied herself and vowed not to be overcome by her emotions; she needed to be stronger if she was going to protect the child.

Melanie made her way back from the fridge with McArdle's Carlsberg. She heard a roar from the living room.

In panic, she increased her pace; as she reached the door she saw her husband sitting on the edge of the sofa with his head in his hands. She moved into the space between the now-sleeping baby and her husband and turned herself towards the screen. There was a young reporter talking about a shooting in the centre of Edinburgh, by the Water of Leith. Two drug addicts, one a known prostitute and the other a career criminal, had been targeted in a professional hit.

The reporter stated: '*Police were already looking to interview Barry Tierney, of Muirhouse, in connection with missing Pitlochry schoolgirl Carly Donald. The case took a strange twist when the bodies of Tierney and long-term partner Vee Durrant were found in the early hours of this morning.*'

The camera panned away from the reporter and showed police officers combing a small wooded area beside the water banks. Melanie turned to McArdle – he was shaking his head in his hands, gripping the skin on his neck so tight white crescents showed in the red flesh.

The reporter continued: '*Tierney was spotted earlier on CCTV cameras at the city's bus station with Carly Donald and her young baby daughter, Beth. After an appeal on the* Six O'Clock News *Tierney was identified, but underworld figures got to him before the police and both he and Durrant died in what officers have described as a professional killing.*'

McArdle rose from the sofa. 'This is out of fucking order!'

'What is it?' said Melanie.

He looked at her, snatched the can from her hand and pointed at her nose. 'Keep that out!'

Melanie felt her pulse quicken as McArdle threatened her. She took a glance back at the baby and slowly edged towards the kitchen door. As she stood inside the doorway, she could still see her husband, his face contorted and reddened as the news item continued.

The reporter was now introducing a man from the church; Melanie leaned forward to glance at the screen and saw that the minister was seated behind a table with police officers. He was reading from a piece of paper: *'My wife and I cannot possibly describe the devastation we feel at the loss of our beloved daughter, Carly. She was a beautiful young girl, kind and well loved by all those who knew her.*

Nothing will ever fill the void in our hearts that has been created by her passing but we beg of you, if you know something that can help the police in their inquiries, to please, please get in touch. Our granddaughter Beth went missing the day Carly left our home and hasn't been seen since. The police have assured us that they are doing all they can but they cannot be everywhere at once and we need the help of you all to find Beth. My wife and I are desperately worried for our granddaughter now. The police have reason to believe she may have been in the hands of the people who were shot this morning and I would again urge anyone with any information, however insignificant, to please, please get in touch.'

McArdle was out of his seat, shaking a fist at the screen. He took a sup from his can then threw it aside. Melanie edged further into the kitchen as he ranted. She had seen him angry before; she had seen him rage and hit out but this was different. He looked desperate, like a cornered animal. Melanie felt fearful. She retreated towards the kitchen table and opened the drawer; as she stared into it her hand trembled but she managed to pick up a long knife. It suddenly went from being a familiar item she had often used without a thought to something that had the potential to change everything she had come to accept in her life. She held the haft close to her thigh and then turned it behind her back as she walked towards the open door.

When she entered the living room, the minister had gone from the television screen and a police officer was talking to the reporter. 'We are now extremely concerned as to the fate of young Beth,' he said. 'We know these early hours and days are extremely important in an investigation such as this and we need to harness all the support of the public that we can get.'

The reporter asked, '*What do you think has become of the baby?*'

'*I'm not prepared to speculate. All I will say is this: if you have any suspicions, however tenuous, you must call the police right away.*'

McArdle spat out, lashed at the television. He pushed the off switch and the screen fizzed but it didn't satisfy him. He swung an arm and brought it from its cradle on the wall. The television smashed on the floor; the noise woke the child.

'And you can shut the fuck up!' McArdle turned for the child, roared again: 'I said "Shut the fuck up!"' As he went to move forward, Melanie stood in front of him.

'What's going on?' she said.

'You can fuck off too.'

'It's their baby, isn't it?' She looked towards the screaming child. 'She's the one off the television, isn't she?'

McArdle drew fists. His face creased as he yelled, 'Who are you to ask me anything?'

He stepped forward, put out a hand to grab her throat. Melanie swung with the knife and caught him near the elbow. A red arc of blood escaped as he flinched back and held his arm.

'You fucking bitch!' McArdle looked at her, his eyes wide, his brows pushing on his hairline. 'Give me that fucking knife.'

Melanie swung out again – this time she caught the open palm of his other hand. He screamed out as blood trailed down his fingers and onto the white carpet. He leaned over for a moment and tucked his hand under his arm. As he did so Melanie gripped the knife in both hands and raised it over her head. She brought it down quickly, aiming for the space between his shoulder blades. She could feel the force of her body weight getting behind the falling blade. Her hands held tight; there was no doubt in her mind she wanted to kill him. She didn't know whether it was because she was too slow, or too weak after her beating, but she seemed to have given too much of her intention away with her movements and McArdle turned with just enough time to avoid the blade. It ripped through his shirt and embedded itself deep in his right arm.

He yelled out, screaming in pain.

Melanie watched as McArdle staggered away. He knocked a picture off the wall then collided with the edge of a small cabinet, tipping a table lamp to the ground.

'You bitch! Look what you've done.' He had his hand on the knife's handle; blood covered his shirt and the top of his jeans.

Melanie stared, then stepped back towards the screaming baby.

She knew she had blown her chance. She tried to think what to do next. She looked at the bawling child and thought about picking her up and running but McArdle was between her and the door. He pulled at the knife, removed it. The blade dripped with blood. He turned to her, stared with bulging eyes. 'You fucking bitch!'

Melanie ran for the kitchen. As she went she heard McArdle take off behind her. She reached the table in enough time to yank open the drawer. There were more knives than she could remember; she put in her hands and tried to grab one but her fingers felt numb to the touch. The knives rattled noisily as she tried to pick one up.

'You bitch! You fucking bitch!' McArdle roared as he entered the kitchen. Melanie turned to face him, saw the knife in his hand, blood still dripping from it onto the floor.

His mad wide eyes burned into her; she didn't recognise him at all now – he was crazed – he was like someone she was seeing for the first time. As he drew closer he seemed to grow in size. She felt the impossibility of any challenge she could make and turned away to run.

The last thing Melanie McArdle heard at that moment was her own screams, as her husband sank the knife into her back. The length of it passed clean through her. She toppled over, and for a second or two the blade showed as she lowered her head towards her stomach, and fell onto the hard, cold floor.

Chapter 42

DI ROB BRENNAN WAS HALFWAY down Leith Walk when he spotted the two dogs eyeing each other. They went nose to nose, tails up. For a brief instant it looked like war. Then one of the dogs lowered ears and conceded its inferiority to the dark cross straining on its lead. Brennan watched the small tan terrier drop its tail next, allow the larger animal to dominate it completely. As he took them in, the detective wondered how different people were to dogs. They were both all about strutting, posturing. As he got closer he watched the dogs' owners nodding and greeting each other – one leaned out a hand and brayed loudly as the other stood still. How different indeed? He recalled some advice from Wullie, back in the early days. A pub fight was never the place for police to go charging in – you were always better sending in a couple of WPCs. His theory was that the presence of females always brought in some civility: 'It's just the same with dogs, Robbie … See dogs fighting, throw in a bitch; that'll separate them.'

As Brennan approached the black graffiti-covered door he wondered how Wullie would receive him. It had been a long time; too long, perhaps. But what were you supposed to do? It seemed like an intrusion now that Wullie had left the force. When they had worked together, it had been inconceivable to Brennan that there would come a day when he wouldn't see Wullie, but now the days had stretched into weeks, months even, and he felt guilty to be calling on him now. He needed his help, though. Brennan knew there were people in his situation who would be too proud to ask for help, but he was bigger than that. Wullie was always the man with the answers; if Brennan was missing something, however small, Wullie would spot it.

He pressed the doorbell and retreated from the step. There was no response. He wondered should he give it another minute or try again right away. An old man across the street left a newsagent's and started to rub at a scratch card with a coin. Within a few seconds his face went from a barely contained optimism to showing a lifetime's disappointment; he let the card flutter to the ground.

'Hello?' It was Wullie.

'It's Rob.'

'*Rob?*' He sounded incredulous – had it really been that long? 'Come away in, son.'

The buzzer sprang the lock on the door. Brennan entered.

The steps were grey and dank, like all Edinburgh stairwells. A mish-mash of bikes cluttered the landing alongside assorted rubbish. There was a lingering smell of urine and only a few bulbs fizzed on the wall lights. How did people live like this? thought Brennan. At what stage did everyone in this part of the country settle for a one- or two-bed-room rat-hole shared with strangers who never spoke to you? This was tenement living – for most, it was all the city offered, so what could you do? Half a million for a three-bedroom house wasn't an option for them.

As Brennan reached the second floor he saw Wullie's door sat open, but there was no sign of the man. He knocked. 'Hello, Wullie.'

'Come away in.' His voice sounded frail, tired. As Brennan entered the small flat he was immediately taken by the lack of air. The place seemed almost too stuffy to accommodate life. He walked down the hall, watching the dust dance in a shard of light, then pushed open the living-room door. There was a small kitchen at one end, pots and carry-out tins piled high. On the other side of the room Wullie crouched over on an old armchair. He wore a white vest and grey slacks; a pair of black braces sat over the vest. He seemed to have put on some weight but all of it sat in a small paunch above his waistband. 'Hello, Robbie.'

Brennan smiled. Though his heart seemed to be galloping, he held himself in check. 'You look well, sir.'

'Fuck off with the "sir" shite.'

Brennan nodded. Made for a seat on the other side of the small living room. 'How are you keeping?'

Wullie started a hacking cough, rubbed at his chest. Brennan noticed how defined his shoulders still looked – the rest of him hadn't kept up. 'I'm as rough as aul' guts,' he said, 'but thanks for asking.'

Brennan knew Wullie had lost his wife and had a strained relationship with his two children but he didn't want to ask about personal matters; even if the old man was doing it hard, on his own, he'd settle for that in front of sympathy from his peers any day. 'Well, there's none of us getting any younger' – he tapped his stomach – 'or fitter.'

Wullie let out a howl: 'Ha, you've a way to catch me yet, pal!'

Brennan brought out the last of his Marlboro pack, showed it to

Wullie. 'Mind?'

'Fire away.' He sat back in the chair. 'I'd offer you a cup of something but I've nothing in.'

'It's okay. Spend enough time drinking tea as it is.'

Wullie took a cigarette from the proffered pack, sparked up, said, 'I heard you'd had a bit of a break from duty.'

Brennan had been starting to settle but the remark jolted him. 'I, er, had some leave after my brother's death.'

Wullie took a deep drag on the cigarette. 'I heard about that too – nasty business ... I'm sorry.'

'No need.'

Wullie tapped the filter with his thumb. 'Have they made any progress?'

Brennan tutted. 'Ian Lauder on the case? You joking me?'

'Not improving with age, then?'

Sneers. 'Like a fine wine, you mean? I don't think so.'

Wullie smiled. His face creased with myriad lines that radiated from the corners of his eyes and covered almost every inch of his skin. His face seemed to have darkened since the last time Brennan had seen him, but his hair had lightened, become greyer. Even the stubble on his chin poked through in white spikes. The sight of him made Brennan suddenly conscious of the passage of time. He had never been aware of Wullie ageing in the job; even when he picked up the sobriquet Auld Wullie, it had passed him by. But now he was an old man. Brennan wondered if he had done the right thing coming to see him. Would he want to hear about what was going on out there now?

Would he care? Was he even up to it? As Brennan toyed with these thoughts his mind was quickly made up for him.

'So, Rob, what can I do for you?'

Brennan reached out, flicked ash into the tray on the mantel. 'I'm working a case, tough one.'

'I saw you on the news the other night.'

Brennan grinned. 'Fame at last.'

Wullie sat forward. 'That's some job you have on your hands. Very dirty business indeed ... Makes me glad I'm out of it.'

'Do you mean that?'

A laugh: 'Fuck no!'

Brennan creased out a wry smile. 'I need your help.'

Wullie leaned back, squared his shoulders. 'Don't know I can be much good to you ...' He waved hands over his midriff. 'You seen the kip of me?'

'There's very little coming together on this one, Wullie. There's a lot going on but nothing slotting into place.'

The old man reclined further in his chair. 'Go on.'

Brennan recounted the main points of the investigation; he left nothing out that he thought could be of any use. As he spoke, Wullie seemed thoughtful. Rubbing at his chin once in a while and allowing his fingertips to wander through the hair on the sides of his head. He didn't interrupt, but Brennan knew there were going to be questions. When he was finished speaking he stood up and stretched his legs in front of the mantelpiece. Wullie looked down towards the window, out into the street. He seemed about to speak and then he stopped himself, flagged Brennan to sit again.

'What is it?'

'This Sproul character ...'

'Yes.'

'You didn't link him to anyone in Edinburgh?'

Brennan curled his toes in his shoes. 'He was Paisley.'

'No connections down this way?'

'None we've turned up.'

Wullie's eyes rolled. 'It's probably nothing, then.'

'What were you thinking?'

Wullie crossed his fingers over his stomach. 'There's a child missing; he was a beast.'

Brennan spoke: 'It was his child, I'm almost certain of it.'

Wullie huffed, 'Since when did that fucking bother them?'

'Even if he was connected to Tierney – say they did some time together – that doesn't help me when the bastard's dead and nobody else is talking about him.'

'Maybe his connection wasn't Tierney, then.'

Brennan touched the crease of his trouser, brought it into a tent point. 'Or maybe he was ... but Tierney was a middle man.'

Wullie pointed at him. 'That makes more sense.'

'But none of this helps me. I still have four dead bodies and a missing baby.'

Wullie got to his feet. He eased back his broad shoulders, spoke: 'Well, take a few steps back the way, Robbie ... What were you telling me a minute ago about your inquiries?'

Brennan crossed over his leg, twisted his ankle in his hand. 'Well, we've had Tierney's known associates in, put the thumbscrews on them ... Nothing.'

'How hard have you turned them?'

'Bloody hard.'

Wullie put a hand on the wall, leaned over and punctuated his words with the point of his finger. 'Then you have to ask yourself why they're not talking.'

Brennan let go his ankle, showed palms. 'That's obvious: they don't want to go the same way as Tierney.'

'Correct!' Wullie took a long cigarette from a packet of B&H 100s, put it in his mouth; it moved up and down as he spoke. 'Tierney's connection is higher up the tree than you've been looking.'

'You think I should start climbing a bit.'

Wullie lit his cigarette, pointed to an ancient television screen in the corner of the room. 'After last night's performance, the bastard might be climbing down himself ... Make sure you bump into him on the way up, eh.'

Brennan put both feet on the floor. He kept an eye on Wullie as he removed his mobile phone, dialled the station.

'Lou, it's Rob.'

'Hello, sir.'

Brennan kept his tone businesslike, but his mind was sparking. 'Any movement from those scrotes you brought in again?'

A pause on the line. 'It's like they're in shutdown, boss.'

Brennan nodded to Wullie. 'Right. Turf them out. All at once – I want them to be bumping into each other in the fucking street as they go.'

'Yes, sir.'

Now he let the emotion into his voice: 'And when that's done, I want every dealer who might once have sold Tierney an ounce of puff hoiked in.'

Lou couldn't hide the doubt in his voice. 'That's a lot of dealers. There must be dozens of them he could have scored from.'

'Start at the top. Ones known to be dealing skag in Muirhouse. Don't go to their delivery boys – right to the top, Lou, and go in hard ... I want them rattled until their ears bleed, get me?'

'Yes, sir.'

As Brennan was about to hang up Lou spoke again: 'Sir, I don't know if there's anything in this, but we took a call and ...' He stalled, seemed to be searching for the right words.

'Go on,' said Brennan.

'We took a call from a woman in Dean Village who says she saw someone on the night of the shootings.'

'*And?*'

'It's not much of an ID, but she insists she saw a limping man soon after the shots were fired.'

Brennan felt as if he'd been punched in the gut. 'How sure is she?'

'Very. She seems reliable too.'

'Okay, Lou, circulate that to the team ... And all the other channels.'

He laid down the phone, put eyes on Wullie. The old man seemed to be a step ahead of him already.

Chapter 43

BRENNAN CHECKED HIS WATCH WHEN he got onto the street
– it was approaching 6.30. Bryce's celebration for Lauder and their
team would be in full swing at the Bull. He really didn't fancy it; just
thinking about seeing Lauder and Bryce gloating was enough to
make him want to throw up. His mind was awash with thoughts of
the Limping Man; Lauder had never traced him, never came close.
Brennan knew he was better than Lauder, he had more invested in
catching the bastard, but pros had a way of ducking under the radar
and this guy was obviously good, very good.

Brennan crossed the road at the Foot of the Walk. The town was
being dug up to make way for trams that never seemed to materialise. He played with the idea of skipping Bryce and Lauder's celebration, but there was a definite advantage to be had from seeing
them with their guards down. He made his way to the Bull. The tram
works had been going on for years, had driven some of the firms on
the Walk out of business, and now there was talk about the trams
only going as far as York Place because of a financial crisis. It made
Brennan shake his head as he looked at the statue of Queen Victo-
ria. What the hell was going on with this city? he wondered.

In Pitlochry he had been reminded that there were other places to
live, places with clean air and clean buildings. Green spaces and bins
that got emptied. Drunks safely tucked away in their middle-class
homes instead of spilling from every shopfront. He had grown tired
of the city, was exhausted by it. As he put his hand in his pocket he
felt the picture that Lorraine had given him. He toyed with the idea
of removing it, looking at his growing child, but he didn't want to risk
being seen by someone. Instead he removed his mobile phone, dialled
Lorraine's number.

'Hello, Rob.'

'This is getting ridiculous.'

'What is?'

'Oh Christ, stop with the shrink-speak.'

'If you like.'

Brennan moved the phone to his other ear. 'I need to see you.'

A note of sarcasm: 'At last a window opens in your diary.'

'Say when.'

'Tonight?'

Brennan sighed. 'I can't make tonight.'

'Brilliant! Why did you call, Rob?'

'Look, I do need to see you. I just can't make tonight.'

'Well, when?'

'How about Monday?'

She raised her voice: 'Are you trying to be funny?'

If he was, he didn't get the joke. 'What do you mean?'

'Rob, you have an appointment with me on Monday ... I am still your doctor, remember?'

He had forgotten about the session, must have pencilled it in before he was handed the case by Galloway. 'Well, Monday it is then. I'll try to be on time.'

'Don't try too hard.' She sounded harsh. 'Goodbye, Rob.'

She hung up. Brennan watched the phone's light go out, then moved off at a slower pace than before.

The Bull was a cellar bar, dark and dingy. When he arrived DC Stevie McGuire spotted him coming through the door and went to greet him. 'Hello, sir.'

'You can drop the honorific, Stevie, we're off duty.'

'Okay, boss ... I'm kidding! What can I get you?'

'A pint, heavy.' Brennan watched McGuire order up the drinks and scoped the bar for familiar faces. Lauder and Bryce were already knocking them back, holding court in the window seats. Prominent positions so no one could miss them. As Lauder caught sight of Brennan at the bar he raised a glass in salute. Brennan nodded, pressed out a weak smile. The bastard was having a laugh with him.

McGuire brought his pint, sat it on the bar counter; Brennan retrieved it, supped. He always stuck to just one pint on these occasions. It didn't do to get drunk in front of colleagues. It was a weakness and that was the one thing everyone on the team was looking out for. Wullie had always told him, 'Have a drink, enjoy a drink, but don't let the team know about it.' Getting drunk meant getting out of control and when that happened, mistakes were made. Brennan couldn't afford mistakes in his position. Mistakes were for people like Lauder; he'd make one soon enough, and when he did Brennan was going to be there to roast his balls over a hot spit.

'You'll have heard the good news, then?' said McGuire.

'About Her Majesty?'

'Yeah ... Think that's her official title now, isn't it?'

'She fucking thinks it is already.'

'Still, better for us if she's sweet. And she'll be off to the top floor … Slim chance of us bumping into her.'

'She's not off yet.'

'True. And neither are we.'

Brennan brought his pint up to his mouth again, sipped, lowered it. 'We still have some moves.' He looked at the glass in McGuire's hand. 'How many of those have you had?'

He jutted his jaw. 'Two. This is my third.'

Brennan took it out of his hand. 'Get yourself an orange juice.'

'What? I thought I was off duty.'

'You are … And I'd like it to stay that way for both of us, so orange juice for you tonight.'

'Yes, sir.' McGuire slumped off.

'And I told you about that before.'

A nod, thin smile, paired with a wink.

Brennan walked over to the table where Lauder and Bryce sat. He took his pint with him and put it down as he greeted them. Bryce stood up. 'Sit down, Brycey,' said Brennan. 'Just coming over to give my best to the team.'

Lauder looked away, sneering. He picked up a glass and tipped it back; the ends of his moustache caught stray static around the rim as he lowered his drink. 'Very kind of you, Rob. I'll be sure to bear it in mind when I'm making up the duty roster next week.'

Laughter rung out around the table. Brennan looked at Bryce, who seemed embarrassed; he was a good enough sort, but Lauder was digging a grave for himself.

Brennan picked up his pint again. 'Don't get too cocky now, Ian. There's a bit of time left before you get your feet under the table.'

Lauder smoothed down the edges of his moustache.

'You're joking, aren't you? … Expecting to clean it up on the weekend?'

'Stranger things have happened.'

'Not fucking many. I think you're delusional, son. We want to get that Fuller woman a more powerful torch to shine in your ear.'

A couple of sneers turned to laughter, but most stayed quiet around the table now. Lauder had stepped over the line; Brennan knew it and so did everyone else. Bryce got out of his seat. 'Come on, Rob, I'll get you a drink.'

Brennan put a cold eye on Lauder as he turned for the bar. His pulse kicked, adrenaline spiked, but he had mastered keeping those out of sight long ago.

'Sorry about Ian,' said Bryce. 'He's a prick sometimes.'

'Just sometimes?'

'Well, most of the time. Look, don't let him get to you, eh.'

Brennan touched the detective's elbow. 'It's fine, Brycey.

Go and enjoy your night. You had a good result, the boys deserve it.'

Bryce returned to the table and McGuire approached, orange juice in hand. 'What was all that about?'

'That? … Nothing at all.'

Brennan took another sip from his pint and watched an exchange of words between Bryce and Lauder; there seemed to be a disagreement. Brennan wished he could place money on the outcome. Lauder rose from his seat and plucked his drink from the table. A beer mat stuck to the base of the glass as he quaffed the last few swallows. The mat hung on for a few seconds then floated to the floor. Lauder slammed down the glass and stomped for the door. Bryce raised his hands in mock defiance but he was flagged down.

'Right, Stevie, you ready to roll?' said Brennan.

'What? I just got this orange juice – two fucking quid it cost.'

'I'll buy you one later, come on.'

Brennan followed Lauder out onto the street. He watched him get into his car and put his phone to his ear.

'You parked nearby, Stevie?'

'Yeah, back of the pictures.'

'Right, get your car. Stay in contact on the phone, not on the radio.'

McGuire looked at Brennan, turned his cheek away.

'What's going on here?'

'Just do it, eh. And hurry up. I'm over there so I'll be on his bumper. I'll phone to let you know where he goes.

If I think he might have picked me up, I'll hand over to you. Okay?'

'Yes, fine.'

'Good. Now move it. We don't want to lose him before he gets rolling.'

Brennan dashed across the road and got into the Passat – the car started first time. He waited a moment for the traffic to clear and then turned the vehicle round in the street. He was sitting in the road, three or four cars back, as Lauder pulled out.

Brennan took out his phone as he drove, placed it in the hands-free cradle on the dash and called McGuire.

'Stevie, that's me following behind Lauder now. He's heading out towards London Road …'

'Right, I'm not too far behind you – just at the junction, waiting for a break.'

'Fine. I'll keep you tuned in.'

Brennan followed Lauder down London Road, through two sets of traffic lights, and one set of roadworks. Council contractors had earlier removed diseased trees from the London Road Gardens and loaded them into a truck bed that sat in the road, cutting the four lanes to two. Lothian Buses were tailed back all the way to the junction with Easter Road and the driver at the front of the queue looked ready to ram the bus into the truck bed.

Brennan kept an eye on Lauder's car; he seemed to be slowing down. 'Stevie, think he's pulling up.'

'Right. Where are you?'

'Just at the minimart on the corner. I'm going to pass him – can you take over? He's getting out now.'

'Yes, sure. I'll stop in the bus lane till he moves off again. Stay on the line.'

'Will do.'

Brennan drove down to the Sainsbury's at the end of the road, turned in the car park and headed back in the opposite direction. He was behind a yellow Hyundai as Lauder got back into his car, pulled out.

'He's on the move again, sir.'

'I see him.'

'Okay. I'll stay with him. He's turning at the lights, going up the hill towards Regent Road.'

Brennan waited for the two cars to pass and swung out in pursuit. He could see McGuire's navy Golf sitting a car behind Lauder; as the indicators came on he was already altering his road position.

'Turning for Calton Hill, now, sir.'

'Stay on him.'

As the cars snaked onto the access road behind the old Royal High, Brennan looked out into the park. It was darker than he thought; pitch black. The lights from the cars lit the gravel road ahead but there was little moonlight up above. As Lauder turned to the left, drove past the Monument and headed for the car park, Brennan told McGuire to pull back.

'Right, ease up, Stevie. Let him get parked.'

McGuire pulled the Golf into the grass verge. Brennan followed behind him, got out and ran towards the driver's door.

'What's he up to?' said Brennan.

'Search me. Scouting for a fucking rent boy?'

Brennan turned down the corners of his mouth. 'Lauder? He's as straight as me.'

'This is Calton Hill. Something you want to tell me, boss?'

'Fuck off ... Come on, and bring that torch.'

Brennan took off for the car park; McGuire jogged behind him. As they passed the National Monument they spotted Lauder parking up. Brennan turned, flagged McGuire to stop.

He crouched behind the base of the Monument. 'What's going on?'

'He's getting out, hang on.' Brennan ducked back down.

'Did he see you?'

He peered over the rim. 'No. He was just checking.'

Brennan watched Lauder walk towards a small hatchback.

He looked round again, then opened the passenger door.

'Right, follow me. Stay out of the road, though.'

Brennan hugged the bushes all the way up the side of the gravel path. When the gravel gave out he stuck to the grass verges and crouched low to the ground. As he got closer to the car he saw there were two people inside. He could make out the silhouette of their heads as they spoke.

Edging nearer, Brennan saw the car was a small red Astra – it looked vaguely familiar.

'Do you recognise that car, Stevie?'

Headshakes. 'No. Should I?'

Brennan smiled. 'Maybe not.' He held out his hand. 'Give me the torch.'

'What are you going to do?'

Brennan looked over to the car; the two heads that had been sitting up had disappeared. 'Wait till you hear those springs going, then follow me.'

'Christ, has he got a bird in there?'

'Better hope it's a bird.'

The car started to move, almost imperceptibly at first, but then with more force. Soon the suspension screeched.

'Right. Let's go.'

Brennan made his way swiftly to the car. He got level with the passenger door before he put the torch on. The windows were steamed up as he tapped on the door. He pointed McGuire round to the other side of the car as he removed his warrant card and leaned over, opened the door.

'Hello, there.'

There was a shriek from the girl on the back seat.

'Jesus Christ,' said Lauder.

Brennan smiled, looked in, warrant card in hand. 'Think you better get your pants on, Ian.'

'Fucking hell, it's you!'

'The very man,' he pointed to the other window, indicated McGuire, 'but not alone.'

Lauder did a quick left-to-right. The girl on the seat started to whimper.

'Hello again … Aylish, isn't it? From the *News* if I'm not mistaken.'

Lauder arked up, 'I'll fucking swing for you, Brennan.'

A laugh, tip of the head. 'I think your swinging days are well and truly over, mate.'

Chapter 44

BRENNAN WALKED AWAY FROM THE car, went to McGuire's side and directed him to start writing down the details. McGuire nodded and made himself busy. As the DC strolled around the vehicle the front door was flung open and Lauder got out. He planted his feet heavily on the ground as he stood and did up his belt buckle. His face was white; Brennan emphasised the point by shining the torch on it.

'Get that fucking thing out my eyes,' snapped Lauder.

'Watch your tone – you're talking to an arresting officer here.'

'Jesus, Rob, you're not serious.'

Brennan looked him up and down. 'Oh, you better believe it.' He peered over Lauder's shoulder, towards the dishevelled Aylish in the car. 'She doesn't look very happy. Mind you, she's probably going to lose her job as well.' He moved towards McGuire, said, 'Aylish Dunn's her name ... Get some details, Stevie.'

'Yes, sir.'

Lauder tucked in his shirt tails. 'Come on, Rob ... We can at least talk about this, surely.' He pulled Brennan away from the Astra.

Brennan smirked. 'You've got to be fucking joking ... You've been feeding this piece more than your boaby, Lauder. Do you think my head zips up the back?'

'You can't prove that!'

Brennan laughed, 'I just found you up to your nuts in a reporter from the *News*, the same paper that's been putting out leaked details on the force's most high-profile murder case in a decade, and you're asking me for proof. Fucking grow sense, lad ... One speck of this dirt is enough to finish you.'

Lauder's expression was unreadable; his eyes seemed to have sunk into his head. There was no colour left in his complexion. He looked towards the car and Brennan followed his line of vision. The girl inside was crying harder now, her face in her hands.

'They'll throw her to the wolves, Rob. She's only young – her career will be over before it gets started.'

Brennan kept his gaze fixed on the reporter. He had some sympathy for her – she'd been used. The one who deserved to pay was

Lauder. 'I'll tell you what I'll do for you, old mate. I'll give Stevie there the weekend to type this up. If your resignation's on Galloway's desk first thing Monday morning, I'll keep her out of it.'

'Resignation!' He put fingers to his mouth, gasped. 'Is it that bad?'

Brennan smiled. 'No, *mate*, it's that good.' He patted the side of the DI's arm. 'Get that girl home.'

As Lauder walked away Brennan's phone started to ring.

'Oh, one more thing, Lauder, before you go: I want all your files on the Limping Man.'

'*What?*'

'You heard – everything. And I want them right away, before your resignation goes in.' He answered the phone, 'Brennan.'

It was Lou. 'Boss, we've had a development.'

'Go on.' McGuire walked to stand beside him, as Lauder joined the distraught girl.

'We sent a unit round to one of the dealers on the list …'

'Who?'

'Serious piece of work called Devlin McArdle.'

'Carry on.'

Lou's voice peaked and troughed; he seemed to be struggling to get the words out quick enough. 'The uniforms found McArdle's wife on the living-room floor. She'd dragged herself from the kitchen with a nine-inch blade in her back.'

'God Almighty.'

'It gets worse. There was a child's cradle … toys and Pampers. Neighbours said they didn't have children but the wife was seen with a baby yesterday.'

Brennan took a deep breath. He could feel his heart thumping in his chest. 'Where's McArdle?'

'That's it, sir. No sign of him. Or the kid.'

'Jesus …'

Lou's voice lit: 'There is an up to this, boss …'

'*What's that?*'

'Melanie McArdle, the wife – she's hanging in. She's in intensive care at the Royal. Lost a barrel of blood but she's still with us.'

'Is she talking?'

'No, sir. Out cold.'

Brennan pointed McGuire to the car. 'Right, I'm on my way there now, Lou. Plaster McArdle's face all over the place; I want airports and ports from here to the fucking white cliffs of Dover on alert and every force in the country notified. Now.'

'Yes, sir.'

He hung up.

McGuire looked quizzical. 'What's going on?'

'We've got our man.'

'What?'

Brennan ran for the car. 'Come on. We've got to get to the Royal.'

On the road to the hospital Brennan relayed the conversation he'd just had with Lou to McGuire. The DC rocked forward in the driver's seat, gripped the wheel. 'I know this guy's name.'

'They call him the Deil ... Nasty piece of work.'

'But he's a dealer, right. What on earth does he want with the kid?'

'You tell me, Stevie ... You tell me.'

Brennan looked at the road ahead, the fizz of orange street lamps, the blur of car headlights as the traffic snaked its way through the city. His heart rattled off his ribs; his mind stumbled from thoughts about the missing child and her murdered mother to the minister and the manse house in Pitlochry where things had all gone so wrong for them. This city swallowed people whole, he thought. Edinburgh took people from all points of the compass and used them for its own end. It was no place for the weak or the insecure, the lonely or the dependent. The city's streets were bright under the street lamps but they hid the shadows and the darkness that lurked there. Carly had come to the city to escape her hurts and the place had taken her in, but on its terms. He saw Tierney greeting her at the bus stop, promising her a helping hand and all the time planning what he could take from her, what he could do with this fragile young life that would benefit him, put a few quid in his pocket. Was life so cheap here? This wasn't some war-torn hellhole; this was Edinburgh, this was the capital of a civilised nation. Or so it was claimed.

Brennan opened the window and tried to grab some air, let the cool night's breeze blow on his face. He felt tired, worn down. Emotionally, he had nothing left to give, but he knew he had to carry on. It was his job, and no one else, he was sure, cared about the job as much as he did.

At the hospital McGuire turned a hairpin, brought the small VW into the cross-hatchings where the ambulances parked at the front door. A man in blue-green overalls shouted at them. McGuire approached and showed him his warrant card as Brennan ran for the front desk.

There was a dour woman in her bad fifties behind the counter. She sternly refused to acknowledge the queue of people in front of her. Brennan swept to the front, ignored the protests and slapped a hand down in front of the woman.

'Melanie McArdle.'

'You cannot just come in here and—'

McGuire appeared, card in hand. 'Police!'

The woman removed her glasses, looked to a small computer screen, spoke as she tapped at the mouse in her hand. 'I really should let you speak to a—'

'Spare us, love. Just give us the ward,' said Brennan.

She shook her head, turned to face them and put her glasses back on. 'It's 202. That's two floors up, turn right.'

The officers took off running for the lifts. They sidestepped an operating trolley as they ran for the sliding doors which were closing. Brennan managed to get a hand inside and prise them back. The lift was cramped, night visitors and nurses. A doctor with a clipboard and an old woman in a wheelchair. Brennan could feel the sweat pooling on his spine; he wiped his forehead with the back of his hand as he watched the floor numbers light up. When they reached the second floor he pushed his way to the front to be first out of the doors.

He turned right and ran towards the far end of the corridor, the leather soles of his shoes slapping noisily on the hard tiled floor as he went. A woman in a white coat pinned herself against the wall as Brennan and McGuire dashed for the door marked 202. She seemed to be in shock as they halted before the small glass window and peered in, and then she spoke: 'What's going on here?'

'Who are you?'

The woman held her ground. 'I should be asking you that.'

Brennan removed his wallet, flashed his warrant card.

'DI Robert Brennan, Lothian and Borders Police, and this is DC Stephen McGuire.'

'Oh.' She put a hand in her front pocket, turned a stray brown curl behind her ear with the other. 'You're here with the others.'

'Others?'

'There's been some officers here already. There's still one in there.'

Brennan turned back to the window, peered in. There was a WPC sitting by the bed. He nodded to McGuire to go inside; the DC opened the door.

'How is she? I mean, what's her condition?'

'She's lost a great deal of blood and is still unconscious, but there's no organ damage that we've found. She's very lucky to be alive.'

Brennan bit his lower lip – this wasn't what he had hoped to hear. 'Is she going to recover?'

The doctor peered down the hall. 'It's really too early to say, Inspector. The next few hours will be critical ...' She seemed to be looking for something, someone. 'Look, this is all very irregular. I'm not sure you should be in there at all. The woman has suffered a near-life-threatening trauma.'

'Do you know who that is in there?' said Brennan.

'A woman who was stabbed, very badly. I know, I treated her.'

'Well, unless you live in a bubble, Doctor, you'll know there's been a child missing in Edinburgh ... I'd say that woman you have through there has been looking after her, so she might just be our best chance of finding the kid alive. Does that make sense to you?'

She backed off. 'Look, I need to see the administrator.

I'm not au fait with the procedures for—'

Brennan turned for the door. 'You go tackle the red tape, love – let me know when you've got it in a pretty wee bow, eh.'

As he stepped inside, McGuire looked round, spoke: 'She's out cold, boss.'

Brennan moved towards the bed, nodded to the WPC. 'No change at all?'

'She's sedated ... She's grumbled a bit and moved about some, but no words,' said the uniform.

Brennan looked over Melanie McArdle's face. She was bruised and beaten. Black stitches sat out proud from her forehead and a white bandage had been taped across her nose; he wondered what horrors it disguised. The woman had been savaged. No one should have to go through that, he thought.

Brennan turned away, walked to the window and looked out into the night sky. The city was sleeping now, but he knew there would be no rest for him until McArdle was found. He removed his coat, pulled out a chair. 'Go home and get some sleep, you pair.'

They looked at each other. 'I think we'd sooner wait, sir,' said McGuire.

Brennan sat down, spread his jacket over himself, said, 'Suit yourselves.'

Chapter 45

IT WAS A COLD NIGHT. Brennan wondered how the patients in the hospital must be feeling. Was there no heating in these places? Were the cutbacks biting so deep? He tried to get comfortable on the chair, but his lower back ached whichever way he turned. He tried not to think about how much rested on Melanie McArdle coming round, revealing what she knew … If she knew anything.

The woman had nearly been killed, brutally stabbed through the back – what were the chances of her talking after that kind of going-over? In Brennan's experience, the wives were often harder to crack than the criminals themselves. It took something spectacular to put them over the edge, into that territory where things like pride and loyalty no longer mattered; was Melanie there yet? He hoped she was, for the child's sake, but he knew for Melanie it meant starting again from scratch. At her age, with her baggage, that was never going to be easy.

Brennan turned in the chair again. A draught blew under the door and caught his ankles; he raised his feet, put them on the edge of the bed. Melanie hadn't moved since he'd arrived. A doctor had come in and confirmed that they could stay; he also said there was nothing else they could do for the woman. It was all in God's hands. They needed to let her rest, let the body try and repair itself. He put her chances at somewhere close to fifty–fifty.

Brennan gave up on trying to get comfortable, got out of the chair. McGuire stirred: 'Boss?'

'Go back to sleep.'

The WPC was awake, watching over the patient. Brennan approached her, whispered, 'If there's any movement, send Stevie for me.'

'Yes, sir.'

'Don't leave her alone – that's important.'

A nod, then a thin smile.

Brennan headed for the white door, turned the handle and walked into the blinding light of the corridor. His eyes smarted as they took some time to adjust and he raised his knuckles to rub at them. He knew he'd gone too long without a cigarette and could feel the empty space in his chest cavity calling out for nicotine. He took the lift to the ground floor, walked towards the car park. Outside the night air was crisp and fresh; there was a hint of rain blowing in the cool breeze and it threatened more to come, a downpour, perhaps.

Brennan took out his mobile phone, checked his messages: there was one, from Sophie. His daughter rarely texted. He took the sight of her name in his inbox as a jolt, quickly opened up.

The message read: 'I saw you on the telly, about the missing girl. I'm sorry for disappearing, Mum said you were worried about me but I'm fine and going to be on my best behaviour now. Sophie xx.'

Brennan knew Joyce had put her up to it, but it didn't matter. In a strange way, it meant more. He had support, people, a family. He thought about the picture of Lorraine's baby in his pocket and wondered what that was going to do to them. He didn't want to hurt Sophie, or Joyce. He didn't want to hurt Lorraine either, but he knew that whatever he did was going to hurt someone.

Brennan put his phone back in his pocket and removed his cigarettes. He only had Silk Cut left again and the taste didn't match his craving. He smoked one almost to the filter, then lit another from the tip of the last. He took long drags on the cigarette, taking the smoke deep into his lungs, but it did nothing for him. He had a spinning sensation in his head; his thoughts wouldn't stop racing around after each other. When things were going well, he didn't worry about this state of mind, but when things were a mess, *everything* started to get messy. The thought process seemed to speed up, chase more and more unrealistic solutions to the problems he occupied himself with.

In his mind right now the situation with Devlin McArdle was uppermost; he wanted to know where he was. He wanted to get McArdle into custody right away, because he knew that, at this minute, McArdle's only thought was to dispose of the child. Brennan didn't like to think how he was going to get rid of it; he knew there were people who would pay big money for a child, but the type of people McArdle was dealing with wouldn't want to buy the kid cuddly toys from Mothercare.

Carly Donald had died. Then there was Sproul, Tierney and Durrant – no loss there, but he didn't want to see Melanie McArdle added to the list. He knew she'd been attacked for getting in the way. McArdle was obviously keeping the child at home – had Melanie grown attached to it? Had she discovered what he planned to do with it?

Whatever it was, she had paid for trying to intervene.

Brennan dropped his cigarette, stamped it out. He looked to the night sky; he could see the lights of the city reflected on the low covering of cloud. He shook his head and tucked his hands in his pockets, dug deep. Galloway was going to go off like a bloody rocket when she heard about this turn of events. The media would be chasing for weeks to get the full story; it would be pandemonium at the office. Somehow the thought didn't faze him. After the time off, the bustle actually appealed. What he didn't want to look ahead to was the wrong outcome – he tried to stay focused, imagine the best possible sequence of events. He concentrated on things playing out how he wanted them to. To do anything less was to invite the worst into your ambit, he thought. He wouldn't do that. He would keep his eye on the outcome he wanted to achieve, which was catching McArdle before he split. Brennan wanted to hand that child back to its grandparents and to have the satisfaction of knowing it was safe. Her mother had died, he could do nothing about that, but poor Beth, she still had a chance.

Brennan turned away from the car park, headed back to the hospital. He pressed the button for the lift and looked up to see that it was already coming down. As the doors pinged, he was nearly mowed down by DC Stevie McGuire.

'There you are … It's Melanie. She's coming round!'

Brennan pushed him back into the lift. 'Then what are we waiting for?'

They listened to the machinery above pulling them upwards, and watched the floors light. The process seemed to take much longer than Brennan remembered.

'Has she spoken?' he said.

'Just a few words.'

'*What*? What did she say?'

McGuire took his eyes off the dial, looked at Brennan then returned his gaze. 'She asked for water … She was parched.'

'Who's with her now?'

'The WPC.'

'You'll have to call the doctor in.'

'Have done; he's on his way down.'

'Good.'

The lift stalled, then came to a halt. Brennan moved a step closer to the door, leaned in, waited for the gap to appear. 'Come on. Come on.'

As the doors sprung he squeezed through, leapt out to the corridor.

Brennan ran towards the door. The bright lights didn't bother him now. As he ducked inside the room, he caught sight of a man in a white coat leaning over the patient; he turned round, flashed large brown eyes at them. 'Can you give me a moment, please?'

Brennan nodded.

The doctor rose. '*Alone*, please, with the patient.'

'I'd like to see her, if that's all right.'

The doctor raised his arms, put one hand on Brennan's elbow and the other on McGuire's shoulder. 'Out! Right now. There'll be time enough to see the patient once I have examined her. Now please, gentlemen, a bit of decorum if you don't mind.'

Brennan and McGuire walked backwards towards the door they had just come through; the doctor shut them out.

'Jesus,' said McGuire.

'He's just doing his job.'

'But still, did he have to be so blunt?'

Brennan walked to the wall, leaned his back against it, tapped his heel off the skirting. 'How did she look?'

McGuire huffed, 'Not great. What do you expect?'

'He's giving her fifty–fifty to pull through.'

McGuire moved to the wall beside Brennan, leaned his shoulder there. 'I think he's being generous. I don't think I've seen a worse battering.'

Brennan nodded. 'She looks like she's been hit with a steamroller.'

They stood staring at the door for a moment, then the handle dropped and the doctor appeared. He was putting a pen in his top pocket, removing his white coat. As he greeted them he threw the coat over his shoulder.

'Sorry about that, gentlemen. There's a way I like to do these things – you get a bit tetchy as you get older.'

Brennan nodded, blinked. 'How is she?'

The doctor pinned back the sides of his mouth, sighed. 'I can't say there's any improvement. She's coming round and she's in a lot of pain. I've given her something for that but she has lost a lot of blood and there's always so much you just can't know when someone's been so badly hurt ...'

'What are you saying?'

'Inspector, she's lucky to be alive.' The doctor took a few steps down the corridor, turned. 'Don't spend more than five minutes in there –

she needs to rest.'

'Yes, Doctor.'

Brennan walked back to the room. The WPC was sitting down beside Melanie McArdle; the woman's head was turned towards the window. She seemed to be strapped in by the tight white sheets and blankets.

McGuire spoke first: 'Melanie, my name's DC Stephen McGuire and this is Detective Inspector Brennan. We'd like to talk to you about what happened.'

Brennan waved the DC away, moved round to the other side of the bed and sat down in front of Melanie, blocking her view of the window. He could see her eyes were bloodied, dark fraught tangles of ruptured capillaries. There were tears too, welling below the irises, waiting to roll down her face.

'Hello, Melanie,' said Brennan. 'Can you speak?'

She opened her mouth slowly, a whisper: 'Yes.'

'I don't want to tire you out, so let me know if I am asking too much … Can you tell me, did Devlin do this to you?'

She seemed to sink deeper into herself at the mention of her husband's name. Her eyes misted some more, then a tear ran down her cheek. 'He … stabbed me.'

Brennan watched her slow breath; each gasp seemed to be an agony. He edged closer. 'What happened?'

Melanie's breathing reached a sibilant wheeze. 'The baby …'

'What about the baby?'

She looked directly at Brennan. 'Where is she?'

Brennan caught McGuire's eye. He turned back to Melanie. 'We don't know.'

She curled her lower lip; it trembled for a second or two and then her whole body seemed to shake as she descended into tears.

The WPC leaned over, touched her hand. 'It's okay, Melanie, it's okay.'

'No, he's taken her … He's taken her.'

Brennan spoke: 'Where's he taken her, Melanie?'

She paused. Then: 'I don't know.'

Brennan watched her in misery. He could see it was painful for her to think of what McArdle must have done with the child. 'Do you have any idea?'

'No. No.' The tears continued.

'Melanie, you must have heard something. You must have seen something … Who was he holding the baby for?'

Melanie pushed away the WPC's hand; she brought her fingers to her eyes, wiped away the tears. 'The news … he saw the news on the television and went mad. He was panicked.'

'Then what happened?'

She seemed to be trying to retrace her steps. 'We fought, over the baby. I had the knife – he took it off me.'

'Go on.'

Melanie's words gathered power. 'He came after me, stabbed me.'

'Then what?'

Her breathing seemed to have stilled. 'I fell. I lay on the ground. I could feel the knife in my stomach.'

'Where was Devlin?'

'He was in the kitchen, then the living room … He was shouting, speaking to someone on the phone.'

'Who was he speaking to?'

Melanie curled her fingers, touched her lips with the tips of her nails. 'It was the German … Günter.'

Brennan nodded to McGuire; he wrote down the name.

'Carry on, Melanie, you're doing fine.'

She removed her hand, looked at Brennan. Thoughts and memories seemed to spark behind her eyes. 'He said … he was going to … Liverpool.'

'Liverpool?'

Melanie turned her face towards the pillow. She looked exhausted now. 'Yes. I heard him say it – he was meeting the German in Liverpool.'

Brennan got out of the chair. He touched Melanie's hand.

'You've done very well, love. Now get some rest.'

She opened her eyes again; they were thin slits as she spoke: 'What about the baby?'

Brennan couldn't answer her.

Chapter 46

DEVLIN McARDLE HAD DRIVEN THROUGH the night with a screaming child and a sense of the world closing in on him. In the space of a few hours the comfortable life he'd known in Edinburgh had ended. He knew there was no way back; even if he offloaded the baby, took full payment and moved on he would be running for years. The plea on the television by the minister played over and over in his head. 'Fucking telly,' he roared. 'Fucking telly's onto me.'

He gripped the wheel tightly. There was a hint of rain in the air, the sun was up and that made him feel even more nervous. In the dark, at night, the blackness made you feel safe. He'd never understood people who were afraid of the dark, he thought; dark was good. No one could see you in the dark. It was when the place was all lit up, when people started to take to the streets that you got nervous – that's when you got caught.

'Bastards stitched me up!'

He cursed Tierney and Vee for getting him involved; it was all their fault. He'd told Tierney if he was up to something it would be the last trick he ever pulled and he was right about that. 'Told you, didn't I, Barry? Told you nobody messes with the Deil.'

Tierney got his, and Vee, he thought.

Stupid pair of bastards, out on the razz when the television folk are all over them. Out drinking it up, smashed out their heads. What were they thinking?

If the police had got hold of that pair, they'd have been coming down with the sweats in a few hours, begging for a hit. They'd have told the filth anything they wanted to know. They knew he wasn't going to take that chance.

'No way. No way.'

The road ahead narrowed as McArdle came off the motorway; he kept his eyes alert to the signs for the turnoff he'd been told about. There was a service station, a Little Chef, with a big car park and a BP garage somewhere on this road. If he could find that, one of his problems would be solved.

'Shut the fuck up!' he yelled at the child in the back seat.

The baby screamed louder, kicked her feet.

Did she know? Had she been listening to all his talk on the phone with Günter?

'What you on about?' McArdle wondered if he was cracking up, losing his mind. Of course the baby couldn't understand – she had no idea what he was doing.

But he knew.

'Not my problem. No fucker looked out for me.'

Life was hard, you had to be hard. He couldn't afford to think about what he was doing; it was survival of the fittest. He'd heard that phrase once before and it made sense to him. Life was survival – it's what his had been all about.

When McArdle spotted the sign for the turn-off he dropped a gear, went into fourth and brought the needle under fifty. He was surprised to see so many cars, and trucks. Lots of truckers. Lazy bastards, truckers, he thought. All those mad murders he'd read about in the papers were truckers. Beasts and murderers. Had to be mad to be a trucker, spending all that time driving up and down the same road day in, day out. And then, sleeping in a cab the size of a bloody toilet cubicle. They were all beasts and murderers, that's what they were.

As the thought subsided, McArdle's mind returned to the moment when he'd put the knife in Melanie's back. For a second he felt something for her – was that shame? Hurt?

He blocked it out. 'The bitch asked for it!'

The baby screamed louder.

He turned, roared, 'Shut it! Shut it!'

She did ask for it, Melanie. She'd taken a knife to him; he couldn't have that. He was Devlin McArdle, the Deil. People knew him. He couldn't have his own wife showing him up.

But what would people say about him if they knew?

'Nothing. I'm the Deil! Who would mess?'

There was a voice in his head that jeered him. The voice taunted him with what he'd done. He'd killed his wife, Melanie. He'd had Tierney and Vee killed too. And he'd taken a child, a child he didn't know a thing about, and was going to hand it over to a gang of paedophiles.

'So fucking what? It's not my lookout! It's not my kid!'

Did it matter whose kid it was?

He didn't think about the baby he'd taken from Tierney and Vee, two junkie lowlifes from Muirhouse. Why would he think about a kid like that? So what was it that was different about this kid? Was it because she had been talked about on the television? The minister, on the news. The police, everyone looking for her. This was big news

– big, big news.

McArdle smacked the side of his head with the flat of his hand. 'No. No.'

He wanted the rolling of thoughts to stop. He knew if he was caught now, he was finished. He'd be in Peterhead.

He'd be in with the beasts.

'I'm not a fucking beast!'

He'd be in with the beasts, because that's what they'd say he was. He'd have to be separated from the other prisoners because every day someone would be trying to kill him, stab him. That's what they did with beasts.

'I'm not a fucking beast!'

As McArdle lowered the speed, put the needle under thirty, he steered into the car park. The Little Chef was open but there didn't seem to be anyone inside. He drove around to the BP garage. There was a green Skoda being filled up by a man in a grey suit. A sales rep; there were always sales reps about these places, no matter what time of the day it was. McArdle felt comforted by the sight of the man – he was a connection to the safe, normal world. A rep, just a salesman. Someone like him, sort of. That's all it was – a transaction. He would hand over the child and take the money, then disappear. It was a sales job, that's all.

He drove round past the overnight truck stop and spotted what he was looking for. The silver Citroën estate, with German number plates. He could see Günter behind the wheel, staring out from behind those thick dark glasses of his. He wore driving gloves, brown leather ones with rope backs. As he spotted McArdle he raised a hand, waved.

McArdle nodded, put in the clutch and selected third gear.

The German didn't move again as McArdle drew up beside him, rolled down the window.

'Günter,' he called out.

The German kept eyes front, pressed a button to lower the window. 'Put the baby in the back with Frank.'

The child was screaming. McArdle didn't want to go near her but he wanted rid. He removed his seat belt and then turned to open his door. When he got out of the car he felt his knees buckle; his legs had grown weary after the long journey but he stamped some life back into them.

The baby screamed louder as he removed the fastenings on the cradle carrier. Her face was red and her eyes tightened as she wailed out. 'Christ Almighty, can't you shut the fuck up?' It was almost at an end; he was about to hand the child over. He felt relieved – why couldn't she be quiet? The baby let out an ear-splitting shriek. How could something so small make so much noise? And why? Did she know? Why did he keep thinking that? Why did the thought keep pressing on his mind?

The man in the back of the Citroën leaned over and opened the door; McArdle passed in the screaming child. Her face was scarlet as the man called Frank took her. McArdle caught sight of the smile he gave to the child and then he watched him wet his lips and place a small kiss on the baby's mouth. McArdle didn't look back after he saw that. The sight of the red-faced howling baby with the smiling beast made him feel uneasy.

He moved towards Günter. 'Well, that's that.'

'Is it?' said the German.

'What do you mean?'

'I mean you failed to inform us of the current situation with the police.' Günter touched the rim of his glasses; the lenses were dirty.

'Look, you wanted the fucking kid, you got it, now turn over the cash or I'll have to get nasty.'

Günter looked in the rear-view mirror, seemed content with the noisy bundle back there. He reached under the front seat and removed a small package. 'Here it is. Less than we agreed.'

'It better fucking not be—'

Günter raised a hand. 'We will incur some expenses to evade the police on our return – we now have to drive back through France. We have deducted the extra costs, and something for our inconvenience.'

McArdle leaned in, grabbed his throat. 'You never fucking said anything about that.'

The German choked out his words: 'And you never said anything about the police. If you like, we can give you the child back and go our separate ways.'

McArdle turned for a final glance at the noisy baby. As she roared, her round cheeks darkened and her tiny fingers pressed the air. As quickly as he had turned, he looked away. McArdle wanted to strangle the beast where he sat, but more than that he wanted to leave. 'Get out my fucking sight.' He grabbed the money and then, stepping back, he pushed the German's head against the steering wheel.

The Citroën sped off. McArdle watched the fumes pouring from the exhaust. He tucked the small bundle of notes inside his jacket and headed back towards his car. The rain had started to get heavy.

Chapter 47

DEVLIN McARDLE WATCHED A LORRY manoeuvring through the car park. It looked awkward as the cab reversed its giant tail through more lanes than he could count. He could see the driver struggling to right the truck, make sense of where he had come to rest, and McArdle felt at ease.

He was over the worst of it, surely. The child was off his hands; all he had to do was lie low for a time and then he could think about his next move. He had some money; he had no ties. McArdle knew he had always done okay on his own. He didn't need Melanie. In fact it was better she was out of the way because she would only go blabbing to the police.

'She had it bloody well coming,' he mouthed to himself. 'Better off without the bitch.'

McArdle started the car's engine, rolled slowly through the gears until he hit the small network of roads that connected up the service stops. He spotted the Little Chef – he was hungry now – and pointed the wheel towards the front bays. He could see there was a drive-through hatch but it was too early in the day to be manned. He parked up, listened to the engine cooling for a moment and then he went inside.

The restaurant seemed instantly familiar, although he'd never actually been there before; it was the same as every other one of a thousand restaurants like it. Blond-wood laminate flooring, geometrically arranged tables and chairs with wipe-down menus everywhere. He spotted the sign for the Gents and made his way past what looked like an artificial plant to get cleaned up.

The toilet room was bright, harsh lights reflecting off clean white tiles. At first he felt uneasy there, as if he was in a spotlight, but after he'd relieved himself, washed his face and neck, splashed water on his scalp, McArdle started to feel calmer, more like his old self.

The bandage he'd put on his hand had begun to seep blood again. He scrunched his fingers into a fist and watched the red ooze from beneath the cotton. He knew it would need to be replaced; the cut probably needed stitching – the worst one on his arm definitely did – but he would live without that. He couldn't risk visiting a hospital and being questioned by the medical staff about how he'd come by such serious wounds.

McArdle put his hand under the dryer, let the warm air remove the moisture. When he was satisfied he tipped his head under the dryer, let the hot jets massage his aching neck for a few minutes. McArdle's hand still needed attention. He went to the cubicles and removed a roll of toilet paper, wrapped a long stretch round his hand. It looked bulky now. He tried to pat down the tissue paper but it only sprang back. He looked at himself in the mirror: he seemed to be wearing one white boxing glove; it made him laugh. He fronted up to his reflection and started shadow boxing. 'Yo! Rocky! Rocky!' He laughed as he swung a final hook on his way to the door.

The restaurant staff were stationed behind a long counter. As he approached he checked out the menu. There were a lot of breakfast combinations: beans, bacon, toast, eggs. As he made his mind up he became aware of a television playing to his left, a small screen like the one Melanie used to have in the kitchen. He tried not to think about home, but when he turned to have a look he couldn't help but be reminded.

The staff in the Little Chef were crowded round the end of the counter as they watched the breakfast programme's newsreader going through a spiel. McArdle had little interest; he watched desultorily as the young reporter talked about a Liverpool murder hunt. If she had said Edinburgh, he might have been more interested, but who knew he was in Liverpool?

'Hey! ... Any chance of some service here?'

The staff turned away from the screen in unison, then one of them separated from the small pack of bodies and slouched towards McArdle, glancing back at the others as she went.

'About time,' he said. 'My belly thinks my throat's been cut.'

He made his order but the waitress struggled with his heavy Scots accent, made him repeat it.

'Beans. Toast. Bacon.' He said the words slowly, as though he was talking to an infant, or an imbecile. 'And coffee ... You get all that, or you want me to write it down?'

He rolled his eyes, caught sight of the rest of the staff watching him. He'd raised his voice and attracted attention to himself. They looked at him and he raised his bandaged hand in a salute, touched his right eye and smiled before ducking and weaving for show. 'Rocky, innit!'

They didn't get the joke, or didn't find it funny.

The group had no interest in him; they were too taken with the tragic series of events being relayed by the newsreader and returned to the screen.

'The latest victim attached to one of the country's most high-profile murder cases is a thirty-four-year-old woman who passed away in hospital early this morning.'

McArdle rested against the counter, waiting for his breakfast to arrive. The waitress who had taken his order returned to the crowd at the other end of the room, transfixed by the television.

'Police have not named the woman but say she was directly linked to the case of the murdered Pitlochry schoolgirl Carly Donald.'

McArdle registered the name at once. He turned around, senses alert.

'The schoolgirl's mutilated body was found in an Edinburgh housing scheme earlier this week, but her baby daughter, Beth, has not been seen since. Police have now issued this picture of a man they are seeking in connection with the murders. Devlin McArdle is believed to be extremely dangerous and members of the public are advised not to approach him.'

As McArdle heard his name, saw his photograph flash on the screen, his knees went weak. His heart seemed to have stopped beating in his chest and relocated to his throat. He felt a tight band gripping him round the neck as he watched the news report continue with images of armed police officers stationed at various points around the city. *'Police say they have definite information linking McArdle to Liverpool and have increased their presence in and around the city centre and main transport hubs.'*

McArdle didn't wait for his breakfast to arrive. He backed away from the counter, at first slowly, then, turning, he broke into a sprint. As he dashed for the car, he didn't look back. His heart had started to beat in his chest again, much faster than he could ever remember it. When he got the door open, he was shaking so hard he could hardly get the key into the ignition. He tried but his trembling fingers wouldn't obey him and he dropped the bunch down beside the pedals.

'Oh, fucking hell,' he hollered. He had to open the door again and get out to retrieve the keys. When he had them, he used both hands to locate the slot, and then got back in the car. He spun tyres as he left the parking space and raced through the intricate connecting roads back to the motorway. As he travelled, he felt himself rocking in his seat; he gripped at the lever with his left hand and tried to work his way up the gears. He knew he risked being caught for speeding, but he also knew he needed to get far away from the city of Liverpool.

'Fuck!' He pounded the wheel with his head.

How did they find him? Who knew? There was no one except the beasts. Had they been lifted already? He couldn't think straight. Nothing made sense any more. All McArdle wanted to do was hide, to find somewhere where no one could get him.

He overtook a bread van heading out of the city and then weaved back into the left-hand lane. He sat there for only a few seconds before he was close enough to read the bumper stickers on a Nissan and then he pulled out again. He decided to stay in the middle lane for as long as he could – traffic was still quite light but it was building. He could see the commuter belt starting to feed in; but they were going into the centre and he was fleeing.

As McArdle pumped the wheel, the wound on his hand started to weep once more. He saw the blood run down his wrist and towards his shirtsleeve. The sight of the red stream made him nervous, but he didn't know why. There was no real reason for it. Everything seemed to be conspiring against him. He felt trapped by fate.

He passed under a flyover and noticed a sign for a slip road. He eased out to the fast lane to let in any traffic that was entering; there didn't appear to be any. He seemed to have the road to himself. For the next few minutes he pushed the needle higher and kept his eyes straight ahead, waiting, expecting to see some more traffic, but none appeared. Soon the sight of the empty road played on his mind: where was everyone?

'Why the fuck is the road empty?' he mouthed.

He passed another slip road, then spotted something in front of him – what was it? As he came closer he thought perhaps his eyes were playing tricks on him. For a moment, it seemed to McArdle that there were two cars, identical mirror images of each other, blocking the lanes in front. As he tried to focus his eyes, another one of his senses was assailed by loud sirens wailing from behind him. When he looked in the mirror McArdle saw that the flashing blue lights speeding from the slip road were police cars; turning forward again, he could see the two cars blocking the road ahead were also police cars.

'Shit! Shit! Shit!'

McArdle tried to think, but his mind shut down.

Chapter 48

DI ROB BRENNAN COULDN'T REMEMBER the last time he'd
been to Edinburgh Airport. If it was for a holiday, he couldn't place
it. For some reason, those moments – the ones everyone else lived
for – never sat so near the repeat button on his memory. He could
still channel the summer holidays he'd spent with Andy, when they
were boys: the trips to Banff, the boat rides across the water to Ar-
ran. But they were remembered for an altogether different reason;
Andy hadn't been so close to his thoughts when he was alive and the
guilt burned Brennan every day.

He looked at his watch – the Liverpool detectives were due in now.
He'd managed to get out of the station without being tripped up by
any of the press pack and he was grateful for that, but he didn't want
to be seen hanging about mob-handed in such a public place for too
long. Brennan had brought three officers and four uniforms in an un-
marked wagon. The windows were blacked out and he was pleased
about that; there would be enough pictures of McArdle circulating
soon.

The Liverpool police had said the prisoner was subdued, no bother
at all, but Brennan knew they hadn't got the tough job of prising information out of him. He was prepared for a long night of it. He was
prepared to give it whatever it took to crack the bastard.

McGuire sidled up, looked about the place, spoke: 'This is taking
too long.'

'Ease up, Stevie,' said Brennan.

He looked at Lou and Brian; they were shuffling their feet nervously.

'I can't believe we picked him up,' said the DC.

Brennan nodded. 'It was touch and go there for a bit.'

'Pure luck, I'd say.'

'Do you think so?'

'That or somebody was looking out for us.'

Brennan dismissed the suggestion, turned to face McGuire.

'The daft bastard walked into a Little Chef and started acting the
Big I Am whilst his picture was being flashed across the airwaves.
Who or what do you think was looking out for us – the ghost of

Tommy Cooper? It was bloody comical.'

McGuire sniggered. 'If you put it like that.'

Brennan didn't know who was right and who was wrong; he cared even less. He had McArdle in custody and any minute now he was going to have him in an interview room.

'The Scousers say he isn't talking,' said McGuire.

'We'll see about that.'

'He must know he's going down for Melanie's murder at least.' McGuire scratched the back of his head, sighed.

'We've a lot to thank her for.'

Brennan agreed. 'If it wasn't for her ...' He cut himself short. What was the point? Brennan wasn't the kind of man to dabble in what-ifs. 'Look, we've nailed this bastard and if he knows what's good for him, he'll turn that child over to us quick smart.'

McGuire looked away, dropped his gaze to his shoes.

'You think she's still alive?'

'Jesus Christ, Stevie ... We've got to stay on top of this. There's nothing to suggest she isn't.'

McGuire raised his head. 'There's nothing to suggest she is, sir.'

Brennan didn't have time to reply – the Scouse detectives appeared with the handcuffed McArdle. He watched the prisoner from across the airport barrier. His every step suggested to Brennan that he was scum. His appearance only confirmed it. The short stocky frame. The square shoulders and squat neck. The jailhouse tats on the arms. He was trash. He had killed his own wife in cold blood and then made off with an innocent child to sell into the most depraved trade on earth. Brennan clenched his jaw. He wanted to smash his fist into McArdle's eye but he resisted. He had higher plans for him; he'd see him suffer for his actions soon enough.

The detectives brought over the prisoner, nodded to Brennan. 'All yours, Inspector.'

Brennan reached out a hand to take the paperwork. 'Thank you, lads.'

McGuire stepped forwards and directed Lou and Brian to take McArdle away. There was already a significant crowd gathered to look at what was going on.

Brennan turned back to the Scousers, spoke: 'Safe journey home, lads. And thanks again.'

'No worries, mate. Glad to see this charmer off our patch.'

Brennan and McGuire exchanged brief stares, then watched as Lou and Brian bundled the prisoner down the concourse towards the waiting wagon.

'Now for the hard yards, Stevie.'

'Haven't they all been hard, sir?'

Brennan nodded; the DC had a point. It had already been the most difficult case of his career – and it wasn't over yet. He tried not to think about how it might now play out – how hard it was going to be to get information out of McArdle and how hard it was going to be to find Beth.

When they arrived back at the station the waiting officers and uniforms cheered. Brennan raised a hand; McGuire patted him on the back. It all seemed a bit premature to Brennan – had everyone forgotten about Beth? There was certainly no cause for celebration after Carly's murder. Then there were the others, and the missing child; at least one good family had been destroyed, whatever happened.

The interview-room door looked as it always did, but somehow as Brennan approached it he stalled before the handle. His mind whirred as he took in the prospect of what he was about to do. This was a killer; he had to put him away, but he also needed him to reveal where Beth was. There was no straightforward way to achieve this; there was no manual he could turn to. If he got McArdle on the wrong foot, he could blow it. He could cost the child her life – if she was still alive. He had played criminals like this before and found a way in, a weak spot or some common ground – he hoped he would again.

Brennan brushed his shoulders, straightened his tie. The handle of the door felt cold and firm as he turned it. McGuire was waiting with his back to him, his shoulder blocking the face of McArdle. As he closed the door, Brennan removed his coat and hung it on the back of the chair next to the DC. He poured himself a glass of water and placed a fresh packet of cigarettes, Marlboro, on the table in front of where he planned to sit. For a moment he contemplated rolling up his sleeves, but thought better of it. He pulled out the chair slowly, letting the sound of its legs dragging on the hard floor play out. When he sat, he stared for a moment into McArdle's eyes; the prisoner looked away.

Brennan raised his hands from beneath the table and opened the blue folder in front of him.

'Speak,' said Brennan.

'*What?*' McArdle crumpled his features, grimaced.

Brennan put his hands down on the open folder, splaying his fingers. 'I'm giving you a chance.' He looked over to McArdle, made sure his eyes were on him. 'A chance to save yourself.'

McArdle sniffed. 'That'll be fucking right.'

Brennan tapped the pages. 'Do you know what this is?'

A shrug, no answer.

'This is a story, a story about a little girl from the north who came down here with her baby hoping for a new life and ended up in a communal bin at the end of a dark lane with her legs and arms cut off.'

McArdle banged a fist on the table. 'That's fuck all to do with me.'

Brennan continued, 'The little girl's baby went missing, still is missing, and along the way four other people died. Do you recognise that story?'

McArdle's mouth widened; he showed teeth as he spoke: 'You can't pin that fucking lot on me ...' He rose up, leaned over the table and pointed. 'I'd like to see you fucking try.'

McGuire got out of his seat, went round behind the prisoner and grabbed his shoulders, forcing him to sit down.

McArdle brushed off the DC, tried to assert himself; McGuire shook his head.

Brennan looked at the pages, turned one over, then another. He let McArdle's temper cool a little, then: 'Tell me about Tierney and Durrant.'

'Never heard of them.'

McGuire sniffed, looked away. Brennan read from the file. 'Says here you've been dealing to them for years; even served time for it.'

'Bullshit ...'

'I've got statements from quite a few people.' Brennan allowed the edge of his mouth to curl into a sneer. 'Funny – at the start of this investigation nobody wanted to speak but when you became public enemy number one we couldn't shut them up.'

McGuire laughed out, 'Yeah, funny that. Seems your popularity's slipped a bit since you started hanging about with beasts.'

McArdle rose again, slapped the table. 'Now you wait a minute—'

'Sit down!' roared Brennan. 'You get out of that seat again and I will throw you to the wolves, McArdle. Are you so stupid? I'm doing you a favour here.' Brennan stood up, went round the table to shout in McArdle's ear.

'You killed your own wife – you're going down for that. Don't you get it? There's no door on that wall leading to a magic kingdom where you start living a fairy-tale existence. It's over! ... You're going down. Whether or not you go down for the lot,' he picked up the folder, slapped it in front of McArdle, 'that's what we're debating here. Nothing else! Don't you get that? Are you that fucking thick, man?'

McArdle brought his hands up in front of him, started to play with his fingers. His complexion smoothed; there were no grimaces as he spoke. 'I'm not a beast.'

'That's for the courts to decide,' said McGuire.

Brennan nodded, straightened his back and loosened his tie some more. 'You run with dogs, you catch fleas. That's what they say, isn't it, Stevie?'

'It is indeed.'

McArdle looked at the cigarettes. 'Can I have one of them?'

Brennan pushed over the packet, watched him light up.

McArdle's hands shook as he drew on the cigarette. The DI spoke: 'Tell me about Tierney ... Did he know Sproul?'

'Who?' McArdle took another pelt on the cigarette.

'Peter Sproul – Paisley buddy and hardcore paedo. Did time in Peterhead ... Place you might be paying a visit to soon if you don't loosen up that tongue of yours.'

'I-I've never heard of him, I don't know. I only knew Tierney a-and Durrant.'

'What's their story? From the beginning, and don't leave anything out because I'll know if you have and I'm keeping count.'

McArdle tapped the cigarette on the ashtray. He moved the spilled ash with his finger, tipping it into the tray. His temper seemed to have subsided but the muscles in his neck had tensed. 'Erm, what do you want to know?'

Brennan moved back round to his side of the desk. His chair was already sitting out; he pulled it in as he sat down again. 'How did they kill Carly Donald?'

McArdle looked up. His lower lip was trembling; he sucked it into his mouth, over his teeth. As he tried to speak it was as if the words were stuck inside him. He touched the side of his head; his bandaged fingers trembled. Then he touched his mouth and began to massage the sides of his lips as though he was coaxing himself to speak. 'It, eh, it was Vee ... she killed her.'

'Vee Durrant ... How?'

McArdle's mouth started to spasm, both lips now sucked into the hollow gape that sat beneath his nose. 'There was some fight or other. They wanted to take the baby away – they were going to cut her in and ...' He looked up, seemed to register the seriousness of the situation, of his words, then continued, 'She tried to leave, with the girl, in the night when they were asleep but Vee woke up and there was a fight.'

'Vee struck her? With what?'

'An iron ... It was a steam iron, this is all what Barry told me.' He looked up, eyes wide, pleading. 'I wasn't there ... He spilled this the night I ...'

Brennan noticed McArdle cut himself off. He knew what he was going to say, but let it go. 'Whose idea was it to hack her up?'

McArdle raised the cigarette again, brought it to his mouth. 'Barry's ... made the body easier to move, he said ... It was nothing to do with me. I fucking swear if I'd known ...' He cut himself off again. Brennan picked him up this time.

'If you'd known, you'd never have agreed to sell the child.'

McArdle said nothing. He seemed to be frozen before Brennan's eyes. The Deil sat staring at the cigarette tip for some time and then he spoke: 'I want to know that I'll be looked after if I say any more.'

Brennan turned to McGuire; the DC nodded back. 'We'll make recommendations to the Fiscal ... if you cooperate.'

McArdle dropped the cigarette; stray sparks flew up, landed on the table and went out. He put his hands over his eyes. 'I'm not a beast. I'm not a fucking beast. I hate them. I fucking hate them.'

Brennan watched McArdle struggle. He took no enjoyment from it. His mind wasn't focused on revenge or payback – they affected judgement. Brennan wanted justice, and Beth back; both required a level head. 'Tell us who you gave the child to.'

McArdle removed his hands, placed them under the table momentarily, then produced them again. His jaw twitched as he spoke, face down, towards the table. 'His name's Günter. I don't know his second name.'

'German?'

A nod. 'From Berlin.'

McGuire started to write down the details. Brennan spoke again: 'Where are they now?'

'I don't know?'

Brennan slapped the desk. 'Not good enough!'

'I don't ... I mean, I think they're going back.'

'How ... Train? Plane?'

McArdle looked away. His eyes darted left to right as if he was looking for a way out; when he found none he turned back to the officers. His words were slow, faltering: 'Car. They're going home through

France, he said that to me.'

'Make of car?'

'Er, a Citroën … silver, estate.'

McGuire wrote the information down, rose, ran for the door.

Brennan leaned in; his tone had hardened: 'Is that it? I'm looking for a fucking Citroën in France – am I supposed to use that? Is that supposed to make me happy, McArdle?'

The prisoner couldn't face him. He whimpered, 'I d-don't know. I don't know.'

'No. Neither do I.'

Brennan stood up. He knocked over his chair as he went for the door that McGuire had just left through. As he ran to the incident room he could feel his mind spinning.

McGuire was already on the phones; the rest of the team had followed him.

'Calais. They'll be crossing to Calais … Get every car checked, every passenger with a child, all of them. I want passenger lists and I want searches and I want the French side locked down. I want all of this done now. Go. Now. Everyone move it!'

Chapter 49

BRENNAN LET THE TEAM WORK, returned to his office. As he got inside the door a uniform poked his head in, said, 'What do you want me to do with McArdle, sir?'

'Do you really want me to answer that? ... Put him in the cells.'

Brennan threw his jacket over the chair. The contents of his pockets spilled on the floor. He walked round and picked up his cigarettes, and the little black-and-white picture that Lorraine had given him. He tried not to look at it but he couldn't stop himself. There was a black shaded area at the top of the photograph where you couldn't see anything, but lower down there was a white patch that looked like a little ball; it was the baby's head. Brennan ran a finger over the image and stared. He held it before him for long enough to register that it was his child and what that meant. He had a child that would be coming into this world soon. He knew that once the thought had gladdened him, made him smile, but he couldn't bring himself to feel anything now. He didn't want to welcome another soul here; it wasn't the place for such a young, innocent life. He put the picture back in his pocket and went to sit down.

At his desk Brennan lit a cigarette; the Marlboro tasted good to him as he drew the deep blue smoke into his lungs. His nasal passages constricted as he blew out the strong burn of the tobacco and then he tasted the hot smoke again as it left his nostrils. He wondered if he needed something stronger, harder, but the prospect of a drink seemed a long time away.

As Brennan looked over his desk, he was surprised to see the blue folder with a yellow Post-it note stuck on the front. It was from Lauder – the details on the Limping Man that he'd asked for. Brennan opened it and peered in. He'd visited the files previously but that was before his psych leave, and during the months in between it had been awkward to get hold of. He scanned the contents. There was very little detail that he hadn't seen already. The witness statements – a pretentious bastard who'd used the word *claudication*; the descriptions, estimates of height, weight, build. The calibre of weapons used and the method of dispatch. It was all familiar; depressingly so.

What Brennan wasn't prepared for was the newspaper cutting with the picture of his brother. It was the same cutting as he'd carried around in his wallet all this time; the only difference was that Lauder's quotes had been underlined in red pen.

'Prick.'

Was that the sum of his achievement? Getting a quote in the newspaper? He was surprised the byline wasn't Aylish Dunn's.

Brennan turned over the blue folder. Took another pull on his cigarette. His brother had died, been murdered, and the police investigation had failed him. The sum total of the information on the Limping Man amounted to a few scraps of paper, a few witness statements that went nowhere.

He had killed, clinically, and then disappeared. What kind of a society allowed paid assassins to operate on their streets? His brother had been innocent, he'd gotten in the way of an underworld killing and paid for it with a bullet in his head. Were the streets so out of control that this kind of thing went on unchecked?

Brennan tapped the folder, got up. He stubbed out his cigarette and lifted the phone on his desk, dialled 0.

'Cells, please.'

The line was connected. 'Hello.'

'Bert, it's Rob. Have you got McArdle settled?'

'As quiet as a lamb.'

'Right, I'm coming down. I want a word with him in private.'

'You sure about that, Rob?'

'Sure as shooting.'

Brennan knew there was little to connect the Limping Man to his case. He had no proof that he was the same assassin that killed his brother but his gut told him otherwise. Did he need proof? The killer was walking free as it was; if he could get him for Tierney and Durrant, wasn't that good enough? Brennan knew he should probably be thanking him for taking that pair off the streets but he didn't think he'd be shaking his hand. There was no hope of connecting the Limping Man to Andy's murder, he knew that – did it matter? It mattered in one respect: if it affected the ongoing investigation into Carly Donald's death. He knew he couldn't risk that, but he had his brother to think about.

As he walked down to the cells, Brennan toyed with the idea of doing this by the book, calling McArdle into an interview room and posing the question in front of Stevie or Lou. But what were the chances of getting the result he was after? McArdle was a hardened criminal. Getting him to lynch himself was one thing; getting him to hang someone else was an altogether different proposition.

Brennan stood before the cell doors, knowing he had only one chance to find his brother's killer. If he came out of there without a name, Andy's murderer was never likely to be found. He nodded to the jailer, listened to the rattle of the keys and the heavy iron hinges singing out. He stepped into the cell.

McArdle was sitting on the edge of his bed. Most cons, by his stage, have learned to chill out inside a jail cell, but McArdle was tense.

'What now?' he said.

Brennan nodded for the door to be closed. McArdle watched carefully, started to raise himself. He rubbed at the front of his jeans, then turned his hands behind his back.

His mouth drooped.

'Sit down.' Brennan put a hand on his head, pushed him back. He paced the small cell and soaked in McArdle's fear. 'You know, I've seen just about every kind of scum and piece of shit that the world has to offer in my time, McArdle, but you take the fucking prize.'

McArdle looked at the floor. 'Should you be in here?'

'Shut your hole.' Brennan walked over to the bed, placed a foot on the rim. 'Paedos are one thing, but selling on kids, that's something else. You're like a trader, a beast trader.'

'I'm not a beast.'

'Tell it to the judge, McArdle.'

'I will. I will.'

Brennan leaned over. 'And do you think he'll listen?' He laughed, watched McArdle turn away and then he grabbed his face in his hand and twisted it round. 'Have you looked at your record recently? And now you've got murder to add to it, and fuck knows what else by the end of the day.'

'I gave you all I had ... You said you'd help.'

Brennan released his grip, took his foot off the bed and walked to the other side of the cell. 'A French car, in fucking France, McArdle ... that's what you gave me.'

'It's all I have. Look, what do you want from me?' He tried to eyeball Brennan but couldn't hold his stare. He kept dropping his gaze, his head bobbing on his meaty neck as if he couldn't support the weight of it any more.

'You're taking the piss, is what you're doing.'

'I'm not,' he pleaded, turning his bandaged palm upward.

Brennan moved in, pointed. 'You know what you've done and how it's going to play out.'

McArdle looked down again. 'Leave me alone. Just leave me alone.'

Brennan laughed, 'Leave you alone? Think you're going to get much privacy in Peterhead, on the beast wing?'

'I'm not a beast.' He stood up, inflated his chest.

Brennan walked towards him, fronted up. 'Then you better start playing ball with me or that's what the court and everyone else in this country is going to think. Devlin McArdle – child trafficker. Wife murderer. Beast!'

A light went out in McArdle. His frame shrank as he sat back down. He was broken; there was no fight left in him. 'What do you want from me?'

Brennan looked towards the door, walked for McArdle, got down on his haunches. 'I know what it's like out there, how your kind of people operate. And you know how I operate.' McArdle looked up. Brennan continued, 'Now, I know, if I get you up there in that interview room, with a DC as witness, you're not going to tell me a bloody thing that I can use because there's a chance it'll get out to the people who know you.' Brennan lowered his voice: 'That's why I've came down here on my own.' He leaned in further.

'Give me something I can use, and no one needs to know where it came from.'

McArdle shook his head. 'I've given you everything. What more can I give you?'

Brennan stilled his nerve, said, 'Give me the Limping Man.'

Chapter 50

OUTSIDE THE CELL DI Rob Brennan leaned his back on the door. He felt a dull ache in the middle of his forehead where his brows pinched; a pulse in his temple kept pace with his ramping heart. He stood for a moment, tried to gather a semblance of reason but the task evaded him. As he eased himself off the door Brennan's knees felt loose. The walk to the front of the station now seemed longer than usual, each step demanding a greater exertion than the last; it was as if he carried a great load, a burden.

In the foyer Charlie looked up from his *Daily Record* and spoke but Brennan failed to comprehend his words. A burning in his chest had started to demand the cooling, calming effects of nicotine and nothing could detract from the craving. As he opened the door he was slapped by the brisk air and the line of sweat above his lip slid towards his mouth – the salty taste made him grimace and then wipe it away with the back of his hand. The empty, hollowed-out emotions that accompanied the fear of never finding an answer to long-held preoccupations was suddenly gone. It wasn't euphoria – never that – but it was an ending, and in the nebulous flux of life that was certainly something to hold to. Wasn't that what we all longed for, every day? Some shape to the monotonous trawl through the misery of existence; the daily questioning of life's lack of order, the absence of structure. There was no law. There was no meaning. There was no justice. The universe didn't care about loss of life, about the shooting of innocent bystanders; the dismembering of young girls, or the perverted trading of innocent infants. Any chance to halt the rut, to find a moment in time, however brief a pause in proceedings, was a reminder that he was alive and the fight went on.

As Brennan removed a cigarette from the pack he noticed how white his hands were; the dark hair on his knuckles accentuated the fingers' cadaverous appearance. For a moment he stared at them, spread them out in front of him; they started to tremble.

'Everything okay, Rob?'

He heard the words, turned: it was Charlie. As he held the station door open he stared into Brennan's eyes. The DI felt the cigarette slip from his mouth. He watched it fall, roll a few feet, then get carried off in the breeze. The action snapped him back to reality.

'Fine. All fine.'

Brennan pushed past the desk sergeant, went for the stairs.

There was suddenly a new purpose in his step; it was the quickening of thought, the realisation that the long period of doubt was over.

As Brennan reached Incident Room One he saw a huddle of bodies round the television screen. He knew at once there had been a break – when these things occurred it was like observing a sea change. The team's collective unconscious altered immediately. The faces morphed from their previous expressions of dogged resilience towards hope – something experience had taught Brennan he was better off doing without. As he walked in he was tempted to clap his hands together and ask what was going on. He felt like he'd missed out; he was a spectator.

McGuire turned round and spotted him, spoke: 'Here he is!' The DC trotted towards him. 'Where have you been?'

The question poked Brennan, made him defensive. 'Nowhere.' As he answered he immediately felt stupid; at once he realised the question was innocent. 'What's going on?'

McGuire grinned like a schoolboy as he grabbed Brennan by the arm. 'Get over here. They've got them!'

Brennan didn't understand. He knew what he wanted the words to mean, but wasn't sure if he'd processed them correctly. Since he had been with McArdle his mind had tripped back to his brother's murder. The realisation that he still had another case to solve brought back a sudden dose of present-day reality. He pushed his way to the front of the crowd and stared at the television. 'Can someone turn this up?'

A small yellow triangle appeared on the screen; the number beside it increased as the volume rose. It was a breaking news report. Brennan sensed the tension mounting all around him; the incident room felt like the terraces of a football stadium as the supporters of the leading side waited for the final whistle. He hushed his team quiet. The room stilled as all eyes turned to the television.

'*And can I remind you these pictures are live …*' said the news reporter.

The scene was of a town Brennan didn't recognise – as he tried to adjust, to take in what he was seeing, absorb the information, he scanned the street and the faces in the crowd.

He noticed there was a strap along the bottom of the screen that confirmed what he'd been hoping: MISSING BABY CASE ... LIVE PICTURES FROM CALAIS. It took him a moment to process the information; his thoughts raced away and became tangled in a net of emotions. He wanted to punch the air, to smack the desk with his fist or make some other expression of relief but he held himself in check; he had to.

'Jesus, we've got them!' His mind calmed as he said the words. He was almost light-headed. A smile spread across his face – it was impossible to hide it. On the screen, images of French gendarmes surrounding a silver car appeared. The camera was shaky, the lens going in and out of focus, but Brennan kept his eyes fixed on the dark-suited officers, armed with assault rifles, as they approached the car. The French officers were fast, brisk and businesslike. They knew the routine and took no chances as they swooped. Two men inside were removed whilst a small bundle with furiously waving arms and legs was taken from the back seat.

Brennan's chest tightened, his throat constricted.

'Look, it's the kid,' said a PC.

'They've got her! She's alive!'

A loud cheer swept round the office. Arms were raised; a blue folder was thrown in the air. Brennan turned to McGuire and grabbed him by the shoulders. 'We did it! By Christ, we did it!'

A wave of bodies started to sway as uniforms and detectives hugged and leapt. Tables and chairs were pushed aside as the team crossed the floor and flung arms round each other. Brennan laughed as he watched Lou slapping Brian's beer gut, and then a round of cheers went up. It was like a party, thought Brennan, but as he stared at the relieved, smiling faces he knew that they still had plenty to do.

The case had been tough; it had taken a lot out of the team, and him. Brennan knew he didn't look at the world in the same way any more. Another part of what made him human had been surrendered. How he would deal with that was a problem for another day, though. He moved off just as the room's pitch intensified.

'Where are you going?' said McGuire.

'Got a couple of calls to make. Don't worry – carry on without me. Enjoy the moment.'

Brennan closed the door to his office and moved towards the desk. He could still hear noise outside as he drew up the international directory on his computer screen and started to tap in the number of the Garda Síochána in Dublin. His thoughts left the celebrations immediately as he announced himself to the telephonist and asked for the special investigations team. It always surprised him how quickly things came together in the end. No matter how many times it happened, the DI never quite accepted the sudden transformation from bewilderment to cheering the successful resolution of an investigation. It was as if the period before, the groundwork, the heavy lifting, had never happened. The effort expended and the toll it had taken on everyone seemed insignificant compared to the accomplishment. He knew there was a low coming – the payment for such a high – but it didn't matter at this stage. He allowed himself a smile, some sneaking admiration for the result.

Brennan was still smiling into the phone as his call was passed on; in four rings it was answered.

'Hello, this is Wylie.' The accent was familiar, thick Celtic tones.

'Ah, yes, hello … DI Robert Brennan, Lothian and Borders CID.'

'And what can I do for you today, sir?'

Brennan tightened his grip on the receiver, wondered how to put this, went with: 'It's more what I can do for you.'

'Oh, really now …' The Guard paused, then his voice indicated a change of subject: 'You sound like there's a bit of a do going on there.'

'We've just wrapped up a big case … The team are in high spirits.'

'Congratulations,' said the Guard. The moment passed; he got back to work. 'Now, you said you had something for me …'

Brennan revealed the details that McArdle had provided in the cell. He kept his tone low and serious as he detailed the whereabouts of the Limping Man.

'I know the place well,' said the Irishman. He cleared his throat, rustled some papers. His tone remained flat. 'I'll get on this right away.'

'Best of luck,' said Brennan.

'Be more than luck we'll need … by the sounds of him.'

'I'd expect him to be armed, and very definitely dangerous.'

A huff. Hint of a raised inflection. 'Oh, yes. I'd say so.'

As Brennan looked out to the office, lowered the phone, he could see the revelry was likely to continue for some time yet. He didn't feel like celebrating. Too much had happened lately to make him feel more than a little unsociable; he felt like withdrawing from the world. He sensed a prolonged period of analysis queuing in his mind. There were facts to be chewed over, digested. There was never a definitive 'why?' – he knew that well enough. But it didn't stop him challenging for an answer. Was there something to be learned? Something to be revealed about the human condition? He doubted it. There would only be black hours of rumination, more data to add to the sum of his knowledge, but little understanding. The mysteries he preoccupied himself with were inscrutable, and as perennial as the Edinburgh rain.

As he thought about the Irish force apprehending the Limping Man, Brennan reached into his wallet and removed the newspaper cutting he'd carried around for so long. He placed the thin paper on the desk in front of him and read the headline through one more time. He had done it – he had found his brother's killer, but the achievement did not register the kind of elation he had hoped it would. That was the problem with his job, thought Brennan. All the sense of achievement came after the tragedy had taken place – there was no altering what had happened. There was no medal to pin on his chest. As Wullie had told him long ago, 'There is no winning in the force, only degrees of losing.'

Brennan picked up the cutting and stared at it, touched its curling edges, ran a finger over the grainy image of his brother. Then he crumpled it into a ball and dropped it in the waste-paper basket beneath his desk. He rose, walked to the filing cabinet on the other side of the room and removed a bottle of Talisker from the bottom drawer, put it under his arm. He picked up his jacket, switched out the light, and went to join the team.

A wide-eyed McGuire, his face flushed and glowing, stopped Brennan as he came through the door. 'What's this?' He pointed to the bottle. 'Prize for your favourite DC?'

Brennan nodded. 'Yeah, something like that.' He handed over the bottle. 'Enjoy yourselves. Because tomorrow we start the paperwork!'

McGuire held up the Talisker, turned on his heels, then made a show of cracking the seal. A voice in the corner of the office roared out, 'Come on, three cheers for the boss.'

Brennan turned away, flagged them down. 'No. Don't ...' He headed for the door as the cheering started.

McGuire called after him, 'You not staying for a drink, sir?'

'No, I've got someone to see.'

'Secret rendezvous, is it?'

A weak laugh. 'Something like that, yeah.'

'Don't do anyone I wouldn't do, sir.'

Brennan dug his hand in his pocket, waved with his other one. He was glad to see the team so pleased; they had done well. Despite everything, they had achieved something worth being proud of. For a moment he wanted to be part of it all, then he remembered who he was, and what position he occupied in the hierarchy. 'Look, don't stay up too late. Be a big day tomorrow.'

'Listen to Dad,' said McGuire.

Brennan headed for the door. He turned once, twice, as he was wished well, but when he was out he kept his head low and focused on each step he took. He needed to get away, to taste different air.

In the car park Brennan picked out the Passat, directed the key and unlocked it. He had a stop to make before going home; it was another one of those stops he didn't want to make, but he knew that he had to do it. The case had demanded his attention, had drawn him away from everything, and everyone, else – but now it was time to shift focus back to the areas he had ignored.

As Brennan pulled out of the station car park the radio news was relaying the arrests in Calais. By tomorrow the case would be all over the front pages. The papers would call it a result. His superiors would be pleased. But Brennan just felt cold. At the outset a young girl had died and, along the way, more people had followed her. He knew that too many people had been hurt and damaged by the events that had sprung from Carly Donald's disappearance, and all of it could have been avoided. He didn't know who to blame or why things had turned out the way they had, but he felt some sense of relief that it was now over. The killing would stop, and Beth was safe.

The voice on the radio started to relay the details of the case from the start, when Carly Donald was found in a communal bin in Muirhouse. *'The grim find was made by schoolgirl Trish Brown, who said she would never be able to get the image out of her mind.'*

Brennan knew how she felt. He could still see the pale, mutilated figure abandoned in the rubbish, the life drained from her like a rag that had been wrung out.

'Father of the murder victim, the Reverend John Donald, earlier spoke of his joy upon hearing his granddaughter Beth had been found safe and well. A one-time contender for Scotland's top church job, the minister confirmed he would no longer be considered for the Moderator's role, as he would be concentrating his efforts on his family life.'

Brennan cursed. 'Jumped or pushed?' He leaned forward and switched off the radio. 'Arsehole.'

Chapter 51

AS DI ROB BRENNAN ARRIVED outside Dr Lorraine Fuller's
home, he brought the car to an abrupt halt, turned the key in the ignition and listened to the engine coming to rest. It was a cool night
and the breeze bit as he opened the door and walked up the path.
He could see a light burning in the front room as he rang the bell.
A curtain moved and Lorraine appeared at the window. She seemed
flustered, not expecting to see him, but then she made for the door,
rattled the chain and lock as she opened up.

'What are you doing here?' she said. 'Our appointment's not until
tomorrow.'

Brennan didn't bite. 'Can I come in?'

She widened the door, motioned him inside with a flourish of her
hand.

In the living room, Lorraine folded her arms. 'So, is this a flying
visit or should I offer you a drink?'

Brennan didn't answer, removed his coat and sat down.

'Wine okay?'

He nodded. Lorraine had never been one for small chat and he was
grateful for that, but he knew they had things to say to each other.

The television was on but the sound had been turned to mute.
Brennan watched a few seconds of *Antiques Roadshow* – an old man
had brought along a collection of toby jugs and twitched every time
the presenter picked one up. Brennan lasted nearly a full minute before he got out of his seat, briskly, and turned the television off.

Lorraine returned with the wine. 'Make yourself at home.'

Brennan took the glass. 'I want you to know this is the first chance
I've had to see you since I took this case.'

She stared at the orange juice in her own glass, swirled it round
the base. 'I saw the news. It's over, then?'

Brennan sighed. *'Really.'*

'What do you mean by that?'

He sipped the wine. 'Nothing.' He reached to place his glass on the
table, retrieved his jacket from the back of the chair. He was about
to remove the picture he'd been carrying around but something occurred to him. 'Do you remember those sessions we had, ones where

we talked about my brother?'

'Yes. Of course.'

'I got him … Andy's killer.'

'*What*? I mean, how?'

Brennan fiddled with a button on his jacket; the words felt trapped in his throat. 'It doesn't really matter.'

Lorraine put down her glass, moved closer. 'You still don't like talking about this. You know, if you've found some kind of closure, then maybe now's the time to tell me.'

Closure? What was that? Shrink-speak. Brennan looked at Lorraine. Her hair was up; she had no make-up on. He hardly recognised her. 'Okay. What do you want to know?'

'Whatever you'd like to tell me.'

Brennan stopped himself, let the last twenty-four hours' events flood into his memory banks and mix with what he knew about Andy.

'There was a man, Grady …' he said.

'Go on.'

Brennan took a breath, hesitated, then continued, 'He was a businessman, one of those with fingers in several pies. I had seen his name mentioned a couple of times when … well … does it matter?'

Lorraine leaned forward, took his hand.

'Andy had this job, a roughcasting, big payer but you need the weather for it so … Am I boring you?'

She shook her head.

'He was telling me about it and it came out that it was for Grady.' Brennan tightened his hold on Lorraine's hand. 'I told Andy not to take the job. I told him Grady was bad news, his name was coming up in investigations again and again. There were connections to Ulster and—'

'Grady sounds serious.'

Brennan frowned. 'Serious trouble. But Andy didn't want to know. He took on the job and we rowed. I told him he had a family to think about and he shouldn't do it … heavy stuff. He wouldn't listen.' Brennan could hear his voice growing weaker as the memory played. 'We argued and argued and eventually I wore Andy's patience down. He broke. It all came out: how he resented me for leaving home and making him give up his ambitions to paint in favour of the family firm; he said he had to do the job because I wouldn't … He blamed me for everything. He'd never said any of this before.'

Lorraine put her free hand on Brennan's face; it felt cold as she spoke: 'It's okay. People say things they don't mean all the time.'

Brennan felt the hurt welling in him again. 'No. Andy meant it. I could tell. And do you know what I did? Nothing.

I left it. I never said another word. I should have pulled him from that job with my bare hands but I let my ego get in the way.'

'Rob ...'

Brennan pushed Lorraine aside. He stood up. 'I could have saved Andy, but I was too bloody pig-headed. I let him get killed.'

Lorraine stood up too; there were tears in her eyes. Brennan put his fingertips to her face, wiped a drop away. 'That's not going to help anyone.'

'Why are you telling me this now, Rob?'

'You asked.'

'No. I mean, why now?'

Brennan watched her rise, take a tissue from a box on the shelving by the wall. She went to sit down again and he leaned over, picked up his jacket and removed the picture. 'Maybe this is part of it.'

Lorraine froze for a moment, then snatched the picture, tore it in two.

'You don't get it, do you, Rob?'

He watched the two pieces of the image he'd carried around fall to the floor. Then turned his gaze to her. 'Lorraine?'

Her shoulders shook as she cried into her hands. For a moment Brennan was confused, then something sparked in him as Lorraine raised her head and showed her flushed cheeks. 'There is no baby.'

Brennan thought he'd misheard. '*What?*'

She turned, screamed at him, 'I printed it off! It's just a picture!'

The words didn't make sense to him. 'Lorraine, what are you saying?'

She got up, turned away to face the wall. He watched her wipe her eyes with the sleeve of her cardigan. 'I wanted to hurt you. You'd hurt me. I wanted to build up your hopes and then let you down, like you'd done to me.'

Brennan listened but couldn't believe it – when it had sunk in he knew he couldn't look at her again. He collected his jacket and walked for the door.

Lorraine chased after him. 'Rob, I was wrong.'

He turned the latch, pulled. Lorraine stepped in front of him, blocking the door. 'Rob, I was wrong. It was a mistake.

I'm sorry.'

'Get out of my way.'

'I'm sorry.'

'So am I.'

'Rob, I-I didn't realise—'

He pulled her by the arm, flung her back into the hallway. 'Neither did I.'

In the street Brennan felt the cold sting at his eyes. There was more moisture in the air now. As he got in the car he turned back to see Lorraine on her doorstep; she was still crying, wiping at her tears with her hands. He looked away, started the car.

The traffic was light. Brennan worked up to the speed limit and then felt his temperature rising; he touched his brow – he was sweating. His hands were clammy on the steering wheel and he felt a shortness of breath. He followed the row of cars he was in to the traffic lights, passed through them and took a left into a residential area he didn't know. For a second or two he felt lost, but he didn't care.

Brennan pulled over the car, killed the engine and got out.

He walked to the end of the street and turned down a darkened path that led to open playing fields. It was raining now. As he walked he could feel his warm brow cooling. His shirt front was wet. A woman with a West Highland terrier on a lead smiled at him as he reached an open grassed area. He looked away from her, headed for a bench under a street lamp. When he reached it he sat and tried to settle the mash of thoughts he now carried around; but he knew it was beyond him.

How? Why? He had no answers any more.

Brennan felt the wind cut into his arms; his shirt and hair were wet now, soaked through. He'd left his jacket behind in the car, hadn't even taken the keys out of the ignition. He stood up, looked back towards the path and started walking again. It seemed easy enough to do, so he continued, kept going. As he went, his phone started to ring. He took it out, looked at the caller ID – it was Sophie.

'Hello, love,' he said. 'I'm on my way home.'

THE END

CPSIA information can be obtained
at www.ICGtesting.com
Printed in the USA
LVHW041535081020
668326LV00013B/1117